Ferdinand Whittingham

Four Years in the Ionian Islands

Vol. 2

Ferdinand Whittingham

Four Years in the Ionian Islands
Vol. 2

ISBN/EAN: 9783337735265

Printed in Europe, USA, Canada, Australia, Japan

Cover: Foto ©Andreas Hilbeck / pixelio.de

More available books at **www.hansebooks.com**

FOUR YEARS

IN

THE IONIAN ISLANDS.

THEIR POLITICAL AND SOCIAL CONDITION.

WITH A

HISTORY OF THE BRITISH PROTECTORATE.

EDITED BY

VISCOUNT KIRKWALL,

LATELY ON THE STAFF OF SIR HENRY WARD, SEVENTH LORD HIGH COMMISSIONER.

IN TWO VOLUMES.

VOL. II.

LONDON:

CHAPMAN AND HALL, 193, PICCADILLY.

1864.

CONTENTS OF VOL. II.

CHAPTER III.

CHAPTER IV.

CHAPTER V.

CHAPTER VI.

CHAPTER VII.

CHAPTER VIII.

CONTENTS.

CHAPTER IX.

EARTHQUAKES IN CEPHALONIA IN 1862-3.

CHAPTER X.

CHAPTER XI.

FOUR YEARS

IN

THE IONIAN ISLANDS.

———

CHAPTER I.

In June, 1859, I first arrived at Corfu, and put
up, with my family, at the Hôtel de l'Europe, till
we could find suitable apartments. M. Grima, the
landlord, kept a very good cook, and did his best
to make us comfortable. But the noises at night
were intolerable, from the much frequented café
below, where the customers, in summer, sometimes
remained till daylight. Soon after our arrival, however, we obtained excellent rooms in the second
story of the house of Sir Spiridion Valaoriti,

which was situated on the Esplanade close to the palace.

On the beauty of Corfu I shall not dwell. From Homer and Xenophon down to the Frenchman About, the American Taylor, and the English Earl of Carlisle, countless pens in verse and prose have celebrated its varied and lovely scenery. Many ranges of mountains form the background in the great distance. Nearer to the north is the famous *Istone* of antiquity, the modern *San Salvator*. The frowning citadel, the olive-woods, the wild roses and beautiful oleanders, the planes, and graceful pepper-trees, with the rich vineyards, complete the picture. The snow on the distant mountains (which often remains as late as May) forms a delightful contrast to the verdure and richness of the landscape. The roads have ever attracted the praise of the traveller.[*] San Salvator, the highest summit of which is 2591 feet above the level of the sea, is not only a fine object to the view, but it also stands a perpetual monument of the terrible internecine quarrels of the ancient Corcyræans, related by Thucydides; conveying admonition for the past, and warning for the future. It was about half way up that mountain, that the oligarchical party entrenched itself.

---

[*] Ce qu'on devine encore, et au premier coup d'œil, c'est que Corfou et les six autres îles sont mieux cultivées, et plus florissantes qu'aucune province du royaume de Grèce : les communications sont faciles par terre et par mer, *le pays est traversé en tous sens par des routes admirables.*—About's *Grèce Contemporaine.*

There, occasionally assisted by Sparta, they, for two years, bade defiance to the democrats of the town, who were in alliance with Athens. Having finally surrendered, their treacherous massacre by their Corcyræan brethren, added another link to that chain of horrors which excited the anger and indignation of the Greek historian. Perhaps to the influence of this perpetual monitor, the fact that the Corfiots of the present day are the most peaceable and civilized of all the Ionians, and consequently of all the Greeks, may be partly attributed.

But the charms of external nature are not sufficient for the complete happiness of civilized man. He requires other things. The living in Corfu was of course inferior to that of countries in the West of Europe. But such things can be borne by most persons with patience, and by some, perhaps, even with indifference. The worst evil to me was the difficulty of sleeping. This was very great, indeed, at all times, except in extreme winter, for then people at night remained in-doors. But usually (and especially in the hot weather) the town was alive with noisy pedestrians from about eight in the evening till three or four in the morning. As the heat necessitated, of course, open windows, the external sounds had free entry into the houses. The loud conversations, the sharp disputes, and the irritating laughter, teazed and tormented the ear and brain struggling vainly for sleep. But worse remained behind. The whole Greek race are heaven-born songsters. But the nasal tone of their performances, as well as the melancholy monotony of their favourite airs, are not calculated at first to charm strangers. Monsieur About complained of this nuisance in continental Greece. But during my brief stay in Athens, I heard nothing that could rival the Dutch concerts of Corfu.* Countless small parties perambulated the town nightly, affrighting "Nature's soft nurse" with intolerable twang. The police only interfered so far, as to insist that the parties should "keep moving." They were not allowed to stand singing before a house. But nothing was gained by this regulation. On the contrary, if one must hear singing, it had better be something like a tune. Whereas the medley of sounds, caused by the voices of the peripatetic songsters, was positively excruciating. Under these torments the hapless Briton tossing on his bed, with the thermometer, perhaps, at 90°, writhed with mingled anguish and despair. He had work to do by day, and if he slept at all, he must do so by night. His tormentors slept for half the day, and walked and sang during the greater part of the night. The Englishman truly felt that he had no

* These nuisances were found so intolerable by a very gallant, able, but eccentric warrior, that, on certain occasions, he adopted very strong measures to procure rest for himself and family. One night he dropped flower-pots, and another night shutters, upon the heads of the musicians. On another occasion he descended to the door of his house with a stout stick, with which he proceeded to keep time with the music upon the backs of the singers.

business there. "*Que diable alloit-il faire dans cette galère?*" Trades also were often carried on noisily in the dead of the night. On the ground-floor of the great house, on the second story of which we lived, coffins were occasionally made at midnight or later. The hammering was fearful and incessant. In my despair I sometimes almost longed to slip into one of these coffins—there, at last, to find the coveted repose. Oh, ye Britons, who have filled columns of the *Times* with your sad complaints of little organ-grinders playing by day, had ye passed some summer nights in Corfu, ye would have been ashamed to mention your slight and insignificant vexations! The ringing of the harsh church-bells was another nuisance. But this was far greater in some of the other islands than in Corfu.

The society of the capital would have been more agreeable to persons of intelligence, had the Greeks and English mixed together freely and cordially. This, however, was far from being generally the case, and never less so than during the four years which preceded the cession of the islands to Greece. It was a matter of general remark that the English were asked to dinner at the palace only to meet each other. The Ionians made a similar observation as regarded themselves. To divide, and thus to govern the more easily, appeared to be the established rule. It is not at occasional crowded balls that interesting acquaintances can be formed or cultivated by rational men, whose dancing days are over. And this must especially be the case when the general want of a common language is superadded. But other circumstances combined to prevent the amalgamation of the two nations, and to facilitate the plan for separating them, if such really existed.

Every one knows that in England the dinner-table is the great lever by which social intercourse is raised to the highest pinnacle of human perfection. But the dinner-table, as we understand it, is not one of the institutions of the Ionian Islands, nor, indeed, of Greeks in general. That temperate race certainly dines, but how? where? and when? has usually remained a masonic secret for Englishmen. Except his Highness the President of the Senate, and the Regents in each island, who *ex officio* give two or three prandial entertainments annually, it is rare, indeed, for an Ionian to have a dinner-party. Almost equally rare is an evening entertainment. English officers have passed years in the Islands on good terms with many Greeks without once breaking bread in any of their houses, nay, sometimes without having seen the inside of a Greek mansion. Moreover, many Ionian gentlemen, who willingly cultivate the acquaintance of Englishmen, never think of introducing the latter to their families; though this remark applies less to Corfu and to Zante than to the other islands. Poverty may prevent their ever giving dinners such as

Englishmen are accustomed to reciprocate even in the middle classes. But when I pleaded this excuse in answer to the complaints of my countrymen, they would answer, "They can at least introduce us to their wives and daughters." The Greek gentlemen had no objections to visit Englishmen, nor to dine with them; but there society ended. The young Britons desirous of other company, of metal more attractive, were naturally disgusted, and gradually broke off intercourse with their new friends.

The ancient ideas of the necessary seclusion of women have not entirely disappeared from the Islands. The evil is certainly greatly mitigated. But it exists to a degree of which the Ionians themselves are apparently unconscious. For they always give an indignant denial to such a charge. To many families, as I well know, it no longer applies. With the great majority it is still evident to every impartial observer. In Cephalonia, Zante, and the other islands where the Turks held sway for many years, the fashion of the Mahomedan rulers may have had its influences. But the seclusion of women is an ancient Greek custom, and its maintenance is one of the proofs of the Hellenic descent of the Ionians. The Zantiots, who were formerly expressly blamed on that account,* are considered now as most free from this blot on Christian civilization. But they are also of the least purely Greek origin.

* Dr. Davy, who published more than twenty years ago.

The Greeks do not appear fully to understand even now that general preference for the society of the fair sex which is so prevalent in the west of Europe. That intercourse with virtuous ladies serves to polish and to purify the mind, is not one of their maxims. Amongst the Greeks the males have nearly monopolized society, and have not gained by the custom. There are some charming exceptions. But the fact remains, that the Ionian ladies do not hold that position which is their right, and for which they are naturally as well fitted as their sisters of France and of England.

The want of large and even of considerable fortunes is another impediment to the pleasures of society. The laws of succession—entailing perpetual subdivision of property—produce evils which are more quickly felt in a small community like the Ionian Islands than in a great commercial country like France. In the former, 500*l.* a year is now considered as a fair fortune. There are very few rich men, in the English idea of the word. A man with 4000*l.* a year is looked upon as a Rothschild or a Marquis of Westminster is regarded in London. The English consider a good dinner or supper, seasoned with the company of elegant ladies, as the perfection of society. Whereas the Greeks prefer the company of men, and habitually eat only in their own houses, or at their club, and that with great temperance and moderation.

But the Ionians are *naturally* an agreeable, generous, quick, and hospitable people. If they cannot give champagne dinners to the English, it is for want of something less easily attainable than good will. They are also very charitable. Their governments have not sufficiently attended to the wants of the poor; but the people make up for this neglect. A poor peasant rarely passes a beggar without contributing a trifle to his wants. Amongst the gentry love and kindness to kindred are very conspicuous. An Ionian does not shun a relation because he is poor, in order to cleave to a stranger because he is rich. But it must be owned that he sometimes carries too far his respect for the ties of blood. Great moral turpitude, and even infamous conduct, does not always destroy the sentiment. " What can I do? We are connected, he is my distant relation," said one of the most honorable of men to me, to excuse his friendly behaviour to a notorious liar and shameless impostor. This too charitable manner of cloaking iniquity has a sad tendency to encourage a general immorality, one exemplification of which I shall here narrate.

There are in the Islands about fifty families, all the males of which enjoy the title of Count. Most of the genuine Counts can prove their descent from persons upon whom the Venetian Government conferred their titles, as a reward for public services. Properly speaking, however, the Ionian nobility is untitled, as was also the case with the ancient Greek aristocracy. The Venetian nobles, as is well known, prided themselves upon the simple nobility of birth, and despised, so far as regarded themselves, the titles of Count and of Marquis. Nevertheless, in the case of its dependencies, Venice made use of the natural love of titles as a means of honorable recompense. In the Islands themselves, where the histories of the nobles are well known, the title of Count has not much consideration, but it is otherwise in the West of Europe. There, if an Ionian proclaim himself noble, the absence of a title is apt to throw discredit on his assertion, or at all events it renders his nobility of little value in the way of deference and social privileges. It is on this account, I presume, that some persons of not over delicate sentiments, and fond of travelling, have assumed of their own accord the title in question. At one time the Senates, with the Lord High Commissioners, endeavoured to stop this scandal, and those who could not legally establish their titles were officially deprived of them. But in process of time exceptions were made, and some impostors were allowed to retain them, in consideration of their services to the Protectorate. One false Count, indeed, attained to the highest dignity which could be held by a native. Thus the Ionian Government committed two errors. First it assumed a right to confer titles which it did not possess; and secondly it greatly encouraged shameless imposture. The genuine Counts were naturally indignant at these proceedings, but were unable to rectify the evil. Meantime, the originally self-made, and finally officially recognized Counts, contracted wealthy alliances in the West of Europe. For the title of Countess has ever had, it cannot be denied, great attractions for all womankind.

Of living people I shall not speak, although some of them richly merit exposure. But, as a tale of past times, I will briefly describe the notorious career of an impostor, who never ceased up to his death to be well received by his countrymen. This person was of good family, but neither himself nor his fathers had ever been titled. He travelled to England, where he assumed the title of Count, and soon after succeeded in marrying a lady of property. On his return to his native island, he went to the municipal minister of religion, in order to have the title inserted in the baptismal registers of himself and of his father. The official was a Roman Catholic married to a Greek. He objected to be a party to the transaction. But his countryman persuaded him that he had been made a Count in England; though when in England he had declared that he had obtained his title in the Ionian Islands. The not over scrupulous municipal was prevailed upon to falsify the register. But the books of a certain church still prove the imposture. Before he returned to England he endeavoured to get his passport signed as Count. The Resident had deputed the Captain of the Port to give passports in his stead; but that functionary, a man of high character, refused to insert the usurped title. The Resident was next appealed to, but he was an Englishman, and not likely to sanction roguery. The self-made Count was obliged to return to England unacknowledged. But he was not a man to yield to fate whilst anything could possibly be done to avert her decrees. Through his wife's friends, therefore, he made great interest to obtain strong letters of recommendation to the Lord High Commissioner of the day. He also procured a document to be skilfully manufactured in Italy in support of his claim. He affected, moreover, on his arrival at Corfu, with his recommendatory letters, the utmost zeal for the Protectorate, boasting of his great personal interest in his native island. His unwearied labours were at length crowned with success. The deceived Representative of Majesty, by means of the Senate, granted to the impostor the ratification of his usurped title. The remainder of his life was perfectly consistent with his above-recorded conduct. But I shall here trouble the reader with only one more sample of his extraordinary career.

In one of his adventurous journeys the Count

found himself in Rome with a very slender purse. He required a carriage to convey him to Ancona, but he had not sufficient money to pay the fare. A bright idea struck him, at the expense of the *rettu- rini* of Rome. It was the law at that period that any one hiring a coachman might demand from him the deposit of a sum of money, in order to ensure the non-violation of his agreement. The Count passed a busy day in hiring as many travelling carriages as he could find, putting into his pocket all the pledge-money. The sum was very considerable, in consequence of the distance from Rome to Ancona, by which it was calculated. The coachmen were ordered to be at the Count's hotel next morning at 9 A.M.; all, except one happy man, who was directed to be at the same spot at daylight. At 9 A.M. accordingly, on the following day, a long line of carriages was stationed at the hotel; all the drivers of which were inquiring for the gentleman who was going to Ancona. When the trick was discovered, above a hundred voices filled the air with their clamours. But the noble Count had departed at daylight; and in those days when telegraphs and even railways were quite unknown, it was not possible to overtake him. That the Count had not taken the trouble to give a false name, was characteristic of his almost incredible effrontery, and also of the impunity upon which he was accustomed to reckon.

The toleration of such conduct as above described is a sad stain upon any society. The want of moral courage, at least, which it displays is very discouraging to those who take a warm and sincere interest in the Ionian people. If the Greeks are in earnest in their desire to cultivate the friendship of the English, they must turn over a new leaf in their manner of treating such delinquencies. These are not simply to be laughed at as good jokes. They must be denounced as a national abomination and disgrace, unworthy of any country calling itself Christian, and anxious to obtain all the moral as well as material advantages of civilization.

With regard to what is ordinarily called immorality, I do not myself believe that the Ionians form any striking exception to the general rule laid down by Monsieur About. That writer praises in very strong terms the chastity of the Greeks. The higher state of civilization of the Islanders over the continental Greeks probably makes the virtue in question less pure amongst the former. But assuredly the Ionian ladies can in this respect well bear comparison with their sisters in the more civilized West of Europe. As far as the experience of myself and my family extend, I cannot speak too highly of the virtues and amiability of the Ionian ladies. But the fatal facility of divorce has an undoubted tendency to evil. Not that it really increases actual crime; but it causes the sacredness of the marriage tie to be less respected than it ought to be, and is injurious both to the happiness and to the morality of the children. Of the two extremes, easy divorce or total refusal of the indulgence, I must myself prefer the Roman Catholic doctrine to that of the Greek Church, which is so totally at variance with the express commands of the New Testament.

The sanction of the archbishops or bishops is all that is requisite to legalize a divorce. If the husband desire to live in the country and the wife prefer to reside in town, and they cannot agree, a divorce is granted.* But this subject will be further discussed in the following chapter.

The English families generally set an excellent example of the fidelity and affection which in their own country are usually the characteristics of domestic life. The rare exceptions have principally occurred in those high places where they would naturally be the least expected. This is a subject upon which it is not agreeable to dwell. But as English writers have frequently denounced the immorality of the Ionians, I must in candour observe, that certain notorious facts in the past history of the Protectorate should make us hesitate to publish such accusations. To three only of these notorious facts will I now briefly allude. One Lord High

* A wedding occurred whilst the author was in the country, one of the parties of which had been divorced for the above-mentioned reason. The divorced wife, of spotless character, was residing close by, whilst her husband was espousing with great festivities another and younger lady.

Commissioner made use of the Patriarch of Constantinople, and of the forms of the Greek Church,
in order to marry a lady already the wife of an
Ionian gentleman. A 'second Chief of the State
publicly paraded his utter disregard of appearances.
A third did not scruple to desecrate the palace (in
which he misrepresented the pure Majesty of England) by converting it into—

" that which I am unwilling to mention."*

But very excellent men have sometimes been betrayed into sad breaches of morality. The stain of
injustice is a graver charge, and more disgraceful to
England than any of the above-mentioned facts.
The affair of the injured Ionian judges has excited
the indignation of an illustrious Assembly. Not so
as yet the case of Count Dusmani. Nevertheless,
this gentleman, after long and invaluable services to
the British Protectorate, was dismissed from his
office by an act of caprice, as good in law as it was
bad in equity. In this sad business the real culprit
must, I fear, be sought for in England.† A great
and verbose despatch came from *London*. And who
dares to oppose the wrath of genius armed with
power? Let us hasten along, and whilst he lies in
the dust, let us kick the foe of——Cæsar.‡

* Illud quod dicere nolo.—*Juvenal.*
† Vide vol. i., page 276.
‡   Verbosa et grandis epistola venit
A Caprels.
Quam timeo, victus ne pœnas exigat Ajax,
Ut male defensus! curramus præcipites, et
Dum jacet in ripâ, calcemus Cæsaris hostem.
                              Juvenal.

CHAPTER II.

Loss of Corfu will be greatly felt—Prince Alfred's Visit—The Duke of Brabant—The Author of " Pelham"—Lord Elgin—The Empress of Austria—The Emperor Francis Joseph—The Emperor at a Regimental Parade—The Empress of Austria in Venice—Visit of the Prince of Wales—A grateful Palace Guest—English Colony, Male and *Female*, denounced—Danger of rapid Elevation—Tribute of Respect to the General and Garrison—A quaint Revenge—It is an ill Wind that blows Nobody Good—" Let us swear eternal Friendship."

THE loss of Corfu, as a naval and military station, and as a pleasant winter abode for civilians, will always be deeply and generally regretted. As regards English society and hospitality it was a second Malta, whilst in every other respect it greatly surpassed the attractions of that " military hothouse."[*] With regard to the subalterns of the army, the excellent shooting in Greece and Albania, with the delightful yachting excursions, and the paper hunts of the ladies and gentlemen, rendered Corfu in their eyes a kind of earthly paradise.

* Byron.

English civilians and distinguished foreigners also visited with pleasure, especially during the winter, the beautiful capital of the Seven Islands.

On the 5th December, 1859, his Royal Highness Prince Alfred landed at Corfu under a royal salute, and with all due military honors. During his stay the Prince lodged at the palace, with another young midshipman of his own selection for a companion. Official dinners and a ball celebrated his arrival. The Royal midshipman, apparently, found the dinner slow; but at the ball he evidently enjoyed himself. The kindness of his Royal Highness in procuring partners for his brother midshipmen was much observed. His personal qualities increased that popularity which is the birthright of all her Majesty's children.

The idea of making Prince Alfred King of Greece had not yet become general. But from the date of this visit, the fact that King Otho had no direct heirs, turned the general attention to future possibilities. Long before the fall of Otho, the hope that Prince Alfred might one day reign in Greece (bringing with him the Ionian Islands), had become the general sentiment of the Hellenic race. In 1862, after the revolution, it was announced that his Royal Highness was coming in a vessel of war to pay a second visit to the Islands. But this intention was suddenly changed; in consequence of the reports of the enthusiastic desire of the Greeks to have the Prince for their King. It was, therefore, judged imprudent to encourage, by his presence, hopes which it had never for a moment been the intention of the British Government to gratify. The Prince, therefore, remained at Malta, to the great disappointment of the Ionians, who were prepared to give him a most flattering reception.

In the spring of 1860, the Duke of Brabant, eldest son of the King of the Belgians, paid a short visit to Corfu, the fortifications of which he duly inspected. Over those at Fort Neuf I had the honor of being one of the party which accompanied his Royal Highness. The Duke much admired the extensive works, which he examined in detail; and he would have been much astonished, I believe, could he have supposed that within three years from that time, Great Britain would cede of its own free will the magnificent fortress of Corfu.

In the same year, the author of " Pelham" passed some weeks in the island; gracing with his presence many dinners and balls. I heard that he was much struck with the handsome faces of the Greek men, but that he was disappointed in regard to the appearance of the females.

On the 26th March, 1861, the Earl of Elgin (on his way to be Governor-General of India) landed for a few hours. A guard of honor and a salute of nineteen guns were the honors he received. He

wore a complete suit of white plain clothes, with a
wide-awake transformed into a white turban, in
early preparation for the hot latitudes he was bound
for. With us the weather was quite cool. The
decidedly plethoric aspect of the Viceroy of India
was not promising as regarded his future health,
considering that he was proceeding to India, for the
first time, at an advanced period of life.

The longest visit paid to Corfu by a Royal personage, during the last four years, was that of the
Empress of Austria in 1861. Her Majesty came to
enjoy the mild climate; and she resided for several
months in the *Casino*, or country-house of the Lord
High Commissioner. There she lived in the simplest
manner, with very few attendants, and happily re-
leased from all the trammels and fatigues of Imperial rank. Her Majesty might be seen, almost daily,
walking on the beautiful sea-side road at Castrades,
which was constructed by Sir Howard Douglas
when Lord High Commissioner. Accompanied by a
single lady, the Empress enjoyed the mild air and the
beautiful scenery; whilst delighting both the Greeks
and the English by her graceful yet dignified simplicity of manners. Her Majesty was a constant
attendant at the little Opera House, and at the
palace balls. Young, beautiful, interesting, and
good, it is pleasing to imagine that she may have
contributed to that great change in policy which

has so raised, in general estimation, the already high character of her Imperial husband.

When the time had arrived for the Empress to return to Vienna, the Emperor of Austria, like a true knight, came in person to escort his fair lady. His Majesty stayed a few days in Corfu. He inspected the fortifications; one of the new batteries of which was called "Francis Joseph," out of compliment to the illustrious visitor.

On one occasion, soon after the arrival of the Emperor, he proceeded to the Esplanade, whilst Lieutenant Middleton, Adjutant of the second battalion 4th Foot, was drilling his soldiers. That officer seeing a gentleman too near, as he thought, to his men, galloped up to him to request him to move a little out of the way. As he approached the tall upright individual in a white hat, it suddenly occurred to him that it was the Emperor, whom he had not yet seen, but of whose presence in the island he was doubtless aware. He, however, with great presence of mind, continued his course, and asked his Majesty if he had any orders to give. The Emperor, on learning that the battalion would be at drill under its officers in the afternoon, arranged to meet it again, and kept his word. Owing to the absence of the field-officers, the command devolved upon a captain named Eccles, who had the honor of manœuvring the battalion before the Emperor. His Majesty appeared to take great interest in the drill of the English soldiers: but he strictly preserved his incognito, and would not receive a salute or compliment of any kind.

A few days afterwards the Imperial couple departed in a steamer for Trieste. The loss of the Empress was felt as a great blank in the island, from which her Majesty carried away the heartfelt and respectful good wishes of all the inhabitants, whether British or Ionian.

The Empress of Austria spent the following winter at Venice; at which the author stayed a week on his return to the Islands from a visit to England. Not all the virtues of the Empress, nor all her personal advantages, could extract from the Venetians any marks of interest or respect towards one who so nearly represented the hated power of Austria. The sentiments of the inhabitants of Venice must have formed a painful contrast with the recollections of Corfu in the mind of her Majesty. The poor Venetians are probably expiating the crimes committed by their ancestors during many centuries of misrule. But let us hope that the expiation is nearly completed, and that Venice may, before many years, be united to the Kingdom of Italy. The English, by the cession of the Seven Islands, have given a noble example to that Emperor, who has already exhibited, under very difficult circumstances, so much good sense and magnanimity. Perhaps his Majesty may yet spontaneously grant to Venice a restored nationality, which will otherwise doubtless be one day extorted by violence.

In the spring of 1862, his Royal Highness the Prince of Wales visited the capital of the Seven Islands for two days, on his way to the East. Owing to stress of weather, the Prince put into Zante, also for a few hours. On the return voyage his Royal Highness visited Cephalonia in June; of which last visit more will be hereafter recorded. In consequence of the very strict orders of the local Government, there were not many demonstrations of any kind. On his Royal Highness proceeding to Malta, the same exceedingly strict reserve was not carried out. The Ionians sensibly felt the difference. It appeared to them that they had been debarred from testifying their enthusiasm for the Queen and Royal Family of England. This circumstance helped to increase, if anything could do so, the great unpopularity of the local Government.

The society of Corfu suffered materially from the absence of any lady to do the honors at the palace, although the Secretary Sir Henry Wolff, and Lady Wolff, endeavoured to mitigate the evil. The latter strove to draw together the Greek and English families, but she was not greatly encouraged in the highest quarter.

The society was frequently enlivened by the presence of English visitors. These, when of any distinction, were most hospitably entertained, and generally lodged at the palace. They naturally returned to England fully satisfied that the Lord High Commissioner was one of the ablest and most popular of men. One of these gentlemen, whose experience had been confined to the vice-regal dinner-table, wrote, in 1863, a letter to the *Times*. In it he stated that he had dined repeatedly at the palace, and had there never heard a word in favour of the displaced Ionian judges; as if it were likely that the truth on that subject would be intruded on his Excellency by his own guests.

The chief ruler at Corfu appeared, on his arrival, to be ambitious of establishing an universal despotism. It was to be over the English, as well as over the Ionians—over the ladies, as well as over the gentlemen. It did not wholly succeed, and his Excellency was compelled to modify some of his views. It is, however, needless to enter further upon this contemptible subject. But, in a celebrated official memorandum, dated 18th November, 1862, the Lord High Commissioner made an extraordinary charge against the English at Corfu. They were accused of being too partial to the Ionian Protectionists, who " had filled all the public departments with their creatures." As the Protectionists were the only party in favour of England, it was only natural that the English should be glad to see them holding offices. But they had no power whatever of carrying out their wishes. Yet his Excellency reported to the Colonial Minister that the Protectionists were "*backed* by the English colony, male and female." The memorandum continues: "The difficulty of the enterprise which has been attempted may be imagined, and the opposition which has been experienced is not to be wondered at." The enterprise of his Excellency was, it appears, to put down corruption and monopoly, which the English colony, male and female, supported.

I may begin by inquiring what is meant by "the British colony male and *female*," which "backed" the Protectionists? I was not aware that there ever was a colony of English in Corfu. The fact is that, except a very few merchants, the English have been limited to civil or military officials, and to temporary visitors. The few English permanently settled in the Islands are, moreover, not persons of any influence. Especially, I may ask who were the *female* colonists who assisted to throw obstacles in the way of the virtuous plans of his Excellency? But it is needless to endeavour to explain an attack upon English ladies, which admits of no rational interpretation. I can offer no other solution of this incomprehensible calumny than the following sentence in Lord Macaulay's History : " One of the most severe trials to which the head and heart of a man can be put is great and rapid elevation." The trial was too severe for the tenth Lord High Commissioner.

But let justice be done, Sir Henry Storks has well fulfilled his destined task. The union of the Islands with Greece being a preordained fact, the more unanimously it was voted for by the Assembly the better ; and the last British ruler assured by his conduct (as we have already described) a wonderful degree of unanimity.

Let it not be supposed, however, that the Ionians hate the English generally. That is very far from being the case. In 1862, before the death of the deeply-lamented Major-General Sir John Inglis, the commander of the forces, the Ionian Parliament snatched at an occasion of paying to him and to the troops under his command a friendly compliment. They had passed a resolution to keep her Majesty's birthday as a holiday. They now forwarded a copy of that resolution to the Major-General, with a written communication. The latter expressed their feelings of loyalty and sympathy for her Majesty the Queen, and also their friendly sentiments to the British troops in the garrison, notwithstanding their desire for union and nationality.*

* Thus the Radical Parliament showed itself as well disposed to the English generally as were the Protectionists, though the English are accused of *backing* the latter.

The excellent example, and the amiable social qualities of Sir John and the Honorable Lady Inglis (though, unfortunately, but briefly exhibited), were displayed at the right moment for the honor and reputation of the departing Protectorate. No English pair could have more worthily represented to the Ionians those qualities of heroic valour and of moral worth which have contributed so much to the glory and greatness of England.

Of the English colony (as Sir Henry Storks styled it), his Excellency had no right to complain. It always treated him with the respect due to the position which he held. The only exception was the case of a gallant and excellent officer who had considered himself personally ill-treated by the Chief of the State. The officer in question, walking one day on the Esplanade, met the band of his regiment proceeding to the garrison ditch to meet the Representative of Majesty, who was then landing from his steamer after a tour of the Islands. "What are you going to play?" inquired the colonel. "*God save the Queen*," replied the surprised musician. "You will do no such thing," retorted his commander; "you will play a simple march." The order was duly obeyed. At the first note of the music, his Excellency's hat was raised as usual in acknowledgment; but, after a bar or two, it was replaced, and he entered his palace greatly annoyed. A sharp correspondence followed. The general referred the case to the Horse Guards. The Lord High Commissioner then discovered that he was not quite so great a man as he fancied himself to be. He was not a first-class Representative of Majesty, like an Ambassador, a Viceroy of Ireland, or a Governor-General of India. He had no right to have *God save the Queen* played in his honor. He had fallen in some measure from his high estate. He could no longer proudly say,

> " To me sole monarch Jove commits the sway,
> *Mine* are the laws, and *me* let all obey."

The officer who had thus bearded the lion in his den became, strange to say, an object of honor and of respect, rather than of anger, to the vanquished ruler. His friendship was most eagerly sought, although for a long time vainly. But a happy opportunity at length occurred to regain the good opinion of a man, who was supposed to have great influence in certain circles in England. The reconciliation was duly effected over the broken but classic head of a poor Ionian, who had ventured to pelt a military band in the open street, and who, prostrated by a Homeric blow upon the skull, fell supine upon the shore, unwept, unhonored, and unrevenged. An English judge, who thought proper to point out to his Excellency the illegality of the inflicted punishment, was informed that the matter, not having taken a judicial form, did not concern him. Care was taken to acquaint the gallant officer of this friendly act on the part of the highest authority. In consequence, a meeting at the palace took place, and " Let us swear eternal friendship," was the anti-Jacobinical termination to a deadly two years' hostility, which had long diverted the public. This anecdote cannot but delight every benevolent mind, for it is a consolatory proof that true Christian forgiveness is still sometimes nobly practised in the somewhat selfish and calculating nineteenth century.

CHAPTER III.

Upon the subject of the Ionian Church I shall not enter into many details. For the difference in the several Eastern Churches is very slight, whilst the general subject has been fully described by various writers. I shall confine my observations, therefore, chiefly to those points which appear to me to be peculiar to the Ionian Church; although the union of the Islands with Greece will doubtless include also that of their Churches.

An able author states of the Oriental Church: "For the clerical body, marriage is not only permitted and frequent, but compulsory, and all but universal." He excepts only the bishops. His remark hardly, I think, applies to the Ionian Islands.

There, marriage is permitted amongst the priests; but far from being compulsory, it is not, I am credibly assured, even encouraged. The character of a priest who remains single is considered more holy than that of one married; other things being equal. It appears to be in the Russian, which is an independent Church, that marriage amongst the parish priests is rendered compulsory. But the Ionian Church is still dependent upon the Patriarch of Constantinople, though it will probably soon cease to be so. If a married Ionian priest loses his wife he cannot marry again. A married priest cannot be promoted. Nor can a priest marry after he has been ordained. It is clear, then, that marriage is not encouraged: but it is, nevertheless, generally contracted.

Various other causes besides infidelity can occasion divorces, at the discretion of the local Bishop or Archbishop. "Those whom God hath joined," *can* be "put asunder," for various trifling reasons. Incompatible tempers, or personal infirmities, are sufficient causes. It is all for *better*, and not at all for *worse*, apparently, that marriage is contracted in the Islands. So that if any *worse* subsequently creeps in, the compact is considered broken, and its dissolution justified. Marriage is allowed only beyond the seventh degree of relationship. This is a most inconvenient restriction; but it is a law more conducive to the health and vigor of mankind than that which permits in other countries the union of near relations.

There are archbishops without suffragans in the four principal islands, and bishops in the three smaller ones. Each of the archbishops is in his turn appointed Exarch, or head of the Septinsular Church. But no additional salary, and but little additional authority appertains to the office, which is at this moment held by the Archbishop of Cephalonia. There are still a great number of monasteries in the Islands, although many, and those the richest, have been suppressed by the British Government. The latter has been charged with using the funds for secular purposes, and allowing the convents themselves to fall into ruins. I am not acquainted with the total number of monasteries: but some idea may be formed from those of Cephalonia, where six of the first and eight of the second class still exist. The monastery of San Gerasimo contains the greatest number of monks—namely, twenty-nine. They are, for the most part, merely labourers, free to leave or to remain, and not bound by any oaths. Even the monasteries which are not suppressed are placed under the charge of Government, which lets them out to tenants, who are bound to maintain them in good order. They have been the occasion of very great abuses; fully justifying the constant intervention of authority which has taken place. There are considerably more than 2000 churches in the Island, public, conventual, and private. There are 900 priests with Government salaries, amounting altogether to about 5000*l.* a year.* The moral character of the clergy is generally good, but the same cannot be said of their intellectual state. The free permission to marry is the great safety-valve from temptations to infringe the rules of morality, properly so called. But very inferior education (from the absence of strict examinations) has subjected the Ionian priesthood to the secret but certain contempt of all the enlightened laymen. There are, of course, exceptions ; but, as a general rule, the clergy are extremely ignorant, bigoted, and unscrupulous. A distinguished English writer, well inclined also towards the Greek Church, has admitted "that the Oriental forms of Christianity are more exposed than others to the danger of uniting the form of godliness with the mystery of iniquity."† My own experience corroborates this opinion. The boasted morality is limited to a single kind of abstinence. Falsehoods, gross deceptions, sham miracles, are a part of the system on which the priesthood depends. The Ionians hope to set the example of civilization to the rest of Greece. But the first indispensable step is a spontaneous internal reform of the Greek Church, founded on the basis of the New Testa-

---

* Vide Appendix F for further ecclesiastical details.
† Stanley's *Eastern Church.*

ment. The great love displayed by the Greeks all over the world for Prince Alfred had in it a deep meaning, which, though chiefly political, is not, I think, exclusively so. Liberty of thought, as well as of external forms. was probably amongst those characteristics of Englishmen which attracted Greek homage. It is, at all events, notorious that had Prince Alfred accepted the throne he would not have been expected to change his religion. The Greeks everywhere declared that they had no objection to a Protestant, although they were strongly opposed to a Roman Catholic King. In spite of their degenerate state, the Greek clergy have deserved respect and gratitude for their past services in the national cause. But they must not now be permitted, by their ignorance and superstitions, to clog the progress of the resurgent nation on the path of Christian civilization and of national development.

Many Englishmen are inclined to believe that the Greek Church in its doctrines approaches nearer to the Church of England than to that of Rome. But I do not think that facts bear out such opinions. It is true that, like the English, the Greeks believe neither in the Pope nor in purgatory ; yet, like the Roman Catholics, they pray to the Virgin and to the Saints. Like them they adore pictures* and

* They do not, indeed, worship statues ; which, however, are surely as worthy as pictures of receiving divine honors.

relics, and believe that miracles have not ceased ; proving, moreover, their faith occasionally by fabricating them.   In essentials I can see little difference between the tenets of Rome and those of Constantinople.   But the Roman Catholics have the advantage of that sounder faith, which is proved by laborious works.   Whilst the Greek Church is, and has long been apathetically indifferent to the spread of its doctrines, the missionaries of Rome have carried the banners of their faith through every region of the habitable globe.

I am of opinion that it is political and not religious motives which now induce the Greeks to regard the Protestant religion without hostility; whilst their hatred of Roman Catholicism is stronger than ever.   The sentiments of the priesthood corroborate this view; for whilst it shares in the hatred against Rome, it is far from leaning towards Protestantism.   In their hearts, the clergy still incline towards Russia, as the most powerful chief of the so-called Orthodox Church.   But as prudence compels them to conceal their opinions, the general aspect of the Greek race is at present favourable to Protestant England.

In 1805, Colonel Leake recorded a state of opinions very different to that now existing.   Speaking of a Macedonian Bishop, he says : " In common with many of the Greek clergy, my host is desirous of an union of the Greek and Latin Churches."   In the present day, an union of the English and Greek Churches would certainly be the more popular idea. But much must be done before this can be accomplished. The Greeks, like the English, profess to found their religion and morality on the New Testament, yet Signor Lascarato persists in asserting that the volume in question is seldom or never to be found in any Ionian house. A little of it is, indeed, read weekly in churches in the original tongue, which, however, few of the natives understand. Whilst learning modern Greek, at different times in two different islands, under clever masters, the modern Greek Testament formed part of my study, as an easy way of learning the language. On both occasions I found that it was an almost unknown book to my fellow-readers. One of them was startled by the passage in the Revelations where the angel from heaven forbids St. John to worship him or to kneel to him, and commands him to worship God alone. He confessed that the passage was directly opposed to the worship of saints and relics, as carried on in his Church. I found, however, that the majority of educated men did not really believe in the superstitions which they practised. But they considered them necessary for the people. I was assured by some persons that the peasants, who will lie when they swear by the Almighty, will yet tell the truth when they swear by the patron saint of their island. But others have confessed to me that the peasants are quite as ready to break the one oath as the other, which I firmly believe to be the case.

I have occasionally attended Divine service at the Greek churches during my stay in the Islands. At Cephalonia I should probably have done so frequently had I not feared to give offence. On the Sunday after Easter, the 27th April, 1862, I was taken by a friend to the little church of the Archangel. The men all stood below in the stalls without seats. But there were not twenty men in the church. The women were chiefly in a latticed gallery above, though I observed the Countess Anino, with her son, underneath the gallery in the body of the church. The service began with chanted prayers and hymns. A priest then read from the Acts of the Apostles the miraculous escape of St. Peter from prison. Next he read from the 20th chapter of the Gospel of St. John from the 19th verse to the end.* All these passages were read clearly in the original Greek. With occasional help from my friend I was enabled to follow easily. There is but little difference between the original Testament and the modern Greek version which I possess, and was at that time studying. When the service was over, boxes and purses were handed together round the church for different objects of charity, into all of which one was expected to put a

---

* In our own Church the Gospel for the day was from the same chapter, from the 19th to the 23rd verse.

trifle. I, however, who was then ignorant of this necessity, had about me only one piece of coin, which I gave to the leader of the alms-bearing procession. I was not much impressed by the service. It appeared to me to be a very formal affair, in which crossings, and holy water, and bows to saints supplied the place of prayer and supplication. There was not much pretence of solemnity, or even of ordinary attention.

I afterwards learnt that my visit to the church had given rise to much gossip and criticism. It was suspected that I had only gone in order to laugh at their proceedings, which was very far from being the case. However, I deemed it best in future to abstain from entering churches during the performance of service, at least in Cephalonia.

The Earl of Carlisle, who visited Corfu in 1853, remarked, in the work he then published, that the Greek Church " encourages the perusal of the Holy Scriptures." This remark does not, I think, apply to the Ionian Islands ; at least, my own long experience does not confirm the statement even as regards the capital. And it must be remembered that the attempt to disseminate a few printed extracts from the Gospels occasioned disturbances at Corfu, in the time of Sir Howard Douglas.* I believe there is very little, if any, circulation of the Scriptures in Cephalonia. In that island, an

* Vide page 148 of the History of the British Protectorate.

English Scripture-reader gave, about a twelvemonth ago, a Greek Testament to a native, who was sick at the time. The gift was thankfully received. The recipient was shortly afterwards visited by a priest, who, seeing the sacred volume, inquired by whom it had been given. The priest examined it and said, "It is just like ours ; but you ought to read the Gospels only as printed in our books." Yet he made no offer to lend the invalid an orthodox copy. On another occasion a portion of the New Testament was read to a priest in the country, who said, "We have all that, but we have also some valuable additions." He did not, however, exhibit any of his books, nor indicate what was the nature of the so-called additions.

The English have not always sufficiently respected the religious prejudices of the natives, and have sometimes treated the clergy rather harshly. In the correspondence of Sir C. Napier, there is an amusing account of a priest who, after fighting in party quarrels, had secluded himself in a convent for twenty years. At this period a Colonel Travers was the Resident, and had been informed that the priest had concealed arms in his possession. The evidence of the fact, however, was very doubtful. "Be that as it may," continues Sir Charles, "Travers *shaved and flogged him* at Argostoli, and again at Lixuri. During his flogging he summoned all good Christians to the rescue." Yet of this priest Sir

Charles speaks rather favourably, as regards his general character.

The Ionian bishops are, at present, generally very respectable men. Some of them are greatly venerated and esteemed ; although they are usually too violent in their politics to accord with English ideas of holy men. In former days they were less respectable. About forty years ago, Napier thus announced a new bishop : "Meanwhile to bless us, we have got a bishop appointed ; an excellent pious man, who formerly lived by sheep stealing, which he now calls his pastoral life."

That the clergy of the Eastern Church are apt to be ambitious is not surprising, when it is remembered that the proud house of Romanoff sprang from a parish priest. The Archbishop of Corfu has great influence, which will probably be increased by the union with Greece, of which he has ever been the staunch and unflinching advocate. He is generally believed to be a secret partisan of Russia. But his popularity with the people is greatly increased by his devotion to the patron Saint Spiridion, whom he loves to style "the miracle-working saint."

The loss of time and money occasioned by the numerous holidays and fasts (which together swallow up more than a third of the Greek year) is an evil not confined to the Ionian Islands. The first day of Lent is always kept as a great holiday. In

1863, it occurred on the 23rd of February. At Cephalonia, nearly all the inhabitants promenaded the whole afternoon on the road leading from the back of the town to the sea. The military band attended; and the scene was very lively and gay. But it could not be compared to similar festas in Corfu, owing to the absence of picturesque dresses amongst the peasantry. 'The Cephalonian women rarely exhibit ornaments of any kind, whilst the males usually wear the plainest Turkish dresses. The most astonishing sight which I witnessed on this occasion, was a number of Greeks riotously drunk; a very rare case in that most temperate of countries. They appeared to select a day dedicated to religion, to break out into the most unusual excesses; thus reminding the stranger of the complete independence which exists between religion and morality in superstitious and half-civilized countries.

There is reason to hope that the majority of the Greek gentry are no longer the dupes of the pretended miracles of the priests. But many still deem it politic to appear to be very superstitious. One usurer, who had enriched himself at the expense of the people of a certain island, endeavoured to counterbalance his unpopularity by the exhibition of extreme piety. By the display of abject submission to the priest, by constant voluntary candle-holding, and by slobbering with his kisses every picture or holy relic that came in his way, he sought to win the admiration of the populace.   But it was all in vain.   He felt that his safety depended entirely upon British protection, and he gave out, therefore, that, when the English should depart, he also would leave the country.   It was pointed out to me, as one of the many horrors which would result from the Union, that this rich man would be compelled to expatriate himself to save his life.   But I was of opinion that if the people, when left to themselves, should tar and feather such a compound of hypocrisy and roguery, they would not be very severely condemned by any honest man.

On the 1st of November, 1862, in company with a Greek friend, I proceeded in one of the usual rattle-trap carriages to the Convent of San Gerasimo,* which lies in a picturesque valley at the foot of the Black Mountain.   It was the feast day of the patron saint of Cephalonia, to whom the convent was dedicated.   The saint, on occasions such as this, was, if in good humour, in the habit of performing a celebrated miracle; the approximation of his relics causing the water to rise in a certain holy well.   No one, not even the English, appeared to doubt the fact that the water did rise.   Had not Caralambo, the farmer who lived close by the well (and who was such a useful friend and agent of the British officers), repeatedly seen the water rise in different years?   The only question for those who

* Usually so called, though in fact it is a monastery.

did not believe in miracles was, what were the scientific causes of the rising of the water? The most approved solution attributed the result to great pressure. It was supposed that the mass of visitors crowding round the well at the critical moment might by their great weight account for the phenomenon.

My friend and I were politely received at the convent, in the reception-room of which we sat for a considerable time. At length a procession was formed in the court, in the rear of which we walked to the holy well. Arrived at the sacred spot with the able Judge-Advocate-Fiscal and the Municipal Minister of religion, I, as the only Englishman present, was treated with great politeness. Way was made for me through the crowd, and I was permitted to look into the well, surrounded by a dense crowd of persons, chiefly peasants. The day was fine, but plenty of rain had latterly fallen, so that water ought not to have been scarce. The saint, in his case, was there; so were the priests, the monks, and the nuns. One of these last, moreover, was so pretty, that her eyes might have worked miracles with some people. *But no rise was to be got out of the water.* I have not a shadow of doubt that my heretical presence bore all the blame of the failure, and that I performed for that occasion the part of a land-Jonah. However, I cannot consider my visit to have been wholly unprofitable. I firmly believe that I that day solved the question which had puzzled so many Britons. The solution in question is simply this—*that the water never does, and never did rise at all!* I was assured, on excellent authority (since fully corroborated), that no respectable Cephalonian—no man worthy of credit—had ever really seen the water rise. The latter, indeed, is down at such a depth (apparently some twenty or even thirty feet), that I do not believe that all the inhabitants of the island standing around it could have the slightest influence on its action.

But, although the miracle is a recognised imposture amongst sensible people, the gentry are generally of opinion that it is advisable that the peasants should continue to credit such fables; a theory which has sometimes been endorsed even by English clergymen. As if any good thing could ever arise from the wilful dissemination of falsehood and imposture!

My friend and I were pressed to stay, for the usual dinner given on these occasions, at the convent, to the Municipal Minister of Religion, and to the other officials who might be present. But being in a hurry to return to Argostoli, I declined the hospitable invitation, and thereby lost, I believe, a good dinner, served in the most approved Greek fashion.

CHAPTER IV.

A candid French Author, and One the Reverse—The Latin Princes protected the Jews—Judas Iscariot the supposed Corfiot—Author's narrow escape of being taken for Judas—Venice grants the Jews privileges—Cruelty to them of the Greeks—Venetians denounce the Desecration of Graves—Marshal Schulemberg befriends the Jews—Their Numbers in the Islands—Sir Charles Napier protects them—Their Treatment at Zante—Accuracy always rare amongst Greeks—A self-deluded old Woman—Peasant's Greek Language—Magic-Lantern Lecture in Italian—A Parricide—An Execution in Corfu—Reported Fate of the Executioner.

MONSIEUR ABOUT informs us that there are very few Jews in the kingdom of Greece, and that the Athenian people are not formed to attract them. He declares that "In the Ionian Islands, the Jewish race lives and prospers under the protection of England."* One would imagine that the notoriety of this fact would render its contradiction, by any rational person, utterly impossible. Yet there exist men of some position in the world, who not only deny the fact in question, but maintain the very contrary to be the truth. A certain French writer has

* "Aux Iles Ioniennes, sous la protection de l'Angleterre, la race Juive vit et prospère."

not been ashamed to print the statement, that it was the British who persecuted the Jews, and that it was the Ionians who advocated their cause.   This writer observed that the Jews in Zante, were regularly shut up every night in the *Ghetto*.   He immediately decided (on the evidence probably of his friend Signor Lombardo), that it was the English Government which illiberally enforced this treatment upon the Jews.   But on these subjects, M. About is an infinitely better authority than his ill-informed, prejudiced, and grossly deceived fellow-countryman.

M. About thus describes in a few words, simple and truthful, the affair of Pacifico, so falsely represented by the other French Author: "On a certain Greek Good Friday, the rabble of Athens, who were accustomed to celebrate the day by burning a Jew in effigy, and who were deprived of that orthodox diversion, consoled itself by plundering the house of a Portuguese Jew protected by England." Even the uncandid French author is obliged to confess that very few Jews are to be found in Athens, while 6000 of them reside in Corfu; although he wilfully shuts his eyes to the obvious causes of this striking disparity.

Two Ionian authors confirm the testimony of M. About, as regards the past conduct of Greeks towards Jews.

In Count Lunzi's history, there is much interesting information on this subject. We find that the Jews were already numerous in Corfu in the time of the Princes of Tarentum. Many decrees were promulgated in their favour ; but their frequent repetition is a proof of their general insufficiency. One order, still preserved, is dated the 6th of March, 1323, another is of the 12th of March, 1324. In 1336, Robert of Tarentum, then lord of the island, issued a proclamation to mitigate the sufferings of the Jews. Similar steps were taken by other Latin princes in the course of the fourteenth century.

The late Chevalier Mustoxidi informs us, that Philip of Tarentum, the successor of Robert, titular Emperor of Constantinople, reiterated, in 1366, the orders of his predecessors for ensuring the toleration and good treatment of the Jews ; " which," continues the candid historian, " were probably always inefficacious to save them from constant violence."*

An old Italian writer (quoted by the same author), declared that there were in his time some descendants of Judas Iscariot living in the island of Corfu, where the house and country villa of the traitor still existed. This, of course, was a mere fable. But it is certainly curious that the modern Corfiots appear to cherish against the memory of Judas, a hatred greater than can be traced in the customs of other Christians. On every Easter Eve, a gun is fired as a signal at eleven, A.M.; and, at the

* *Delle Cose Corciresi.* By A. Mustoxidi.

same instant, from the windows and tops of all the houses in Corfu, great quantities of crockery are discharged into the streets. For this memorable occasion, all broken or cracked earthenware jugs and dishes are carefully preserved throughout the year. The supposition is, that good Christians are stoning, in imagination, the traitor Jew. The Greeks will not readily confess this fact to strangers, yet it is generally believed. On Saturday the 14th of April, 1860, I (to use a sporting phrase) very nearly *came to grief*, from a misunderstanding in regard to this custom. I had been led to believe that operations were to commence at noon. But about two minutes to eleven, I was riding quietly along the Line Wall, on my way home, when I observed that the streets were unusually empty. My suspicions being excited, I asked of a man in a doorway if it were not at twelve that the gun would be discharged. He replied that it would be fired in a minute or two. I instantly set spurs to my horse, and galloped to my house at racing speed. Just as I had dismounted, bang went the gun, and down came the crash of crockery from the houses. From the moment the crockery falls, guns and pistols are fired in all directions. This part of the ceremony lasts for three or four days, and is by no means agreeable to ladies, or quiet strangers. But I must now return to the subject of the Ionian Jews.

In 1386, Venice (in the same year in which she

took possession of Corfu) directed the Jews in the island to be treated with especial kindness; forbidding that greater taxes should be imposed upon them than upon the rest of the inhabitants. In 1560, the Jews, quoting this order in an appeal to the Serene Republic, obtained the revocation of a tax imposed upon them by the local Government. When in 1571, the Venetian State decreed the expulsion of the Jews from all its territories, a single exception was made in favour of those of Corfu. These, moreover, were granted certain privileges. They were permitted to follow the profession of advocates, as well as to become traders. They were also organized politically, after the manner of the other citizens. They had a council which elected its own functionaries. The Venetian Baillie (and in after times the Proveditor) presided at the elections, at which four syndics, two censors, and two directors of Synagogues were duly appointed by the majority of votes.

For some time the Jews and Christians lived together in an amicable manner; which, however, scandalized some of the Proveditors. Anthony Foscarini, complained to the Senate in 1588, of this disgrace (as he called it) to all good Christians. In 1760, the Jews in Corfu were calculated at 1171 souls. The laws were not always made in their favour. On the contrary, harsh edicts were sometimes directed against them, at all events in appearance. They were ordered to wear yellow caps and yellow badges on their breasts, to distinguish them from Christians. But this act may have originated in sentiments of compassion; for it expressly substituted these badges for *stoning*, which it forbade for the future. It was evidently, therefore, the practice of the Greeks at that period, to throw stones at the Jews whenever they appeared in the streets. These badges were afterwards practically converted into taxes; an annual fine being imposed on all those who did not obey the order.

The cruel manner in which the poor Hebrews were treated, in spite of protective decrees, is candidly narrated by Count Lunzi. In 1614, the Syndics, Giovanni Pasqualigo and Ottavius Bon, published on the 14th of September, the following proclamation in Corfu : " As persons are found in the city who (from their own fancy or out of contempt for the Jews, who have complained to us) are accustomed to enter the cemeteries by night, and to take the dead bodies of Jews out of their graves; stripping them and committing other indecent and disgraceful acts, barbarous, inhuman, and repugnant to nature, which forbids such treatment of corpses; and as these acts are also repulsive to the pious sentiments of the Serene Republic, which impartially cherishes all her subjects without exception; it is, therefore, necessary to make due provision for the remedy of such great evils." The penalty of death was then threatened to offenders; whilst informers were promised (if not principals) a reward of 200 sequins each.

The desecration of the graves of those whom they consider as heretics or unbelievers, is still one of the greatest stains upon the moral character of the Greek race. The English tombs in the Islands have frequently furnished indisputable evidence of these uncivilized barbarities.

On the Greek Good Friday night, there is always a grand torch-light procession, in which the remains of St. Spiridion are carried; whilst the Archbishop moves in state under a canopy, followed by the inhabitants of all ranks, bare-headed, and carrying huge lighted candles. On the following morning there is another procession, which terminates a little before the annual imaginary stoning of Judas Iscariot takes place. There are two other processions of the patron saint in the course of the year in the capital. They are interesting sights. The picturesque appearance of the peasantry, and especially of the females (with their jackets profusely embroidered with gold, and their massive ornaments of the same precious metal), add greatly to the beauty of the spectacle. But I must return to the Jews.

When Marshal Schulemberg was raising the new fortifications, in 1719, he caused the Venetian

Senate to grant a general permission for all Jews to settle in Corfu on payment of a tax. The Marshal, being a Protestant, exerted himself greatly in favour of universal toleration, and his brilliant services gave him effective influence both with the Venetians and with the Ionians. To the hero who had saved them from the Turks, it was difficult to refuse any request. Moreover, the Jews had earned indulgence by their valour against the Mahomedans in 1816, on which occasion, one of them was promoted for his merits to the rank of Captain.* It is highly probable (although I have no authority for asserting the fact) that Fort Abraham derives its name from the desire of Schulemberg, both to record the valour, and to recommend the toleration of the Jews.

When the French first occupied Corfu in 1797, the number of Jews there appears to have been only 2000. At present there are about 6000. In Zante there are 274, in Cephalonia only 34; in the remaining islands there are few or none permanently settled. Corfu being the capital, and also containing the mass of the English, has attracted to itself most of the resident Jews. It has been reserved for the British Government to abolish the *Ghettos*, formed centuries ago for the protection of that persecuted race. The *Ghetto* of Zante was the last to disappear. In May, 1862, when

* Daru.

I visited that city, the gates had been removed some days previously, and I found it difficult to observe a trace of their past existence.

It is generally believed that when the English leave the Islands, most of the Jews will also take their departure. But I hope better things of the Ionians (enlightened as I trust they are by the effects of half a century of British rule) than that they will return to their old habits of bigoted persecution.

The Jews have never been numerous in Cephalonia, but when Sir Charles Napier was Resident they were 130 in number; and that distinguished officer exerted himself strenuously to protect and encourage them. On the 3rd of February, 1823, he issued a proclamation in Italian, a copy of which is in my possession. It accused the citizens of Argostoli of conspiring to drive the Jews out of the island, by refusing to sell necessaries to them, except at very exorbitant prices. The document threatened to punish all those concerned in such disgraceful proceedings, " in order that the citizens of every religion might be able confidently to rely on the protection of the government and the laws." It was added that four citizens had been arrested and sentenced to imprisonment for having ill-treated certain Jews. The original cause of this proclamation was the discovery of the body of a murdered youth. The Greeks accused the Jews of being the murderers, and loudly demanded vengeance. But it was retorted that the lad had been murdered by Greeks, who had then endeavoured to transfer the guilt to the detested Hebrews. The greater portion of the latter after Napier's departure appear to have emigrated to Corfu, as there was little scope for making money in Cephalonia; where, moreover, the Jews were held in great detestation.

At Zante, as late at all events as 1862, the Jews were obliged to shut themselves up in Passion-week (according to the testimony of a most respectable English eye-witness) to escape the insults of the populace. At Corfu they were safer, owing to the strength of the English garrison. But even there they did not show themselves much in the town during the Holy Season, although, as they made it a holiday, I often met them out walking in the country. I one day said to a party of them, " How is it that you are all out of your houses at such a time ?" They simply replied : " Thanks to you English." On my mentioning this occurrence to a Greek gentleman (an enlightened man who speaks English perfectly), he somewhat sneeringly replied : " It was said only to please you as an Englishman." A Greek will never confess any fact which appears to tell against his country. Indeed, the general disregard of accuracy by that nation, is one of their most lamentable characteristics;* but it is no proof of the degeneracy of the race. The Ancient Greeks had the same failing. The Spartans, indeed, had little respect for either truth or honesty ; the greatest virtue with them being to steal or to lie so skilfully and audaciously as to escape detection. Even Homer did not consider the circumventing of a friend disgraceful to one of the noblest of his heroes. On the contrary, he rather chuckles over the simplicity of Glaucus, who was prevailed upon by Diomed to exchange, in proof of reciprocal affection, his gold armour, worth a hundred oxen, for the Greek's armour, which cost only nine. Here, as the Irishman observed, the reciprocity was certainly all on one side.

The Greek peasantry have an especial horror for Jews, which was formerly fanned by the priests into occasional riots. But, thanks to British influence, though there is still a Jews' quarter in Corfu, disturbances no longer occur. Having mentioned the peasantry, I must here record my opinion of them. The children were nuisances who constantly rushed after the Englishmen whom they met, shouting for "*fardings;*" but the grown men were always very civil. As for the women, they generally ran away if spoken to by Englishmen. One day an officer

* An Englishman once defended in my hearing the ignorance of Greek in a certain Resident, by saying, " if he could converse with the people *he would hear nothing but lies !*" an absurd exaggeration!

having alarmed an old woman by firing a gun on a hill near her house, went up to her to give her a trifle as a compensation; but at his approach she moved off. He increased his pace, upon which she fled up the hill, as hard as her tottering legs could carry her. Old as she was, her modest timidity had not abandoned her, though she certainly greatly exaggerated the power of her personal charms. My young friend gave up the chase in despair.

I found the middle-aged and elderly peasants, generally speaking, very polite, to those especially who could speak a few words to them in their own language. At my request they have brought me handfuls of grapes out of their fields, and have refused the proffered remuneration. As a general rule, they have always most civilly replied to all the questions which I have put to them. They are a people easily led, either towards evil or towards good; and sufficient steps have not been taken to ensure their preference of the latter. To ride out and converse with them was one of my constant diversions, with a view to the practice of modern Greek. It is true that the lower the grade in life of my interlocutor, the more difficult I found it to make him understand me. At first, whilst I was quite a beginner, he would either shake his head at me, or (if he knew a few words of English) would reply, " *No speakee Eenglish!*" That was a very mortifying answer. But as I advanced in fluency, I frequently obtained the more flattering reply in *Greek*, " I cannot speak Greek, but only Romaika."* This proved to me that my masters both in Corfu and in Cephalonia taught a language very superior to those peasant dialects, which for centuries formed the sole Greek of the Ionian Islands. It enabled me to understand the remark of a Corfiot gentleman, who said to me: " You are learning Greek ? You will soon know it more correctly than we do ourselves." But though his speech was a natural one, I cannot say that I myself realized its truth.

Whilst in Corfu, I occasionally gave to the soldiers magic-lantern lectures on elementary astronomy and comic subjects. To please some of the native families, the lecture was translated into Italian chiefly by my wife, and the lantern was exhibited at several evening parties. It was my ambition to give the lecture also in modern Greek ; but a year or two elapsed before I ventured to carry out this intention, with what results will be narrated in a future chapter.

Although murders occasionally occurred in all the Islands, and were frequent in Zante, yet partly owing to the lenient system established, and partly to the absence of convictions by the inefficient police, executions were very rare events. I myself only witnessed one case, and never had the opportunity of witnessing another. It was for the crime

* Δὲν ἠξεύρω Ἑλληνικὰ ἀλλὰ Ρομαίκα.

of parricide. A farmer had divided the greater part of his property amongst his three sons, who expected upon his death to share the remainder. He, however, quarrelled with one of them who was a bad character, and therefore prepared to make a will which should deprive him of any further part of the property. For the Ionian law permits a father to dispose as he pleases of a certain portion of his property. The wicked son, therefore, killed his father in order that he might die intestate, in which case the rest of the property would be equally divided between the brothers. The murder was effected with an axe, in a grove of olive trees. His bloody shoes and stockings, betrayed and convicted the murderer, and he was sentenced to the gallows. The day before the execution, I saw him marched through the town from the prison to the church, in which he was, according to custom, to pass his last night. A priest sat up with him to prepare him for death, and he was liberally provided with refreshments. People were permitted to enter the church to see him, and to witness his callous indifference to his fate. He was a coarse, stout, middle-aged man of a dark complexion, and with a heavy cast of countenance. He wore a monkish gown, upon the back of which appeared a placard inscribed with the word *parricide* in Greek. He was a hardened villain, and, though his guilt was undoubted, he to the last obstinately asserted his innocence.

The next morning I rode out with a military friend at six o'clock to see the execution. The prisoner was marched from the church, accompanied by many priests, to an elevated piece of ground, situated between Fort Neuf and Fort Abraham, where a small scaffold had been erected. A strong body of armed police kept the place clear; the spectators lining the road. The people were suspected of an inclination to rescue the victim of the law, if they could sum up sufficient resolution. But I never saw the slightest signs of any such intentions. When the culprit arrived at the scaffold he ascended the two or three steps, and was suspended in a few seconds, with his feet only just clearing the ground. The business was quietly conducted, but considering that an immortal soul was being despatched from this world, the brevity of the proceedings had an appearance of indecent haste. However it must be remembered that he had had many hours of preparation if he chose to make use of them, whilst waiting in the church. I was also told afterwards that he was employed in mentally praying while ascending the scaffold. The executioner, always an object of intense hatred to Greeks, had to be escorted to the water's-edge that he might enter the boat which was to convey him back to Albania, from whence he came, carrying away with him the wages of his nefarious work. It was afterwards reported that he had been waylaid on landing at the other side, and robbed and murdered by some Albanians. But whether this report were true, or merely an embodiment of the general wishes, I never could ascertain with any degree of accuracy.

CHAPTER V.

The "*magnanimous* Cephalonians" of Homer—First at a Feast and last at a Fight—Attractions of the Black Mountain—Beautiful and extensive View —Black Mountain rarely visited by Natives — Population — Salt Water below the level of the Sea—Strangers reminded of "*Puss in Boots*"—Sir Charles Napier—Cephalonian Society—An Apostolical Archbishop—A Romantic Visit—Murder in High Life—A sleepless Night—Use of Garlic, and neglect of Soap.

I ARRIVED at Cephalonia on Sunday the 16th of February, 1862, from England *viâ* Corfu. Little did I then imagine with what warm feelings of friendship for the inhabitants I should take my departure, the following year.

Of the Seven Islands, Cephalonia and Ithaca are at the present day the two most purely Greek in blood and language. Indeed Ithaca (the inhabitants of which were at one time reduced under the rule of Venice to little more than 2000*) is said to have been chiefly repeopled by Cephalonians.

Ulysses, King of Ithaca, sailed to Troy B.C. 1193, with twelve ships, containing probably about 2400 soldiers, composed of Cephalonians, Ithacans, and

* Lunzi.

Zantiots.   That wise prince could not have failed to maintain his troops in excellent discipline.   His friends, the aged Pylian Nestor, and the youthful Athenian Menœstheus, were masters of the ancient tactics, and he doubtless imitated their examples. We may therefore believe, that he placed his best troops in the front and in the rear, whilst the soldiers least to be relied upon occupied the centre. The front rank, especially, must have been deemed the post of honor; as affording the best opportunity for distinction, in an age when personal strength and valour opened a rapid career to military fame.

Now, we find that the "*magnanimous* Cephalonians"[*] formed the first line of the division of the King of Ithaca.   Homer is silent as regards the occupants of the rear and centre.   I must therefore leave the modern Zantiots and Ithacans to settle the knotty point of the comparative merits of their respective ancestors.   To the Cephalonians alone was applied the flattering epithet of the immortal bard. Nor have their descendants degenerated in valour; as has been amply proved whenever the opportunity to display it has been granted to them by Providence.

As to the blame laid upon the Cephalonians by Agamemnon, that angry martinet was frequently in

* Αὐτὰρ Ὀδυσσεὺς ἦγε Κεφαλλῆνας μεγαθύμους.
Pope's translation omits the flattering epithet.

the habit of abusing his bravest soldiers by way of encouragement. We must not therefore attach too much importance to his satirical remarks upon the conduct of Ulysses, and of his valiant soldiers. He mentions the Cephalonians by name probably because they were in advance of the Ithacans and Zantiots; and were also the strongest in number. According to Agamemnon they were at first rather backward in coming forward. The king of men did not scruple to utter severe reproaches against Ulysses and his generals. They were eager, he declared, to accept his invitations to dinner, and " to consume at his banquets plenty of roast meats and sweet wines;" and yet when a battle was to be fought they preferred to play the part of spectators "until other divisions of the Greeks should advance and commence the battle." First at the feast, and last at the fight; such, in brief, was the royal accusation.* Ulysses, however, repelled the charge with generous, though somewhat insubordinate, indignation; and the glory which he subsequently acquired (up to the fall of Troy on the 11th of June, B.C. 1184) amply vindicated his character and that of his valiant Ionians.

The external appearance of Cephalonia, rugged,

---

* Perhaps Molière had this passage in view, when he made one of his *valets* exclaim to a pugnacious master, who wished him to join in his quarrels,

> " A table comptez moi si vous voulez pour quatre,
> Mais comptez moi pour rien s'il s'agit de se battre."

mountainous, barren, and gloomy, presents a strange contrast to the singular and soft beauty of Corfu. Yet in the interior of the former island there are some picturesque valleys; whilst from the top of the Black Mountain may be enjoyed, in clear weather, a magnificent view, embracing all the Ionian Islands except Cerigo, as well as a considerable part of the continent of Greece. But this subject, as well as the classical and other objects of interest in this and all the other islands, are fully described in Murray's Handbook; so that I need only mention, and that slightly, such objects of local interests as have particularly attracted my special notice.

The Black Mountain of all Ionian localities presents the greatest charms to an Englishman, especially during the hot weather. There, at the Resident's Cottage, shaded by a forest yet accessible to the breezes, the thermometer is in summer usually sixteen, but often twenty degrees of Fahrenheit lower than in Argostoli. The cottage (which I repeatedly visited and stayed at) is about 3800 feet, and the highest summit is 5246 feet above the level of the sea. To this last point, I, to my great regret, only once ascended; but I was well rewarded for my trouble. I rode on a mule, in some places alarmingly near the edges of deep precipices. It was a most beautiful ride through picturesque woods of lofty dark pines* with occasional glimpses of the

* It is from its peculiarly beautiful dark pines that the mountain obtained the epithet of *Black.*

valley below. From the summit, at which I arrived before sunrise, I had in spite of a mist (which rose at the same time as the great luminary) a very extensive view. Corfu was indeed concealed in a fog; but Cephalonia itself, Zante, Ithaca, and a part of Acarnania were visible. The light shone beautifully on the silver line of the Achelaus as it flowed winding to the sea. I sat upon the pile of stones which crowned the highest peak, and on which the ancients were wont to sacrifice to Jupiter. At the foot of the heap of stones lay innumerable minute fragments of the bones of the animals which had been offered up on the rude altar.

To pass a day or two at the Resident's Cottage, on the beautiful mountain, appeared to me, during the hot season, as the summit of human happiness. So great is the force of contrast between such a cool spot and the sultry stifling plains below. The natives (except municipal officers and other official persons) were never known to ascend even as far as the cottage. But it always was the favourite resort of English visitors; whether civilians, or naval, or military men. As the loftiest, freshest, and most bracing spot in the Seven Islands, his Majesty the King of Greece would do well to make it his summer residence in July and August, the two hottest months of the year. He would then, without quitting his own kingdom, enjoy a climate as pleasant as that of France or England. At a small expense the cottage could easily be converted into a rural retreat, where Royalty with a few attendants might find a grateful temporary repose from the cares of state.

The modern town of Argostoli began to be built in 1680. But Fort George was then, and continued long afterwards to be, the seat of Government. Argostoli has about 10,000 inhabitants. Lixuri, the second town, situated on the other side of the harbour, has 8000. It would, I think, have been an advantage to Cephalonia if the two towns could have been concentrated into one large one. Such a want of concentration has ever been the bane of the island. One of the principal reasons which prevented the latter from playing so great a part in ancient history as was played by Corfu, was its then division into four independent cities. These were Cranii, Pale, Samos, and Pronos.

Nearly all visitors were in the habit of inspecting the two mills, which are situated less than a mile from the western side of Argostoli. The earliest established was discovered by Mr. Stevens, an Englishman long resident in the island. He was walking one day (as he informed me) along the shore, when he fancied he heard water falling under ground. He soon perceived a small hole, by which the salt water trickled into what he believed to be a natural stream of fresh water, which was a few feet below the level of the sea. He opened out the hole, built a mill, and regulated by artificial means the flow of salt water from the harbour. When the mill was stopped for twenty-four hours, Mr. Stevens was of opinion that the water became fresh. To this day he believes in the fresh water theory. A Signor Migliaressi built another mill near to that of Mr. Stevens, which he also afterwards purchased. He is still, and has long been, the proprietor of both mills. He totally disbelieves that there is any fresh water in the stream that works them. He feels confident that the apparent freshness of the water after the mills have been stopped for many hours, arises partly from its filtration through the rocks, but chiefly from the salt falling to the bottom of the stagnant water. I am inclined to believe that the Greek is right, and that the Englishman was deceived by appearances. In either case, the difficulty of comprehending why this water is below the level of the sea remains a mystery to every one. Admirals, generals, bishops, and distinguished civilian visitors seldom failed to examine minutely this interesting phenomenon. The late Bishop of Gibraltar, whom I accompanied to the spot, took an especial interest in the subject, in connexion with the theory of earthquakes, which will be related in a subsequent chapter.

The stranger, on his first arrival in Cephalonia, may, by certain circumstances, be easily reminded of the well-known fairy tale called "*Puss in Boots*."

There the King of the country, when constantly inquiring the name of the owner of this field, of that wood, or of this palace, receives one universal reply, namely, *the Marquis of Carabas*. The traveller to Argostoli, Lixuri, or to any other part of the island, usually enacts the royal part. When he asks who constructed this mole, or that road? who built this court-house, that jail? who introduced that reform, or this improvement? the answer is always one and the same name. The sole difference between the fairy tale and the reality is that for the Marquis of Carabas we must read Sir Charles Napier. Had the general government of the Islands been administered by a series of Lord High Commissioners resembling the famous Resident of Cephalonia, the desire for a union with Greece would never have so speedily become almost universal.

If, as we have seen, it was difficult for the English and Greeks to amalgamate in Corfu, this was still more strongly the case in Cephalonia, where Englishmen have always been very few in number, in addition to the officers of the annually changing garrison. However, I determined, if possible, to form an exception to the general rule, and before my departure, I succeeded in making a great many acquaintances, and I confidently believe, not a few friends. The English ladies were generally ignorant of any language but their own, and were thus deprived almost entirely of the society of Greek ladies.   Such of the latter, however, as knew Italian well, commenced gradually to attend our evening parties, and we established a very pleasant society. In the case of those who could talk nothing but Greek, I enjoyed one great advantage.   I was afforded an excuse for practising from politeness that difficult language, which I might otherwise have feared to attempt in company.   By thus mixing with the inhabitants, I was enabled to acquire more information, and more insight into the native character, than are usually accessible to Englishmen. I had also the good fortune to be of some service to the gentry.   I was the means (as many of them afterwards gratefully acknowledged) of their children being taught English at very little cost.   By this and other trifling acts of civility, I became popular with the Cephalonians to a degree that perfectly astonished me.   They are an amiable and easily pleased people, when kindly and considerately treated.   " The English," said Lascarato often to me, " have been generally disliked, because they have treated the Greeks with contempt, and contempt never did any good."

The Archbishop of Cephalonia was made Exarch, or Chief of the Ionian Church, in 1862.   He was a very old man, and not very popular.   He had been forced upon the clergy as Archbishop many years before, instead of a certain Unionist named Typaldo, who had received the majority of votes. · I had not

the good fortune to make the Archbishop's acquaintance; but I believe him to be a most gentle-
manly, and at the same time most truly charitable,
man.　There was a shabbily-dressed madman, of a
respectable family, who used to walk about the
town.　The poor fellow, whenever he chose to do
so, dined with the Archbishop, going in and taking
his seat without any invitation, and being always
hospitably entertained.　After hearing this anecdote,
I could not help feeling great respect for the Exarch,
as somewhat of a true apostle; his claim to which
title is not lessened by the fact that he has not the
reputation of great learning or abilities

The beggars of the lower orders, even when not
insane, are what we in England would call *very cool.*
The following specimen will suffice:　On the 13th
December, 1862, I was startled by a knock at the
door of my cottage, resembling (in length and loud-
ness) the knock of a London footman, impressed
with the greatness of his noble master.　It turned
out to be a blind beggar, led by a boy, who demanded alms, and who all down the street pursued
the same plan.　The Greek beggars are proud of
their calling; and the absence of poor-houses, and of
parish relief, gives them a kind of right to the support of the benevolent-minded population.

The active and locally well-informed young Resident was ever the ablest guide to the prettiest
scenery and most interesting curiosities of the island.

Happy those persons, whether visitors or temporarily stationed there, who obtained the benefit of his company. The most accomplished of pedestrians, an indefatigable horseman, and a good sportsman, he knew all the places that were worth seeing as well as the best and quickest mode of visiting them. With him I had many pleasant rides and walks, repeatedly visiting the walls of Cranii and other interesting localities. On one occasion I accompanied him on a visit to the country, to a certain romantic spot, which I shall, for excellent reasons, not very accurately define. The distance was some twenty-six miles, of which we drove fourteen in a carriage. The rest of the way the Resident walked over nearly the most difficult stony hilly ground that I ever encountered. His Greek cook and I preferred riding on mules. My sure-footed animal carried me up and down rugged hills without slipping, in a truly wonderful manner. It was dark before we reached our destination. As we neared it, a house was pointed out to me through some trees, which had, about a year before, been the scene of a terrible tragedy. The victim, an unpopular gentleman, had paid his addresses to, and then abandoned, the young lady of the house which we were about to visit. Her brothers had, it was fully believed, on a certain night, ascended a tree which faced the window of the fickle Lothario's house. Through the latter the assassins had fired

at their victim, whilst he was seated at a table. He
fell dead on the spot. I learned that anecdote for
the first time when we were close to our destination.
Had I heard it before I started, I should certainly
have declined such a visit. When I arrived at the
house, all that I saw of the wild manner of living,
and of the absence of books and other signs of civilization, gave an air of probability to the romantic
story. The unsophisticated state of the rooms, like
those of a low pot-house, the queer looks of the
men seated in the principal apartment, partly composed of inmates of the house, and partly of persons
who had come to greet our arrival, had certainly
the charm of novelty if no other. When a little
later the two young men entered with their guns, I
could not help thinking, as I sat watching them, of
that neighbouring house, and of the fatal tree and
murdered man. Our host, however, was an excellent fine old man; and if his sons had really done
the dark deed for which they were universally given
credit, the father had certainly not been to blame.
The supposed fair cause of the terrible affair in
question, adhering to the ancient manners of the
country, never joined the society of the men. But I
caught a glimpse of her before leaving the house
next morning. In consequence of the great unpopularity of the murdered man, none of the peasantry
could be induced to come forward to give the evi-

dence which many of them, it is believed, were able to supply.

As to the room I slept in—no, that is a mistake, for I never slept a wink that night, notwithstanding my long day's journey, which had made me very tired; for a mule's back, with a hard so-called saddle and rope stirrups, is a somewhat trying mode of equitation. The walls of the room given to me by my kind-intentioned host, literally swarmed with bugs in all directions. Nor were they confined to the walls. One glance at my coverlet made me resolve to pass the night on one of the little cane chairs, which formed part of the scanty furniture. But after sitting for a few minutes, troops of the enemy came crawling up my trousers in such irresistible numbers, that I fairly rushed out of the apartment. In the large room, I stumbled over a lot of men sleeping in their clothes on the floor in various postures, intermingled with dogs, as to whose probable treatment of a stranger, I felt rather nervous. But all remained quiet, and I escaped into the open air. As I could not have well endured a second similar night, my friend and I shortened our visit, and returned to Argostoli. I shall not easily forget that expedition, although we fared well as to living. The plan, when Englishmen make such visits, is that the host supplies you with the raw material, whilst you take your own cook, who prepares all your meals. Thus you escape the oil and garlic flavour which usually permeates all native cookery. The garlic grown in the island is insufficient for home consumption; and I was assured that, to supply the deficiency, 25,000*l.* worth of the unsavoury comestible is annually imported into Cephalonia. The constant use of garlic, and the rare use of soap, impress an Englishman very disagreeably. As to the latter evil, where water has to be purchased (as is the case in all the Ionian towns, except Corfu and Zante), there is naturally a difficulty in keeping up those habits of ablution, which, desirable everywhere, are in hot climates especially indispensable to civilized comfort.

CHAPTER VI.

Signor Focca, the Archivist—Proveditors—Making up for lost time—Good Dinner due to bad Memory—Napier's summary Justice—Great Extension of the Franchise—Lord Collingwood's Fleet, 1809—Deputation sent to General Oswald—Unconciliating Conduct of Sir Hudson Lowe—A bragging Commander—An Englishman of few Words—Major de Bosset, Governor of Cephalonia—The dying Beauty and her wicked Brothers-in-Law—Rascal Notaries—A Land of Savages—De Bosset's summary Justice—Illuminations for Count Caruso, and Signors Zervo and Montferrato in Cephalonia— A Cephalonian Picture-Gallery.

DURING my stay in Cephalonia I made the acquaintance of Signor Focca, the Archivist, the oldest and staunchest friend of the British Protectorate. I inspected with him a number of old documents, and he imparted to me much interesting information. He possessed a considerable repertory of anecdotes, some of which I shall here relate. Signor Focca well remembered a Signor Valiero, a Cephalonian, who had passed much of his life under the rule of the Venetians. This gentleman told Focca that when he was unable to obtain his rents he was in the habit of applying to the Proveditor for the services of a soldier, who was sent to live in the house, and at the expense of the debtor, till the latter was brought to terms of submission. The fruits of extortion (for in these cases something more was demanded than was due) were divided between the landlord and the Proveditor. Proveditors were usually poor Venetian gentlemen sent by great protecting nobles to make their fortunes in the island in two years. They generally carried away with them a thousand sequins, which in those days was thought a considerable sum to be extorted out of a single island. It was customary also for the Proveditor to give great dinners of a very remunerative kind. For the invited guests were all expected to leave under their plates either sums of money or, more generally, orders for oil or currants. In return for these tributes paid to the Venetian rulers, the Ionian gentry were allowed to rob at discretion their poor and ignorant peasants.

A certain Proveditor passed his two years in a manner quite exceptional to the long established rule. He acted most honorably, was not guilty of extortion, and took only what was voluntarily given to him. He acquired great respect, and was .universally beloved. When his period of office was about to expire, every one bewailed his approaching departure. But he adopted an excellent plan for consoling the Cephalonians for his loss. The day before he sailed away, all the police were employed in inspecting the weights and measures used in the island. They were all found to be false, and consequently their owners were severely fined; and the Proveditor, carrying away the total amount of the penalties, made up in his last twenty-four hours for the time previously lost.

The Proveditors were often good-natured men, who were disinclined to do more evil than was actually necessary, in order to enrich themselves. One of them attained to celebrity from his singular want of memory, of which failing some wily Greeks often took advantage. One Cephalonian particularly distinguished himself in this respect. He went almost daily to pay his court to the great man, taking care to inspect his kitchen at the same time. Whenever he found a good dinner preparing, he stayed till it was served up. The Proveditor would then say to him: " What is your business, Signor ?" " My business? I am come to dinner, according to the invitation which you gave me yesterday." " Oh, indeed," replied the other, " I had quite forgotten it. Well, sit down."

Signor Focca related to me several stories about Sir Charles Napier. Here is one which I do not remember to have previously heard or read. A fair Turkish slave robbed her master's Seraglio, and fled with a Cephalonian Captain from Constantinople; entrusting him with all her property, consisting both of money and valuable jewels. Arrived at

Cephalonia, the Captain denied the deposit, and retained everything for himself. The girl appealed to Colonel Napier, who at first replied that it was a case for the courts. But he afterwards reflected that if the parties went to law, the lawyers would eat up all the property. He therefore sent the chief of the police for the Captain, whom, on his arrival, he thus addressed: "Captain you have most gallantly saved this poor girl from slavery at the risk of your life. That action" (he continued, addressing the girl) "deserves some remuneration from you. Captain, she has entrusted to you 700 sequins and valuable jewels. I decide that she shall give you 200 sequins. Go and bring the money and jewels, and I will give you the reward your gallantry deserves." The Captain had not the effrontery to deny the facts, and he was accompanied on board his ship by the chief of the police. The money and the jewels were brought to Colonel Napier, who gave the 200 sequins to the Captain, and restored to the lady the rest of her property.

According to Signor Focca, before the treaty of Tilsit a Russian Colonel, named Stepano, commanded in Cephalonia, where he lived with a certain native Countess. This lady sold all the official posts, and thereby greatly enriched herself. With regard to General Berthier, though he governed despotically, Focca said that he did so by means of the Senate of Corfu.

Before 1817 there were not 400 voters in Cephalonia, according to the same authority. There appeared to have been the same number in the time of Napier. The printed list of the electors of the island for 1862 (now lying before me) has recorded opposite the last name, the number 3563. As the population has very slightly increased since Napier left, the enormous difference is due almost entirely to the reforms of Lord Seaton. Thus in Cephalonia the constituency are more than eight times as numerous as before the reforms took place.

The Venetians left the Islands in the hands of a small and ill-organized aristocracy. The English have handed over the political power chiefly to a democratic and uncivilized peasantry. British bayonets, and British ships restrained the effects of these changes to liberty of speech, and of voting; unaccompanied by commensurate action. But the new King, with a sadly disorganized army, may very possibly have some difficulty in preserving peace and order in his newly acquired territories.

Signor Focca was an *eye-witness* of the taking of Cephalonia by the English in 1809. A petition requesting the restoration of national independence by the English arms had been circulated for signature amongst the inhabitants, and was subsequently despatched to the British Government. All the Islands were at that time incorporated with the French Empire. The troops in Cephalonia were chiefly composed of Neapolitans in the service of France. In October, the English fleet, under Lord Collingwood, sailed into the harbour, carrying with it a military force under the command of General Oswald. The weather was remarkably fine; and Focca, standing on the heights above the town of Argostoli, beheld the magnificent spectacle. A battery then stood on the spot where the inner lighthouse of the harbour is now placed. From it, one gun was discharged at the distant ships; and then the defenders fled. The fleet continued to advance, sailing majestically in two parallel lines. Signor Ladico, of Naples, commanded at Lixuri; and he caused a gun to be fired at the enemy. Upon this a single frigate detached itself from the fleet and deliberately fired a broadside at the town. The inhabitants fearing that the latter would be destroyed, prevailed on Ladico to cease firing. Upon this the frigate rejoined her comrades, and the whole fleet advanced and anchored in the harbour of Argostoli. A Greek named Zerbini was then administrator of the island for the French, under the Chief Commissioner at Corfu, whose name was Bessier The governor, General Donzelot was the supreme authority in the Seven Islands; but commissioners carried out the details of civil government under his supervision. Focca held the post of chief clerk to Signor Zerbini. The military commandant of Cephalonia was a Corfiot named Colonel Pierri.

He retreated with his men, only 100 in number, to Fort St. George, declaring that he would defend himself to the last extremity.

Zerbini now sent a deputation on board to General Oswald, to inform him that no opposition would be made to his landing. The General referred the deputation to Colonel (afterwards Sir Hudson) Lowe, whom he had appointed Commandant of Cephalonia. But the Colonel refused to treat with it because the principal person, Colonel Corafan, "wore the uniform of the French usurper." For though a Cephalonian, he held the Emperor's Commission as Colonel of Militia. The emissaries returned discomfited to Argostoli. There, Zerbini and Focca found it difficult to persuade any one to go on board the General's ship. The wrath of the French in Corfu, where the garrison was then composed of from 10 to 12,000 men,* was greatly dreaded. Signor Paul Valsamachi and Focca himself at length volunteered for the duty. But in the meantime they learned that the British troops had quietly landed.

Colonel Lowe distributed his forces in the Lazzaretto and about the town, and then proceeded to the house of the administrator. Signor Zerbini offered him dinner, which was however refused.

* Such was the belief of Signor Focca. I have somewhere found the French garrison of Corfu, in 1814, estimated at 14,000 men, but that amount appears improbable. Under the British Protectorate all the troops in the Islands rarely exceeded 4000 at a time; 3000 of which usually formed the garrison of Corfu.

A servant brought their food from the ship to the Colonel and his aide-de-camp. The unfortunate administrator repeatedly entered the room, where the surly Colonel stood, with profuse offers of service. But he returned after each rebuff to his own apartments. All his attentions were rejected, Colonel Lowe would take nothing, not even a bed. He said he should sit up all night; and he was as good as his word. In the morning he sent his aide-de-camp to Fort St. George to summon Colonel Pierri to surrender. That officer replied that he would defend himself to the last, unless he were permitted to march out with the French colours flying, and with all the honors of war. Colonel Lowe, on receiving this reply, sent a threatening rejoinder, and instantly started for the fort at the head of a British regiment. On his approach, Colonel Pierri marched out to meet him, and surrendered without further difficulty. The Corfiot was perfectly justified in not resisting greatly superior numbers; but he made himself ridiculous by uttering bombastical threats, which he could have had no intention of carrying out into practice.

Colonel Lowe now despatched Zerbini to General Oswald to resign his office of administrator; but the General referred him back to the Commandant. The latter now sent him on board as a prisoner. Zerbini expostulated (through a Zantiot interpreter, who was the friend of the English), maintainin g that as a civilian he was not subject to military law; but Colonel Lowe, who appears to have been a man of few words, and of a disposition the reverse of conciliatory, remained immovably firm. Zerbini was carried on board as a prisoner, but General Oswald subsequently liberated him by sending him ashore at Corfu, which the fleet proceeded to blockade after the capture of Santa Maura by the British troops.

General Oswald issued a proclamation in the Italian language which Focca read to me. It promised protection, good government, and liberty of commerce; but it did not hold out any hopes of independence to the Islands. From Cephalonia the expedition proceeded to attack Santa Maura, which surrendered after a defence of some months duration; but, for further particulars, the reader is referred to my History of the British Protectorate.

Colonel Lowe was appointed by General Oswald civil and military chief of Cephalonia, Santa Maura, Ithaca, and Zante. A Swiss in the British service, Major De Bosset, was appointed Lowe's deputy in Cephalonia. He was an excellent person, of great abilities and firmness, and was animated by a love of the strictest justice. Colonel Lowe invested him with full powers; and punishments were inflicted, without trial, on such officials as were guilty of bribery, corruption, or other crimes. A perfectly despotic system appears to have been introduced in

the southern islands, by the future jailer of the
great Napoleon. But as war was raging all over
the world, and a large army of Frenchmen occupied Corfu, it was not the moment for establishing liberty. Major De Bosset, however, endeavoured
to maintain justice and good order. He found the
peasantry oppressed by their landlords. Homicides
also were frequent (though not so much so as at
Zante), and general confusion prevailed. It appears,
indeed, that although Corfu itself was well governed
by General Donzelot, the absence or paucity of
Frenchmen in the other islands, had left the chief
authority in the hands of incompetent and untrust-
worthy persons. De Bosset laboured hard to re-
establish better government in Cephalonia, where
he remained from 1809 to 1813; leaving behind
him a reputation destined never to be surpassed,
except by that one Englishman whose name it is
not necessary for me to repeat.

One romantic trait of Major De Bosset's conduct,
as recorded by Focca, is worthy of mention. In a
small house, in the beautifully situated village of
Svoronata, which lies in the larger of the two
drives* near Argostoli, and about six miles from the
latter, there lived, more than fifty years ago, a young
married lady dying of consumption. She was

---

* The larger circle is called the *Great Giro*, and the lesser circle the *Small
Giro.*

twenty-two years of age, singularly beautiful, and possessed of considerable property. Her husband was absent from the country, but his mother was living with her. It appears that, as she had no children, if she died intestate, her husband's brothers would eventually inherit some of her wealth; but she desired to leave everything to her husband. A Dr. —— acted for the brothers, and he took measures to prevent the village notaries from obeying the sick lady's summons to make her will. The mother-in-law of the latter tried vainly to induce them to change their minds. She at length went to Argostoli, and laid her complaint before De Bosset. The latter sent for Focca, and gave him detailed instructions for his conduct, which were faithfully carried out. The Town Major with a party of soldiers left for the village. Focca preceded them a little, accompanied by a notary from Argostoli. He arrived at the house, and pretending that he was accidentally passing by, sent a message to say that he would be glad to see the lady if convenient. Being admitted, he inquired of the invalid whether it were true that she desired to make her will. She replied in the affirmative, and shortly afterwards the notary was brought in, and the will duly made and signed. Focca then requested the lady to tell him who were the notaries who had refused to give her their professional assistance. But the dying beauty earnestly requested to be excused. " I shall soon be dead," said she, " and I do not wish at such a moment to be the cause of unhappiness to any one, since all is now arranged as I desire."

But Focca would not give his consent to the generous request of the lady; and, as he had strong claims upon her gratitude, he persuaded her that it was her duty to give the required information for the sake of justice. A reluctant aquiescence was at last extorted. The soldiers had now arrived in the village, and Focca caused the two guilty notaries to be arrested and placed upon mules, and to be carried as prisoners into Argostoli. The indignant De Bosset had given orders that the notaries were to be put in chains, but Focca did not carry out this order till they were close to the town. They proceeded to the house of the Governor, who had sat up all night waiting for them, he having declared that he would take no rest until justice were done. " I thought," he had exclaimed, " that I was in a civilized country, but I find that I am in a land of savages."

The notaries were old men. The justifiable plea of sickness, saved one of them from punishment. The other was suspended for six months from the exercise of his profession. The doctor who had acted as the agent for the wicked brothers was al-

lowed to escape; De Bosset and Focca agreeing, for
the sake of his many influential relations, to keep
silence regarding his conduct. This termination of
the story is the point least honourable to the worthy
Swiss. It can be accounted for only by the fact
that morality was generally at that time at so low
an ebb in the Islands, that it would have been impossible to punish every one who deviated from the
paths of honour and honesty. It is not, however,
thus apologetically that similar misconduct treated
by Sir Charles Napier would have to be recorded.
But we must now revert to present times.

The expiration of a quinquennium occurred in
March, 1862, whereby all the official posts held by
the Ionians became legally vacant. The entire re-
arrangement of offices was an affair of some months,
but some of the new appointments took place immediately. Amongst the latter, Count Caruso (formerly Regent of Cephalonia) was appointed President of the Senate by her Majesty the Queen, on
the recommendation of the Lord High Commissioner. In consequence of his elevation, all the
public buildings and Government offices in Argostoli and Lixuri were illuminated on the 10th of
March. But on the 15th of the same month, there
were far more extensive and general illuminations
in favour of Signor Zervo, the new President of the
Assembly, and of Signor Montferrato, the new Vice-

President, who were also Cephalonians. Portraits also of those martyrs, as they were styled (on account of the exile which they had endured under Lord Seaton and Sir Henry Ward), were hung up in various parts of the town. But perfect tranquillity and good humour everywhere prevailed. Perhaps the great earthquake of the season, which had occurred on the previous day, had left behind it a certain sedative influence on the masses.

In the month of April, we were invited one day to see the largest and best gallery of pictures in the island. A more comical proof of the decadence of modern Greek art, could hardly be conceived than was furnished by this collection. It was as if some speculator had taken advantage in England of the ruin of the country inns (by the immense influx of railways), to buy up all the signs, usually the works of village artists, for the benefit of the Cephalonian market. When called upon to express our opinions, we did not know which way to look or what to say. As my companion could not be induced to open her mouth in praise, I at length, pointing to a portrait, broke out with, " *There* is rather a nice-looking picture!" Immediately the master of the house eagerly exclaimed, " Well, it is something to possess *one* good picture." I could not say less in return for the excellent ices with which we were regaled, and which we greatly enjoyed after a sultry walk through the town in the heat of the day. A gallant field-officer, who, a day or two after visited the same gallery, was compelled, in order to avoid impolite convulsions, to cram his handkerchief into his mouth. Yet the gallery was one of which the Cephalonians generally were very proud, regarding it as an honor to the country.

CHAPTER VII.

IF the nuisances of Corfu were trying to an Englishman, those of Cephalonia were even less endurable to him. It was a case of Saul and David—
of thousands against tens of thousands. In Corfu,
although the living was bad, yet excellent cooks
were to be had, and we had had the good fortune
to enjoy the services of one of the best. But in
Cephalonia tolerable fresh meat was very difficult to
procure, and the cooks had been trained in a school
of grease, garlic, and oil, which Western nations

cannot appreciate. Our Cephalonian was as remarkable for his bad performances as our Corfiot cook had been distinguished for his skill and success. The butter, also, always fresh in the capital, was now salt and bad; and, worst of all, the bread was coarse and sour. Moreover, our house on the Mole in the harbour was exposed to many discomforts. The boatmen, proceeding to or returning from Lixuri, made a terrible noise when embarking or landing their passengers. This was especially the case during the summer months, when the disturbances usually commenced at daylight, awakening us, and rendering all further sleep impossible. There was no necessity that these boats should stop exactly opposite to our house. Indeed, it was more convenient for the inhabitants to embark and land higher up in the town. Some Residents had, therefore, ordered the nuisance to be removed by directing the police to warn the boats from the house, which was usually filled by English officers, married and single. But, unfortunately for me, two years before I arrived, the Commandant of Cephalonia had been on very bad terms with the Lord High Commissioner. His Excellency, therefore, directed the Resident to cancel his orders, and he thus virtually sentenced the Colonel and his officers to be deprived of sleep and rest. The Commander in question, however (a character to whom I have more than once alluded, and who, from his antipathies, may be styled a *Mis*hellenist), was not the man to undergo martyrdom without a struggle. He therefore took the matter into his own hands, and, by means of his military police, he kept the mob clear, in spite of Resident, Senate, and Lord High Commissioner. Not, however, that he always succeeded in repressing the harassing noises, which sometimes caused him to lose his temper. On one occasion he was heard exclaiming to a number of Greeks below, "Oh, *what* have I done, what *have* I done, that her Majesty should banish me to this vile and abominable place?" But it is not every one who can successfully set at defiance superior authority, and I was doomed to obtain very little success in my attempts to secure sleep and rest for my family.

Our house on the Mole was, from its height and doubtful foundations, very subject to earthquakes, and 1862 was an unusually bad year in Cephalonia for those terrible visitations. But an account of my experiences in this respect will be mentioned in a future chapter. Our apartments on the second story had one great advantage, that of being very cool, as they faced the usually prevalent north-west winds. It appears that when on the 9th of August, 1862, the thermometer was 92° in the shade at Corfu, it was only 82° in our drawing-room at Argostoli on the same day. But the almost perpetual storms, gales, and hurricanes of that year lessened the comfort of our airy situation, although they blew away the mosquitoes, which were troublesome in other parts of the town.

I will finish at once the history of my Cephalonian annoyances whilst I am in the vein. Partly from ill-health, and partly from the dread of earthquakes on their account, I sent my family to England in August. No longer requiring many rooms, I changed houses, and went to reside in a small detached cottage farther from the sea. I now hoped to dwell in comfort and safety. I was out of the sound of the boatmen, and living near to the ground. Earthquakes had become much less dangerous; and now I had no family with me to increase my anxiety. But, as far as the boatmen were concerned, I gained little by the change, for their place was more than supplied by the nuisance of dogs, owls, and bells. Of these evils the dogs were the least; but they were bad enough. Whether shut up by themselves in outhouses or yards, or roaming wild about the town all night, the howling and barking were incessant. The civil police with their guns, myself and servant with pistols—everything was tried. But the evil, though occasionally abated, was never entirely remedied. The perpetually repeated plaintive cry of the owl (half sigh, half squeak) was another nuisance which frequently kept me awake for hours.

But in what language can I speak of those terrible tortures which, in my second solitary abode, at times drove me very nearly frantic? Most assuredly I could not have survived two years of such an existence. I can give no idea of the demoniacal sounds which proceed from a Cephalonian bell. To compare them with the harmony that can be extracted from poker and tongs, is a gross calumny upon those useful articles of domestic furniture. Signor Lascarato assails them severely in his " Mysteries of Cephalonia." He denounces the inhabitants as worse than Turks—" for these, at least, respect sleep." But the satirist, " native and to the manner born," could hardly feel the nuisance in the degree in which it is felt by an unfortunate Englishman, especially if a light sleeper. I find my journal for the autumn, winter, and spring of 1862-3 full of the most heartrending complaints of these bells. My state of mind appears to have been terrible. But I will not now, in cold blood, repeat all my impolite lamentations.

I can still picture to myself the little boys, standing on the small balcony, holding in their hands the long iron tongs, and striking them on the bells with all their might and main for hours at a time. The bells were double. Sometimes two boys were at work together, and sometimes they relieved each other. One night my servant procured me a little peace by creeping out in the dark, and pelting my torturers with stones.*   But this was too hazardous a mode of defence to be permanently employed.

At Zante (as I afterwards experienced) the bells were annoying; but an order had been given in that island that they should not ring for more than five minutes at any one time.   Whereas in Argostoli twenty minutes were reckoned a trifle, and two hours at a time was a frequent dose.

When I applied to the Resident for some relief from these terrible bells, he was at first horrified at my application; dreading all imaginable evils, " if religion were interfered with."   But a Greek official displayed more courage.   He was a very clever fellow, whom I was glad to consider my friend. He boldly spoke to the Bishop on the subject, and not without effect, as will shortly appear.

My chief tintinnabulary enemy was a little chapel, nearly opposite to my cottage, called the " *Church of the Entrance*,"† built in honor of the Virgin.   I was told that the Archbishop had sent a message to the priests to make less noise.   At all events, for a time the nuisance appeared to have abated; but eventually the bells were nearly as bad as ever.   No hour of the night nor of the early morning (any more than of the day) was safe from those worrying sounds.   It was too evident that the priests " of the

* An able Greek official recommended me always to adopt the plan in question ; but I thought it even better to endure the torture.

† 'Ο Ναός τῶν Εἰσοδίων.

Entrance" considered it amongst their good works to torture heretics. But all Cephalonian priests were not of the same stamp. A certain Father P. disliked the bells as much as any one, and would sometimes leave the town for days together to avoid them. He, too, used his influence to induce the Archbishop to check the nuisance. My official Greek friend—a worthy Protectionist—went much further. He told the most reverend gentleman that he was ashamed of his country, when Englishmen made complaints to him of these barbarous customs.

I shall not easily forget the Greek Christmas-day at Argostoli, on the 6th of January, 1863. The bells began about an hour after midnight, utterly destroying all sleep, and continuing, with brief pauses, all night and the following day. But it is useless to speak of days. Throughout that month sleep was for me an almost unattainable luxury. I grew ill, and began to fear that the bells would literally be the death of me.

Taking from my journal one of many records of anguish, I find: "*Sunday, 18th of January.* From midnight to two A.M. bells *raging*" (not ringing, you will observe). "I wrote to ——, and was too ill from want of sleep to go to morning church."

I will here give an extract from the letter alluded to.

Cephalonia, Sunday, 18th of January, 1863.

"MY DEAR SIR,—Last evening it was remarked

by the officers how much the nuisance of bells had been mitigated of late, and I acquainted them that it was chiefly to you that we were indebted for such a mitigation of our torments. Alas! I spoke too soon. Last night and this morning my sleep was utterly destroyed by a ringing of bells, hitherto unequalled even in Cephalonia itself. . . . I hear that the water was being blessed by the Greeks. I am sure that by Englishmen the very contrary operation was actively performing. My health would not permit me to stay here much longer. So that I am truly thankful I am about to leave so barbarous a rest-and-sleep-destroying country."

The next paragraph of my letter expressed my surprise that with such habits they could expect an English Prince to reign amongst them. I could not strike a harder blow than that given by this remark. For at this period all my Ionian friends, gentle and simple, old and young, male and female, were positively certain, in spite of my constant assurances to the contrary, that Prince Alfred was to be the future King of Greece and of the Seven Islands. To such an angry state did the terrible priests "of the Entrance" bring an Englishman, who, when of sound mind (that is, when not within sound of the endless bells), felt more interest in, and friendship for, the Cephalonians than any other Briton had, probably, ever experienced. It was a kind dispensation of

Providence, I believe, that caused the annual relief of troops in the six minor islands, thus preventing too long a strain upon the nerves of the sleepless officers.

On arriving at Cephalonia, in February, 1862, I had been very anxious to make the acquaintance of Signor Lascarato, whose chief work had formed my principal Greek study at Corfu. I found that he was my near neighbour, whilst my family was with me, and we lived in the upper rooms of the great house on the Mole. But I soon learned that he was very shy of the English, and that it was difficult for any of them to know him. However, I was bent on doing so. I succeeded, ere long, by means of a friendship formed between one of his little girls and my eldest daughter. In return for asking the former to tea, Signor Lascarato and his lady called one day about noon to thank us. But I was out, and my wife did not receive visits in the morning. The only man in the house when they called was our Greek cook. He had, unfortunately, overheard his mistress give the order that she could not be at home before luncheon, as she did not wish to waste her time. Now the cook had an exalted idea of English people, and very little respect for his own countrymen. I suspect, also, that he regarded Signor Lascarato with especial horror, as the opponent of the priests and as an excommunicated man. To the inquiry, there-fore, of whether we were at home, he replied that—

" His mistress was, but that it was not the proper hour for calling, and that *she could not waste her time.*" That afternoon I received a letter from Lascarato, detailing the ludicrous affair with great indignation. I immediately went over to his house and explained the mistake; and I afterwards sent the cook to apologize. Such was the commencement of a friendship, which I trust, nevertheless, will become permanent. Signora Lascarato spoke our language perfectly, having been brought up by an English step-mother. She has the manners and accomplishments of a well-educated English lady, combined with the laborious character of the mother of a numerous family with limited means. They live on the produce of their currants from his small estate at Lixuri, the little house on which is not fit for their residence. Their dwelling, therefore, is in Argostoli. He periodically visits his property, residing on it for some weeks, at the time of the gathering in of his currants. He is a man of good family, and a nephew of that late Count Delladecima, who so nobly resigned the highest office which a Greek can hold, in the vain hope of extricating his friend Lord High Commissioner Mackenzie from his political embarrassments.

Lascarato became my principal companion in my walks, and he used occasionally to attend our evening parties, and to dine at the officers' mess. I read nearly all his works, some in Italian, but most of them in modern Greek. IIis " Sufferings in Prison," was written in the former language, and I found it a very interesting pamphlet.* The innocent simplicity of his character had added greatly to his troubles. When, on the 17th of August, 1859, he gave himself up to undergo his imprisonment for libel, the then Director of the jail received him at first very civilly in his private apartments. He was promised that his punishment should be as light as possible, and that his cell should only serve as his dormitory. He was to pass the day in the Governor's rooms. Finally, he was to be allowed some private furniture in his cell, with full liberty of writing. Unfortunately, however, they began to talk politics, and to discuss the merits of Signor Lombardo, and they became very heated in argument. Lascarato was a staunch Protectionist, who, if he did not love the English, at all events respected and admired them. The jailer was a fierce Rizospast, and an enemy to England. The disputants lost their temper, and finally the Director rushed out of the room. But Lascarato was not left long alone, for a warder came to conduct him to his narrow, military-looking cell. From that time every attempt was made to break his sensitive heart by harsh and harassing treatment. His jailer, assisted

* *Le mie Sofferenze* . . . . *nelle Prigione di Cefalonia*, written in Italian, for the sake of the tenth Lord High Commissioner, because " *egli non intende il Greco.*"

by the prison priest, played the part of a Spanish Inquisitor. Lascarato was compelled to listen to long, insolent, and bigoted exhortations, and to answer endless questions. The Director, a brutal wretch, equally devoid of morals and of manners, gravely assured his victim that it was his (the Director's) duty to attend to the moral as well as to the physical well-being of his prisoner. The latter pleaded that, being excommunicated, he ought not to be compelled to attend the prison church. But his tormentor retorted that as he belonged, by his own confession, to the orthodox Church, he should be compelled to attend its services. He threatened, in case of refusal, to shut him up in a solitary cell, and to cut him off from all communication with others in order that they might not be contaminated. " I repeat," continued this barbarian, "that our establishment has for its object the moral recovery of the persons" in its charge, and " when your imprisonment is terminated you will acknowledge the beneficence of our measures!" Yet this man, so moral in theory, was afterwards expelled from the public service for infamous conduct, as I have already narrated in the History of the British Protectorate.*

Thus did the prison Director avenge on Lascarato the expression of opinions unfavourable to Signor

* Vide page 254 of vol. I.

Lombardo and to the ultra-Rizospastical party. For, amongst the really honest Liberals, Lascarato, as I can myself testify, has many friends, notwithstanding that he differed with them greatly in regard to the merits of the British Protectorate. It was only the insincere and unprincipled demagogues, who disgraced the national cause, whom Lascarato eloquently and justly denounced; men who from sordid motives grossly deceived the bigoted and uneducated peasantry.

When the jail subordinates observed the conduct and tone of their chief, it can surprise no one that they imitated his example, and treated their gentle prisoner with contemptuous harshness. One of them had the impertinence to write in one of the few books he was permitted to read: "*Andrea Lascarato, the Protestant.*" For "Protestant" is still, from long habit, a term of reproach in the Islands.

Half-starved, and living chiefly on stale black bread, and treated like a felon, the health and nerves of the prisoner soon broke down. He made, however, a friend and confidant of the jail physician, Dr. Avrandino, and thus probably saved his life. He had caught a fever in spite of his starvation; but by affectionate care he was restored to health. The improvement of his diet especially contributed to this result. The insults of his keepers, however, still continued. Even his wife and daughter were mocked when they came to see him.

About the end of August, borne down by the persecutions of his brutal jailer and his obsequious myrmidons, Lascarato began to dread the possibility of personal violence. He in consequence appealed to the humane physician for assistance in case of need. His attempts to communicate with superior authority were for a long time frustrated by the prison authorities. But my space will not permit me to dwell longer on the contents of his pamphlet, the truth of which has never been impugned, and which revealed practices not unlike those which existed in English prisons a century or more ago. To live with prisoners of all kinds, poor half-starved wretches; to be robbed and ill-treated in a filthy, disorderly jail; such was the fate of an honest man, who, had he received a good Western education, would very probably have established an European reputation as an original and benevolent man of genius. Unfortunately, modern Greek, as used by the peasantry, and Italian, which is rather Venetian than Tuscan, are the only vehicles in which he can convey his ideas to the public. These are thus sealed to the great majority of readers. But his great object is to reform his own countrymen, and not to acquire fame and distinction for himself. Neither does he wish to expose his countrymen to the world in general. Therefore his writings, it may be said, fully answer his purposes. I was credibly informed that even in Constantinople his name is respected, and his works are read with pleasure by the Greek people.

On the 17th of April, 1862, Lascarato kindly accompanied me to the jail of Argostoli. His cousin, the new Director, the Count Spiridion Delladecima, showed us over the premises. The prisoners (whose position had been greatly improved in consequence of the exposures in Lascarato's publication) greeted my friend with affectionate respect. They had all been incarcerated since his release; but they knew him, because he had often visited the prison. The new Director kept everything in the most excellent order. We entered the cell in which Lascarato had passed two and a half of the four months to which he had been originally sentenced. We found the total number of prisoners to be sixty-three. In the female department there were only seven. Two of these had burned a female relative alive, yet, strange to say, were not condemned to death.

Sir Charles Napier built this excellent prison upon an American model. It is a far superior building to the prison at Corfu, both as regards strength and convenience. Only half of the original plan is completed, or likely ever to be so. It has five departments, which branch like rays of the sun beneath the semicircular office of the Director, in which five windows overlook the five departments, which are divided by high walls. If the building were completed, there would then be ten departments, overlooked by the ten windows of a circular office. Sir Charles intended it to form the principal prison of the Seven Islands. The cells were not unlike those of the military prisons in England about thirty years ago. There was nothing particular in the one which Lascarato had occupied, but which I regarded with interest on his account. I believe that if all Greeks were like him in regard to truth and honesty, the speedy re-establishment of a great Greek Empire would be a more probable event than it now appears to be to men of restricted imagination.

Within the enclosure of the prison walls are a hospital, a church, and rooms for instruction in various trades. We saw tailors, shoemakers, and carpenters at work. But, except in the case of minor offences, this method of treating criminals is open to many objections. A good garden is attached to the premises, cultivated by two of the prisoners, not only supplying the whole establishment with vegetables, but clearing a small annual sum for the municipality. All these proceeds had been appropriated to himself by the former Director, who had been so relentless an enemy to Lascarato.

I was an almost daily witness for some months of the respect with which the author of the "Mysteries of Cephalonia" is beginning to be held by the respectable part of his countrymen. I was surprised, when walking with him, to observe the friendly salutations which he received; he, who had been obliged only a few years before to fly for his life from Cephalonia and Zante successively. On the subject of greetings, no people are more polite than the Ionians generally. Persons who have an extensive acquaintance (especially when in company with others who have also many friends) must, in places of public resort, have their hats perpetually in their hands. In Cephalonia, where the carriages are very few indeed, the people habitually walk in the middle of the streets and roads. This is generally the case even in Corfu, where vehicles and equestrians are, comparatively speaking, plentiful; but it is especially so in Argostoli. The foot passengers, instead of making room themselves for carriages and riders, always expect these to move out of *their* way. The gentlemen sometimes walk five or six abreast. Should such a party meet another containing one friend of the six, the perhaps dozen hats rise simultaneously in the air. You must acknowledge all the salutes made to your companions as well as to yourself without distinction of sex. I used to think seriously sometimes of inserting a little plate of brass in the front rim to save the permanent dent which this custom inflicted on my hat.

" Many good men," said Lascarato to me one

day, "are in favour of the union with Greece, not because they wish to please the mob, nor yet because they think the Islands would benefit by the measure, but from a generous feeling of self-sacrifice for the sake of the Greek race in general. These persons believe the Ionians to be greatly superior to the Continental Greeks in morals and in civilization, and consequently that the latter will be considerable gainers by their union with the Islanders."*

Lascarato remembered the time when glass in the windows was a great rarity in Argostoli. The young doctors returning from the Italian colleges often brought with them small window-frames fitted with glass to put up in their rooms, and thus to astonish the natives by their unwonted luxury.

He told me some curious characteristics of the seclusion of the ladies in Cephalonia in former times. When the British officers were first quartered in Argostoli about fifty years ago, as they never saw any ladies, they inquired if it were a city inhabited only by men. On learning that the town really contained fair ladies, but that custom secluded them from the sight of strangers, the young officers resolved to obtain a peep of them. They adopted a notable scheme. They hired a number of donkeys, to which they appended plenty of bells. Then,

* Lascarato himself, however, was strongly against the Union to the last; considering the Protection of England necessary to the well-being and security of the Seven Islands.

mounting upon these animals with their faces towards the tails, they proceeded to ride through the streets. The ludicrous scene brought the whole population to the windows, and the officers returned to their quarters, joyfully exclaiming, " At last we have seen the ladies!"

When my friend was a youth, the shoemakers were not allowed to see young ladies who required their services. The doors of the rooms were provided with holes through which the ladies passed their feet in order to be measured.

Lascarato had been educated at the college of Fort St. George, at the expense of Lord Guildford. When a boy, he had seen Lord Byron in 1823. The noble poet called one day on his uncle, the late Count Delladecima. His Lordship, having on great muddy boots, was too polite to enter the sitting-room, and conversed in the hall with the lad till his uncle had dressed himself. The noble poet's kindness and affability left a very pleasing impression on my friend's mind. The principal Signori gave dinners to Lord Byron, at which the ladies of the house did not appear, but dined alone in their own apartments. His lordship arrived in Cephalonia late in 1822, and remained there some months. He lived very retired in the picturesque village of Metaxata, about six miles south of Argostoli, not far from the sea. My wife and I visited the house on the 22nd of May, 1862. We found the road very bad, but the scenery was very pretty, and rich in flower, foliage, and fruits, being one of the least barren parts of rocky Cephalonia. The village, from the regularity and neatness of the houses, might be called a small town. The arms of Russia appeared sculptured in stone on one of the houses, reminding us of the period when the Seven Islands obeyed the great Northern Autocrat. We were taken over the house by a lady, who was certainly the handsomest person I ever saw in Cephalonia. The only relic of Lord Byron shown to us was a broken jug which he had used. The house, enclosed in a court-yard surrounded by walls, was well calculated for tranquil seclusion. It was not inhabited, and we had at first to wait till the beauty above named appeared with the keys. She spoke not a word of any language but Greek; but I contrived to make myself understood.

Although I do not believe that the fair sex is held at present in the same contempt as when Lascarato wrote his book, yet even at the present day the birth of a girl is considered a family misfortune in Cephalonia. It is an event which demands condolences from friends, and is the subject of congratulations only from enemies. The girl, despised as an inferior being, is often hated for a more rational cause. Every father in the Seven Islands is compelled to give a dowry to his daughter on her marriage. The amount must always be in proportion

to his means. If he do not obtain her a husband
before she is twenty-one years of age, she is then at
liberty to marry without his consent.   If he refuse
to give her a proper dowry, she may employ against
him legal means of compulsion.   It would seem as
if the laws took especial charge of daughters to
supply the deficiency of love in parents.   Yet they
are calculated to increase the hatred of the latter for
the former, for fathers of small means naturally regard their daughters as heavy incumbrances. They
are tempted to neglect and half starve them, and to
leave them uneducated, in order to save up the
necessary dowries.   Even sons, when they become
of age, frequently expect to receive a share of their
father's property. They, however, generally all live
together, or use one common purse, even when the
property is nominally divided.   Eighteen centuries
ago a similar custom prevailed, it appears, amongst
the Jews.   The prodigal son in the parable of Our
Lord demands of his father his share of the family
property, and, when he has spent it all, he returns
to the paternal mansion with confidence.

I can testify that, as far as appearances go, happy
marriages are not rare in Cephalonia.   I will therefore hope that the practice of wooing, as described
in the " Mysteries of Cephalonia," is rather the
exception than the rule.   Indeed, allowance must
always be made for the natural exaggeration of a
professed satirist, however truthful and honest he

himself may be. But his account of the manner in which his countrymen arrange their weddings is deserving of mention.

Marriages for love are rare. A young gentleman takes a wife partly to be well served, and to have his meals well cooked; but chiefly in order to obtain a good dowry. After making inquiries, to ascertain that the girl he proposes to marry is neither deformed nor one-eyed, he proceeds to call on the father, and requests to be informed what he will give with his daughter. Let us suppose that the reply is 3000 dollars. Our hero takes out his pocket-book and notes the amount; says he will consider it, and takes his leave. Not to go home and meditate. No; he proceeds to another house to ask similar questions of another parent. Perhaps at the house Number 2, the reply is 2000 dollars. "That will never do," exclaims the suitor, "I have already been offered 3000." Perhaps the bid rises; if so, he returns to the first parent, to give him another chance, or else he tries other families. It becomes a regular auction, where the bridegroom is knocked down to the highest bidder. When the business is entirely arranged, the young lady is made acquainted with the fact. Parental politeness is sometimes even carried to the length of asking her whether the arrangement pleases her. But this is a mere matter of form, signifying nothing. The marriage takes place, at all events. The husband is, perhaps, a doctor, who has studied in Italy, and has seen the world. If so, he despises his uneducated partner most sincerely. But if he have not been abroad, and be as ignorant as his wife, he still despises her; because the doctors, who set the fashion, despise their wives.

Formerly, parents believed that if their daughters were taught to read and write, the first use they would make of their accomplishments would be to read and write love-letters. At the present day the daughters are allowed to read, and their chief intellectual food is novels. As to writing, they are still backward, for the most part, in that useful art; and many of them find it difficult to answer notes of invitation. The manner in which they are treated at home makes them eager to marry, as a release from bondage. But they too often find, when they have realized their wishes, that they have but exchanged prisons. Such, in brief, is the picture drawn by Lascarato. But I cannot affirm its faithfulness from my own experience. To this I am aware that it may be replied, that the number of our female acquaintances amongst the Greeks was very limited; which cannot be denied.

I will trouble the reader with only one more extract from the "Mysteries of Cephalonia," as especially characteristic of its author.

"What is the love of one's country? Nature did not make Englishmen, Frenchmen, Greeks, and Turks. Nature made men. We subsequently gave to them distinctive appellations, when human weakness did not permit all mankind to unite in one nation, one society. Thus the division of men into nations was a matter of political economy, and not a decree of nature. Humanity must remain thus divided, until a way is found to realize the idea of Christ—' to be united and love one another.' But still the tendency towards that idea will be progressive; whilst the tendency towards exclusive nationality is retrograde, or at least stationary. We Ionians have for some time displayed much fanaticism in favour of nationality, which is at present regarded by many as the first of virtues, and as a sentiment of great generosity. It is easy to prove that the many are in error, but it is difficult for them to understand and sympathize with our feelings.

" Nationality has its generous side; but it is peculiar and circumscribed. The love of one's country has for its origin the love of the individual. He who loves his nation has first loved himself, then his family and neighbours, afterwards his locality, and finally his country. Up to this point the love of one's country is the greatest expansion of the heart, and compared with the love of the individual is certainly a noble sentiment. But the depths of love do not end here; and the love of one's country bears to the love of humanity the same position as the love of the individual bears to the love of one's country. He who sacrifices the rest of humanity to his nation, is as egotistical and mean as he who sacrifices his nation to his individuality."

Unknown to the author of the passage of which the above is a translation, very similar ideas had been expressed before in a condensed form by a speaker illustrious both by royal rank and by personal merit. " Nobody," said the Prince Consort, on the 21st of March, 1850, at the Guildhall, London —" nobody who has paid attention to the peculiar features of our present era will doubt for a moment that we are living at a period of wonderful transition, which tends rapidly to accomplish that great end to which all history points—*the realization of the unity of mankind.*"

A great monarch has lately proposed that Europe should take, what may be considered as the first step towards carrying into practice the sublime theory in question, by means of a Congress, bent on securing the peace of the world. But for any mortal to assume such an initiative, it is necessary that he should not only have attracted the admiration, but have also gained the respect and confidence of the civilized world.

CHAPTER VIII.

Flowers and Foliage—Wine Company unsuccessful—Unpopularity of Cephalonia as a Station—Local Society without a Head—A too secluded Ruler—A Wedding in High Life—Sugarplum Surfeit—Privileged Englishmen—The Marriage Ceremonies—" Let the Wife *fear* her Husband"—Cephalonian Beauty—An unwonted Dance—How Unionists were sometimes Manufactured—A too classical Partner in the Dance—Visit of H.R.H. the Prince of Wales—H.S.H. the Prince of Leiningen—A Crown refused by a Naval Captain—The Prince's Ride—A Royal Dinner Party—The Mysteries of Cephalonia—The Royal Departure—The Ionian Steamer and the Ionian Assembly—The President of the Assembly—Offer of a Country-house—Begging Boys—Count Roma, Mr. Stevens—Zante, second in Beauty only to Corfu—The Pitch Wells—Luncheon of Grapes—Advantage of a Knowledge of Greek—Superior Clubs of Zante—The Archives—The Ghetto—First Visits made by Strangers—Count Lunzi's Country-house—Appropriate Present to a John Bull—How the Greek War-office employed the Military Staff—" Hair Mattresses for Private Soldiers"—The Resident and the Rizospast—Mr. Stevens' Mistake regarding the Mills—Tempting Offer of a Passage to Athens—A Greek Regent of British Descent—The Alfred Mania—Obstinacy of the Greeks—A Rash Promise.

ALTHOUGH the general aspect of Cephalonia (especially as viewed from the harbour and town of Argostoli) appears barren and rugged, it yet contains some fertile and picturesque valleys and slopes. There is also in some parts of the island an abundance of trees, flowers, and fruits, sufficient to attract the admiration of travellers who have not seen Corfu. Besides the lofty pines of the great mountain range; the plane, the olive, the oak, and various other trees are frequently seen. The cypresses (as in Corfu) usually raise their upright forms like sentinels round the village churches. The almond-tree, so beautiful both in blossom and bloom, is a most agreeable object. Palm-trees and cactuses give, in some places, a tropical tinge to the scenery. The Orange groves (the bright fruit contrasting with the dark foliage) also form a pleasing variety. The olive, it must be confessed, is very inferior to that of Corfu, where that tree in the formation of its trunk and branches attains to an unrivalled beauty. Flowers are scarce in Cephalonia, and the deficiency in society is usually supplied by Zante. Fruits are excellent; the largest melon that I ever saw was one presented to us by a gentleman of Argostoli. Figs of two kinds are excellent. Baskets of these and of grapes were frequently sent to us by the Regent's wife and other Greek ladies.

Grapes, which in their season are a drug in Corfu, are considered at all times a luxury in Cephalonia; where the ground is chiefly occupied by currant vines. Riding one day with my wife near the little light-house early in June, the old proprietor of the currant vines in that neighbourhood, with whom we were not acquainted, ran after the horses in order to present to the English lady the first bunch of currant grapes of the season, a fact which I mention as a corroborative proof of the good feelings generally prevailing towards our nation.

With the exception of gooseberries, I believe that all European fruits grow in the island. The Cephalonians moreover are not accustomed so constantly to gather them unripe, as are the Corfiots; who from the fear of thieves, never wait till their fruits ripen. Caviare was a common luxury in Argostoli. The wines of the country were passable considering their cheapness. For sixpence a bottle a tolerable white wine was procurable. The wine company newly established was not (up to my departure), very successful. The manner of keeping Ionian wine without injury does not appear as yet to have been discovered. The company sold for a shilling wine no better than that which could be procured for sixpence, or even fourpence, from the farmers; so that the English officers with every desire to patronize local enterprise, could not employ the company.

There was little to attract or to please the young Englishmen in Cephalonia. The shooting involved a great deal of walking, with very little sport. The yachting, except in the small harbour, was all in the open sea, instead of being everywhere, as in Corfu, sheltered by the vicinity of land. The mountainous country would have made paper hunts impossible, even had there been a sufficient number of Englishmen to establish such a pastime. Dinner parties were almost entirely limited to the tables of the Resident, the Regent, and the mess of the officers. Lastly for those who could only speak English, even the few Greek ladies who went into society were sealed books. The regiment previously stationed at Argostoli, had given a ball; but only eight Greek ladies, and most of these married, had been induced to honor it with their presence. Plenty of Greek gentlemen did attend it, and they doubtless considered the ladies to be superfluous. Games at cards and a good supper were more to their taste than the society of the fair sex. But the English officers were greatly disgusted with their ball experiment, and they left an example not likely to be followed.

Unfortunately the English Resident did not patronize the local society. Indeed except an annual visit, on New Year's-day, to the principal ladies and gentlemen of Argostoli; the English officers and a few of his Greek official subordinates constituted his sole society. This was a great misfortune. The Residents, as representing the Lord High Commissioner, were the first personages, and the heads of society in their respective islands; the Regents being only the second in rank. When therefore the Resident shut himself up from society, the latter remained without any acknowledged head. What is worse is that England was thereby left unrepresented. For in the small Islands the Resident was usually the sole permanent English official; the annual relief from Corfu of the garrison leaving little opportunity for social influence on the part of the officers, which was still further diminished by the causes we have already enumerated, in a previous chapter.

Although the Resident of Cephalonia was highly esteemed, and even beloved by those who knew him well; yet after what I have above stated, it will not be a matter of surprise that he was by no means generally popular with the Greeks. The stoutest Rizospast could not deny his amiable and honorable qualities. But even his best friends regretted the seclusion which he had adopted as a system. Seeing habitually only three Greeks, whose talents and characters he estimated very highly, it was only natural that the people generally should have believed him to have been the tool of those able but party men. Active, zealous, and efficient in all that related to those external matters, which do not depend upon political knowledge or foresight, the Resident yet by his own choice deprived himself of nearly all influence amongst the gentry and people of the island.

Some of the Greek gentlemen had evening parties at their houses. But these were of men only; cards and light refreshments forming the entertainment. We, however, managed to arrange some evening parties of both sexes at our house. Conversation and occasionally magic-lantern lectures, explained in Italian, served to pass the time.

On Saturday, the 10th of May, 1862, we were present at the marriage of the Regent's eldest daughter in Argostoli. We arrived at eight in the evening, and found a very large company assembled, probably about a hundred persons of both sexes. Besides a covered verandah, there were two large rooms, the one full of ladies, and the other of gentlemen. At the head of one sat the bride, a pretty girl of eighteen, and by her side the bridegroom, the only gentleman in that apartment. The mother of the bride sat near them, and placed my wife next to herself. I at first remained in the same room with the ladies. But it soon appeared that I was either infringing the etiquette, or derogating from my dignity as one of the male sex. For my worthy host came up to me and taking me by the arm led me into the apartment occupied by the lords of the creation. There he left me ensconced in a chair between two stout amiable gentlemen. Ices were handed round in the first instance. Afterwards there followed, throughout the evening, interminable baskets of white and coloured sugar-plums of various shapes and sizes. At first, being unfortunately past the age for relishing such refreshment, I allowed them to pass by me untouched; but I quickly perceived that I must do at Rome as the Romans do. The etiquette was rigid, and applied to old as well as to young. The rule was to fill your coat, waistcoat, and breeches-pockets, as also your pocket-handkerchief (in short every available receptacle), with those *bonbons*. For politeness sake I was ready to do everything—except swallow them. Before the night was over, I had collected enough to open, had I desired it, a small lollypop shop on my own account. We were informed that fifty pounds sterling had been laid out by our hostess upon these strange comestibles. My first idea was to take them home to give to my children; but, on second thoughts, I was deterred from such a proceeding by prudent fears of doctors' bills. I therefore reserved them for the young English drummers, who I felt sure could digest anything. They were certainly tried in this respect. For the following morning the Regent's lady despatched a servant with a large additional basketful of the sugar-plums, as was customary on such occasions. The drummers and soldiers' children devoured, however, the whole without difficulty or inconvenience of any kind.

I should state that the company consisted entirely of the relations of the bridal pair, with the exception of the Resident, myself, and a few others. It is thought a great slur to leave out any kinsman on such occasions. The marriage ceremony commenced about nine P.M., and lasted more than an hour. It

took place in a small room adjoining that first occupied by the ladies, which had been prepared for
the purpose. The only gentlemen admitted, who
had no part to perform, were the two Englishmen.
But the door being open, some of the outsiders
could look in occasionally if they felt so inclined.
Even the father of the bride remained in the outer
room most of the time. A table was spread with a
white cloth, upon which was placed bread and
wine. A priest, magnificently dressed in gold-embroidered robes, officiated with the aid of some
assistants, plainly dressed in black. Before them
on the opposite side of the table stood the bride and
bridegroom, supported by the mother of the bride,
and the friends of the bride and bridegroom.

The bridal pair each held tall lighted candles in
their hands, throughout the tedious ceremony. The
priest rapidly read the service, whilst performing
various little ceremonies. He crowned the pair
with white wreaths, which he frequently transferred
from one head to the other. He also dipped a
pointed piece of bread into the wine, and then al-
ternately put it into their mouths for each of them
to take a small piece. This, constantly repeated,
was the least pleasant part of the ceremony to the
spectators. The wine was then handed to each in
the cup. Afterwards the bride and bridegroom,
with their three or four assisting friends, formed a
circle, and moved together three times round the

table. The pretty young bride could not help laughing at this rather comical part of the proceedings. There were various other ceremonies about the ring, and also about kissing the Bible, and the priest, and the nearest relations. The whole operation appeared to be a very fatiguing one for the fair bride, who, however, went through it all most good-humouredly.

It appears to me that when our version of the New Testament was translated, very chivalrous ideas must have prevailed in England, as regarded the ladies. In the Greek Church there exists no such weakness. In our version, Saint Paul, when instructing married couples in their duties, uses the words : " And the wife see that she *reverence* her husband."[*] The original words used by the Greeks are: " Let the wife *fear* her husband." The modern Greek version of the New Testament, published in Athens in 1850, but very little used by the Greeks, has the appearance (as regards this passage) of being translated from the English Testament; for it adopts the word *reverence*.[†] This verbal difference may appear unimportant; but it is, I think, very significative of the different positions held in society by English and Greek married ladies.

The beauty of the bride, and the still handsome

* Ephesians, ch. v. v. 33.
† *Original.* . . . . . ἡ δὲ γυνὴ ἵνα φοβῆται τὸν ἄνδρα.
Modern version. ἡ δὲ γυνὴ ἂς σέβηται τὸν ἄνδρα.

appearance of the Regent's lady, added greatly to the general interest of this wedding scene. There were also many other pretty faces amongst the assembled Greek ladies. But as all the company, with the exception of the priests and of the servants, were dressed in the fashions of Western Europe, there was not much appearance of nationality on this occasion. The servants, however, were dressed in the Albanian dress, which it is now the custom in Europe to consider as the Greek national costume.

The wedding party broke up amidst the kissings of the bride on the part of the privileged few; in which the Englishmen were, of course, not included. But every one was bound to say to the bridal pair, "*May you live—may you live.*"* The parents of the bride were also greeted with friendly expressions of "*I wish you joy.*"†

The Regent's lady told my wife, in the course of the evening, that far from being accustomed to earthquakes, they prevented her from sleeping, as they were this year so unusually severe as to be very alarming even to the natives. She little knew how severe a shock was then approaching.

We returned home before eleven. It had rained very hard whilst we were at the party. But the day had been very fine, with a brisk north wind

---

* νὰ ζῆσετε.   † εὐχαριστό.

the day before. I was up very early next morning; and at half-past five, we experienced the second greatest earthquake of that shaking season, the particulars of which will be hereafter recorded. In sending (the following morning) the basket of bonbons before mentioned, the Regent's lady kindly inquired if my wife had been alarmed by the great earthquake.

It was on Thursday the 15th of May, that the sole dance I ever witnessed in Cephalonia occurred at an evening party at our house. We had asked a few friends to listen to the music of a string band. Amongst them were the Resident, the Regent with his lady, and one of their charming daughters; and the Austrian Consul and his wife and daughter, the latter of whom was considered one of the belles of Argostoli. We had altogether, ten or twelve Greek ladies present, displaying, for the number, an unusual proportion of beauty. . But the gentlemen, as in all Ionian parties, greatly preponderated. One young lady present, though small of stature, had a very beautiful, regular Greek face; and looked like a pocket edition of a classical Venus. Amongst the company was my friend, Signor Cladan, who speaks English perfectly, and is a great admirer of our country. Nevertheless, he has always been strongly in favour of the union with Greece, in the hope that some career may be thereby open for his only son. He never can forget that when he, in early life, applied to enter the English army, he was refused on the plea of being a foreigner.

I now come to the incident, which alone has induced me to mention this party, out of the many agreeable occasions on which we met our Cephalonian friends. The band had not long played a lively piece of dancing music, before the Regent's wife applied to the hostess for permission to dance. The extraordinary request was communicated to me. I could scarcely belive my ears. A dance in Cephalonia only conveyed to me the idea of a number of dark, hirsute male peasants, jumping or skipping in the *Sirto* or *Romaika*, with their wives and daughters either absent, or, if present, merely looking on at the performance. However, the impromptu dance went off very well; and, considering the little practice they ever enjoy, it was astonishing how well and gracefully the fair ladies of Argostoli danced. The young officers present, however, lamented that, although they could waltz with the little beauty, yet they could convey no ideas into her too classical mind, into which no language more vulgar than Greek had ever penetrated. From what we saw of the native ladies, we decided that their general seclusion from society must be solely owing to the want of taste in the gentlemen. For the ladies we were in the habit of meeting, would have been an ornament to any society in every quarter of the globe.

In the summer of 1862, Cephalonia was honoured by a brief visit from his Royal Highness the Prince of Wales. At about ten A.M., on the 2nd of June, the *Osborne* steamed into the harbour of Argostoli. By the time it had anchored, the President, Regent, and Commandant went on board to pay their respects to his Royal Highness. The flag-ship, the *Marlborough*, and five other vessels of war, had arrived the previous day. But it was now learned that the Lord High Commissioner was not expected until the following morning. Chiefly in consequence of this circumstance, but partly for the sake of General Bruce, the *Osborne* proceeded to Ithaca. The general was lying sick in his cabin of the disease which carried him off soon after his arrival in England; and it was thought better for him that he should not remain unnecessarily long at anchor. When the *Osborne* arrived at Vathy in the pretty harbour of Ithaca, the captain commanding the troops happened to be absent. A young ensign, therefore, had the honor of going on board as commandant to report himself to his future sovereign. The royal steamer did not return to Cephalonia until the following morning.

Meantime, Admiral Sir William Martin, the naval Commander-in-Chief, gave a grand dinner on board the *Marlborough*, to which we were invited. The Lord High Commissioner was present, having arrived at Cephalonia in the course of the day, sooner than was expected. The General also was a guest on board the flag-ship, the Admiral having brought him from Corfu. The dinner was excellent. Indeed the Admiral enjoyed a great reputation both for boundless hospitality, and for the excellence of his cook. If at sea he was a stern disciplinarian, he was ever in the harbour the kindest and most affable of hosts. The Prince of Leiningen, captain of the *Magicienne*, was also of the party. His Serene Highness left early next morning for Malta to precede the Prince of Wales. Not long afterwards, he furnished the striking example of the refusal of a crown by a captain of a British man-of-war; and though there were not wanting persons to blame him for his resolution, it was not the less wise and prudent in the general estimation of the public.

On the following day, the 3rd of June, the Prince of Wales with the Lord High Commissioner, both of them in plain clothes, landed at half-past four P.M., on the Mole opposite to our house. His Royal Highness was received with no military honors, but was met by a great crowd of the inhabitants. Some soldiers were mingled amongst the latter, dressed in their white summer tunics, and they were useful as fuglemen in regulating the cheers of the crowd, who were fully disposed for loyal demonstrations. In consequence of the mourning for the late Prince Consort, the visit of the Prince was treated as a strictly private one. The Royal party walked through the street to the Residency amidst the cheers of the spectators. There several horses had been collected from the small number kept in the garrison. Of these, mine had the distinguished honor on this occasion of carrying his Royal Highness. The Lord High Commissioner, the Resident, and some of the royal suite, mounted the other horses. The party then rode as far as the tents on the south-western coast, where the musketry practice was usually carried on; returning by the Little Giro round by the harbour and barracks. His Royal Highness rode at a sharp pace the whole way; so that some of those who accompanied him exhibited a to them very unusual equestrian fleetness.

The inhabitants of Argostoli, who had expected that his Royal Highness would return, as he had started, through the town, were much disappointed; for they had prepared garlands and flowers to throw on his path as the Prince passed. The royal party dismounted and re-entered the boats opposite our house. Returning sunburnt from his Eastern tour, and being now within six months of his coming of age, the excitement of the first British subjects, who greeted the homeward return of his Royal Highness, may be easily imagined. These feelings were shared by the Greeks; but the brevity of the Royal

visit, as well as the strict orders previously mentioned, deprived them of the opportunity of fully
expressing their respectful and affectionate loyalty.

On the same evening there was a dinner-party on
board the *Osborne*. The Prince of Wales was in
evening plain clothes, but wore the riband and star
of the Garter. On his right sat the Lord High
Commissioner, on his left the Admiral, and in front
the General and Resident. The suite of these
royal and official personages, with the naval cap-
tains, the Commandant, and the Regent of Cephalonia, completed the party. The moderate
size of the state cabin made a larger party impossible. Some of the bands on the decks of the
neighbouring men-of-war played during the dinner,
as did also the infantry band on the parade-ground
close to the harbour. Little etiquette was observed on board the *Osborne*. The Prince was
supposed to be Lord Renfrew, but he was always
addressed by the title of Royal Highness. He
was once, however, accidentally addressed as "my
lord," probably from a confused amalgamation of
the Royal Prince with the supposed peer. Upon
the condescension and affability displayed at that
entertainment it becomes me not to dwell. It will
be sufficient to say that no one present at it could
afterwards be surprised at the enthusiastic loyalty,
subsequently displayed in England, a few months
later, on several memorable occasions.

A distinguished gentleman (who accompanied the princely traveller on his journey) to whom I told the history of Lascarato, requested me to procure for him a copy of the "Mysteries of Cephalonia." I informed him that it was written in the Cephalonia *patois;* and that I feared that he would not be able to read it satisfactorily. He, however, believed he could read any Greek. I therefore promised to send him a copy as soon as I could procure one; for I could not part with the only one I possessed. More than a fortnight passed before I could fulfil my promise, so rare had the work become. But on the 17th of June a Greek friend brought me a copy, which he had obtained with difficulty. A youthful Cephalonian had purchased the book in 1856, when it was first published. His father had ordered him to burn it immediately. He had feigned compliance; but had carefully hid it for six years; and had now been persuaded to give it to my friend. It had never been read by its late owner; for when brought to me the leaves were uncut. I duly despatched it to England according to my promise; and I hope that in judging of it allowances were made for the circumstances under which it was produced in an only half civilized country.

The party on board the *Osborne* broke up at ten o'clock. Half an hour later the Royal yacht left the harbour; its stern beautifully illuminated, and discharging blue lights and rockets. At the same moment the huge flag-ship was splendidly lit up in every part. Two vessels of the squadron followed the *Osborne*, which proceeded on its way to Malta. No earthquake occurred during the Royal visit; but not long after the departure of the *Osborne* a slight shock appears to have occurred.

The Lord High Commissioner remained for a few days in the island, on one of his biennial visits.* His Excellency now for the first time ascended the Black Mountain, and visited the Resident's Cottage; near to which had been built a beautiful arbour of forest pines, in the hope that the Prince of Wales would have there taken luncheon. On witnessing the beauty of the scenery and the climate, Sir Henry Storks is reported to have expressed his regret that he had not visited the mountain in his earlier visits to Cephalonia. Had he done so, he declared that he would have laid out some money in improving the cottage as a summer residence.

This year the Assembly refused to renew for the future any grants of money for the Ionian steamer, which was chiefly employed in carrying His Excellency on his tour through the Islands. For the rest of his stay he had consequently to make use of a man-of-war on such occasions.

On Sunday the 8th of June the Ionian steamer was lying at anchor in the harbour of Argostoli,

---

* By the English, this functionary was called *The Lord High*, which a mail-servant once converted into *The Lord Mighty*. By the Ionian gentry he was styled *il Lord Alto*; and by the Greeks in general ὁ Ἁρμοστής, the Harmost, the ancient title of the Spartan governors of colonies or dependencies.

when the Greek steamer (on its bi-weekly passage from Corfu to Greece) came in for a few hours. Before it came to anchor, it was surrounded by crowds of boats, decorated with Greek and Ionian flags; the persons in which commenced cheering most vociferously: making a strange contrast with the solitary unnoticed steamer, which contained the British Representative of Majesty. We soon learned that Signor Zervo, the eloquent President of the Assembly, was returning in triumph to his native island, after the close of the parliamentary session. With a portion, however, of the extreme democrats the President was no longer in favour. For he had this year declared himself a reformer; and had ceased to join in the agitation for the Union. He had maintained that it was useless for the present to do so; as the Ministry in England had again announced in the English Parliament, that the Protectorate was to be firmly maintained. Although an able man Signor Zervo took on this occasion a course rather unfortunate as regarded the future permanence of his popularity. But no one could then have foreseen that in a few months the plans and opinions of the English Government would have undergone so mighty a change.

In July a Greek friend offered to us the loan of his country - house, in the neighbourhood of Orphanata; a pretty village in the south of the island, about nine miles from the capital. We drove out to see the place, through a pretty picturesque country; carrying with us the ponderous house-keys. We found the mansion at a little distance from the road; and before reaching it we had to pass on foot over some rugged ground. A poor old man in a neighbouring cottage took us over the premises, whilst a boy bore the keys. The little house was entirely empty, without a particle of furniture; the supplying of which last would have occasioned to us much trouble and expense. In short we soon gave up all idea of profiting by the obliging offer which had been made to us. The old man would accept nothing for his trouble; but the little boy, after taking the keys back to the carriage, readily accepted sixpence. Before we started on our return a good-looking young girl presented my companion with a bunch of little leaves resembling thyme; and she positively refused any recompense. The boys alone in the Islands are usually greedy about money, even when they have done nothing to earn a recompense. In passing and repassing through Orphanata we were pursued by a number of these little urchins, with cries of—" Fardings! fardings!" I gave them my usual reply on such occasions: " You ought to work, and not to beg." But they evidently did not see the point of my observa-tion.

In the month of August I was introduced at a weekly reunion of Greek gentlemen, to Count Roma, the Resident of Ithaca. He is father-in-law to Sir George Bowen, formerly secretary at Corfu,

and now Governor of Queensland.   He is the only
Greek, I believe, who ever filled the post of representative of the Lord High Commissioner.   It was
rather an anomalous position for a native to hold
under the Protectorate of England.   But he appears
to have performed its duties loyally and efficiently.
It was at this same party that I first met Mr.
Stevens, who has resided for the last fifty years in
Argostoli, under the rule of all the ten Lord High
Commissioners, and from whom I obtained a good
deal of valuable information.

On Sunday the 24th of August I started with an
English friend by the Austrian steamer at about
eleven A.M., on a trip to Zante, which I had not
yet seen.   I arrived there about four in the afternoon.   The Resident was on leave in England,
and the late lamented Major Ansell, who commanded the garrison, was also Acting-Resident.   He
kindly took us ashore in the Sanita boat, and we
proceeded in a carriage up to the Castle.   There
we slept that night in a comparatively cool atmo-
sphere.   But I cannot say that I had much rest; as
the huts occupied by the officers were generally
swarming with rats, whilst the mosquitoes also
abounded.   I was glad therefore to sleep the two
following nights in town; where the chief medical
officer of the garrison hospitably gave me a bed in
his house.

In beautiful scenery and fertility, and richness of
flowers and foliage, Zante is second only to Corfù

At this time the currants had not been all gathered in, and were still lying in heaps exposed in the fields. The troops were very inconveniently located, partly in the town and partly on the steep hill which was defended by the Castle; the old Venetian walls and battlements of which form interesting subjects of study to military men. Very curious also are the immense rents caused by the earthquakes in the cliffs beneath the Castle. From the latter there is a very beautiful view of nearly every part of the island, which appears amply to deserve its title of " the flower of the Levant."

On Monday morning, S—— and I started in a carriage for the pitch wells, which form one of the principal sights worth visiting. We drove along a good road for about nine miles. We then left our carriage, I to mount a mule, whilst my friend preferred walking. Our drive had been through a beautiful cultivated plain, and extensive groves of ólives, almost as fine as those of Corfu. We passed, though at some distance from us, the picturesquely situated house of Count Ermanno Lunzi, the historian. On leaving the road our way led over some wild and barren hills for about three miles. The path was very rugged, and the heat very great for some time. At last we reached the shady wood through which the wells are approached. Being pressed for time, we only saw one well. It was a little pool of water, in which the pitch was perpetually bubbling up in a small stream forming a shiny black surface. The pitch partly subsided and partly remained floating on the water. The latter appeared clean and good to the taste with the exception of a slight bituminous flavour. It is generally believed that there is some connexion between these pitch wells, and the causes of the frequent earthquakes which have shaken the island. These visitations, however, had been less severe than usual, owing to the apparent change of their subterranean course in 1862. A peasant was standing near. the wells, whom I desired to fetch us some grapes, whilst we seated ourselves under the shade of an olive-tree. He brought us a handkerchief full of fine large grapes, such as in the London season would probably have cost at least a sovereign, but for which I found that sixpence was an ample remuneration. Currants forming the staple in Zante and Cephalonia are in those Islands of course much cheaper than the large grapes. But in Corfu, where currants do not grow, and where grapes are plentiful, a hatful of the latter may be obtained in the country for a penny. A few bunches were always procurable for nothing but simple thanks ; and were often indeed taken by the passers-by without even that kind of payment.

At the pitch wells, with a thermometer more than 80° in the shade, the grapes brought to me formed a very refreshing and sufficiently substantial luncheon. Besides the muleteer who had accompanied me, two other peasants waited on us. I found it as easy to converse with them, as with Corfiots, and more so than with Cephalonians. One of these men was constantly employed in fetching water, out of the clear part of the pitch well, which we made use of to cool our grapes, to drink, and finally to perform our ablutions with. My indifferent Greek was of good service, saving us much trouble in satisfying our wants. Moreover it made the people inclined to oblige us. A Greek always likes to be addressed in his own language, however imperfectly spoken; a simple fact which unfortunately was never sufficiently appreciated by the British Government.

We returned to the town by five P.M.; when a Zantiot gentleman showed us over the two clubs situated in the principal square. One of these was quite new and really astonished us by its English appearance of cleanliness and comfort; so superior to anything that I had ever before seen in the Ionian Islands. Of this club, the English officers had been made honorary members. Many of the gentlemen and even of the ladies of Zante spoke English well, and mixed cordially in society with our countrymen. That evening I dined again at the Castle, but slept in the town. The noise of the church bells was very harsh, and disturbed my morning sleep. But as the torture was not allowed to continue for more than five minutes at a time, it was more endurable than in Cephalonia. Next morning, Tuesday, the 26th, a Zantiot friend took me to the office in which the archives are kept. I saw copies of " The Golden Book," containing the names of all the Zantiot nobility. The original consisting of many volumes, had been burnt in 1797 after the arrival of the French Republicans. My friend pointed out to me, his own name, and that of his relatives in the list of nobles. I also read some of the correspondence between the Marquis Riva-rola, then in the British service, and General Campbell, at that time Governor-General and Commander-in-Chief at Corfu. These letters amply proved the complete, but as I believe most neces-sary, despotism established by the English in 1815. The corruption of judges, and other officials in those days, and the general state of the Islands, after their many vicissitudes, made a strong government indis-pensable for the welfare of the inhabitants. A constitutional rule, in the English sense of the word, could have ensured neither the security of life and property nor that distribution of justice which form the main objects of all rational governments.

We next proceeded to the Jews quarter, which till lately bore the name of the *Ghetto*. But about a month before my visit, all the gates had been removed by order of the local Government, with the consent of the Senate. The gates had been erected centuries ago by the Venetians to protect the Jews from the Greeks, and had been always carefully closed at night. So effectually had the barriers been removed, that I was unable to discover any trace of their past existence. Zante is the largest, as well as the handsomest town of the Seven Islands, and its principal street, the Strada Larga, is the longest. There are in it some curious old houses, one of which dates as far back as the Byzantine period. There are porticoes along the principal street superior in extent and number to those of Corfu.

Later in the day, my Zantiot friend called for me in a carriage. We drove first to the church of St. Dionysius, the patron saint of Zante. It is a handsome, clean, and neatly ornamented building. The church tower was a separate structure on the opposite side of the road, lofty and well-proportioned. In the church itself, besides a number of paintings of a curious old style, I was shown a great number of gold and silver lamps and chalices, and other valuable articles, many of them set with precious stones. There was altogether an appearance of wealth and refinement unknown to the churches of Cephalonia.

We next proceeded some miles into the country to call on Count Lunzi, the elder brother of the historian. For it is the hospitable custom in Zante for strangers first to call on the native gentry; and thus respectable persons have no need of introductions. Through ignorance of this fact, the amiable and excellent English Commandant had deprived himself of some very agreeable society. For he had persisted in expecting the first visits to be paid to himself. We had a beautiful drive through the fertile valley of Zante, and were most kindly received by Count Lunzi in his handsome and spacious country-house; he being an old friend of my companion. In front of the house the currant crops were lying collected in heaps on the plain. To the back of the house was a large picturesque ornamental garden, rich in flowers and fruits; and which would have been perfect had there been a sufficient supply of water. But the excessive dryness of the soil somewhat disfigured the beauty of the scene. The hostess was out driving with her family; and our hospitable host was quite uncomfortable because she had carried off the keys of the ample well-filled commissariat stores. But as it was already near six P.M. and I had to dine in town at seven, it may easily be supposed that the absence of the keys did not greatly afflict me; especially as abundance of ripe grapes were offered to us, as well as some simple cooling drinks. The Count asked me to dine with him on the following day; but unfortunately I was obliged to return to Cephalonia, and so was compelled to decline the invitation. On our way back to town we called on Count Salomos, father-in-law to Count Lunzi, and a gentleman highly respected by every one. That evening I dined with an English family, where I met the lady and niece of the absent Resident. Upon my arrival at the house where I slept I found awaiting me a neat little barrel of currants, as a present from my Greek friend to be sent home to my family. What greater attention could be paid to a John Bull than thus to supply his family with the means of making an unlimited number of plum-puddings?

Early next morning, the 27th of August, my sleep was put to flight by a very grating peal of church bells. In tones they were if possible worse than those of Cephalonia; but fortunately the advance of civilization in Zante, had limited to five minutes at a time these excruciating noises. At eight A.M. the Sanita boat took me and my English friend on board the steamer, where we had an excellent *déjeûner à la fourchette*. A Greek Major of Artillery, proceeding to Corfu on his way to Italy, introduced himself to me. He informed me that he was now on the staff; and was employed on a special mission by the King's Secretary of War.* Subsequently he was kind enough to acquaint me with the purport of his mission; which was to engage female singers for the Opera at Athens! It appears that the theatrical committee there is partly composed of military officers. Notwithstanding the peaceful staff

* The major spoke English perfectly.

duties for which he had been selected; Major R. was a soldier-like man, and appeared to be a really zealous officer.   As the steamer remained for more than an hour at Argostoli, the Major landed, and was shown, at his request, over the English barracks by a young officer.   He afterwards came to my cottage, and took a glass of wine before re-embarking.   He related to me, the great interest which he had taken in inspecting the barracks.   He also expressed his delight at everything he had seen, especially at the privates having meat every day and separate beds with hair mattresses.   Boards and blankets and hard biscuits formed, it appears, the bed and food of his own soldiers.   He seemed to think that English privates were better off than Greek officers.   But with all his inclination to admire our liberal system, he yet appeared almost scandalized with what he called the luxuries with which the private soldiers were indulged.   The hair mattresses especially appeared to puzzle him. He could not get over the idea, and kept repeating: " *Hair mattresses for private soldiers!*"   It is my belief that he dreamed that night of those wonderful hair mattresses: so entirely had they taken possession of his excited imagination.

The year 1862 was a bad one as regarded the production of currants, from the effect of the blight, which the use of sulphur mitigated, but did not wholly remedy.   I was assured that in some cases the price was so low as to be barely renumerative.

The quantity produced both in Cephalonia and Zante was in 1862 less than the average. From the former island only 17,000,000 lbs. and from the latter only 14,000,000 lbs. were exported. Cephalonia has for many years produced more currants than Zante; but whilst the latter produces a considerable quantity of oil, the exportation of the former in that respect is hardly worth mentioning. I was informed that about 100,000 barrels of oil were exported from Zante in 1862, and from Cephalonia only about 3000 barrels.

Walking on the 20th of September in company with the Resident, we met the rich ultra-Rizospastical owner of the famous mills of Argostoli. Whilst we were discussing the mystery of the water below the level of the sea, the Rizospast observed: "Why don't you as governor have the matter explored?" The reply was that nothing could be done without the consent of the Senate and general Government of Corfu. "Napier," retorted the other, "did everything himself, and so ought you to do. You English ought either to govern us or to go away." This speech accurately represented the general feeling of the people; who held the Protectorate responsible even for details, which had been legally left to the management of the Ionians themselves. In my opinion, constitutional ideas, as cherished by Englishmen, are simply absurd when applied to modern Greeks, in their present state of incomplete civilization. The best form of government for them, for at least the next fifty years, would be, I am convinced, an enlightened and popular despotism, if such a thing were possible.

The mills had been stopped for a day at this time. The Resident and I, therefore, tasted the water, after it had ceased to be supplied from the harbour, and had subsided to its natural height below the level of the sea. It was still decidedly salt, so that no doubt remained on our minds that the venerable Mr. Stevens was mistaken in the theory he had so long established in his own mind.

Towards the close of October, the news reached us of another Greek revolution. But the actual dethronement of Otho, took place a little later in the year. About this time, Sir R. S. arrived in his yacht in the harbour of Argostoli, where, owing to the violence of the gale then raging, he was detained for some days. He finally proceeded to Athens on the 14th of November, and must have arrived there just after the fall of Otho. He had kindly offered me a passage in his yacht, but I could not then absent myself from the island. It was a most tempting offer; for the little craft was fitted up in such a luxurious manner, that the baronet's daughter, who accompanied him, could miss few of the comforts even of a wealthy home.

On the 18th of November, the Regent Inglessi, gave one of his periodical dinners to all the principal officials. The tables groaned under the solid meats as well as made dishes, all of which were successively handed round. This arrangement is very suitable with light French cookery; but with a dinner of English solidity, to expect every one to eat of everything implies, I think, enormous gastronomic powers. I once heard the wife of a French general in Paris say to her husband, who was recommending me some particular dish at his hospitable table, "*Nous mangeons tout, nous mangeons tout.*" The exquisite cookery, however, exhibited on that occasion, justified the lady's sanguine speech. But in Cephalonia, I was far from being able to adopt this plan, in spite of the good example set by my neighbours. Our host, the Regent Inglessi, had more the appearance of an Englishman than of a Greek. He is said, indeed, to be of English descent. A British merchant named Inglis was wrecked, it appears, on the island about two centuries ago. He settled in Argostoli, married a Greek lady, and left behind him numerous descendants. In the list of the *Sincliti** of Argostoli for 1862, there are more than sixty persons of the name of Inglessi. It is one of the peculiarities of the Islands, that the inhabitants appear to be composed of few but very large families. In the lists of the Sincliti of Lixuri for the same year, I find 110 Typaldos, more than 50 Zervos, and nearly 70 Macris.

* The *Sincliti*, as explained in vol. i., are the voters.

The Greek revolution and the dethronement of Otho, was rapidly followed by what may be called the *Alfred mania*, which raged in Cephalonia as fiercely as in any other part of Greece. It pervaded all parties, except a very small fraction of the extreme democrats, whose hatred to everything English appeared to be inextinguishable. But even that small, contemptible party, if it could not share the general enthusiasm, was at least silenced for the time. The Greek ladies were especially enthusiastic for the English Prince; and the Greek youths still more so, if possible. Some of these last, to whom I had been the means of facilitating the learning of English, visited me occasionally to confide to me their ardent aspirations. Steady, sober-minded men, though less enthusiastic in their hopes, were yet anxious that Prince Alfred should become the king of an enlarged Greece. But neither old nor young, male or female, would credit my repeated assurances that they never would obtain this desire of their hearts. They persisted in believing that the determined will of the whole Greek race could not possibly be denied. They also quoted to me the encouraging tones of the English ministerial papers, which their journalists had translated for their benefit. In vain did I point out that Russian intrigues were the probable causes of the apparent hesitation of the English Government. No one heeded me, and for a long time King Alfred the

First was looked upon as the inevitable termination of the Greek revolution.

On the 26th of December, I gave, chiefly for the benefit of some young gentlemen of Argostoli, a magic-lantern lecture on astronomy in Italian, explaining subsequently the comic slides in Greek. The latter part of the performance gave much satisfaction. But the majority of my audience were either ignorant of Italian, or knew it very imperfectly. It was the general wish, therefore, that I should give the performance entirely in Greek. To obtain my consent, three of my young friends called on me at my cottage. I promised to accede to their wishes, should I find the scheme feasible. I, in consequence, commenced at once with my Greek master the translation of the lecture into the best modern Greek, which our joint labours could manufacture. I say *joint*, because, though I was but a beginner in his language, yet he was not quite perfect in mine. So that our united efforts were necessary in order to perform the task in anything like a satisfactory manner.

CHAPTER IX.

EARTHQUAKES IN CEPHALONIA IN 1862-3.

Classical and Biblical Earthquakes—Former Shocks in the Ionian Islands—Destruction of Fort St. George—My first Earthquake worthy of the Name—Four Days of Shocks in one Week—The worst Shock known for Years—Damage done—*Saltatory* Motion most dangerous—Discouraging Friends—General's House shaken at Corfu—Barometer no Guide—Extracts from my Journal—An unfulfilled Prophecy—The second Shock, in Severity, of the Year—Comparison of the two greatest Earthquakes—The late Bishop of Gibraltar—Send my Family home—My new Habitation safer—A violent but partial Hurricane—British Soldiers fly for their Lives—Why Greeks have always built strongly—Water, Fire, Wind, cause Earthquakes.

OF all terrible human sensations, I know of none equal to those aroused by serious earthquakes. The fear which I once endured on board a condemned ten-gun brig for some eighty hours, from the continual expectation (shared by the captain, crew, and passengers) of immediate foundering, was less appalling than at least two of the earthquakes which I experienced in Cephalonia.

The ancients regarded these visitations as signs of the Divine displeasure. The New Testament represents them as heralding, or accompanying its most important events. Thus, at the crucifixion of

Our Lord, the earth was shaken by an earthquake;* and at the resurrection there was "a *great* earthquake."†

Lastly, "a great earthquake" leads the way, after the opening of the eighth seal, amongst the horrors foretold as the signs of the judgment-day.‡

Homer, Thucydides, Xenephon, and the classic authors generally, regarded the ocean as the great cause of earthquakes. In their writings, *Earth-shaker* is the usual epithet applied to Neptune.

I was in London on the 6th October, 1863, but knew nothing of the earthquake till I read of it in the *Times*. Those Englishmen who felt the shock can probably, for the first time, appreciate Pope's translation of Homer's magnificent description of a great earthquake.

> "Beneath, stern Neptune shakes the solid ground,
> The forests wave, the mountains nod around,
> Through all their summits tremble Ida's woods,
> And from her sources boil her hundred floods.
> Troy's turrets totter on the rocking plain,
> And the tossed navies beat the heaving main.
> Deep in the dismal regions of the dead
> Th' infernal monarch rear'd his horrid head,
> Leap'd from his throne, lest Neptune's arms should lay
> His dark dominions open to the day,
> And pour in light on Pluto's drear abodes,
> Abhorr'd by men, and dreadful to the Gods."

The Ionian Islands have probably been always subjected to earthquakes. But wholly unrecorded

* "ἡ γῆ εσείσθη," Matt. c. xxvii. v. 51.
† "Καὶ ἰδοὺ σεισμὸς ἐγένετο μέγας," Matt. c. xxviii. v. 2.
‡ Rev. c. vi. v. 12.

in ancient times, they have even in modern history been very rarely noted. About twenty years ago, Dr. Davy wrote a chapter on them in his voluminous scientific work on the Seven Islands. He records three serious earthquakes, two at Zante and one at Santa Maura, all attended with loss of life, but still more with destruction of property. The dates of those which occurred at Zante are 1791, 1820, and 1840. The greatest shock experienced in Santa Maura happened in 1825. It occasioned the greatest loss of life recorded in the Islands for nearly a century. Fifty-eight persons were killed on the spot, and ninety-two were wounded, many of whom died afterwards from the effects of the injuries which they had received.

The earthquake of 1791 at Zante, by which thirty persons were killed, lasted half a minute. That of November, 1840, in the time of Sir Howard Douglas, did damage estimated at 300,000*l.* No less than ninety-five shocks were counted during the day. But this visitation, doubtless on account of its diffusion into so many shocks, was not attended with much loss of life. At least, Dr. Davy records none. The inhabitants had, probably, ample time to leave their gradually falling houses. It appears that the great mass of them slept afterwards for two or three nights in the open air.

Zante and Santa Maura have long been subjected to frequent earthquakes, whilst Cephalonia has stood the third amongst the Seven Islands as regards the severity of shocks. But in 1862 an alarming change took place, Cephalonia being far more shaken in that year than any of the other Islands. It began to be feared that the horrors of 1765 were about to be renewed. In that year Fort St. George, the ancient capital of the island, about six miles from Argostoli, had been destroyed by a shock, with the loss, it was said, of 700 lives. 1833 had also been rather a bad year, especially in Lixuri, where houses actually fell, and a few lives were lost.

Previously to my arrival in Cephalonia, I had only once experienced *one* earthquake, and that was hardly deserving of the name. In the spring of 1861, I was sitting with my wife in our drawing-room at Corfu, with my back touching the wall. Suddenly, I felt the latter move very slightly. I exclaimed, "That is an earthquake!" My wife, however, sitting in the middle of the room, never felt anything, and believed that I had been mistaken. However, we happened to call that morning at Lady Wolff's, who lived in Condi-terrace, in the higher part of the town, and we found that there had been an earthquake, which had shaken a large chandelier.

On the *8th of March*, 1862, I experienced the first shock worthy the name, in our loftily-situated apartments in the great house on the Mole at Argostoli. A series of violent storms of wind and rain had prevailed for some time, but the day itself was very fine. I had been up very early, and at a quarter before eight A.M. I felt the dreadful sensation. The moving walls and rattling doors announced the mysterious stranger. The shock lasted only a few seconds; but it cracked some of the ceilings in two or three places.

Our house was considered, as regards earthquakes, the most unsafe habitation in the town. It rested partly on the Mole, built by Sir Charles Napier, the ground being formerly under water. Its height of three stories added to the danger. It had been built about twenty years, and there were some splits in the outer wall facing the north, which had been occasioned by shocks fourteen years ago. The shock of the 8th was only the beginning of troubles. Before a week had elapsed we had experienced four earthquakes—one of them more severe than any since 1833. On *Monday, the* 10*th,* about two P.M., I fancied that my eldest little girl was playing with the handle of the door of my room. This was the first sign of our second earthquake. As in the first case, the weather was fine after a day of wind and storm. The temperature was cold, and the barometer appeared to be wholly unaffected on both occasions. Earthquake No. 3 happened on the 13*th at ten* P.M. The motion was something like a steamer rolling at sea. My wife was sitting at the time alone in the drawing-room.

When the shaking began, she, with great presence of mind, and a laudable eye to economy, seized hold of the moderator lamp to prevent it from falling.

I began to be seriously alarmed. With a wife and two children at the second story of a house reputed unsafe, my position was by no means enviable. It appeared bad, indeed, but worse remained behind.

Few of the English then in Cephalonia will ever forget *Friday, the 14th of March*, 1862. At half-past four that morning occurred the greatest earthquake felt for some years past in the Ionian Islands. In our house every one was fast asleep, in profound darkness; but all were suddenly and startlingly awakened by a tremendous crash. It appeared to me as if the end of all things were at hand, and that I was hastening to eternity! It was as if everything and everybody were falling and crashing together. A violent hurricane of wind, with a noise like the discharge of a huge piece of ordnance, accompanied the shock; whilst the house, rattling, shaking, bounding, completed the terrible sublimity of the moment. There was, I feel sure, few Englishmen who did not pass those seconds, which appeared like minutes—that is, if their minds were sufficiently clear—in recommending themselves to the care of him who "rides in the whirlwind and directs the storm." When those ten or twelve seconds of horror had passed away, the sense of relief was beyond the power of description.

The damage done to our house by this shock was far less than I expected, but it was sufficiently alarming. The ceilings of our eight rooms were all more or less cracked and split, with a good deal of mortar on the floors of some of them. The ceiling of one room was opened out from the wall, as if the house were slightly leaning towards one side. In one corner of our dining-room a crevice had been opened all down the partition. The outer wall of the house was bulged out which faced the north-west, from which the earthquake appeared to come. Some new splits were made outside, and some old ones widened. The rooms below occupied by young English officers were still more injured and shaken, with the exception of our dining-room wall, which was the worst of all the damage done to the house. One young Briton rushed as quick as he could out of the house in his night-shirt; and I am not sure that I would not have done the same if I had had no wife or children to take care of. The motion of this shock was of the most dangerous kind—the "*saltatory*," or up and down movement. Had it lasted a minute, I think that the house must have fallen. Of many a mortal it might then have been truly said,

"A fate so near him chill'd his soul with dread."

The general opinion was that another *similar*

shock would bring the house down. Few houses in Argostoli escaped considerable damage. In Lixuri, which lies to the north-west of Argostoli, on the other side of the harbour, the houses were much more injured on this occasion. The small detachment of soldiers stationed there abandoned the hired house which they occupied in great alarm. They were brought in the course of the day to Argostoli, till arrangements could be made at Lixuri for encamping them outside the town. The house which they had occupied was reported as wholly untenable, so split and opened were the walls, and so unsafe appeared the roof.

I began now to make preparations for removing from my apartments in the great house on the Mole of Argostoli. Every one, except my landlord, advised us to seek a safer habitation. My wife and I, therefore, commenced house-hunting; but we could nowhere find quarters so suitable for an English family as those we already occupied. We therefore finally determined to remain where we were. In coming to this resolve we were far from meeting with general encouragement. Our friends shook their heads, and looked serious. The amiable Resident gave me the very unpleasant information, that whenever a severe earthquake occurred his first operation was to ascend to the flat of his roof to see if the lofty house on the Mole were still visible. The Professor also, who instructed me in modern

Greek, kindly imparted to me similar consolation. Nay, he went further, and said that he always hastened to our house to give assistance if necessary, so probable did he consider the fall of our house. Other gentlemen assured me that the boatmen coming from Lixuri, after a severe shock, always looked out for the great house, satisfied that if that were still standing no house in the town could have fallen.

The same earthquake was felt in Corfu, though with much less violence and with very little damage. Still it created great alarm in the capital, where shocks of any severity had not been previously felt for very many years. Zante and Santa Maura, the usual sufferers, escaped violent shocks in 1862. It looked as if those subterranean visitations had slightly changed their line under the Islands, to the alarm of Corfu, but still more of Cephalonia. In the famous citadel of the former island the mortar dropped from the ceilings of the General's house, and the chimneys were so shaken that two of them fell shortly afterwards during a gale.

In superstitious times this selection of the General's house for its chief fury by the earthquake would have been considered ominous of a coming event; for a few months later the General, Sir John Inglis, the hero of Lucknow, died whilst on temporary leave in Italy, amidst the universal regret of both the English and the Corfiots.

Small shocks were so frequent in the spring of 1862 in Cephalonia, that it would be tedious to the reader were I to record them all. Generally speaking, the barometer gave no warning of their approach, and appeared to be rarely affected by their presence. It fell considerably on the 14th of March, but that was fully accounted for by the terrible storm-bursts which accompanied the earthquake. I observed that north, or more often northwest winds, almost invariably preceded, accompanied, or followed the shocks which I experienced in Cephalonia.

Perhaps for the benefit of those who desire to study these phenomena, I cannot do better than to give some extracts from my journal written at the time.

Monday, March 17. Earthquakes nightly, or rather between 3 and 4 A.M. Slept through them to-day and yesterday.

Monday, 24. I learn that at $3\frac{1}{4}$ A.M. to-day there was a slight shock, but it did not awaken me. Dr. Lane said there were several at midnight.

Thursday, April 3. At 2 A.M. awakened by an earthquake; weather calm, barometer when I went to bed rising. A little fallen this morning, though very fine. The great storm yesterday morning (from N.E.) a great deal to do with it.

Friday, April 4. (This day I wrote my journal chiefly in modern Greek. It records that the wind

was very strong from the S.E., and that Mr. ——
an Englishman, had told me the day before that the
Greek Almanack prophecied for to-day a terrific
earthquake in Argostoli. I also heard that the
Patriarch had dreamed at Constantinople that one
of the Seven Islands was to be swallowed up this
year. And as Cephalonia was suffering unusually
from earthquakes, which else could be the victim?
My countryman was amusingly alarmed and angry.
He thought there must be something in it. I, however, could not understand why God should take
the Greeks into his especial confidence. And I told
L.—speaking from experience—that so long as
the wind continued S.E. there would be no earthquake. My double-languaged journal thus con-
cludes): "10 P.M. Glass rose a trifle in the afternoon. L. and I rode the little *giro*. . . . . Up to
this hour the Greeks are false prophets about the
earthquake. The bells have been ringing frequently
to-day in expectation. *One must fear God alone.*"*
(The wind being S.E. I felt sure that the prophecy
would not be fulfilled in the night.)

Saturday, April 5. No earthquake yesterday, so the
Greeks and their Almanack—as usual. A very fine
day to-day. —— and —— and I rode to the Convent of St. Gerasimo, situated in a beautiful valley

---

* Classical readers may be amused with the specimens of doggrel modern
Greek in which I recorded the last reflection:

Πρέπει νὰ φοβοῦμεν μόνον τὸν θέον.

at the foot of the Black Mountain, near a village called *Frangata.* A pretty ride—many picturesque villages on the mountain side; talked Greek with some peasants.

(This was a year of almost perpetual gales. With the exception of these, all was quiet for a month after the last-mentioned date; signally refuting the Greek Almanack. I find that I recorded, as a singular fact, on *Good Friday,* 18*th of April,* that), " The north wind has brought no quake this time" (so much had I then identified this wind with earthquakes).

Thursday, May 8. Thermometer 69° (cool weather for that time of year in the Mediterranean). Barometer rose high yesterday. Fell a little to-day. Blew nearly half a gale, part of the time from the north. I was reading the paper in the drawing-room (my family out at the band-playing on the Esplanade), when a little rushing sound announced a slight earthquake.

On the 10th of May, a very fine day, we were present at the marriage of the Regent's daughter, described in a former chapter. The barometer fell a little that day, but not during the night I believe.

Sunday, May 11. At ½ past 5 this morning, a severe earthquake lasting many seconds, and all in a perfect calm, upsetting all my theories. But the wind had previously been from the north. A second shock came about an hour afterwards. . . . N.W.

wind brisk in the afternoon. W—— came in from Lixuri at 3 P.M. He informed me the first shock had been at midnight. They had had a very severe one this morning, at the same time, probably, as ours . . . . From thence to about 9 A.M. they had a succession of smaller shocks, perhaps a dozen he says. Many houses split at Lixuri; one down, or nearly so. The old servant of the Regent's wife, who brought L. this morning a basket of beautiful sweetmeats from last night's wedding-party, does not think this shock so bad as the great one of the 14th of March last. But generally, it is thought worse, because if less violent, it was on the other hand more protracted. . . . The soldiers encamped on the rising ground above Lixuri scarcely felt this shock, W—— says. Mr. H. called on me to-day. It appears that there were minor quakes during the night here at Argostoli, as well as at Lixuri, though they did not awaken any one in my house.

I may here observe that the two great earthquakes of the 14th of March and the 11th of May were very dissimilar. The first came in a violent storm, the second in a perfect calm. The motion of the first was rapid and saltatory, that of the second slow, undulating, and oscillatory. The one came accompanied by fearful noises; the other was comparatively silent, except the creaking of the walls and furniture as the house swayed slowly to and fro for many seconds, that seemed like minutes.

The first had suggested to my mind some monstrous giant seizing and shaking our house in a paroxysm of fury. The second was more suggestive of a rolling vessel, insufficiently ballasted. If the second appeared to have done the more mischief, especially at Lixuri, it must be remembered that its work of destruction had been facilitated by its one great and its many minor predecessors.

Our house on the 14th of March, judging from some of our ceilings, appeared on the first occasion to have leant towards the sea. On the 11th of May it more than returned to the perpendicular. Where the mortar in the ceiling had, after the first great shock, overlapped, it left an open space after the second.

Monday, May 12. A slight earthquake about 4 A.M., followed soon by a great ringing of bells (as usual). Went on board the *Trident* with Mr. Fisher (the chaplain). Bishop Tomlinson lunched with L. and me at ½ past 1, and dined at mess with the officers at ½ past 7. He drove in the day to the mills and Little Giro. *Trident* off at 10 P.M. (The Bishop took great interest in the mills, especially as regarded certain earthquake theories. But no earthquake occurred whilst he was ashore or at anchor. As the friend of Sir Robert Peel, and the attendant of his death-bed, as well as from his own amiable qualities, the Bishop was an interesting character to

meet with in Cephalonia, and little did we think
how nearly he had reached to the end of his career.)

Tuesday, May 13. Thermometer only 73°. Slight
earthquake at 2 A.M. (An earthquake the day before
and the day after the Bishop's visit; but none on the
day itself to gratify his laudable curiosity.)

Friday, the 16th of May. Went with Resident,.
Regent, President of Tribunal, and others to Lixuri.
Sir C. Napier's Court-house, and many houses, split
and shaken in various parts. Part of the roof and
front of one house had actually fallen into the
street. Another quake would bring down some
houses entirely.

The next earthquake was on the night of the *3rd
of June*, after the departure from the island of the
Prince of Wales. But it would be tedious to detail
all the earthquakes recorded during that year.

On the 21*st of June* there were three separate (but
slight) shocks in the course of the day. *On the* 26*th
of June,* 9*th, and* 23*rd of July*, there were other
similar shocks, with the N.W. wind generally prevailing. Perpetual storms were also characteristic
of this year. *On the night of the* 11*th*, and on the
morning of *the* 12*th of August*, fresh shocks took
place, sufficient to keep up the alarm still prevailing.

On the 16th of August I had the satisfaction of
seeing my family embark for England. The fear on
my part of earthquakes on their account, more than

their state of health, made me rejoice that they should leave the island.

After their departure, not requiring many apartments, I left the big house for a small cottage, built chiefly of wood. Here I felt perfectly safe, although I succeeded an Englishman, who had hastened his departure to England, mainly from the dread of these terrifying visitations. The cottage was built on arches; and the hollows below it, and its nearness to the ground, certainly caused the subterranean sounds of the shocks to be very clearly distinguished. But the risk of death or serious injury was small indeed when compared with that which my family and I had so long incurred in the large house on the Mole. Yet my predecessor had been sadly tormented with visions of his future descent into the huge cellar, with the cottage collapsing over him.

On the 30th of August and the 26th and 27th of September there were shocks; one of which I did not feel, being out walking at the time with a friend.

On the 16th of October I heard, in my solitary detached cottage, a strange underground sound during a perfect calm. A slight, scarcely perceptible earthquake followed. I have read explanations of the sounds that generally precede earthquakes, as arising from the shaking of the timbers and furniture of the neighbouring houses before the earthquake arrives at one's own house. But no houses were now near me, nor was there much noise even in my own house; though the underground rumbling and rushing were tolerably loud. I fully believe myself, that earthquakes are subterranean, and are never caused by electricity.

The early spring of 1863 was very different from that of 1862, which was an exceptional year in Cephalonia. But there are slight earthquakes every year. Writing home on the 11*th of January*, 1863, I was disagreeably interrupted by a smart brief shock, and then inserted at once an account of my visitor.

On the 16th of March, there occurred in Cephalonia the most violent hurricane ever known in the memory of the oldest Greek inhabitant. The glass fell wonderfully low. The storm raged for about twenty minutes. Its breadth was fortunately never more than a few hundred yards. It destroyed or injured a considerable number of olive-trees, chiefly belonging to a gentleman who, with his wife, formed a part of the pleasant society in which we moved. It came from the S.W. Had it come from the N.W., I should have expected some terrible earthquake. It tore up whole trees by the roots. It carried off huge branches, cutting them neatly as with a knife. It nearly destroyed and rendered quite uninhabitable one of the houses employed as a soldiers' barracks; so that the men had

to sleep in the school-room till sufficient tents could
be provided for them.

Thus an earthquake at Lixuri and a hurricane at
Argostoli had caused the British soldier to fly for his
life before them within the space of a few months.

A slight earthquake on the *25th of March*, 1863,
was the last I was destined to experience in Cephalonia. On the 10th of April I left for Corfu.
During the fourteen months I had been on the
former island, I had recorded twenty-six days on
which earthquakes took place. But as on some occasions two and even three shocks occurred in the same
twenty-four hours, there is little doubt that I may
reckon at nearly fifty the total amount of the earthquakes which I experienced.

Of the duration of shocks it is difficult to judge.
But my belief is that no single shock that I ever
felt lasted fifteen seconds, and very few more
than five or six seconds. My belief also is, that
houses built as modern houses frequently are in
England at present, would fall like packs of cards
before such earthquakes as the two worst that I
experienced. The houses in Argostoli are usually
built with double walls of stone, with the inter-
stices filled with rubble, or fragments of stones;
and thus are not easily thrown down. When well
shaken, however, the loose interior lining of the
wall helps to create the awful sound of falling and

breaking, which on one occasion deceived me into believing that much more damage had been done than was really the case.

Were not these visitations the chief cause of the strength and solidity of the ancient Greek architecture, as they also are of the gradual disappearance of those mighty works of art? In June, 1863, I saw what was a few years ago one of the few remaining pillars of Jupiter Olympus lying broken on the ground at Athens, from the effects of an earthquake,—still beautiful though fallen.

The ancients believed, as I have stated at the commencement of this chapter, that the sea causes the earthquakes. Experience without science may, perhaps, give hints to science without experience. Living for months in no slight fear of these always alarming, and at that time constant visitors, it is impossible not to form some opinion on the matter. I believe, then, that by the action of the winds, the ocean is forced occasionally into contact with the realms of fire that occupy the centre of the earth ; and that the waves, repelled by the flames, generate enormous volumes of steam, which rush furiously along the hollows, conveying with them the lava of those dark regions. This mass of steam-propelled lava seeks everywhere to escape and makes for the volcanoes ; and on its passage breaks through or violently shakes the crust of the earth where it is weakest.

In proportion, then, to their nearness to great volcanoes, or to main channels leading thereto, countries are more or less affected by earthquakes. In a calm, I imagine that the sea may then be retreating from the fires, which it may have before approached. Steam may then still be generated, but not with the same violence as when, in the inimitable manner described by Homer, Pluto

> " Leap'd from his throne, lest Neptune's arms should lay
> His dark dominions open to the day."

Comparing ideas with the respected and amiable late Bishop of Gibraltar, at Cephalonia, he assured me that he had long entertained the same opinion as to the manner in which earthquakes probably originated. I hope, therefore, I may be excused for having given vent to a theory which science may possibly prove to be wholly unfounded, and which, indeed, must be so if the mystery of earthquakes can be fully explained by electricity.

CHAPTER X.

The Greek New Year—An exciting Tour of Visits—Unreasonable Complaints of England—My strong Belief in the approaching Union—Author requested to make an Address—Motives which actuated Him to comply—" Hop o' my Thumb"—A successful Hit—My supposed Speech printed at Athens—The true Speech—Greek Hospitality—Projected Address to the Author—The English Honorary Members of the new Club, the *Kephellenia* —A Greek Christening—Barbarous Treatment of the Baby—Legal Necessity of the Custom—Festivities in honour of the Royal Wedding—Dinner, and Illuminations—Cephalonian Taste calumniated—A romantic Story— The Theatre—Modesty at a Discount—The Prima Donna's principal Friend —An unchivalrous Exploit—The Prince of Denmark to be King of Greece —Beauty to the Rescue—A vainly wished-for Riot—Unfounded Rumours of intended Disturbances—The Clubs and Illuminations—Excellent Behaviour of the Masses—Greeks not yet fit for Constitutional Government— My Departure on the Greek Good Friday—The Address from the Gentry— Reluctantly rejected Addresses.

On our Christmas-day, 25th of December, 1862, I received a great many visits from my Greek friends : and on the 6th of January, 1863, the Greek Christmas-day, I returned the compliment. Having had no sleep all the previous night, on account of the dreadful bells, I did not start on my visiting tour in the best of humours. But the very flattering manner with which I was received in all the houses that I entered, made me soon forget past annoyances. Most of my friends were staunch Protectionists, who were all in terrible dread of possible separation from England. If, indeed, Prince Alfred were to be King of Greece, they might be reconciled in some degree to the Union; but upon no other terms whatever was such an idea tolerable. In spite of the many visits which I had to pay, one lady would not let me go for half an hour; during which she poured forth copious streams of eloquence which amounted to this,—that the beloved Prince Alfred was the only proper or practicable solution of the Eastern question. In my visits I found many gentlemen also who were furious with the British Government for having so suddenly and unexpectedly announced that under certain conditions the Islands would be ceded to Greece. It was maintained that even the demagogues themselves did not really wish the cession to take place, and would find some excuse for finally voting against the measure. My friend Lascarato, who had himself experienced the necessity of British protection, especially maintained this opinion. I, however, could never believe that the Rizospasts in the Assembly would dare to belie all their past words and acts in the manner contemplated by their enemies. I unreservedly assured my friends that if that were their sole hope of the maintenance of the Protectorate, I considered the cession of the Islands as good as carried. I asked them why they did not petition against the Union, and thus prove to the English that their views were supported by numbers and respectability. But the reply always was that they could not venture openly to oppose the wishes of the majority. In fact intense moral cowardice was always the principal feature of the Protectionist party. " If," I remarked, " you will neither speak nor act, nor vote against the Union, how can you find fault with the British Government for sanctioning the measure?" But their idea always was, that if the question were settled by secret voting the cession would never be carried. I at once saw how impossible it was for so timid a party to have much effective influence in the country.

A few days later the same party were rejoicing greatly at the announcement in the papers that the Great Powers were generally opposed to the cession contemplated by England. Again the confident belief prevailed that England would never really part with the Islands. But I myself never doubted that from the moment that the British Government had held out to the Ionians even the conditional promise of the Union, this measure had become a certainty which could not be much longer delayed.

Meantime I was preparing to fulfil the promise

which I had made to my young Greek friends, to give them an astronomical and comical magic-lantern lecture in their own language. At this lecture not only my friends, but the friends of my friends were desirous of being present. Fresh petitions for tickets came to me daily, and I found my small party was swelling into a very large one. At that time I was expecting in a few days to leave the island, probably never to return. My lecture would, therefore, necessarily partake of the nature of a final entertainment. On that account I was requested to close the proceedings with a farewell address. As much for the novelty of the idea, as for any other cause, I consented to undertake the difficult task. The published intentions of the Government, known to the whole world, rendered friendly allusions to the almost certain cession both innocent and natural between an Englishman and his Greek friends. I desired also to make the Protectionists of Cephalonia understand that their cause was hopeless if they persisted in their *moral cowardice* spirit of listless inactivity. At the same time I could not help feeling for them, thus abandoned as they were by the Protectorate which had so long supported them. On the other hand, I was,. as the reader of my History must be aware, strongly impressed with the false position of England as regarded the Islands. Moreover I could not help feeling some sympathy with the ardent aspirations of nationality, which, in the young men of Argostoli, appeared to me, to be as sincere as they were natural. It was with such feelings that I composed my farewell speech; little imagining that the good wishes and friendly feelings of an individual, unconnected with politics, could give rise to any erroneous interpretations. Moreover I naturally attached no importance to the fact of my alluding, as it were privately, to the friendly intentions which the Government of England had publicly proclaimed.

The success of an evening party in Argostoli, where carriages were scarce and bad, and people usually walked, depended greatly on the state of the weather. Friday, the 9th of January, the day on which I gave my entertainment, was very threatening in the morning, and about five P.M. occurred a tremendous thunder-storm, accompanied with floods of rain. The latter indeed ceased before eight o'clock, the hour of invitation; but the state of the roads, the darkness of the night, and the probability of more rain all tended to diminish the number of my friends. Nevertheless (including some persons who slipped uninvited into the large room) the company amounted to about two hundred ladies and gentlemen.

With the Professor at my side behind the sheet,

the lecture went off pretty well. First came the astronomical part of the performance. Then, for the benefit of the younger portion of the audience, followed
" *Hop-o'-my-Thumb*," illustrated by many slides. I
had ample proofs that here I was well understood ;
by the continual laughter which greeted my ears.
At one moment the giantess intercedes with the
giant, to spare Hop-o'-my-Thumb and his brothers
for that night in order that she might make a pie
of them for a party of giants expected next day to
dinner. I placed in the mouth of the giantess
(whilst coaxing her hideous lord) the most tender
terms of endearment. Of these "*my soul*," ἡ ψυχήμου
(a familiar expression with Greek lovers), produced a peal of merriment which would have
excited the jealousy of Mr. Buckstone in his most
palmy days. The subsequent comic slides explained
in Greek, were received with roars of applause. At
last the time came for me to read off, still behind
the sheet, my farewell speech. The audacity of
such an undertaking in Greek, by one with no pre-
tentions to learning, made me naturally somewhat
nervous. I spoke, therefore, as fast as when, many
years before, I had played the part of *Young Rapid*,
in " The Cure for the Heartache." This, with the
great size of the room, and the fact that the Professor's Greek resembled the ancient more than the
modern dialect, prevented my speech from being

generally understood by the audience.   At most,
no one carried·off more than a sentence or two.
For many days afterwards I was importuned for
copies, with a view to publication.   This I steadily
refused; reminding my visitors that it was a private
party at which I had spoken.   The Cephalonian
editors behaved like gentlemen, and kept silence in
accordance with my wishes.   But pretended copies
of the farewell speech found their way to the
journals of Corfu, of Zante, and finally to one in
Athens.   In this last I was ridiculously described
as officially announcing the cession of the Islands;
I thought it, therefore, necessary to send a refuta-
tion to the Athenian editor, which he duly inserted.

In consequence of the fuss which had been made
of so trifling a matter, I destroyed both the Greek
and English copies of my speech.   My Greek
master also assured me that he had destroyed his
copy.   But some time afterwards, when the affair
had passed into oblivion, he found some fragments
of the first rough of the translation which he had
made of my speech in modern Greek; and he
brought it to me.   It is thus that I am now able
to give almost the exact words of my speech, for
the benefit of my friends, whether Englishmen or
Ionians.   For there are many of the latter who can
read English perfectly, and may like to know what
I really said on that occasion, even in the English
version.

Translation of the farewell address delivered by the author in modern Greek at Argostoli, on the 9th of January, 1863, at a private entertainment.

"LADIES AND GENTLEMEN,*

"I thank you for your company on this occasion; and I hope that, in spite of my imperfect knowledge of your beautiful language, you have been both amused and interested.

"I believe that the time is rapidly approaching, when the connexion of fifty years' duration, between Great Britain and the Ionian Islands, will cease for ever; and that ships will soon arrive to bear away the British army from these classical shores. But this separation will be neither of an unpleasant nature, nor will it be the result of violence or intrigue. It will, moreover, occasion no humiliation to either party.

"An electric spark of generous sentiment suddenly struck the hearts of England, and of Greece with the pleasant shock of an agreeable surprise, and soon spreading into a powerful flame, diffused genial warmth amidst former coldness, and burned up, like chaff, the remains of past misunderstandings. This electric spark was the sudden and unanimous cry of Greece, demanding for her King Prince Alfred of England; the son of the deeply lamented Prince Consort, and of that illustrious

---

* A Greek friend recommended me to change this to "Gentlemen and Ladies," according to the custom of those whose language I was using, and whom I addressed!

lady, who as a sovereign is a model to kings, and in domestic life is an example to all womankind.

"It is deeply to be lamented that insurmountable obstacles impede the realization of the hopes of Greece, so flattering to England. Aspiring Greece, like an ardent lover, offers her hand to England. The reply conveys sincere regret that the offer cannot be accepted; and carries with it also much consolation. For Greece, though refused the hand, obtains the dowry in the shape of the most beautiful islands in the world. Soon shall we English bid you all farewell. I am confident that our separation will be that of friends, whose memories will be mutually preserved in pleasing recollections. I am certain that I shall always take great interest in Greece, and in the Ionian Islands; and especially in Cephalonia, where I have made so many agreeable friends and acquaintances.

"May Greece progress rapidly in civilization and good government. May she be one day restored to more than her former glory and greatness. I say to *more*, because her ancient glory was tarnished by the countless evils of a cruel and immoral paganism. May Greece henceforth advance on firmer ground under the enlightened banner of Christianity. For Christianity has power, not only to raise up fallen nationalities, but to bear them onwards to the highest pinnacle of freedom, of virtue, and of happiness."

The Greek revolution, towards the close of 1862, was the occasion of the arrival at Cephalonia of many of the partisans of Otho. With two of these, General Milios and Captain ———, I at different periods in January, 1863, made acquaintance. The general at the time of the revolt was Minister of War. He appeared to me to be a quiet and respectable man. To the captain I was also inclined at first to show some attention ; for he had done his duty loyally, and to the last had gallantly fought for his king. But his personal appearance was very wild and unrefined, and appeared to corroborate the stories circulated regarding his conduct. He was declared to have himself cut off the heads of some of the rebels, whom his men had shot down. It is possible, however, that these stories were greatly exaggerated by the Ionians, who sympathised with the revolutionary party. The captain, and other fugitives were, however, hospitably treated by the people of Argostoli, in spite of the general poverty of the country, and of a bad season.

I had expected to leave Cephalonia at the latter end of January. But for various reasons, with which it is unnecessary to trouble the reader, my departure was delayed for more than two months. On the 27th of January I was privately informed that the inhabitants intended to present to me a farewell address. On learning this fact, I requested that they would wait until the actual day of my departure. Meantime, it was resolved that the wording of the document should be of such a nature as to obtain the signature of all parties in the island; which was done accordingly.

On the 4th of February I was happy to learn that my friend, Lascarato's late sister, had, notwithstanding his supposed unorthodox opinions, left him a thousand dollars. The sum was small indeed, compared to that which the testatrix had bequeathed to another brother, but it was nevertheless very acceptable.

About this period a new club was established in Argostoli, called the *Kephellenia*, of which the officers of the garrison and myself were courteously made honorary members. Its President, the amiable and gentlemanlike Signor Dallaporta, kindly announced the fact in a letter to the Commandant. The club was better than I expected, as regarded the rooms and the furniture. But it was very inferior to the clubs of Zante; where the gentry are richer than those of Cephalonia, and, associating more with the English, imbibe their ideas of comfort.

On the 18th of February two English visitors arrived in a yacht at Argostoli; a rare event, as strangers travelling in the islands usually omitted Cephalonia in their tour. Their names were Lord Garlies of the Blues and Lieutenant Luck of the

Inniskilling Dragoons. They were the guests that evening of the officers, and on the following day of the Resident. They had left Corfu impressed with the belief that the union with Greece was not the general wish of the Ionians. Englishmen entertained at the palace invariably imbibed these absurdly erroneous views.

On the 19th February I was present at the christening of the second son and eighth child of Signor and Signora Lascarato, which took place in their own house. Except the officiating priest and his attendant boy, I was the only person present who was not a relation of the family. The brother of Lascarato officiated as godfather. The ceremony commenced at 4 P.M. and lasted about an hour. It was a truly tedious and, I may say without exaggeration, a disgusting affair. The priest gabbled over a great number of prayers in a most irreverent and unimpressive manner. Perhaps this was the custom; but it is possible that he considered it useless to pray for the child of an excommunicated man. The uncle godfather held a large lighted candle in his hand throughout the ceremony. His chief task appeared to be the answering of numberless questions. The proceedings were opened by a long exhortation by the priest to the devil, who appears to be considered as especially present and active on such occasions. Amongst other performances the dirty little boy who officiated as clerk squeaked out the Creed, three times successively, with the most wonderful rapidity. The last twenty minutes of the ceremony were actively employed in torturing the baby. After various crossings and benedictions it was stripped naked, and carried in a cloth by the nurse. The priests then burnt a quantity of incense, and poured plenty of oil into a large iron caldron, previously half filled with tepid water. His reverence now seized the baby, and plunged it three times into the caldron. The shrieks and piteous moans of the victim may be easily imagined. It was next laid, still naked, on its back; and the priest, with a piece of rag soaked in oil, crossed its face, breast, and stomach. After this it was turned on its face, and the same ceremonies performed on its back. It was now put into a cloth, which was held by the priest at one end, and by the godfather at the other. In this hammock-like position the baby was carried three times round the caldron and incense pan. It was then handed to the godfather by the priest, and passed on to the mother, and finally to the nurse; all of them successively kissing it. I cannot pretend to recollect all the details of the baby's martyrdom, but the above description of what I do remember will give the reader some idea of the cruel barbarity of a Greek christening. The enlightened parents would of course have gladly dispensed with such abominations. But for the sake of the legal rights of their child, it was necessary to conform to the custom, and to leave everything to the priest.   Lascarato assured me that children are usually very ill for some days after their christening. But my only surprise is that they do not frequently die.   One can easily fancy the ancient Spartans having established similar practices in order to be rid of weakly children; but they appear to be sadly out of place in these days of Christian humanity, and of sacred respect for human life.

The 10th March, 1863, was loyally celebrated at Argostoli by the British garrison; which was the more necessary as no entertainment of any kind was given by the civil authorities. These contented themselves with lighting up their own houses and arranging the illumination of the government buildings.   The troops assembled on the parade ground at 11 A.M., in the presence of a great number of Greek ladies and gentlemen, as well as of the few English in the island.   At twelve o'clock a *feu de joie* was fired, and three cheers given for the royal bridal pair.   In the evening the officers gave a grand banquet to the principal civil authorities, including the Resident, Regent, Judges, and other important functionaries. There were about a dozen Greek guests, and the utmost loyalty and good fellowship prevailed. The Resident proposed the health of the Queen: and the Commandant that of

the Prince and Princess of Wales. The toasts were
drunk with enthusiasm by the Greeks as well as by
the English; the military band outside playing
appropriate airs. The cheering was taken up by
the Greeks in the street, and no one who witnessed
the scenes that evening could doubt of the general
good feeling that prevailed towards the Queen and
people of England. The company broke up early
in order to see the illuminations and fireworks,
which, with the numerous transparencies in honor
of the Prince and Princess, were very well arranged.
It was reported to me by some Protectionists that
one of the transparencies, put up by the Municipality, was disrespectful to Her Majesty the Queen.
The translation of the inscription was given to me
as, " Long live the Queen, *because* she promised the
Union." This appeared to me to be so incredible
that I hastened myself to read the inscription, which
I found to be, " Long live the Queen *who* promised
the Union."* Thus the promise was not represented as the cause of the good wishes expressed
for the Queen, but only as one of her Majesty's
benevolent actions deserving of gratitude. So
readily will party feelings misrepresent the best
intentions. All the inscriptions, without exception, were exceedingly loyal. That in the trans-
parency which ornamented my cottage was in

* " ἡ προτείνουσα τὴν ἕνωσιν."

Greek, out of compliment to my Cephalonian friends.

It was about this period that Lascarato told me an anecdote characteristic of the loose morality of even the best intentioned Ionians. An elderly gentleman of fortune resided at Lixuri a few years ago, where he married a pretty young lady. Soon after his marriage he discovered that his bride was attached to a young gentleman whom her friends ' had not permitted her to marry in consequence of his poverty. Her husband, finding that the attachment was mutual, and that the gentleman was of good character, adopted an extraordinary resolution. He immediately applied for and obtained a divorce. He then married his late wife to her lover; himself giving away the bride. He next took them into his house, and became a father to them; and finally (having no natural heirs) he left them his fortune. The generosity of the affair in Greek ideas made the irregularity of the proceeding a matter of no importance. Such facility of divorce is very conducive to romance, but not equally so to the sanctity of the marriage tie.

Although Cephalonia could boast neither of a hospital nor of a poor-house, it yet possessed a theatre in which operas were performed during the winter months. Both externally and internally the theatre of Cephalonia was superior to that of Corfu. The only established amusement of the ladies of Argostoli appeared to be attending at the Italian opera; almost all the boxes in which were the property of the noble families. Those occupied by the Resident, the Regent, and the officers of the garrison, were charged for very highly. In fact the officers complained that they and the soldiers chiefly defrayed the expenses of the performances. Every one paid sixpence nightly to enter his own box, and this was supposed to be the only payment made by the Greek gentry in general. However this may be, the constant attendance at second-rate performances, with only about six different operas in the whole season, is but a poor substitute for the absence of balls, dinners, and evening parties. Moreover the keeping up of a theatre in a town whose population does not exceed ten thousand, can only be done at the expense of better things. Certainly hospitals, poor-houses, museums, and such like institutions, should take precedence of a theatre in civilized countries. It was reported that when Captain Murray was the Resident, he frankly told the Cephalonians that the theatre was the curse of their country. Both in Cephalonia and in Zante there were frequent disturbances on theatrical matters; involving the committees of management, the police authorities, and the audience in general.

In Argostoli, in the winter of 1862-3, there was a Prima Donna and a Seconda Donna, each of whom was supported by a strong party. The

Prima Donna, as might be expected, had the better voice; but, as was generally supposed, had the worse character. The Seconda Donna was the better actress, and maintained a spotless reputation. She had attracted respect from the few admirers of modesty, by declining presents whenever there was reason to suspect the motives of those who proffered them. Strange to say, this unusual virtue was far from enhancing the popularity of the young lady with the natives generally. With the English, however, it was otherwise, especially as it was believed, and was indeed apparent, that her health was very delicate, and that she was suffering from consumption. So long as the Resident and the British officers and soldiers were amongst the audience, the small native party of the Seconda Donna was well supported. She even divided with her rival the applause of the public. The same remark is true as regards her benefit; and she bade fair to finish her engagement with triumphant success. Unfortunately the very last night of the opera season was on a Sunday; on which account only one or two English persons were present on the occasion. The consequence was, that free scope was given to the unmanly and unchivalrous machinations of those who wished to degrade and insult the Seconda Donna, as the most flattering proof of their devotion to the Prima Donna. The whole story of this persecution is a sad corroboration of that unchristian treatment of the feebler sex, of which Lascarato has brought such severe charges against his countrymen.

Amongst the principal supporters of the Prima Donna was Signor ———. He was a man generally respected, and possessing considerable influence in the Government. He was also a married man. Yet the great partiality which he displayed in favour of the Prima Donna gave rise to evil reports which nevertheless I believe were unfounded. The improper use, however, which he made of his official position, on the evening in question, was a matter of universal notoriety. He appears to have thought it necessary to the complete triumph of his favorite, that her rival should be inhumanly and publicly sacrificed. In the absence of the Resident and of the English generally he was, for that evening, completely master of the situation. In consequence the Seconda Donna was not merely slighted and hissed, but insulted and pelted, till she was actually driven off the stage, with ignominy, never to return. Those in the theatre who endeavoured to support her were forcibly ejected by the police. So notorious was the part played by the official patron of the Prima Donna, that one of the English officers congratulated him on the next day upon the skilful manner in which he had secured the success of his favourite. Nor did he disown the compliment. As I myself only occasionally visited the theatre, and as I never was personally acquainted with any of the performers, male or female, I cannot be suspected of any partiality in thus recording my opinion of this disgraceful affair. The reader may judge of the social and political civilization of a country where, after fifty years of British protection, such conduct on the part of respectable officials could pass without any serious notice.

Towards the end of March, 1863, there were great rejoicings in Cephalonia at the news that Prince William George of Denmark was to be King of Greece. The speedy union of the Seven Islands with Greece was consequently considered as certain. On Good Friday, the 3rd April, the Greek steamer entered the harbour covered with flags, and bringing with it the confirmation of the good news. Soon afterwards a crowd paraded the town with Greek flags, and raised enthusiastic cries in favour of union and of the King of Greece. The best feeling, however, prevailed towards the British garrison. Nor was this lessened in consequence of an unpleasant report that the Lord High Commissioner had forbidden a meeting at Corfu, under the Archbishop of that Island, on the absurd pretence of an apprehended riot.

On Sunday the 5th a *Te Deum* took place in the principal church in honor of the supposed new King. I say *supposed;* because it was not till several months later that the Crown of Greece was definitively accepted by the Prince of Denmark. After the *Te Deum* a slight disturbance arose in the streets in which the youthful son of President Zervo was a chief performer; and in which he was somewhat roughly treated. His anxious mother and his beautiful sister rushed into the crowd to rescue their assaulted relative. The head of another gentleman was broken on the occasion. It was however only a slight and partial affair; although some persons, endeavored to misrepresent its importance. There had long been a very small and contemptible republican party, entirely limited to this Island, which was composed of some twenty or thirty tradesmen, but whose chief was a member of the Assembly. This party, whilst the people were shouting "Long live the King," attempted to raise the counter-cry of "Down with the King." At such conduct, some young men naturally took offence, and angry words were soon exchanged for blows; but the combatants were speedily separated, and quiet was restored without difficulty. Yet old feelings of jealousy between the townspeople and the peasantry were still supposed to exist, and rumours of coming troubles were prevalent. Many staunch Protectionists evidently wished for what they pretended to fear; hoping that if disturbances should arise the English Government would abandon their intentions to grant the cession. Moreover it is probable that many demagogues of the Lombardo school were not really sincere in their expressed desire for that Union, which could not fail to place many of the Assembly politically on the shelf. Nevertheless the great mass of the people were, I believe, sincere Unionists; who now felt much gratitude for the kind intentions of the English Government. The Protectionists, however, assured me confidently that disturbances were to be apprehended; and indeed at one time the military had notice to be ready if required. I have explained in my history the absurdity of these pretended fears as regarded Corfu; and they were almost equally absurd as regarded the more restless Cephalonians. People, who have hitherto been tranquil, do not rise against governments at the very moment that these are conceding to them all their fondest wishes.

The anniversary of the Greek Revolution* gave occasion to celebrate the acceptation of the Prince of Denmark. The rejoicings consisted of peaceable processions by day and of brilliant illuminations by night. The clubs too were most gaily decorated, and were kept open night and day. The processions of the peasants and of the artisans, which it had been feared would quarrel, acted together harmoniously. An excellent spirit of quiet satisfaction reigned in the town. Party spirit and

* The 6th April (which the Greeks style the 25th March), 1821.

personal hatreds appeared everywhere to have given way to feelings of general contentment and of universal philanthropy.

As I was fully convinced that there was no foundation for the rumours of probable disturbances that night, I amused myself, in company with an English and Greek friend, by walking through the streets to see the illuminations and transparencies, and to read the inscriptions. I also went again into the clubs, which I had visited in the morning. They were very elaborately decorated with flowers, flags, and various devices. There was also an extraordinary number of handsome prints, displaying the deeds of the Greek and Philhellenic heroes of the war of Independence. Amongst these figured Lords Byron and Dundonald and other Englishmen. At the three principal clubs we partook of the ices which were hospitably handed to us, and we were everywhere received with the most polite and friendly attention. The night scene was very gay and exhilarating. The streets were crowded with persons of all classes, especially in the neighbourhood of the clubs; in one of which a band of amateurs played very agreeably. All the public were admitted into the clubs freely; and there was a perpetual succession of visitors of all ranks crowding the rooms and staircases. But everywhere room was made for us, at times under the greatest difficulties, but always with complete success. I was very much surprised at the quiet, regularity, and perfect sobriety with which this great national rejoicing was conducted. There was nothing to annoy the most refined Englishman, unless an exception must be made as regards the occasionally overpowering odour of garlic. But I hasten over scenes, which at the time of their occurrence I found both interesting and amusing, but which it would be tedious to describe in detail. All that I saw convinced me that the Greeks are a people who, if still somewhat uncivilized, are yet not difficult to manage by those who are acquainted with their characters, and who take a real interest in their welfare. I may, however, believe all this, and yet doubt the fitness, at the present day, of the Greek race for constitutional government, in the English sense of the word. The most rational and best educated Greeks cherish the same doubts; and of the whole race it may be truly said that the enthusiasm for a great nationality is greater than that for mere liberty, for which, in the extended sense, the mass of the nation are assuredly not yet sufficiently prepared.

A few days before my final departure from Cephalonia I was shown the address which was to be presented to me by the Cephalonian gentry. I also saw another address signed by fifty boys of the public school of Argostoli. This last, however, upon due consideration, I thought it best to decline. For, written with the frankness and open-heartedness of youth, it contained expressions which, however flattering to me, would certainly have excited jealousy in quarters whose feelings I was then in some measure bound to respect. But the address signed by 105 gentlemen of the first families of the island, I gratefully consented to receive. For its expressions of respect and affection were of a private nature, at which no reasonable being could possibly take offence.

The 10th of April, 1863, the Greek Good Friday, was the day of my departure. This was a misfortune in the eyes of my Greek friends, as regarded their intended demonstrations. A great part of that holy day is always passed in the churches by the natives; which fact would be an impediment on this occasion to their proceeding to the place of embarkation. However, when the time came, notwithstanding that I departed somewhat earlier in the afternoon than was generally expected, more than fifty gentlemen were in time to be present at the farewell scene. The address and the reply were both read in Greek, and an additional verbal speech was made by one of the principal gentlemen. All the speeches were followed by hearty cheering. I embarked after a most affectionate leave-taking and amidst renewed cheers. I had not long left the landing place before I perceived a large additional party of gentlemen advancing from the town, whom the sacred duties of the day, or the mistake

regarding the hour, had made too late to bid me
farewell. The address was signed only by such
persons as were considered to be nobles; in consequence of which the middle classes were desirous
of presenting another address to be sent after me.
But this proposal, like the intended address of the
boys, and from similar motives, I reluctantly requested a friend to negative with my grateful thanks.
Enough had been done to prove the facility with
which an Englishman could win the affection of
Greeks; by substituting warm sympathy for cold
contempt, and by making due allowance for the
errors and weaknesses of an incompletely developed
civilization.

CHAPTER XI.

ON the 11th of April, 1863, I was once more located in Corfu. Contrasting the latter with Cephalonia, I was more than ever struck with its unrivalled beauty. An equally agreeable contrast was presented by the bustle and liveliness of the people, the numbers of carriages and equestrians, and the social gaiety of the place. It was quite a relief from the monotony and tranquillity of Argostoli. Nevertheless, I missed my many Greek friends of the latter town; and associating now chiefly with my own countrymen, I returned almost entirely to the ordinary routine of colonial life. I landed on the Saturday forenoon after the annual discharge of crockery had just taken place; thus missing my opportunity of again witnessing this curious old custom.

The following day (the Greek Easter Sunday) I dined with Sir Spiridion and Lady Valaoriti. Although it was Lent, and the entertainment chiefly consisted of orthodox dishes, yet good meat was provided for the heretics. Everything was nicely cooked in a Greco-Russo fashion. The company consisted about equally of Greeks and English. One of the dishes was full of coloured eggs, which were used in the following manner. Every one pressed his egg against that of his neighbour, and the person whose egg was broken in the encounter was considered defeated. I suffered several reverses, till I discovered that half of the eggs were boiled hard, and the other half soft. The initiated, who knew how to select them, therefore easily gained the victory. Fish, eggs, and vegetables, cooked in various agreeable ways, formed, with fruits and sweetmeats, the principal dishes. But the mutton, for those allowed to eat it, was very good and tender. More excellent specimens of Protectionist Ionians than the host and hostess it would be difficult to find, whether as regards manners and appearance, or ability and accomplishments.

On the 15th and 20th of April there were foot races and athletic sports for the soldiers of the garrison, which took place on the drill-ground out-

side of the town, under the patronage of the General.
Some distinguished English visitors were present;
amongst whom were the Duchess of Montrose and
her daughter, Lady Olivia Graham. Lady Valsamachi was also there, and greatly lamented to me
the intended cession of the Islands; the fact of
which she could scarcely believe. Although now
a Greek by marriage, the widow of Bishop Heber
was naturally grieved at the severing of the last
political tie which bound her to her native country.
This estimable and amiable lady dedicates her time
to charitable purposes, in the cause of which she en-
listed the English residents; the loss of whose aid
she will of course sadly miss.

About this time, Captain Baillie (brother to the
Earl of Haddington), Captain of H.M.S. *Trafalgar*,
acquainted me with the murder of a Greek wine-
shop-keeper in the town.   He had been found lying
dead in the street, alongside of a drunken English
sailor. The latter was at first suspected of being
the murderer. It was afterwards discovered that
a Greek boy aided by his uncle had been the real
culprit; and that the uncle had placed the corpse
close to the sleeping sailor, on purpose to inculpate
the latter. He had then taken his victim's keys,
and carried off all his money out of the till. It was
with considerable difficulty, and after the lapse of
some time, that the murderers were arrested, and
eventually hanged on the glacis in front of Fort
Abraham.

In the month of April, a deputation from Athens, on its way to congratulate the Prince of Denmark, and headed by Admiral Canaris, touched at Corfu, where it created great excitement, and received a popular and enthusiastic ovation.

On the 22nd of April, the Lord High Commissioner, in H.M.S. *Caradoc*, started on his tour of the Islands, where, by all accounts, he was everywhere very coldly received. On the same day the races commenced at Corfu. The first day was a great triumph for the Greeks. For the principal race was won by a horse called " Bella," the property of Doctor Vrassopulo, and which was ridden by Count Andrucelli. The Count came in first in all the three heats of this race. In the second heat, however, he crossed a horse ridden by an English officer. By that act he was, according to strict rule, incapacitated both for claiming the second heat and for running in the third. But the English officers, well knowing the great discontent that would arise amongst the Greeks if a rule were enforced which they could not understand, decided that the Count should be allowed to run for the third heat, and that the second should count for nothing. Count Andrucelli won the race, and Dr. Vrassopulo carried off the cup. But the unsportsman-like decision caused some confusion in the betting arrangements, and considerable dissatisfaction to many of the English. I was glad, however, that the more generous course had prevailed, and that the Greeks had been given the satisfaction of seeing a compatriot carrying off the first honors at essentially English sports. During the races, I received many compliments, regarding the flattering proofs of affection that had been given to me on leaving Cephalonia; and which appeared to make considerable sensation from the rarity of the circumstance as regarded the English in general.

On the 9th of May, there was a sham siege and assault carried on in the island of Vido; where a good luncheon was laid out in the tents for the officers and their visitors. The affair, though well arranged, was on a small scale; as only a part of the garrison of Corfu reinforced, for the occasion, the troops at Vido. But from the picturesque nature of the ground, the attack and defence manœuvres formed a pleasing spectacle, which even ladies could appreciate. The interest was increased by the fact, that some degree of risk was incurred by the troops; as the scaling ladders employed in the attack did not quite reach to the top of the ditch. But as regarded this difficulty no accident occurred. An artilleryman, however, was by the hasty discharge of a gun accidentally blown into the ditch of the principal work; and the poor fellow died a few hours later in the Vido Hospital. Amongst the spectators of the sham fight was the young and beautiful Princess of Montenegro, who on this occasion did not wear any national costume, but was smartly dressed in the Parisian fashion. There was also present a staff captain of the Austrian army. I had the honor of being introduced to the Princess, and the conversation (which was carried on in French) turning upon the Austrian Captain, I remarked, that he could not think much of military movements on so small a scale : as he was accustomed to see large armies frequently manœuvred. Her Highness, however, quietly replied :—"At home he has seen how armies manœuvre which are beaten ; but here he has the opportunity of seeing how they do who win."*

Three days later I had the honor of sitting opposite the Princess, at a grand dinner at the palace. Her Highness looked handsomer than ever, not only because the candle-light suited her complexion, but also on account of the splendour of her national costume. The Greek light cap, the embroidered jacket and vest, with magnificent gold chains and jewels, formed a dazzling whole, which I am not milliner enough to describe. Her brother-in-law, the young Count Roma, added to the picturesque effect of the scene by his richly embroidered Albanian costume. Some noble English travellers of both sexes, and the Greek exile General Milios, whom I had met at Argostoli, completed

* A romantic interest attaches to the history of this young lady, whose husband, the Prince of Montenegro, was assassinated at her side a few years ago.

with a number of civil and military officials the interesting party.

On the 11th of May, accompanied by a Greek friend, I visited the Foundling Hospital, a small private looking building. There were only fourteen children in the establishment, chiefly girls. One of these was nearly twenty years of age, and rather pretty. She was engaged to be married to a shoemaker. There is a circular box, for the reception of babies. It revolves in a hole in the outer wall on a spring being touched, which at the same time causes the bell to be rung. In Cephalonia, there is no establishment of the kind: but there abandoned children are put out to nurse in the country. These institutions may justly be considered as encouragements to vice and immorality: but the small number of infants apparently sent to the hospital in Corfu, forms, I think, an honorable testimony to the general morality of the Corfiots.

On the 13th of May, Captain T. and I embarked in his little yacht, the *Sylph*, to visit the islands of Ithaca and Zante. We started at 1 P.M. with very little wind; and in eight hours we had made less than twenty miles. Calms, or southerly winds, constantly retarded our progress. Until dark we did not lose sight of the Citadel, or Mount Salvator; but we had ample time for enjoying the pretty views to the south of the island. In the night the breeze freshened, and at one moment caused some amusement, as a sudden lurch of the little yacht ejected my servant out of his hammock in the little fore-cabin.   During the greater part of the following day the absence of breezes made our progress slow and tedious.   For several hours we were almost becalmed close under *Sappho's Leap;* and we had ample opportunity for studying the celebrated precipice; whilst Ithaca had been in sight from an early hour of the day.   A breeze sprang up at sunset, but died away about 10 P.M.   Our Corfiot sailors were therefore compelled to use the large oars for the greater part of the night.   At 4 A.M., on the 15th, we at last dropped anchor in the, at first sight, lovely little harbour of Vathy.   As day advanced, the rocky barrenness of the surrounding hills and mountains, detracted not a little from the beauty of the scene.   Nevertheless, to most visitors, the poetical halo with which the imagination encircles the kingdom of Ulysses, gives even to barren rocks an air of fertility.

As it was too early to disturb Count Roma, we sent our cards, and a letter of introduction to the Residency; and started at 6 A.M. on an exploring expedition.   Having obtained a guide we proceeded first to the Castle of Ulysses, on the top of the mountain, which is visible from the harbour.   The ascent, as we made it, was very difficult, and in some places dangerously precipitous.   A Greek hero like Ulysses no doubt habitually surmounted the heights without much risk or fatigue. But it requires considerable faith to believe that Penelope was in the habit of ascending and descending those pathless rocks, whose summit is 2350 feet above the level of the sea. Our guide, Georgio Artalaris (such, as well as I could make it out, was his name), appeared to be an intelligent and respectable man. On our way to the foot of the mountain he pointed out to me some fields which were his property, and he suddenly dashed into one of them to abuse an old woman for trampling down his barley. He appeared to me to speak Greek better than any of the peasantry of the other islands with whom I had conversed. He assured me that the English were greatly beloved in the island: but he confessed that the Ithacans were in favour of the Union. He declared, however, that his countrymen desired it only because they believed that United Greece would be under the protection of England. Speaking of Ulysses he remarked, by way of parenthesis: "One of whose descendants I am." This was said in the quietest manner, and with the utmost gravity; as if there could be no possible doubt on the matter.

Georgio Artalaris pointed out to us what he called the foundations of the once existing Castle of Ulysses. But the huge stones had very much the appearance of natural rocks untouched by art. The exception was a kind of deep underground

pit admirably fitted to conceal the spoils of brigands
or to serve as a dungeon to their victims. After
re-descending the hill, we hired a horse and a
pony in order to ride the greater part of the way
towards the Fountain of Arethusa. We had a long
and pretty ride through the town of Vathy and
alongside of the valley of Ithaca, with its numerous olive-trees and verdant vines. The latter
generally produce an excellent yearly crop of
currants. This fertile valley forms a striking contrast to the general barrenness of the land. When
we at length left the road our sure-footed nags
carried us safely up and down a succession of steep
hills. But for the last mile and a half we were
compelled to dismount and to proceed on foot to
our destination. Here the walking, excepting as
to danger, was much worse, and more rugged and
disagreeable than had been the ascent to the Castle
of Ulysses. When we reached the fountain (un-
classical Goths that we were) we did not think that
it repaid us for the heat and weariness which it
had cost us to arrive there. It is necessary not
only to be a good classical scholar, but to be a very
enthusiastic one in order sincerely to see in barren
rocks, thinly inhabited by peasants and goats, a land
of demigods and the traces of a mighty people.*

* Any one who has actually scaled these rocks and looked down on the
small and barren land must be lost in admiration, when he thinks of Mr. Gladstone's dissertation on *the Ancient Parliaments of Ithaca.*

For myself I can only say that I was as much disappointed with the Fountain of Arethusa as with the Castle of Ulysses. And if the classical reader pity my ignorance and want of taste, I hope he will at all events give me credit for my candour. I am sure that I only express what thousands have felt who have visited the island. But it is too much the fashion with authors to say rather what is expected to be said on such subjects, than what they really think. Why should every traveller tread the beaten path instead of selecting his own? That of the classical past has been trod by thousands, with scarcely any variety. The present and the future of these islands have chiefly interested me; and therefore Corfu and Cephalonia are in my eyes infinitely more important than Ithaca, which was colonized by Cephalonians after it had been very greatly reduced in population and wealth. I was perhaps a prejudiced judge that day, for I arrived dead beat at the Fountain of Arethusa. Yet, on the other hand, never was fountain more welcome to me, than on that occasion: for eagerly and gratefully did I imbibe its classic streams. The views also from the spot of Ithaca itself, of Cephalonia, of Zante, and of Santa Maura formed a whole only surpassed by the magnificent prospect from the summit of the Black Mountain in the largest and most national of the Seven Islands.

On our return to Vathy, we visited the amiable Count Roma, father-in-law to Sir George Bowen, and the only Greek Resident under the British Protectorate. He kindly invited us to dine with him that day, but we were pressed for time, and could not stay. We had therefore to take leave of him at the moment of making his acquaintance. Hospitality was also pressed upon us by the officers of the small detachment stationed in the town, which we had in like manner to decline. We re-embarked at 3 P.M. and sailed at 4; when the yacht had been just twelve hours at anchor. I dismissed our guide well satisfied with his attendance; his charge for which was made in the usual Greek phrase of — "What you please." This, however, is by no means meant to be taken literally. It only, I think, implies that an Englishman on such occasions is often ready to give more than a Greek has the effrontery to demand.

The baffling winds and calms accompanied us to Santa Maura as they had done to Ithaca. At 6 A.M. on the 16th we stuck fast in the mud, a few hundred yards from Fort George. We therefore went ashore in our little boat and walked the four miles into Amaxiki. It was a singularly beautiful walk through olive groves, orange-trees, fig-trees, and almost every variety of foliage and flowers. Cherries, plums, and apples abounded, in tempting luxuriance and ripeness. We skirted by the old Cyclopean walls, which we had not time to examine. Moreover, my long stay in Cephalonia had made me familiar with similar antiquities. After a hot walk we arrived in the town and were most hospitably received by Baron d'Everton, the Resident, who established both of us in comfortable apartments. We had breakfasted on board the yacht: so having taken a little wine-and-water, we proceeded to the castle in the Sanita boat placed at our disposal by the Baron. There we lunched with the officers of the 9th Regiment; with one of whom I afterwards went round the fortifications. These are mostly of an old fashioned Venetian kind; and do not appear to be very strong. Nevertheless the French bravely defended them against us for some months in 1809.

We returned to the Residency, where at dinner that evening the fourth person was the Director of the police. He was a Cephalonian, and he spoke in a flattering manner of the warm feelings entertained for me by his countrymen. I found the conversation of the Baron very interesting. He has been more than twenty years in the Ionian Islands; and he appeared to be thoroughly acquainted with the people and their language. Alone, perhaps, of all the Residents, he was truly the right man in the right place; and both in his public and private capacity he maintained a very high character. Originally in the service of the Duke of Lucca, he had been created a Baron by his

Royal Highness. His family name is Seabright. His first appointment in the Islands had been to the Residency of Cephalonia, from which he had been removed by Lord Seaton to Santa Maura. He estimated the inhabitants of Ithaca at about 12,000; and those of Santa Maura about 17,000. But I have reason to believe that there are not, at any one time, so many as 10,000 souls actually present in the former. For in all the Islands a great many persons proceed annually for months to Greece, or Constantinople, in order to gain money by field and other labours. The Baron gave me some details of the whipping given by Sir Charles Napier to a noble wife-beater at Argostoli. Attracted by cries from a house, Napier had entered it, and found a gentleman dragging his wife by the hair with one hand and pommelling her well with the other. Sir Charles immediately gave him a good thrashing, and then compelled his chief of police to carry a message to his victim, offering satisfaction, with the results I have already elsewhere recorded. Notwithstanding that Napier had built so many public edifices, and constructed so many roads, he yet left (said the Baron) 12,000 dollars in the then separate chest of Cephalonia. I mentioned to the Baron that the son of the gentleman whom Napier had chastised kept Sir Charles' portrait in his house, and highly honored his memory; adding that the fact surprised me. But the Baron replied, " You must remember that if Napier chastised his father, it was solely in defence of his mother."

On Sunday, the 17th of May, Captain T. and I, leaving the mud-stranded yacht to follow us when possible, returned to Corfu by the weekly steamer. The Baron walked down with us to the Sanita boat: and whilst passing through the town (Amaxiki), I was much struck with the generally mean appearance of the houses. The upper parts of the latter are usually built of wood, in a rough fashion, supported by transverse beams and by bars of iron; with the view of withstanding earthquakes. As we neared the boat an elderly man, somewhat shabbily dressed, saluted me, and shook my hand and asked me if I were going to Corfu. When he had passed the Baron told me that he was the father of the Roman Catholic Archbishop of Corfu. It appears that there are still 6,000 Catholics in the principal island.

Amongst our fellow-passengers in the steamer were a senator, his wife, and his pretty daughter. This party embarked under a salute of nine guns from the castle. There was a solid breakfast on board at ten, of which I did not partake, having already breakfasted at the Residency. But we made our appearance at the dinner; which was in the Russian fashion, and by no means bad. I found myself seated opposite the senatorial family. They conversed in Greek; but much too rapidly for me to follow them with comfort. But I comprehended much of what they said; and when they commenced talking of England and Englishmen, I could not help smiling. The lady observing this, said to her husband, still in Greek, "I do believe the gentleman understands what we are saying." "Only a little," was my reply, in the same language. We, however, carried on the conversation in Italian till the dinner was over. Subsequently I talked a good deal with the senator on deck. As he had been very lately appointed to his honorable and well-paid post, I expected to meet in him a cordial supporter of the Government. I was astonished to find him, on the contrary, nearly as much disgusted with the prevalent despotism, as were those Ionians who had been lately ejected from office. At half-past 5 P.M. I again landed at Corfu, the unrivalled supremacy of which had not been weakened in my mind by the sight of either Ithaca or of Santa Maura.

My stay in the capital on this occasion lasted only a fortnight; during which only one event occurred worthy of mention, namely, the two days' Festa at Ascension Hill. The weather was magnificent, and the throng of visitors very great. Ascension Hill, not far from the country-house of the Lord High Commissioner, is one of the prettiest spots in the island. The undulating grounds, the green grass, the fine olive groves, with the occasional openings displaying views of the bay and citadel on one side, and of the Hyllaic harbour on the other, formed a whole indescribably charming.* The festa commenced on the evening of the 20th of May, and lasted the whole of the next day. The crowds of carriages and of pedestrians that visited the scene were truly astonishing. I first visited it at 11 o'clock on Wednesday night on horseback, and was taken by surprise at the brilliancy of the affair. The open space on the top of the hill was nearly encircled with booths gaily illuminated, and containing various kinds of small merchandise for sale, as well as sweetmeats and refreshments. The surrounding trees were lit up with lamps, and every part of the grounds was swarming with both sexes. The carriages were not permitted to advance beyond a certain point. Even on horseback I found myself so much in the way that night, amidst the dense crowds, that I did not remain very long. The next day the general attendance was still greater, being augmented by nearly all the English, few of whom were present the previous night. The playing of a regimental band also added to the attractions of the second day. The chief amusements of the people consisted in the indefatigable dancing of the *Sirto* and the *Romaika;* whilst the ladies and gentlemen walked about or sat eating

---

* This forms the subject of one of Mr. Lear's beautiful sketches of the Ionian Islands, lately published in London.

ices under the olive trees. The rich dresses, gold-embroidered jackets, and picturesque caps of the peasants, especially of the females, gave a national aspect to the exhilarating scene. For strangers who desire during a brief visit to see at a glance the gentry and peasantry of Corfu, no better opportunity could be found than the attendance at the annual Ascension Hill *Festa*.

Being now about to proceed to England, I determined (however much it deviated from the shortest road) to visit Athens by the way. My first operation was to apply to that indispensable agent of the British, Mr. James Taylor. He procured for my friend and me the passports and also the permits, without which even an English official could not leave these Austrian-like governed Islands; and he also recommended to me the best manner in which to prosecute my journey.

CHAPTER XII.

ON the 30th of May Captain T—— and I started
for Athens in the steamer *Byzantium*. Such was
the then disorganized state of the capital of Greece,
and of its rabble army (a detachment of which
had lately committed a horrible outrage in Athens),
that I was strongly advised by every one to defer
my journey thither for the present. Even my

friend T—— (who had visited Athens before, and therefore did not feel inclined to a second journey attended by personal risk) was silent only in consequence of his previously made promise to accompany me.   By the very steamer in which we were to leave Corfu, two officers of the 9th had just returned after having been robbed of everything on the heights of Pentilicus.   Nor was this all. Captain Parker, about an hour before we started, called upon me to say that he had received a telegraphic order to proceed immediately to Patras ; from which he concluded that some disturbances were apprehended.   All my English friends, high and low, male and female, advised me to abandon my resolution, and to proceed direct to England. But I was determined not to lose the opportunity, which might never return ; as the cession of the Ionian Islands to Greece was likely to prevent my revisiting this part of the world.   I therefore turned a deaf ear to all dissuasions.   And with regard to my travelling companion, in whose face I distinctly read decided disapprobation of my obstinacy, I adopted the plan of never appearing to doubt that he meant to keep his promise.   With regard to danger, I argued that the fact that English officers had been so lately robbed made the re-occurrence of a similar catastrophe extremely unlikely for some time to come.   I added that the officers who had been robbed had ventured out of

Athens; whereas we should take care to keep within the town. To be brief, we started.

As we were walking down to the boat, with Sir Spiridion Valaoriti, we met one of the officers lately robbed at Athens, who had just landed from the steamer. It was not a very encouraging meeting. So, especially thought my companion; who stayed to hear particulars; whilst I passed quickly on to the boat, dreading the effects of discussions. It appears that several brigands, with cocked pistols in their hands, had relieved the officers of their watches and purses, in spite of the warning of their guide, who had proclaimed that they were Englishmen. The robbers were overheard by the former proposing to bind the officers: but eventually the latter were suffered to depart uninjured.

Sir Spiridion Valaoriti was acquainted with the captain of the Greek steamer, to introduce me to whom, as well as to see me comfortable, he accompanied us on board. The captain was the first man to impart to us any consolation with regard to our generally condemned expedition. He assured us that he did not think any harm would happen to us if we did not go outside of Athens itself. And as to the Isthmus of Corinth, a strong guard rendered its passage perfectly secure.

We arrived at Cephalonia about six o'clock the following morning, and remained there at anchor till half-past eight. My old friend, the harbour master, kindly placed the Sanita-boat at my disposal for going to and from the shore. The gentry of Argostoli were asleep at that hour with few exceptions. I therefore saw only my friends Lascarato and Rasis, and two other gentlemen, whom I knew by sight. I regretted very much the arriving at so early an hour, which prevented my seeing most of those from whom, six weeks before, I had taken an affectionate farewell. But in the warm weather the Greek gentry walk about or sit up the greater part of the night; and they consequently take their soundest sleep in the early morning. Moreover I had been expected to arrive only by the Austrian steamer which we met at the mouth of the harbour on our way to Zante. At the latter we arrived about noon. That island was looking even more lovely than when I had visited it in the previous autumn. The day was so hot that we remained quietly on board till half-past 4 P.M.

A young Zantiot gentleman, who had relatives in Cephalonia, had been my fellow passenger from Corfu to Zante. We had made acquaintance; and, on his learning my name, he had asked for my card and had given me his photograph. On his going ashore I requested him to acquaint Judge Typaldo that I should call at his house in the course of the day, and he promised to do so. I afterwards learned that he sent his servant to announce my approaching visit; and, that my name might be understood, the messenger was charged to show my card to Signor Typaldo, and then to restore it to his master. The puzzled servant simply told the Judge that I was coming to call on him, and wanted my card back when he had read it!

In the afternoon T—— and I went ashore to arrange about our dinner; as the steamer was not to start till the middle of the night, and it supplied us with no meals while at anchor. We went to the only hotel or rather inn; but we found that we could get no dinner there on so short a warning. However, a guide that I employed took me to the house of Gabriel Macri, the garrison grocer; and he promised to provide us with a good meal by eight o'clock in the evening. The title of grocer inadequately represented the business of Macri. For his shop contained not only the wares of a grocer, but those also of almost every other trade and manufacture. I next proceeded with my guide to call on my friend the President of the Tribunal, and his amiable lady. They kindly pressed me to send for my friend T—— to come to them also. One of their country relations had passed the morning with them: so that, contrary to their usual practice, they had this day followed the national custom of dining early. Their ordinary dinner hour, however, was seven; and had I written to announce my arrival they would have got up a dinner party for us. It was now arranged that we should pass the day with them, excepting for the period which would be occupied by our dinner at Macri's.

After a luncheon of wine and fruit, our kind hosts took us a drive into the country. First we called at the country house of the Resident, on a hill situated above a beautiful grove of olives, which extended to the sea-coast. I have seldom seen a lovelier spot. We found Mrs. Wodehouse and her niece at home, and were most politely received. From thence we drove to the country seat of Count Lunzi, whom I had visited in the previous autumn. On our way we met the Countess and her family taking an airing in their carriage; so that I was again deprived of the pleasure of making her acquaintance.

We found Count Lunzi at home, as polite and amiable as ever. We were shown over his beautiful garden and grounds, and partook of his hospitable refreshments. The Count is a gentleman, of whom the Ionians should be justly proud, as indeed is the case with all persons of respectability. But with regard to the masses, it is as shameful as it is true, that Signor Lombardo, of questionable fame, would any day obtain more votes from the Sincliti even of Zante, than would the excellent gentleman whom Signor Typaldo (no bad judge) described as, in every sense of the words, " *The first man in all the Ionian Islands.*" From the lips of such a man, so universally respected, and well known moreover to be thoroughly independent, I could not but feel proud of the compliment which he paid me. In reply to some observation made to him by Signor Typaldo, the Count turned to me and said: "Had all Englishmen been like you the union with Greece would never have taken place." Such a testimony from such a source I shall always consider as second only in value to the address of the 105 gentlemen of Cephalonia.

After returning to town, T—— and I left our hosts for a time to eat the dinner which we had ordered. We sat down at what would have been considered a fashionable hour in the London season, namely, at half-past eight. Young Macri, a Cephalonian by birth, superintended our meal, whilst his servant waited on us. We fared very well: for rarely in the Ionian Islands have I eaten such tender and well cooked mutton, or drunk better draught beer. Moreover, nothing could exceed the civility and attention with which we were treated. Nor did we consider the charge of five shillings a head to be high, considering the trouble it had taken to procure a dinner for us, on so short a notice. We afterwards returned to the house of the hospitable Chief Judge, to take our coffee, and to pass the evening. Signor Gaeta, lately removed from being Judge of Cephalonia, was of the party, and enlivened us by his agreeable conversation. I was a little joked about the supposed anxiety that I had shown to have my visiting card returned to me. But on my denying the accusation, they at once perceived, from the injunction which he had given to his servant, that the young Zantiot had been determined not to 'lose the only souvenir that he possessed of his new friend.

Signor Typaldo is a Cephalonian, and is proud of his native island. He assured me that a great many of the most thriving shop-keepers in Zante are Cephalonians, whom he considers to be more enterprising than the Zantiots. He had himself, however, lived chiefly in Zante and in Italy. He informed me that there had been five assassinations in Zante within the last week. Yet he did not estimate the annual average of murders at more than twenty-five. When the English first took possession of the Islands, the assassinations averaged one a day in this island, according to Doctor Davy. Its population is very inferior to that of Cephalonia in honesty and morality. But as regards civilization, there is, I think, little, if any difference. The gentry of the place complain that the British Protectorate has shown itself indifferent to the state of the country, taking no proper steps to apprehend or convict the assassins. I was assured that the frequent murders are generally committed with the most perfect impunity.

Captain T—— and I re-embarked at midnight: but we did not proceed on our voyage till six the next morning, the first of June. Amongst our new passengers were the Regent of Santa Maura, and his charming lady, who was the daughter of the Regent of Zante. We touched at Missolonghi in the afternoon, so interesting on account of the death of Byron, and also for its brave subsequent defence by the Greeks. Here a retired Colonel of Infantry came on board, who appeared to me to be quite an original character. He was a rough, large, coarse old man, queerly dressed in a half civil, half military costume. His closely cropped grey hair, and short white bristling moustachios, added to his strange appearance. He had long served under Otho, and he adhered to his king to the last, like a true and loyal soldier. With us, though surrounded by countrymen who enthusiastically favoured the new order of things, he took no pains to conceal his intense disgust against the revolution and all its abettors. A young officer of the regular army also came on board, having been ordered up to Athens. It appears that the regulars and the National Guard at Missolonghi had recently come to blows; the latter desiring to take possession of the barracks, and the former refusing to give them up. Some blood had been shed; but the National Guard had prevailed; and the commander of the small detachment of the regulars had been ordered to head-quarters to explain his conduct. The young officer came on board accompanied by his sisters, and did not appear to be in much distress. Indeed no one seemed to think that he would be punished; and it is very probable that he had only done his duty.

We anchored at Patras about noon. Captain Parker sent a boat to us from H.M.S. *Liffey;* the middy in command of which, after transacting business with our captain, informed me that the boat was at my service to go ashore if I pleased. I decided on first visiting Captain Parker on board his ship; and I took with me the Regent of Zante and his lady, that they might have an opportunity of seeing the vessel. We were kindly and hospitably received. Later in the day the passengers of the *Byzantium* went ashore, to see the town; and six of us, including our captain, and the Regent and his wife, dined at the Great Britain Hotel. A very tolerable dinner was served up to us in the Greek fashion, at six shillings a head. Afterwards we walked about this handsomest of Greek towns, which has about 22,000 inhabitants. Volunteer drilling of the newly enrolled National Guards was the prevalent fashion of the day. I observed one squad at drill; the privates of which appeared mostly to be young shopkeepers. They had no uniforms as yet, but they carried muskets with fixed bayonets; and they marched and performed their exercises very passably. Some of the houses in the streets had a handsome and comfortable aspect,—giving an appearance of wealth for which

I was not prepared. We when tired of walking went and sat at one of the numerous tables in front of the great hotel of the place to eat ices, and to look at the crowds of promenaders. Finally we paid a visit to the Casino or Reading Club, a large and handsome building, where we saw French and Italian as well as Greek journals, and where refreshments were offered to us. On our leaving the building to proceed to the Mole, one of my fellow passengers said to me: "Your name is well known here: for, on my mentioning it to the gentlemen at the Casino, they said, Monsieur ——, of Cephalonia, we know all about him." We were all on board by half-past nine that night. On my way to the vessel, I was informed that some soldiers, who had lately deserted from the 9th Regiment at Santa Maura, had given themselves up to the officers of H.M.S. *Liffey*, in a state of starvation; so little aid or countenance had they received from the Greeks.

Tuesday, the 2nd of June, we started at about half-past eight A.M., just after a boat from the *Liffey* had brought me a despatch from Captain Parker, for Captain Hillyar, of H.M.S. *Queen*, at the Piræus. We reached Naupactus (Lepanto) about half-past nine. The town has about 2500 inhabitants. The scenery in the gulf was very beautiful; but I shall not expatiate on what has been already so often described. At the ten o'clock breakfast on board there were great discussion carried on, in Greek, between the old colonel and some of our other passengers. The former, now, as stoutly defended King Otho with words, as he had been lately ready to do with his sword ; had his officers and men but obeyed him. He boldly accused the Greeks of being wholly devoid of patriotism; and of seeking only each his own interests. He had been placed for the present on the retired list, by the revolutionary government. But this appeared to be no punishment to him; for he declared that he would not again serve in the regular army, where "they had forgotten to obey." He, however, added, that if the new king should ask him to assist in the organization of the National Guard, he would serve his Majesty for that purpose. The colonel took no pains to soothe his opponents, whilst disputing with them. On the contrary, though they were many, and he but one, they were far more polite to him, than he to them. I could not help admiring his boldness, although regretting his want of discretion, which offended the passengers, in spite of their ostensible forbearance. Even the jolly captain of the steamer was, in his good humoured way, indignant at the colonel's language. For he shortly afterwards observed to me, with a sneer, "If you opened his paunch, you would find it stuffed full of Otho." I suspect, in spite of their external appearance of moderation, that several of the passengers would not have objected practically

to test the truth of the captain's suspicions.   But
the frankness of the old soldier amused me.   He
laughed at the idea of the independence of
Greece; which obeyed, he declared, the will of
England, France, and Russia.   Yet there was not
much sense in his reproach: for how could a small,
half-civilized kingdom be entirely independent of
the favour and protection of the Great Powers?   It
is folly and meanness to reproach any one with a
misfortune, which it is impossible for him by any
means to avert.   In the course of this breakfast
my health was proposed as a Philhellene, by the
Regent of Santa Maura.   The toast was drunk in
a most friendly manner by all the company, including the ladies; and I felt already as if I were
amongst old friends.   The great popularity of
England and Englishmen amongst the Greek race
was, at this time, very remarkable; though I do
not pretend that my own case was not in some
degree exceptional and personal.   Still the feeling
that my country was so highly esteemed, and
honored, added very greatly to the interest which,
in spite of all their faults (the result chiefly of circumstances), I already felt for the Hellenic race.

At Vostizza, where we arrived at 11 A.M., a pretty
young Greek bride and her husband left us.   She
was returning with her husband after a week of
their honeymoon spent at Patras.   Here also a
considerable number of fresh passengers embarked,

including some wild looking chieftains in Albanian
costumes.   At all the places at which we touched
everything appeared to be quiet and orderly.   There
were no visible signs of a revolution; nothing to
justify the prognostications which my friends in
Corfu had so liberally pronounced to discourage
me from undertaking my journey.

All the way from Zante to the Piræus, our fellow-passenger, Signora C——, had formed the
principal attraction and ornament of the journey.
She reminded me, but in a pleasing and immaculate
manner, of those charming women of antiquity,
who have been handed down in immortal works
for the admiration of posterity. In the classic ages,
the modest Greek women, jealously immured in
their houses, and almost wholly illiterate, were
unfitted to be the constant companions of highly
educated men.   In consequence, the society of
women better educated, though less modest, became
an indispensable necessity.   Thus a great blow was
given to virtue and morality.   Indeed these qualities, the most precious ornaments of the weaker
sex, began to appear contemptible to men intoxi-
cated with the wit and wisdom of the charming
Aspasias of the age.   The modern Greeks have not
yet entirely shaken off the old prejudice in favour
of immured and uneducated wives.   But even
Eastern Christianity has been sufficient to shake its
empire considerably; and it is to be hoped that it

will gradually disappear altogether. The qualities which exercised so great a fascination in the unprincipled mistresses of pagan antiquity will be enhanced a hundred fold when developed and encouraged in the chaste wives of a Christian age. The charming lady whose character has given rise to these remarks is a living proof that pure morality completes the perfection of mind and body; and that it is no longer necessary, as in the days of Pericles, for a Greek lady to become vicious in order to please, nor to fall morally in order to rise intellectually. Thoroughly well informed in Greek and Ionian affairs, Signora C——, when she discoursed on these subjects was listened to by the passengers with admiring attention. Friendly and affable to all, and familiar to none, young, handsome, and elegant, she contributed greatly to the pleasure of the voyage, and became the centre point round which her fellow-travellers revolved by the laws of mental as well as of personal attraction.

We touched at Galaxidia at half-past one in the afternoon, and reached Salona by two. Mount Parnassus rose visibly to the north-east; and during the whole day we greatly enjoyed the delightful scenery. Passengers in various costumes, landing or embarking at every place we touched at, together with the political excitement and the contradictory rumours everywhere afloat, put to flight all possibility of dulness. We stayed many hours at Salona, where some of us took a long walk into the country. Amongst our party was a stout-looking chieftain in the Albanian costume, with a brother and a little nephew and niece similarly attired. He was a large proprietor at Vostizza, which place he represented in the National Convention. We proceeded as far as the commencement of a most beautifully cultivated green valley, extending further than the eye could see in a chain of bold and picturesque hills. We were informed that it would not be safe for us to proceed far in that direction, est we should be carried off to the mountains by Hellenic brigands; but we enjoyed our walk greatly notwithstanding. We did not steam away from Salona till midnight; and I never quite understood why we thus wasted so many hours opposite to that little village.

Wednesday, 3rd June. We arrived at about 4 A.M. at Acrocorinth, and proceeded to Corinth. There we had a distant view of the Acropolis. We disembarked at 5.30 A.M., after taking leave of the Regent and his wife, who were to return to Santa Maura by the same steamer. Carriages, and an omnibus with four horses, were waiting to take us across the Isthmus. T—— and I chose the latter conveyance. There was a separate conveyance to carry the luggage, which was guarded by some infantry soldiers. Mounted guards were supposed to keep the carriages in sight; but as the latter started separately, the task of the soldiers was not easy, and was not accurately fulfilled. However we found all along the sides of the road, especially amongst the trees and underwood, about every five hundred yards, a couple of soldiers of the line stationed in loose order. Some we found standing; others were sitting or lying under trees; others again were perched, musket in hand, in their branches. We did not meet a single native on the road, and the Isthmus appeared like an uninhabited country.

Soon after we arrived at Kalamaki we were startled by an unexpected episode, but one very characteristic of the state of the country. I was in the upper room of the little inn, when I heard a shot fired about half a mile off. About an hour later two wounded soldiers were brought to the village in a vehicle. It appears that they had formed a part of the luggage escort, and had got up on the waggon to take things easy. Their young sergeant ordered them to descend; and as they hesitated to obey him he fired his pistol at them, and wounded them both with the one discharge. There happened to be a surgeon amongst our fellow-passengers, who volunteered his services to the wounded men in the lower room of the inn. A ball had passed through the arm of one of them, and it was feared that it would eventually be a case of amputation. But for the present his arm was merely bound up with coarse bandages. The other man was very slightly wounded. Whilst the more serious case was being attended to, the sergeant came in to look after his victim. The latter said to him, "We are friends; why did you wish to murder me?" There were plenty of officers and privates of the National Guard standing about; but no one ventured to interfere, or to arrest the sergeant, as he belonged to the regulars. He was a tall, fine young fellow, and took the matter very coolly. Perhaps, considering the mutinous state of the army, he had done after all no more than his duty. But he pretended that the affair had been entirely accidental; and, to cover the national honor, all the natives present accepted the explanation as satisfactory. But the man who was likely to lose his arm took a different view of the case, in which he was supported by the other wounded soldier. The military detachment, including the wounded, proceeded with us to the Piræus. But we had to wait four hours at Kalamaki before we could embark. I never in my life experienced in any part of Europe such a waste of time as repeatedly occurred on my journey from Corfu to Athens. Before starting we learned from a member of the National Convention, just arrived from the capital, that the Prince of Denmark had at length definitely accepted the crown of Greece; and great was the general satisfaction at the news.

While still in the inn, I was surprised by the arrival of my friend the Regent and his fair wife, of whom we had taken leave at Corinth. It appears that finding that their steamer would not leave before the evening, they resolved to take a pleasure trip to Kalamaki, returning with the next set of passengers coming from the Piræus. I could not help expressing my surprise at the courage of the lady in thus voluntarily crossing the Isthmus of Corinth twice in one morning. To be sure there were guards, horse and foot; but, in the mutinous state of the army, the soldiers excited a distrust second only to that caused by the brigands. At this very time the regular soldiers were occasionally amusing themselves by firing off their ammunition; apparently with no other object than to make a noise and alarm quiet people. I began to think that the old colonel was not far wrong in his resolution to have nothing further to do with such an army.

After once more taking leave of my Santa Maura friends, and wishing them a safe return, T—— and I embarked for the Piræus in a small, dirty, and miserably crowded steamer. Constant rain and a violent thunder-storm, accompanied us to the famous port of Attica, so that the classical scenery was almost entirely obscured by mist and darkness. We arrived safely, however; and on my way to shore I left at H.M.S. *Queen* the despatch for Captain Hillyar with which I had been entrusted. There were no less than thirteen vessels of war in the harbour, forming a fine spectacle, and displaying the flags of

England, France, Russia, Austria, Sardinia, Spain, Prussia, Greece, and Turkey.

In the town of Piræus, as at Kalamaki, I was very much struck at the confusion and disorganization of the army. A great deal of time was taken up in getting the small detachment of twenty men out of the steamer. But at last the sergeant marched away to the barracks with his wounded prisoners, and I heard no more either of him or of the Kalamaki episode. We had an agreeable drive of one hour on our way to Athens. The distance is only six miles: but our driver insisted on stopping half-way to water his horses according to custom. At last we reached the *Hôtel de la Couronne*, where we found ourselves more comfortably located than we had expected, and within sight of the glorious Parthenon; without seeing which I had firmly resolved not to return for the second time to my own happy country. Having ordered dinner at seven, I proceeded to make some calls. I had been provided with several letters of introduction, amongst which were two addressed to ex-ministers of King Otho. But in consequence of the brief period of my intended stay, I deemed it useless to deliver them all.

The dinner at our hotel was far better than we had expected to find in any part of Greece. The bread especially was, I think, the very best I had ever eaten in my life; much as I appreciated that of France.   My *Commissionnaire* informed me that the stolen property of the officers of the 9th Regiment had been recovered, and that the police had taken up the chief criminals.   Our Minister had remonstrated so energetically, and the desire to please England had proved so strong, that the Provisional Greek Government had been aroused to wonderful and successful exertions.

Thursday 4th of June.—After an excellent breakfast at our hotel, T—— and I started at 10 A.M. for the Acropolis.   The weather was fine and the rains of the day before had imparted a freshness to the air which caused us to see everything to the best advantage.   What shall I say of the Parthenon? I know not; excepting that to have seen it is to have lived not wholly in vain.   Accustomed as I am, like most persons, to expect more than can ever be realized, I yet do not think that I was much disappointed.   Perhaps I had imagined the pillars to be even larger and loftier than they really are; but on the whole I was extremely delighted.   Such a noble spectacle restores for a moment the fervor of youth, even to those to whom alas the poetry of life has long been a faint glimmer of an irrevocable past.   The views from the Parthenon enchanted me, both as regarded their present beauty, and still more as regarded their past glory, from which in imagination they can never be separated.

The official in charge of the Acropolis abused

the memory of Lord Elgin for having carried off
so many beautiful statues and marbles. But he
soon after confessed to me that many valuable
works had been thereby saved from destruction,
for the admiration of highly cultivated Englishmen.
Since the late revolution, especially, great mischief
had been done, and extensive robberies had been
committed. In consequence many valuable relics
of antiquity had been removed to a little wooden
building, which no one was permitted to enter
without a written order from the Minister of Public
Works. I made only a few purchases at the Acropolis; having been informed that it was better to
obtain in the town the curiosities one desired to
possess. The neat and handsome modern town,
the plain of Attica, the Piræus, with its many ships
of all nations, the sweet Hymettus, and the various
ranges of classical hills and mountains formed a
picture which will not easily be forgotten. Amongst
other sights I was particularly pleased with the
wonderfully preserved Amphitheatre of Dionysius,
which was excavated as lately as May, 1862. Independent of this charm of novelty, it is intrinsically
beautiful and interesting; especially as regards the
front row of carved marble chairs. But the whole
is built of beautiful marble. It is on such spots
that a man is compelled to regret the want of an
early classical education; which can never be fully
supplemented during an active career, in after life.

But on this particular occasion I derived some consolation, and partial satisfaction, from discovering the errors of my guide, which even my slight knowledge of modern Greek enabled me to detect. Miltiades, for such was his classic appellation, was generally very well up in his task of *cicerone*. So far as regarded the old established sights, at all events, I could not detect mistakes, if he made any.   But he was not so perfect in his description of the lately discovered amphitheatre.   He assured me that the family names of their owners were described on the marble chairs.   I however pointed out to him that the names inscribed referred neither to individuals nor to families, but only to the holders of certain offices.   The best seats were appropriated to the priests of temples; the centre chair appertaining to the priest of Dionysius, to whom the theatre was dedicated.   Apollo of Delphi, ·Jupiter Olympus, and many other gods, were also honored in the person of their priests.   I found no difficulty in reading such inscriptions as were sufficiently preserved; and I flatter myself that, in spite of my general ignorance of such matters, I was of some use to Miltiades, whom I found to be an honest and respectable man.

We next visited the Temple of Theseus, and the glorious remains of the Temple of Jupiter Olympus. One of the gigantic columns of the latter had been overthrown two years previously by an earthquake.

A railing had been put up by King Otho to protect the ruins; but had been subsequently removed by order of the Revolutionary Government.

On returning to the hotel I found that two Greek gentlemen had called upon me. I subsequently received from them considerable information on the political state of Athens, with which they appeared to be well acquainted. At 2.30 in the afternoon T—— and I again drove off to continue our tour of sight seeing. We first went to a shop in Eolus-street, named *Minerva*, where we purchased some curiosities. We then visited the interesting Temple of Eolus, with its aqueduct and symbolical figures of the seasons. Next we saw the store of Adrian, and the picturesque *Agora*. Then to the palace, where we were shown over all the apartments, from which much of the furniture and ornaments had been removed for safety by the provisional government. The marble staircases, and the rooms of the same material, were very fine; but the other parts of the building were not in keeping with this splendour. The palace itself resembles a huge square box; but is, I dare say, a comfortable house to reside in. It has a handsome portico, which furnishes the sole specimen of classical architecture in the palace.

Friday 5th of June.—The view from my window in the Hôtel de la Couronne facing the south-west embraces the great street of Athens, Μεγάλος Δρύμος, bounded by the Acropolis, rising high above all. The effect of the latter would be improved, I think, by the removal of the ill-assorted Venetian tower to the west.

At 9.30 Doctor M—— called on me, and we had a long conversation in French. He told me that the army was already reduced to about 2,000 men, an unusual proportion of which were non-commissioned officers. It is the intention, in future, to maintain only the nucleus of a regular army, and to depend chiefly upon the National Guard and upon the police. He described to me the energetic measures which had been taken to recover the property lately stolen from two officers of the Corfu garrison. Parties of soldiers, of National Guards, and peasants, were employed to surround and hem in the village, to which the robbers belonged. The culprits were eventually surrendered, on condition that they might leave the country after they had given up all the stolen property. Doctor M—— assured me that the utmost tranquillity prevailed in Athens and its neighbourhood. He described the army as being in a wretched state, and that, under Otho, promotion had depended almost entirely on interest. He considered the officers a set of ignorant men, inferior even to their non-commissioned officers. Respect for authority and military discipline had almost entirely disappeared. He was of opinion that the union of the Ionian Islands with Greece will be a very beneficial event; because the long Protectorate of England had educated the Ionians for government, and had helped to civilize them, and to make them feel some respect for honor and justice.

At about 11 A.M. T—— and I visited the House of Assembly, accompanied by a guide, and by a clerk of Mr. Scarlett's, to show us the way. We entered into the diplomatic box, which we had all to ourselves, excepting for a few minutes. The building is a temporary one, to be used whilst the permanent structure is being built close by. The President was seated on an elevated platform, with two assistants on either side, and the secretaries below. About 200 members were actually present; but a number of persons, not members, appeared to go in and out at pleasure. I could not follow much of what was said, owing to the rapid delivery of the speakers. One of these was my former fellow-passenger, with the broad form and the Albanian costume. I saw that he recognized me, and I thought that he was not sorry that I should hear him speak. The strange dresses of some of the members, and the shabby appearance of others, made it a curious scene.

At 12.30 I returned to the hotel, and was glad to make a pause at sight-seeing. In the afternoon we drove to the ex-Queen's farm, which is about six miles distant from Athens. It was a very agreeable expedition. There were very neat walks and grounds and leafy bowers. One of these last was built round the trunk and amidst the branches of a fine olive tree, three great stems of which passed through and supported the floor. The ascent was up a winding staircase, and, in a neat little well-shaded room, we found a rural table with chairs, where the royal party used to sit and take their coffee. The Queen had also a menagerie of birds and animals, which had been removed before my visit to the farm. She was in the habit of riding daily to this rural retreat, and must have greatly felt the loss of what had so much occupied her time and contributed to her pleasure. We made this excursion beyond the town of Athens under no fears of being robbed or interfered with, so that I had no reason to regret that I had carried out my determination of visiting the revolutionary capital.

I paid some visits in the course of the day, and discovered enough to make me suspect that Russia had not ceased to intrigue with the Ionians, of whom the Russian Minister appeared to be very fond. In 1862 I had the honor of travelling from Trieste to Corfu with that distinguished individual. Happening one day in conversation with him to mention the Ionian Islands, he surprised me by very abruptly exclaiming:—"Oh, I assure you that I have nothing to do with the Ionian Islands." I thought at the time of the proverb "*Qui s'excuse, s'accuse.*" And I have now reason to believe that my suspicions were well founded.   I do not pretend to understand what sensible object Russia can have in paying such court to certain Ionians.   Perhaps it is merely a specimen of the universal intriguing characteristic of that nation, which likes to meddle in all political matters, and which keeps up the practice even when apparently nothing can thereby be gained.

In the evening I dined with His Excellency the English Minister, where the honors of the hospitable mansion were gracefully performed by Miss Scarlett, to a pleasant party of eighteen persons. This young lady may be said to have been under fire during the Greek revolution; for the bullets occasionally flew over the terrace of her father's house, where she was in the habit of walking.   The minister, supposing that I intended to return to Corfu immediately, had proposed to make me the bearer of the watches and money recovered from the Greeks who had robbed the officers of the 9th Regiment, and which had been sent by the police to the embassy.   I should certainly have made a triumphant entry into Corfu had I arrived there with the recovered spoils of others, instead of fulfilling the evil prognostications of my friends by adding to the number of the victims of Athenian robbers. After dinner the party adjourned to the terrace, which commanded beautiful views, and there the gentlemen were permitted to smoke their cigars.

My friend T—— had been compelled to decline

the dinner at the embassy; as he had parted with his evening suit of clothes, and had despatched it with his heavy luggage to England. The lady of the house was kind enough to express a regret that that obstacle should have been considered insuperable. But it is certain that an Englishman requires to be very intimate indeed with a family in order to venture amongst its guests inappropriately dressed.

If one may judge by the press it is a common complaint that on the continent, except to the distinguished few, the English diplomatic body are more famous for superciliousness than for politeness. I cannot corroborate this opinion by my own experience; but, even if true, assuredly Athens furnishes a most brilliant exception to the rule. It is not possible to imagine an embassy more popular with the English. And as to the Greeks, I learned enough during my brief visit to be convinced of the beneficial influence exercised, and of the great respect acquired amongst them, by her Majesty's representative at Athens.

Captain T—— and I left for the Piræus on the morning of the 6th June, very well satisfied with our fortunate and interesting trip. Our good humour as travellers was not, of course, lessened by the fact that the charges at the *Hôtel de la Couronne*, were not by any means extravagant. We embarked for Marseilles at 11 A.M., and started at half-past 1.

e dinner at the embassy: as he had parted with his
vening suit of clothes, and had despatched it with
his heavy luggage to England. The lady of the
house was kind enough to express a regret that
that obstacle should have been considered insuper-
ble. But it is certain that an Englishman requires to be very intimate indeed with a family in
order to venture amongst its guests inappropriately
dressed.

If one may judge by the press it is a common
complaint that on the continent, except to the distinguished few, the English dirty nails are
more famous for superciliousness than for politeness. I cannot corroborate this opinion by my own
experience; but, even if true, assuredly Athens
furnishes a most brilliant exception to the rule
It is not possible to imagine an embassy more popular with the English. And as to the Greeks I
learned enough during my brief visit to be convinced
of the beneficial influence exercised and of the great
respect acquired amongst them by her Majesty's
representative at Athens.

Captain T—— and I left for the Piraeus on the
morning of the 6th June, very well satisfied with
our fortunate and interesting trip. Our
hour as travellers was not, of course, lessened
by the fact that the charges at the Hôtel de la
were not by any means extravagant. We
for Marseilles at 11 A.M., and started at

We had to pay seventeen pounds each for our fare, for a journey usually of little more than four days, a somewhat exorbitant price.

I have called my visit to Athens *fortunate*, and with good reason. Just before I arrived, revolutionary and republican Athens was considered unsafe; and within a month of my leaving the country fresh disturbances had broken out on the 2nd of July, in which the soldiers of the divided garrison fought against each other; and bullets were again flying through the streets. And yet, throughout my stay of four days in the country, I had met with nothing disagreeable to me, excepting only the episode of the baggage guard at the Isthmus of Corinth. But assuredly all I saw of the unsettled state of affairs, and of the disorganization of the army, confirmed me in the opinion that I had long ago given to my friends in Cephalonia, that it would have been madness in the British Government to send Prince Alfred to be King of Greece, unless he were accompanied by an army of at least 5,000 Englishmen. But such was the desire to have that prince at their head, that I do not believe, that such a condition would at the time have caused any difficulties, except from the jealousies of France and the intrigues of Russia. The present new King of the Hellenes has trusted himself, without a Danish or English soldier, in the midst of the Greeks. It is to be hoped that the latter will never cause him to regret the bold step which his Majesty has taken.   This should be a point of honor with the nation under all the circumstances.   Moreover, the Greeks should never forget that it is the Queen of England and her ministers who prevailed upon King George to incur the great risk of mounting, amidst the whirl of revolution, the throne of a half civilized country.   Let them remember, also, that their sovereign is brother-in-law, not only to the future King of England, but also to the beloved Prince Alfred.

Finally, may the Greeks realize the hopes—faint though they be—of their friends, and falsify the predictions—very confident though they be—of their enemies.   May they learn also, that their true friends are not, as they too readily believe, those who flatter their vices and follies, but those who point them out in a loving spirit, and with a sincere wish to see them eradicated, as the surest means of regenerating the nation, and of realizing its fondest legitimate aspirations.

CHAPTER XIII.

Return to Corfu—Great Change of Opinions—Destruction of the Fortifications—The Ionian Money Contributions—The Demolitions commenced—Uncharitable Greek Wish—A needlessly lost Opportunity—Four English Soldiers Drowned—A Sergeant hanged for Murder—Removal of Guns and Military Stores—The best Explosion—Visit to Pantaleone Pass—A Peasant Anti-Unionist—School of Lascarato—A Prophet honoured at last in his own Country—The Archbishop loses his Knockers—Proceedings of the thirteenth Parliament—Speech of Aristotle Valaoriti—His Tribute to the "Good Inglis"—The Days of Chivalry not over—The Lunette Battery, Vido—Destruction of the Round Tower—The King signs, the Keep is blown up—Acquaintance with Sir G. Marcoran—Paper-hunting—An Officer killed by an Olive Tree—The last of the Paper Hunts—Retreat of his Highness the President—Absurd Reports, Streets flowing with Blood—Anniversary of the Greek Revolution—Isolation of Great Britain—Death of Dandolo—Invasion of Britain by the Corcyræans—Ionian Commission's Visit to Athens—Poem of Aristotle Valaoriti—The Aqueduct of Sir F. Adams—The last of the Explosions—The Protectorate lingers too long on the Scene.

As the reader has probably inferred from the concluding sentences of the last chapter, the author never expected to return to the Ionian Islands, after his departure from them in the summer of 1863. Who, indeed, could then have imagined that nearly a year would have elapsed before the actual cession of the Septinsular State had become a matter of history? It was generally supposed that everything would have been settled by the close of 1863, and I therefore prepared at once my long projected work for publication. But time rolled on, and the Protectorate, though doomed to be abolished, continued .to protract its lingering existence. It became my duty to return to Corfu, and to defer my publication to a time when it could not possibly embarrass the British Government, whether at home or abroad. Meantime, before I left England, my work was already in type up to the end of the twelfth chapter of the second volume. I consider this explanation necessary in case of any apparent discrepancies of opinions and statements; though I trust that these, if they exist at all, are of a very trifling nature.

On the 25th February 1864, I arrived at Corfu from Ancona; after a very agreeable journey through France and Italy, including ten days at Florence. I arrived in the midst of the carnival. Every afternoon the streets and esplanade were crowded with promenaders many of them in masks and dominoes. Nevertheless there was not much real gaiety. For in my absence a great change had taken place in the feelings and sentiments of the Ionian people; and also of the Greek race generally. The neutralization of the Islands by an European treaty had given great offence, and had also lessened the value of the present we were making to the King of the Hellenes, a monarch set up by England. But a far greater indignation arose at the announcement, that, without consulting the

Ionians in the least, the fortifications of Corfu and Vido were to be destroyed before the cession of the Islands. In the conditions laid before the Assembly in October 1863, by Sir Henry Storks, nothing had been said either of neutralization, or of the destruction of the works. It is a pity that the blow was not softened at the time, by any expressions of regret on the part of the Protectorate that it had been compelled to yield to the demands of the Great Powers, Russia, France, and especially Austria. It is true that the original cruel intention was subsequently very greatly modified. The strong and beautiful citadel, though shorn of guns has been otherwise left untouched; and Fort Neuf has lost only a small portion of its works. Even the complete destruction of Fort Abraham was an injury more apparent than real. For in the event of a siege the English themselves would have found it very difficult to defend all the works of Corfu; and any other nation not having the command of the sea would have required from seven to ten thousand men to make a good defence. Moreover, it is only quite lately that Fort Abraham has been restored and enlarged by the English, who have now only undone their own recent work. But the greatest humiliation inflicted on the Ionians was the destruction of the strong and extensive fortifications of Vido, one mile from the citadel of Corfu. These measures brought to a climax the unpopu-

larity of Great Britain in the Seven Islands;. and
if the Ionians were furious, a feeling of shame was
almost universal amongst the English, whether civil
or military. The conduct of Great Britain, under
continental pressure may be palliated on the score
of expediency, but will hardly redound to the
honor either of her justice or of her generosity.

The Ionians (as has been proved. by a very distinguished Corfiot*) had contributed immense sums
towards the cost of the fortifications of Corfu and
Vido. Deducting the debt remitted by England of
90,000*l.* of unpaid contributions, there still remains
about 870,000*l.*, as the military contributions of the
Ionians during. the Protectorate. In 1825 the
Assembly voted, at a sitting, 164,000*l.* expressly for
the fortifications in question, directing the sum to
be paid by annual instalments of 20,000*l.* We have
the authority of Sir Charles Napier, that this vote
was duly carried into effect.† The subsequent
military contributions were fixed by law, and with
a few exceptions appear to have been spent, like the
grant of 1825, on the fortifications. Also, before
the time of the Protectorate, the French had for-
tified Vido at the expense of the Ionians. A great
deal of English money has also been spent on Vido
and Fort Abraham. On the whole it is probable

* "*La Revision du Traité, du 5 Novembre,* 1815, *relatif aux Iles Ioniennes.
Corfou,* 1863," by Sir George Marcoran. Sir George subsequently added an
Addenda, in writing, which I have also consulted.
† *Vide* vol. i. p. 120.

that the Ionians have paid about two-thirds and the English one third of the cost of the defences. The pay and subsistence of the British troops have never it is true been charged to the Islands; but, considering the expense of a British army, it would have been quite impossible to enforce that article of the Treaty of Paris. Even the 25,000*l.* a year contribution was too great a burden on the Islands, so much so that Great Britain at the cession felt bound to remit the 90,000*l.* debt due to her from that source. But, besides fortifications, certain military lodging allowances were formerly charged to the Ionian contribution, so that it cannot be considered as quite exclusively spent on the works. Yet it remains that the Ionians have spent vast sums of money, at the very least half a million sterling on works, a considerable part of which have now been destroyed, without their having been consulted in the slightest degree.*

About the 11th of February, 1864, the work of demolition commenced, by manual labour in the first instance; whilst experimental explosions were also carried on. A few days before my return, the most serious operations had been entered upon at Fort Abraham, and in the Island of Vido. Colonel Wynne of the Royal Engineers, who had been ordered to England, and had returned with instruc-

* *Vide* Appendix E, for the details of the military contributions paid by the Ionians.

tions, had the general charge. But Captain Shaw, R. E., had been sent out expressly from home to arrange the firing of the mines, so as to secure the safety of the spectators. He began with experiments, which, fortunately, were on a small scale; for he very soon furnished an example of an "Engineer hoisted by his own petard." For believing, on a certain occasion, that all his shafts had exploded, he too quickly returned to the place of danger, when suddenly another explosion occurred. For a moment, the gallant captain believed that his last hour had arrived; but though raised from the ground, and thrown upon his face, he was fortunately uninjured. A sapper on the 2nd March, was less fortunate, having been greatly hurt about the head and face by the unexpected explosion of a shaft supposed to have been already sprung. This man remained in hospital many weeks, but eventually recovered.

The earlier mines were fired by long trains of powder laid on the ground in furrows, and slow burning fuses. That was a very picturesque and exciting process. But after the arrival of a Voltaic battery from England, the affair was arranged in the scientific manner, which suited better to this age of wonders. The Engineer thenceforth played the part of Jupiter. The mines were fired, and the works destroyed, by home-brewed lightning. At the sound of a bugle, the mysterious wires were joined, and dipped into the little quicksilver glass, by the operator's hands, causing an instantaneous explosion, and scattering in a second the labours of many years.

Although the English in Corfu sincerely regretted the destruction of the works, yet most of them took great interest in watching the process and its results. During the last ten days of February, throughout the whole of March, and the first part of April, there were constant, and at first almost daily explosions; sometimes there were two or more on the same day. They usually took place at five in the afternoon. Now, it was at Fort Neuf; oftener at Fort Abraham; and oftener still at Vido. The English of both sexes were eager spectators; approaching as near as they ventured, or were permitted. The Greeks looked on the mines of Fort Abraham from a greater distance, and at those of Vido from the Line Wall of the town near the sea. Whatever they felt, I myself never saw or heard them express any anger or disgust. One man, however, was overheard by some one exclaiming, just before a rampart was blown up: "I wish that Lord *Roosel* were on the top of it." But resignation was the prevalent feeling after my return, whatever it might have been at the outset. Probably after their first fears they looked upon it as a boon that the citadel was not to be touched, and that Fort Neuf was to be destroyed at one side only; that next to the sea.

Some of the explosions were very fine sights. The spectators' eyes would be fixed on some escarp or counterscarp, which they were aware was doomed. Then, as soon as the bugle sound of "fire" was heard, a rumbling noise followed, and the huge wall would appear to shake, and to advance, with the centre bulging out, like a war-horse bending his knees for a charge, and then the great mass would jump into the wide and deep ditch; whilst mighty fragments were hurled into the air and sometimes to considerable distances. Torrents of the densest smoke, accompanied, and too often partially concealed, the picturesque effects of the explosions.

Many of the officers of the ships of war in the harbour were anxious to try their guns on some of the walls or towers of Vido. But for fear of offending the Greeks, the permission was at first denied. It was eventually granted by a letter from England, which however arrived too late, and after the round tower, the last good butt for target practice, had been well undermined preparatory to explosion. So the opportunity was lost of trying the power of the Armstrong guns.

There were always a number of English men-of-war in Corfu during the last months of the British Protectorate, and generally also some foreign ones.

On the 4th March, an Austrian frigate quitted the harbour in pursuit, it was said, of Danish vessels; a sight not pleasing to most of us.

On the 5th March, the first step was taken towards removing the British garrisons from the Ionian Islands. The 2nd battalion of the 6th Regiment under Colonel Hobbs, embarked that afternoon on board the *Orontes* transport, and started the next morning for Jamaica. In its march through the town, there were considerable crowds and some excitement. But the wonted cheering of the soldiers was not (as far as I could observe) reciprocated by the inhabitants, although no feelings of hostility were manifested on the occasion.* The destruction of the doomed works was at that time the daily occupation of the troops, and the unpopularity of England was at its highest point, so that the only wonder is, that the troops departed in peace and free from insults. But even at that period, there were many honest Ionians, who still retained their confidence in the British name and people. The following extract from a letter, dated the 14th March, and addressed to me by a Cephalonian official of most estimable character, gives I believe, a just idea of the sentiments of many of his countrymen. " Although the islands have been

* I have been assured, since writing the above, that many of the petty tradesmen were in tears in the town, grieving over the loss of their customers: like the tailor in " *Don Cæsar de Bazan*."

severed from England, there are many amongst us who feel deep sympathy and attachment to your Great Nation, which we hope will never forsake us, but will continue benevolently to grant to us her mighty Protection in every occurrence."

About the end of February, by a melancholy accident, four non-commissioned officers of the 1st battalion 9th Regiment were drowned near Ithaca, by the upsetting of a small sailing boat. On the 7th March, a sergeant of infantry was hanged in the citadel, for the murder of his wife. Drunkenness (as usual in such cases) was equally the cause of the provocation and of the crime. The convict was granted the indulgence of dying in his full uniform, and with his war medals on his breast; as well as with crape on his arm as a tribute to his wife. With his almost last words, he warned his companions of the terrible effects of indulging in drink. He died wonderfully calm, resigned and penitent. The day before, he had said to his chaplain confessor (for he was a Roman Catholic), "would it be wrong in me to die bravely? I should like to die bravely." The worthy priest assured him that if he were truly penitent the braver he died the better. Indeed, I believe the chaplain was greatly relieved by the request, as the previous abject prostration of the prisoner's mind, and his earnest pleadings for a reprieve, had induced fears that he was very far from being resigned to his fate. The execution was a dreadful exhibition. The length of drop appeared to be insufficient, and some ten minutes elapsed before all movement ceased. The imposing ceremonies of the Catholic religion, whose services attended the prisoner, even whilst suspended, imparted a solemnity unusual to such scenes. The parti-coloured dress, and concealed countenance of the Albanian executioner, with his black eyes glaring through the part of his dress that covered his face, completed a picture which will be fixed for years in the brains of many young soldiers. But will it stop them from drink, that terrible curse of the British army? I fear not, and that the example had little, if any effect, except for the moment.

The convict had been condemned to death by a court-martial, as British subjects in the Islands were not amenable to the criminal laws of the Ionians, though they might be sued for debts.

Simultaneously with the destruction of the fortifications, commenced the shipping off of the guns and shot, and military stores. This work occasioned many trifling and some serious accidents. On the 19th March, from the giving way of a bolt, a number of round shot rolled out of a cart—knocked a sailor down, and broke his arm to pieces, rendering amputation necessary. Soon afterwards, the wheel of a cart, which carried a heavy gun, run over the breast of a soldier, who was kept in hospital some days; and then returned to his duty, apparently quite recovered. Before I arrived, a fatal accident had occurred in embarking a gun in a hired Danish vessel; which suddenly turned over on its side—throwing some seventy sailors and soldiers into the sea. Only one man, however, was drowned: the rest were either picked up by boats, or swam ashore.

The expense of destroying the works was not very great, as condemned powder was used for the purpose.; but that of carrying away the guns and stores must have been very considerable. It was even said that the freight paid for the shot exceeded the intrinsic value of the latter, and that to have dropped them into the sea would have been the best economy! The expense of sending away more than 400 guns must have also been very great; for a vessel was frequently hired to carry to England, or to Malta, a single gun—so I was assured.

At the commencement of 1864, there were 430 pieces of ordnance in the Ionian Islands— more than 350 of which defended Corfu and Vido.* Of the serviceable guns, only seven were left behind, which formed the saluting battery

* *Vide* Appendix G, for the details and distribution of the 484 guns in the Seven Islands previous to the Cession. What became of the guns the British found in Corfu, I am not aware. Probably the greater part were long since broken up as useless. But 36 brass guns appear to have been sent to England, their value being credited to the Ionian Treasury.

in the citadel. Five old Venetian mortars, dated 1684, and marked with the Lion of St. Mark and the Doge's cap; and six Venetian guns, probably of the same date, were collected and left on the south parade of the citadel. It was Colonel Wright, of the Royal Artillery, who obtained leave for the saluting battery to remain untouched. He thought it hard that the Corfiots should be denied the pleasure of saluting Saint Spiro. Others were more gratified to think that they would often be more rationally employed in saluting the young king of the Hellenes. A few old Venetian guns were also left in the other islands.

One of the largest, and perhaps the best of all the explosions, took place at Fort Abraham, on the side towards Fort Neuf, on the 23rd March. It destroyed the walls and defences on each side of the soldiers' picturesque little barrack-house, which was purposely spared—though it must have been greatly shaken by the concussion. From the house of Major de Vere R. E., on Condi-terrace, where some of the Anglican beauty and chivalry of Corfu had assembled, an excellent view was obtained of the most successful and finest *blow up* of the season. But the mass of the spectators were on the glacis of Fort Neuf. The little barrack-house left standing alone, after this explosion, amidst the wrecks of Fort Abraham, is of a three-fold construction. The lowest part was built in the time of the Anjous, the centre by the Venetians, and the upper part by the French and English. This occasion, with a few trifling exceptions of small explosions (to level more completely some of the fallen works), finished the destruction of Fort Abraham; but that of Vido was not completed till some weeks later.

The following day, the 24th March, I witnessed the blowing up of Fort George, in Vido, from the top of the citadel of Corfu; and the operation was well performed (like the other proceedings at Vido) under the immediate direction of Captain Craik, R. E.

On the 18th March, I drove, with a friend, to the pass of Pantaleone—from whence there are such beautiful views, both to the north and south of the island. We put up horse and vehicle at a rural house of refreshment (I suppose I must call it an inn), below the village of Scripero; and we walked through the latter to the top of the pass. We had for a guide one of the brothers who kept the inn. He talked only Greek; and I was rather out of practice for getting on in conversation with a Corfiot peasant. I contrived, however, to comprehend him in a great measure. He appeared to me an unusually intelligent man for his class of life—living, as he did, in the hills, thirteen miles from the capital. He was very glad when, in reply to his question, I told him that the citadel was not to be touched at all. He spoke with despair of the approaching departure of the British garrison, both as losing good customers in the market, and also from fear of being left to the mercy of the Signori. Pointing to the rags in which he was clothed, he declared that the little he had left to him would be taken away by his landlord after our departure. The general distress caused by the bad harvest of 1863 had embittered the peasantry against the Signori.

Although I tried to arouse the enthusiasm of my guide by displaying my sympathy with the Greek cause, he did not conceal his dislike of the Union. " But," said I, " who do you vote for ? And why did you all send none but Unionists to Parliament the other day, expressly to vote for the measure you dislike ? " He replied, " Poor fellows, like myself, have no votes." It is not the ordinary peasants, but the class a little above, who have the money qualification for voting—who were the enemies of the British Protectorate. From what I then and since learned, I am inclined to doubt whether, in spite of the influence of the priesthood, the poor peasantry would have voted for the Union, had they possessed the franchise. As in England, so it is in Corfu ; the small proprietors, the petty tradesmen, are the most radical and revolutionary in their opinions. But in Corfu there is no popular and powerful aristocracy to counterbalance the revolutionary class, into whose hands Lord Seaton threw that political power which the English garrisons alone have enabled the Lord High Commissioners to control or neutralize as regards its natural tendencies and results. King George, with a small army—which, moreover, he cannot depend upon—must have in his character some traits of the Emperor Napoleon, if the Islands are to progress and flourish under his youthful rule, and if the profligate and unprincipled men, who have been given too much power of doing mischief under the Protectorate, are not restrained by a firm and just hand. The Greeks are hardly fit, as yet, for an English constitution—far less for one still more liberal. Constitutions must be fitted to those whom they are intended for, and are not, as some Englishmen appear to imagine, like the ready-made garments of certain Hebrews, warranted to fit anybody.

Early in March, I received gratifying accounts from my friend Lascarato of his proceedings in Cephalonia. He and the Signora Lascarato had established a school, or rather had taken and enlarged one already established, for young ladies. The parents only requested that their children might receive the same education as Lascarato and his wife had given to their own children. The chief management of the school was placed in the able and prudent hands of Signora Lascarato; so that I cannot doubt of the ultimate success of the undertaking. To contribute to the enlightenment and civilization of the rising generation, and especially of that sex so long and shamefully neglected, must be a truly gratifying occupation to a man like Lascarato, who has so deeply felt and lamented the moral and intellectual deficiencies of his countrymen and countrywomen. He will give to the humble position of schoolmaster a portion of that philosophic dignity which it formerly enjoyed in the days of his remote Greek ancestors —tempered, however, by that Christian morality, gentleness, and cordial sympathy, to which the pagans were strangers. What a triumph of truth and honesty is the readiness of parents in Cephalonia to confide the education of their children to the man so long shunned and persecuted; to the man who had repeatedly to fly for his life from his own countrymen; to the man who still lies under a sentence of excommunication! And now, at last, it is in his own country—in his own island— that this prophet is appreciated and respected. It appears that even the priesthood have become either friendly or silent. If Greece could but command the services of a score of such instructors of youth as Signor and Signora Lascarato, she would take the first step towards the realization of her fond hopes of the national restoration to Empire.

After the departure of the 6th Regiment, there remained in Corfu the 2nd battalion of the 4th Regiment, and the 2nd battalion of the 9th Regiment; whilst the 1st battalion of the last regiment garrisoned the subordinate islands. The latter battalion was shortly to have followed the 6th Regiment; but the Lord High Commissioner, dreading to have any islands under his authority after the departure of their British garrisons, exerted his influence successfully to effect a simultaneous withdrawal of troops from the Islands. The order, therefore, for the departure of the 1st battalion was countermanded.

On the night of the 20th March, the palace of the Archbishop of Corfu was deprived of its knockers, by the hands of some Corfiots, who were, it appears, offended at his advocating that the same members who had been elected to vote for the Union should be chosen hereafter for the Assembly at Athens.

The report of the debate of the 19th March in the English House of Commons had, on reaching Corfu, considerable influence (but less than it should have had) in allaying the irritation felt against England; for it became clear that France,

Russia, and especially Austria, had insisted on the neutralization of some of the islands, and the destruction of the fortifications, as necessary conditions of the cession. But Great Britain eventually succeeded in saving the citadel, and nearly the whole of Fort Neuf, from their threatened fate.

Until my return to Corfu, I was not accurately informed of the proceedings of the thirteenth Parliament, which, in my absence, had decided the question of the Union; whilst the meagre accounts in the London journals were full of errors. I will now endeavour briefly, but clearly, to explain its conduct.

The thirteenth Parliament opened on the 1st of October, 1863. On the 2nd, Signor Padovan was unanimously elected President of the Assembly. On the 3rd, the Lord High Commissioner delivered his speech. On the 5th, the Assembly decreed the Union by an *unanimous* vote.* On the 6th and 10th, the members of the Assembly met privately, without coming to any decision on the conditions announced by his Excellency; who on the 10th called their attention to the subject. On the 13th, the Assembly carried a proposal to request a modification of the conditions laid down as indispensable to the Union. On this occasion three mem-

* *Vide* Appendix, vol. i. pp. 300-5.

bers voted against the resolution of the Assembly. These dissentients were Signors Aristotle Valaoriti, Socrates Curi, and Count Viga Bulgari. They desired to prove their confidence in England, by confiding to its generosity all the conditions of the Union.

I will now give a few translated extracts from the speech made on this occasion by Signor Aristotle Valaoriti, a poet, an orator, and a man of honor, and always a staunch supporter of the Union with Greece.

"In addressing you upon the important question now before us, rest assured that I have no desire to make an oratorical display. I desire to limit myself to the performance of a duty. . . . . I count myself amongst the foremost (and I mention this as a simple historical fact) of · those who, whilst declaring incessant and unrelenting war against the Protectorate, were yet firmly convinced that without the sympathy of the British nation, it would be impossible for us to realize speedily our national hopes.

"As a member of the twelfth Parliament, I deemed it right, on a former occasion, to publish and explain my views and ideas.* At that period, the battle between us and the Protectorate had

---

* At the first session of the twelfth Parliament in the Spring of 1862.

reached its highest fury; and intriguers taking advantage of the fact, declared that we had put the seal to our inextinguishable hatred—not against the local rulers, but—against the British nation, and its gracious Sovereign. Then, in the midst of the general excitement, I unhesitatingly and solemnly proclaimed that I was still an admirer of the British nation; and that to it, rather than to any other, would I wish to intrust the important interests of the Hellenic race. Because I believed that it would give the best securities for our constitutional liberties, and for our true political existence. I did not shrink from declaring that I desired to have England for our ally and support in the path towards our national restoration, which we were all pursuing. A motion was then made in favour of the Queen; and I witnessed with great satisfaction that, whilst a deep gulf divided us from the Protectorate, still, on the other hand, we were linked to the British nation, and to its gracious Sovereign by ties of the deepest deference, and by the most cordial sympathy. To avoid all misunderstandings, we did not direct our address to the representative of the Protectorate, but to the General commanding the British Forces in Corfu.* For we considered him as the flower of

* *Vide* p. 26, vol. ii.

that generous nation, on which all our hopes were placed. Nor did we stop there. The members forming the majority on that occasion sent their cards through me to the General (on the anniversary of her Majesty's birthday), with their names written in their own hand-writing. These cards remain in the family of the *good Inglis*, as a token of the affection, which the inveterate enemies of the Protectorate bore to the British nation."

The orator then proceeded earnestly to recommend trust and confidence in their new king, leaving to his Majesty to carry out with the British Government all the details of the Union. He endeavoured to make them ashamed of carrying on selfish intrigues at such a moment. Speaking for himself and his friends, he exclaimed: "We place our full confidence in our king. Let him act as he thinks best. I do, from this moment, bow my head to his supreme will; fully believing that the King of the Hellenes will never betray the honour of Greece. . . . . I have sworn to support his throne by laying under his feet, if need be, my own head and those of my children. . . . . I have been asking myself what am I and all my colleagues, compared with the grandeur of the Hellenic name? . . . . I wish to bequeath to my children my name unspotted. I wish to remove the heavy responsibility that weighs upon my head. I wish to be able to say that I have done my duty, that I have not forsworn myself, that I have not only voted for the Union, but that I did my best in favour of the speedy, the immediate completion of the act upon which the existence of Greece at present depends."

Will any one, now, say that the days of chivalry are passed in the Ionian Islands?* Yet, in the face of the Treaty for neutralizing Corfu and destroying its works, the eloquence of Valaoriti was fruitless. Only two members, as already stated, gave him their support. But the Assembly was forbidden to discuss the conditions, and on the 21st of October was finally prorogued, never to reassemble. Only three of its members had shown any confidence in or gratitude to England, and those three were amongst the most inveterate enemies of the local Protectorate.

On the afternoon of Tuesday, the 29th March, numbers of English ladies and gentlemen in spite of wind, heavy rain and rolling seas, crossed over to Vido in order to witness from the keep the destruction of the strong Lunette battery to the west of the island. The job was performed (with about 14,000 pounds of powder) in three successive explosions, with intervals of half an hour. It was

* Signor Aristotle Valaoriti is a native of Santa Maura, and one of its representatives in the Assembly.

preceded by the destruction of some small arches, one of which last I witnessed just before I landed. When we stepped ashore we saw a sapper being carried away on a stretcher, whose leg had been broken by a fragment as big as one's fist, necessitating speedy amputation, from the effects of which he afterwards died. Some accident about the connecting wires prevented the Lunette from being destroyed at one shock as originally intended. Many people sustained a soaking at Vido on that pouring day. The consequence was, that on the next day there was only a small attendance to see the round tower blown up. There was no rain, but the wind was higher and the sea rougher than ever, which contributed to keep spectators away. Yet the explosion of the 30th March was perhaps the most successful operation of the whole. A voltaic battery and an Austrian friction battery (the latter to be used only if the first failed) were placed in a neat alcove excavated under the brow of the hill near the sea. The well-covered double wires were laid from the shafts driven in under the tower, to the voltaic battery, and met in the quicksilver at the sound of the "fire." But the first bugle that was sounded was the "retire" and the second "the alarm," to ensure the safety of the spectators. Sentries also, without arms, were placed so as to prevent any one approaching too near. At the sound of the "fire" the tower rose like a wounded giant with a crash and a roar, and a burst of flames and smoke. The mass of the fragments, fell into and filled the circular ditch; but fragments were also carried up to a great height. One large substance was seen for some seconds sailing majestically through the air to a great height. After its fall it was discovered to be solely one of the earth *tampings* which had closed the mouths of the shafts. Quantities of rubbish also fell into and discoloured the sea. This operation obtained great praise, performed as it was completely at once, and requiring no after explosions to finish it off. But the fact is that, though the circular ditch was of the usual solid stone, the tower itself was merely built of small inferior bricks, and could have been neither so strong nor so heavy as those huge works of masonry which had been found more difficult of speedy demolition.

Whilst still at Vido, we learned that a telegram had been received at Corfu, from Athens, announcing that the King of the Hellenes had at length signed, on the previous day, the treaty of cession. It added the Seven Islands to his dominions, but condemned two of them to neutralization.* It handed over to him also many unsightly ruins, in the place of those works which were so lately the ornaments, as well as the defence

* Corfu and Paxo.

of the country. But one must not look a gift-horse in the face, even if the donor after giving it to you, takes a fancy to extract some of its finest teeth.

On the 8th April the keep at Vido shared the inevitable doom ; and it was successfully demolished at the first explosion. I had a good view of this affair from the citadel, just one mile distant. About 4000 pounds of powder were used on this occasion.

About the middle of March, Lascarato, in reply to my question, wrote to inform me that since I had left Cephalonia, no earthquake, worth men-tioning, had occurred ; thus corroborating my statements, that 1862 had been a very exceptional year. Lascarato added : " The sole earthquake of *the Union* keeps all our minds in suspense ; and God grant that this earthquake may come without great shocks of misfortunes."

I think it right to record here, that I first made the acquaintance of Sir George Marcoran only on the 21st March 1864. Up to that date he was per-sonally so perfect a stranger to me that I did not know him by sight. The reader will also bear in mind that my work up to the end of the twelfth chapter of the second volume, was in type before I left England to return to Corfu. Consequently

no private partiality tinctured my description of
that gentleman's character and conduct; though I
was certainly pleased to be able to portray, with
truth, such an honourable and unimpeachable an
Ionian.

The paper-hunting season of 1863-4 had not
quite terminated on my arrival; so I was glad to
renew my acquaintance with the beautiful cross-
country rides of that delightful island. Saturday
was the hunting day, and I came in for three or
four runs before the sprouting vines put an end to
the diversion. My horse twice down in ditches,
and my saddle once turned round, were all the
accidents I myself sustained, and many had falls
with equal impunity. But a very sad accident
occurred on the 5th of April, which was not a
hunting day. A young officer of the Royal Engineers was killed on that afternoon whilst taking
a ride through the olives with a comrade of the
same corps, who was somewhat ahead of his friend
when the accident occurred, and received his first
alarm by being overtaken by the riderless horse.
Riding back he found the unfortunate youth
lying senseless near the foot of an olive tree, with
one side of his head, near the temple, completely
smashed; probably by his pony running away to
overtake the other rider. Having carried him to
a cottage and washed his face, he put a peasant

on his own horse, and bade him ride hard to the town for a doctor. But he failed to make the fellow understand him; and was, therefore, obliged to ride in himself and leave his friend to the Greeks, after securing his watch and purse. He galloped into town, where I accidentally saw him dismounting to go on foot for a doctor. He was so stained with blood in various parts of his dress, that for some time I believed it was he himself that had been thrown and injured. The sufferer had been dead some time before the doctor could reach him, never having spoken, nor been sensible for a moment, since the accident. The body was brought into the citadel in the evening; and was buried with military honours in the cemetery at Castrades on the 8th of April. Six young Engineer officers acted as pall-bearers, and the officers of the garrison followed the coffin to the grave. It was truly a mournful affair. Young, handsome, and but lately arrived in the country, he was, moreover, it appears, the only son of his mother, and she was a widow. What a task must the breaking of such news to the bereaved and desolate parent have been to a heart of any humanity!

The ponies accustomed to the paper hunts incurred little risk of damage. But the riding through the bare vines (which occasionally it was not possible to avoid) was apt to wound the legs, fetlocks, and frogs of English horses; so hard, strong, and sometimes sharp were the vine branches in winter. After the vines began to sprout, towards the end of March, they could not be trampled on without injury. But those who did ride over them were made to pay so exorbitantly, that the peasantry had little cause of complaint. Yet it was deemed prudent to stop the paper-hunting before April. However, on the last occasion, there was a hunt or two extra, and the final one took place on the 2nd of April, 1864; commencing near Potamo Bridge and terminating on the race-course. As the Greeks are little given to riding across country (though all of them go out shooting), the paper-hunts of Corfu may, I think, be now considered as a matter of history.

In the first week in April, some thoughtless young officers, wishing to try their horses at some fences and ditches, trespassed on some sprouting vines. If damage had been really done, ample compensation would, of course, have been given as usual. But a Greek editor seized the opportunity of abusing and cursing the English (the " departing heretics ") in a style which Billingsgate might envy. I was assured, however, that the writers in the journal in question did not represent any respectable class; that one had been guilty of peculation, and that the other had had an escape from being hanged for treason. It must be confessed that the Greeks themselves had full liberty of the press for the last ten years, at least, of the British Protectorate. Sir Henry Ward having been, I believe, the last High Commissioner who exercised the powers of the High Police to restrain its abuses.

On Saturday the 2nd of April, Count Caruso, the President of the Senate, left Corfu for his native island, Cephalonia, on leave of absence, but never to return to his office. It was then expected that the English would all leave the Islands by the end of the month, and it is supposed that his Highness, the President, did not care to be left in Corfu after their departure. A domestic misfortune furnished him with a reason for retirement, of which he availed himself; and another senator was appointed to perform his duties.

Soon after the above recorded event, I was ordering some olive-wood articles of an Italian carpenter in the town, who began to bemoan the cession, and to declare that he should not remain in the island, after the departure of the English. " But," added he with a smile, " I do not believe that they will ever really go away." He repeated this opinion several times confidently. I considered it, at the time, a ridiculous speech. Nevertheless,

a day or two later (on the 12th of April), it was
known to everyone that Earl Russell had decided
that the troops were not to be moved for some
time, " probably not before July." Of course the
Italian carpenter, and the many who cherished
similar opinions were more than ever confirmed in
the correctness of their views. The stores and
guns having all been sent away, and the fortifications destroyed, no one could comprehend this
apparent reluctance on Earl Russell's part to finish
the transaction.

The mails from England and the continent
occasionally brought us strange news of what was
going on around us in peaceful Corfu. The *Galig-
nani's Messenger* of the 6th April, 1864, had this
startling announcement : "Advices from Corfu
mention the publication of the first number of a
very revolutionary journal. The people attacked
the house of the English Director of the College.
Fresh disturbances were anticipated." It is true
that some College youths insulted Professor Baker
(the English Head of the Greek College) ; but the
affair was of no more importance than the hundreds
of similar boyish outbreaks that have occurred in
English schools, though doubtless the approaching Union gave a political significancy to the ric
of the Greek lads. But its juxtaposition with
the revolutionary journal (and calling school-boy

" *the people*") was certainly amusing. Revolutionary journals were not novelties in the Ionian Islands, and created little alarm so long as British troops remained in the land.   In 1861, I remember some French newspaper announcing imaginary tumults in Corfu, and adding the dreadful intelligence,—"the streets are flowing with blood." For the last report there was some foundation; as I can testify that on the occasion much blood flowed in the streets; but it was the blood of the sheep killed in the customary manner on the Saturday forenoon before the Greek Easter Sunday.

The 6th April (which the Greeks call the 25th March) is the anniversary of the Revolution of 1821, and is always celebrated with rejoicings and ceremonies by the Ionians.   That of 1864, was not however, observed with much enthusiasm in Corfu, in spite of the processions night and day, headed by the Archbishop.   The illuminations were very few and far between; confined indeed, almost entirely to the clubs.   The joy at the approaching Union · was by no means exuberant; and the nearer it approached, the less it appeared to be valued.   It was very different to the celebration of the previous year, which I had witnessed at Cephalonia, and have described in a former chapter.   It was very different also, I was informed, to the last year's festa in Corfu. A few transparencies representing King George in the Albanian costume, and half a dozen inscriptions were all I discovered at half past nine in the evening; when the streets already were nearly empty. "Long live King George." "Long live the Union;" "Long live the 25th March," were the usual inscriptions. But the best was round one of the royal portraits, and made a very graceful allusion to the youth and inexperience of the King. It ran thus: "My Strength is the Love of my People."*

In the months of March and April, the Ionian press teemed with scurrilous articles against England and Englishmen. "Villains, robbers, thieves, monsters," and such like epithets were in daily use. They abused us not only for destroying their fortifications, which was natural enough, but for carrying off our own guns and stores, which was less rational. In their folly and ingratitude, they took no account of the fact, that if the citadel remains whole, and if Fort Neuf has suffered but little, the thanks are entirely due to the kindness and generosity of the British Government, Alas! the Ionians are too like petulant, spoiled, unreasoning children, impervious alike to reason and reflection, and deaf to the accents of truth. But

* Ἰσχύσμου ἡ ἀγάπη τοῦ λαοῦμου.

that they should be so, is certainly a disgrace to that great nation, which, for fifty years ruled the destinies of the Islands, with the aid of a moral and physical force, which had it been well and reasonably directed, must have brought forth better fruits than those which we have left behind us. When I left Corfu, in 1863, the love of the Greeks generally for England, had made even the Ionians friendly by example and sympathy; but when I went back in 1864, the Ionians had returned to more than their former hatred, and the Greek race generally regarded Great Britain with hostile eyes. Our isolation had become complete, and for much of this result we had no one to blame but ourselves, for our ignorance of, and indifference to all matters, not exclusively of domestic interest.

The notorious Signor Dandolo died on the 13th April, and was buried on the following day; his funeral was attended by great numbers of the Greek gentry, and attracted crowds of spectators. He had nearly attained the age of eighty years. Long one of the deputies for Corfu, in the Ionian Assembly, he had not been re-elected for the thirteenth Parliament, but he had been chosen by the people as a Municipal Counsellor of Corfu; he was already a man of about thirty, when the Protectorate of Great Britain was established in the Islands, and he very nearly lived to see its actual departure.

Dandolo was possessed of considerable knowledge and ability, but was utterly deficient in judgment, steadiness and consistency. And though a Venetian in name and origin, he too often displayed, by his exaggerations and inaccuracies, the worst faults of the Hellenic race. His extravagance in private life, in youth and in manhood, resulted in an indigent old age; and his political extravagances left him, at the close of his career, without any followers of character or respectability. His chief notoriety was obtained by a habit of publishing pamphlets, addressed to statesmen or other personages of distinction, in which reckless and unfounded assertions were made with a lively volubility that excited attention, without carrying with it conviction or approval.

Earls Russell and Grey, the Emperor of Austria, and the late King Bomba of Naples, were amongst the personages honoured by Signor Dandolo with letters of advice or reproof. Whilst he abused the English noblemen, he praised and flattered the continental despots. A radical in Corfu, he was elsewhere the supporter and admirer of unlimited monarchies. In short, as a politician, he was the most absurdly inconsistent of men. He had a wonderful confidence in himself, and in his intuitive knowledge of past events was at variance with all known histories. He wrote 'a short account of Corfu, in which we have to believe (on his own unsupported authority) that Thucydides was a liar and a slanderer in all that he wrote about ancient Corcyra. We are also assured that ten thousand Corcyræans assisted Julius Cæsar in the conquest of Britain—a kind of anticipated vengeance for the recent destruction of the fortresses of modern Corfu. But enough of Signor Dandolo. Let his ashes lie in peace, undisturbed by heretic hands. In spite of his constant attacks on British statesmen, and on British policy, he did not dislike, and he certainly respected Englishmen in general; and these, in return, in spite of his inconsistencies, generally cherished towards him feelings the reverse of hostile—regarding him both as " witty himself, and the cause of wit in others."

On the 13th April, the thirteenth Parliament was a second time prorogued for six months; namely, from the 21st April to the 20th October, 1864. Of course, it never reassembled; and his Excellency completed his time, unencumbered by opposition or check of any kind, and ruled despotically to the last by means of his Senate.

On the 16th, the long gallery of masonry, which connected the keep with the Lunette battery at Vido, was most effectively destroyed— the foundations being torn up and turned over by the force of the explosion. Of all the doomed

works, there then remained only the South battery
—the fate of which was deferred for a few days, to
allow of experiments in gun cotton, which was to
be used as the means of its destruction.

On Sunday, the 17th, Signor Padovan, President of the Ionian Assembly, returned from Athens
to Corfu, where he was received with great enthusiasm.   He was escorted to his house by great
numbers of the inhabitants, with a Greek flag and
a band of music.   He, with Signor Lombardo of
Zante, and Signor Aristotle Valaoriti of Santa
Maura, had gone to Athens, as a Commission of
the Ionian Assembly, to consult with Count
Sponneck and the Greek ministry regarding the
future of the Islands.   These deputies had been
well received at Zante, Patras, the Piræus, and
Athens.   At the latter town they had been presented to, and dined with the King.   Of the three,
Signor Lombardo has ever been the most inveterate and unscrupulous enemy of Great Britain,
and Signor Padovan scarcely less so.   Signor
Valaoriti alone, though a staunch Unionist, from
patriotic and honest motives, was inclined to court
the friendship of England.   I much fear that the
Union will bring to Athens from the Ionian
Islands too many selfish intriguers, ready, in order
to obtain place and power, to do the bidding either
of Russia or of France, and to sacrifice for pelf

the true interests of their country. I acknowledge that Signor Aristotle Valaoriti appears to be an exception to the general rule, and to be guided by really noble motives; though he perhaps relies too much upon democracy. But Valaoriti has few followers, and is regarded by his countrymen rather as a poet than as a politician. He celebrated his visit to Athens, and the approaching Union, by a poem in the vulgar modern Greek, which was greatly admired by his countrymen; and deservedly so, as far as I am able to judge. The poem alludes to the Protectorate (especially in Sir Thomas Maitland's time) as one of the powers that have tyrannized Greece; from which it would appear that even Valaoriti had become somewhat hostile to England, in consequence of the neutralization treaty, and of the destruction of the fortresses. But as he is a man of truth and honesty, he will, on due reflection, resume his former sentiments; for he will have to confess that, however much appearances at first condemned the conduct of Great Britain, it is to the other powers solely that the cruel and obnoxious measures which have so offended the Ionians were wholly due.

On the 19th April, I rode with a friend to examine, more accurately than I had hitherto done, the excellent aqueduct which supplies the town and citadel of Corfu with good and abundant water. Starting from the heights above Benitzi, the pipes are carried along the olive groves, from a distance from Corfu of nearly eight miles; and its underground course is marked by little round hollow pillars, which contain locked iron gratings, which are opened when necessary. About half way between the farthest source and the town are first the filtering-tanks, and next the great reservoir. Into this last two different streams are conveyed—the water of one of which is better than the other. From the great reservoir the united stream is conveyed, in separate pipes, to the citadel and to the town. To Sir Frederick Adam (the second Lord High Commissioner) the Corfiots are indebted for this inestimable boon. An English engineer commenced, and an Ionian finished the work. The old man in charge (who opened for me the doors of the filtering-tanks, and of the great reservoir) well remembered the constant visits paid to the spot by Sir Frederick Adam, on horseback, in order to watch the progress of the workmen. Whether by the road or through the olives, the ride to Benitzi is second in loveliness to few of the many beautiful scenes for which Corfu is famous. Assuredly, as regards the aqueduct, the name of Sir Frederick Adam deserves to be remembered by the Corfiots as that of one of their greatest benefactors.

On the 22nd April, 1864, the sad destruction of the doomed fortifications terminated with the blowing-up, by gun-cotton, of the South battery at Vido, just opposite the citadel of Corfu. It had been announced to take place at 6 P.M., and every one was anxious to witness the affair; for not only was it the last of the explosions, but also it was the first and only time that gun-cotton was used instead of gunpowder. But, to the disappointment of most persons, the mines were fired at half past five, instead of at six. Many of us were listening to the band of the 4th Regiment on the esplanade at Corfu, when we were surprised by the sound of the explosion at Vido. Rushing to the draw-bridge of the citadel, we arrived in time to see the light-coloured smoke caused by the gun-cotton clearing away. When it had passed, not a vestige could we see of the masonry of the South battery—a mound of earth alone being visible. Thus the gun-cotton had operated most successfully, although the proportion used had been only as one to three of gunpowder. Had the gun-cotton arrived earlier from Vienna, it would doubtless have been generally, if not exclusively, employed. Altogether, nearly 80,000 lbs. of gunpowder had been used in the work of demolition. Fort Abraham and the whole of Vido had become unsightly ruins, and Fort Neuf was greatly disfigured towards its sea-side. By this time also, nearly all the stores had been removed. Why the English still lingered on in the Islands was a matter of general regret and surprise. But the diplomatic department has ever been of the circumlocution order, delighting in procrastination. Thus the British Protectorate was destined to remain in the Islands without guns and without stores, and to rule for some time longer amidst the wrecks of fortresses, over an indignant and discontented people.

CHAPTER XIV.

SEPTINSULAR STATISTICS.

Area and Population—Incorrect Statistics—Males exceed the Females in num-
bers—General and Municipal Revenues—Proportions paid by the Islands—
How the Revenue is chiefly raised—Bad Fiscal System—Revenue fluctuations
—Statistics of Corfu—Ionians not untaxed—Effects of bad Laws—Where
Nature does Much, and Man Little—Decadence of Cephalonian Marine—
Statistics of Cephalonia—Zante—Of Santa Maura—Of Ithaca—Of Paxo—
Of Cerigo—Queer exports—Cephalonia at fault—Cephalonia shines in the
Statistics of Morality—The Septinsular Debt — English Pensioners of
Greece — Athens surpasses Corfu in Education — A Boon ungraciously
granted.

In order to be enabled to state with confidence
the total number of the Ionian Islands, it would
be necessary first to decide how large a rock must
be to justify its receiving the more dignified appellation of an island. But I am disposed to estimate their number at forty. Of these, the seven
principal, which have given occasion to the title of
" the Septinsular State," are Corfu, Cephalonia,
Zante, Santa Maura, Ithaca, Cerigo, and Paxo.
All these have Regents, and Municipal Councils;

and the six last named had also, under the Protectorate, Residents, who represented the Lord High Commissioner, who resided at Corfu.

The smaller islands and rocks are all dependencies of one or other of the above-named seven.[*] The whole together contain an area of 1,097 square miles, or 702,080 acres, somewhat less than the area of Dorsetshire (720,000 acres), but considerably greater than that of many other English counties. In regard to population, whilst Dorset in 1861, had only 188,651 inhabitants, the Ionian Islands in 1860 had 232,426. Moreover about 20,000 Ionians live in Greece, and in Constantinople, and in the various ports of the Black Sea.

It is generally believed that in ancient times the Islands were better populated than is the case at present. But the inhabitants were greatly reduced in numbers under the rule of Venice, in consequence of the wars with the Turks, and also of the inefficient protection against pirates, and against internal dissensions, afforded to them by the Government. It appears that in 1578, the population of Corfu but little exceeded 19,000.[†] But it must be remembered that forty years previously Sultan Solyman had carried away 20,000 Corfiots into captivity. That in 1578, the population of Cerigo

* *Vide* Appendix II, for the names of all, and for the extent of the principal islands.
† Daru.

only amounted to 3,263 souls,[*] is confirmatory of
the then desolate state of the Islands. Moreover
in 1622 Ithaca possessed only 2,500 inhabitants.
It is not probable therefore that in the sixteenth
or seventeenth centuries, the population much
exceeded 100,000 souls.

In a letter, written in 1808, the then Regent of
Corfu stated that from a census held in 1802, the
inhabitants amounted, at that period, to 44,526.
But he remarked at the same time, that as the
census took place for the purpose of imposing a
capitation tax, the names of indigent persons had
not been inscribed. He was therefore of opinion
that the total population had amounted to about
45,000. It is not consequently probable that the
population of the Seven Islands exceeded 160,000
in 1802.

General Vandoucourt, writing in 1816, estimated
the Corfiots in 1807, at 60,000 a statement only
less absurd than his estimate of Paxo at 8,000, at
the same period. But if the French general greatly
over-estimated the population of Corfu in the early
part of the century, Sir Charles Napier equally
underrated it in 1833, when he stated it at only
40,000. But, an excellent authority as regarded
Cephalonia, Sir Charles is not always to be depended on for Corfu details.

* Daru. *Vide* **Appendix** I, for the population of the **Islands** under **Venice**
and also during the present century.

I am informed that before 1840, statistics were
not very accurately kept in the Islands.   But in
1836, Dr. Davy estimated the total population at
216,689 souls.   In 1854, it rose to 228,981.   In
1858 to 229,706.   In 1860 to 232,426.   Finally
in this year (1864), judging by the census of
Corfu, it cannot be much less than 240,000.*
In all the islands there is a considerable preponderance of males over females.   In Cephalonia
especially, according to the statistics of 1858, this
inequality is very striking.†   There, we find only
31,829 women to 39,918 men.   Bad treatment and
hard work are probably amongst the causes of this
undoubted evil.   For the peasantry everywhere
make of their women beasts of burden, loading
their backs as if they were donkeys.   In the
copious census of Corfu for 1864 (too bulky a
document for publication in this work) the sad dis-
proportion of the sexes may be traced in all the
more than 120 villages of the island. In the village
of Scriperò (where in my last chapter I recorded
my conversation with a peasant), there are 472
males to 415 females.   In the equally pretty and
almost equally elevated village of Pelleca, which I
have also visited lately, there are 462 males to 334
females.   But in the little village of Climatea there
are 138 males to only 7 females!

* A census of Corfu was published on the 1st March, 1864.
† *Vide* Appendix K, for the statistics of 1858.

Great apparent discrepancies and confusion of statistics, have been caused at times, by the varying manner of estimating the revenue of the Ionian Islands. Formerly the stated amount of the revenue meant only that part of the finances which were received by the General Government. But afterwards when the municipal chests of the different islands were all taken under the direct control of the Lord High Commissioners and their senates, it became usual in general statements of the revenue to include the municipal incomes also. The following five years will enable the reader to judge of the revenue and expenditure, towards the close of the Protectorate : omitting shillings and pence.

	1858.	1859.	1860.	1861.	1862.
Revenue	£ 240,828	£ 160,857	£ 172,304	£ 190,236	£ 219,193
Expenditure	£ 198,615	£ 186,943	£ 198,998	£ 190,102	£ 195,307

All the above amounts of revenue include the ·municipal incomes of all the islands. The money which the General Government could lawfully spend, will be known by deducting from the above general total, the total of the municipal revenues. These were (omitting shillings and pence), 39,553*l.* for 1858; 30,596*l.* for 1859; 31,449*l.* for 1860;

37,288*l*. for 1861 ; and 43,439*l*. for 1862.* As the revenue of the municipalities in the Islands are intended for the particular benefit of each of them, it has been an abuse, I conceive, thus to mix them up in the general revenue. But such a system was well calculated to keep up that mystery in finance, which was a part of the secret un-English policy of the Local Protectorate. It was rare indeed to meet any Ionian fully acquainted with the statistics of his country, so long concealed from the public.

Sir Henry Storks arrived early in 1859, just after a year of excellent revenue, with its surplus of more than 42,000*l*. Like most of his predecessors, instead of paying off during his rule a part of the debt, he appears to have increased it, and if the year 1863 were known in all its details, the deficit would probably be greater than it now appears to be.

The revenue of the year 1857 had been as unusually bad as that of 1858 was unusually good. In the former year the whole revenue, including that of the municipalities had only been 140,270*l*., of which the general revenue, was 110,310*l*. The bad year of 1857, as to revenue, was the result of the comparative failure of the olive crops in 1856. And the excellence of the revenue of 1858

* *Vide* Appendix C, p. 299, vol. i., where the revenue of Sir Henry Storks, in 1860, of 140,855*l*. was the real revenue of the General Government, unmixed with the municipal revenue.

was due to the abundant harvest of 1857.   That 1858 was itself a poor year is proved by the revenue of 1859, which, though superior to that of 1857, was yet far below the average.   Since that period the revenue was prosperous till 1863, of which I have no details, but it is well known it was a bad year, though probably the results will appear only in the revenue of this present year.

For the following summary of the average Ionian revenues, for thirteen years which I now present to the reader, and for the study of the admirably arranged details on which it is founded, (which I deem superfluous to publish), I am indebted to that most distinguished and excellent Ionian, Sir George Marcoran.

Average of the Local Government Revenues of the Seven Islands, from 1850 to 1862 both years included:

	£	s.	d.
Corfu	59,309	11	6
Cephalonia	36,567	9	$10\frac{4}{10}$
Zante	32,484	1	$2\frac{4}{10}$
Santa Maura	7,447	0	$7\frac{4}{10}$
Ithaca	3,305	3	$2\frac{2}{10}$
Cerigo	1,649	14	$8\frac{4}{10}$
Paxo	3,573	2	$8\frac{2}{10}$
	144,336	3	$10\frac{2}{10}$
To this must be added the average revenue raised from all the islands for the general treasury*	2,836	9	$6\frac{2}{10}$
Total	147,172	13	$4\frac{4}{10}$

* It appears to me, that of late years, judging by the general statistical table of 1857, which I have seen, the revenue was devoted solely into general and municipal.   The former comprising both the Local and General Government revenues of former days.

Average of the Municipal Revenues for the same thirteen years:

	£	s.	d.
Corfu	17,213	9	$1\frac{2}{5}$
Cephalonia	6,471	9	$6\frac{2}{13}$
Zante	6,474	6	$8\frac{7}{13}$
Santa Maura	2,640	4	$0\frac{2}{13}$
Ithaca	687	10	4
Cerigo	361	2	$4\frac{3}{13}$
Paxo	493	0	$4\frac{3}{13}$
	34,341	2	$6\frac{5}{13}$
Total Government revenue of Islands	147,172	13	$4\frac{4}{13}$
Total revenue	181,513	15	11
The average expenditure, General, Local, and Municipal	185,926	19	$11\frac{4}{13}$
Average annual deficit	4,413	4	$0\frac{4}{13}$
Total deficit in the thirteen years	57,371	12	$5\frac{2}{13}$

The average of what may be called the revenue for thirteen years was therefore 147,172*l.* 13s. $4\frac{4}{13}$d. But the Lord High Commissioners with their Senates have ever equally disposed of and regulated the municipal revenues; besides borrowing from them at will, for the use of the General Government.

By far the greatest portion of the Ionian revenue is raised from duties on exports and imports. Oil and currants form the principal exports:

" Duties on export of oil, on the average form the largest source of the revenue. And currants are next on the list." Both of these staple-commodities are subjected to a charge of altogether $19\frac{1}{2}$ per cent. The great staple of Corfu and of Paxo is oil: of Cephalonia currants; and of Zante currants and oil. Santa Maura exports a little oil, less currants and some flax. Ithaca exports currants. The exports of Cerigo consist chiefly of wine, made of imported Candian grapes. The islands do not produce more than one third of the bread necessary for their own use. Yet all imported grain is subject to duty, and brings in about 10,000*l.* or, 12,000*l.* a year to the general revenue. Mr. Gladstone, when in Corfu in 1859, justly denounced the errors of the Ionian fiscal system.* But such is the force of habit that it will not be easy to introduce the necessary changes; especially as, in spite of bad laws, the people have made some progress in general prosperity. For instance, the value of the imports in 1833 were only 563,611*l.* But in 1859 they were estimated at 1,306,303*l.* And the value of the exports, which in 1833 was only 250,669*l.* rose in 1859 to 649,057*l.*

The fluctuation of the revenue is caused not only by the variation of good and bad harvests,† but also by the fact that the olive-tree only produces a crop every other year. The best years for revenue are those which follow the best years for crops, and in which these are principally sold. The currants are produced every year, but their price is variable, and contributes, though in less degree than oil, to

* *Vide* vol. i. p. 239.

† The revenue of Corfu for 1858 was 103,411*l.* (not including the municipal), while for 1859, it was only 52,728*l.*, scarcely more than half that of the preceding year.

the general irregularity of the revenue. Thus in the Greek war of independence, when the currant fields in the Morea were either destroyed or left uncultivated, the currants of Cephalonia and Zante sold for 100 dollars the 1000 lbs. That fact helps to account for the great prosperity in the time of Sir Thomas Maitland, in spite of the onerous export duties which he imposed. In 1862, when I was in Cephalonia, currants fetched only from 22 to 25 dollars per 1,000 lbs., which may account in some measure, for the poverty of latter times, in spite of the great increase of exportation.

Corfu, ever the richest of the islands, was formerly inferior in population to Cephalonia, but has now begun to surpass it, even in this respect. Much of the prosperity of the capital has been occasioned by the constant presence of British regiments and ships in her barracks and harbour:

In 1844 the inhabitants amounted to 68,000
,, 1848 ,, ,, ... 68,374
,, 1856 ,, ,, ... *67,930
,, 1860 ,, ,, ... 72,967
,, 1864 ,, ,, ... †73,453

Without reckoning the suburbs, the town of Corfu contains a little more than 17,000 souls; but if the suburbs be considered a part of the town, then the population exceeds, at present, 25,000.‡

* The cholera in 1856 reduced the population.

† Of this number more than 8500 are foreigners; about 6000 of whom live in the town and suburbs, and the remainder in the country. The 6000 Jews are of course counted in the native population, of which they form a part.

‡ *Vide* Appendix L, for the population of Corfu in detail in 1848, 1860, and 1864.

The numbers of births and deaths corroborate the fact of the steady increase of the Corfiots. In ten years, the preponderance of births over deaths was upwards of 5,000.*

The details for the thirteen years, and the average struck, as regards the money paid into the general treasury, as distinct both from the Local Government revenues, and from the Municipal revenues, have not been explained to me so clearly as the rest, and I know not how to divide amongst the Seven Islands — the 2,836*l.* 9*s.* $6\frac{2}{10}d.$, in question. Independently of this, the total revenues of Corfu appear to have averaged in round numbers about 76,000*l.* But, in 1861 and 1862 (especially in the former year), the revenue, including everything, exceeded 80,000*l.*; the customs alone producing about 70,000*l.* in that flourishing island. The remainder of the revenue is raised by police fines, stamp duties, sale of powder, tax on coffee-houses, and from similar other sources. Substituting in some islands currants for oil: the manner of raising the revenue is nearly uniform throughout, so that to understand Corfu is almost to understand the Seven Islands.†

It is quite a mistake to assert that the Ionians are very lightly taxed. It would be more accurate

---

* *Vide* Appendix M.

† *Vide* Appendix N, for the details of the Corfu exports and imports, and the duties paid upon them.

to say that their taxes are imposed in an unequal, unwise, and unusual manner. He who studies the fiscal details as I have done, is not likely to be impressed with any great idea of the political or financial talents of most of the Lord High Commissioners. It must be confessed, however, that of late years, the Ionians were but little disposed to be guided in such matters by any Englishman. I have yet, however, to learn that any Lord High Commissioner (except Mr. Gladstone, during his brief visit), ever pointed out the evils of the present system, or proposed the remedy. It is well known that Sir Henry Storks was quite ready to entertain any proposals for that purpose that the later Assemblies might have wished to make; but there is no record of his having had any scheme of his own for bringing the country to that flourishing state which his despatches have painted. A ragged and discontented peasantry, living under a fiscal system which taxes the importation of wheat (in a country dependent on foreigners for its bread), and which concentrates its taxes on the staple commodities.

It is true that many other causes conspire to bring about the poverty of both signori and peasantry, besides the unusual manner of raising the revenue. The mixture of French with Venetian laws; the sub-division of property in an unmercantile and unspeculative community; the many masters living on, and the many persons having claims on, the same lands, with the consequent difficulties in the way of capital acquiring estates, all tend to ruin the signori and to starve the peasantry.

But, when I found fault with the Ionian laws, an able judge said to me with a smile, "Would you have us adopt the English laws?" I own I was silenced: for I felt that only a very rich country could afford to imitate us in our legal luxuries of boundless expense. I could, however, have replied, that the English have grown rich in spite of their laws, which, I fear, will never be the case with the Ionians. *They* must change their laws, and their system of revenue, before they can hope to be a wealthy and commercial people. And their gentry must alter their ideas, and not consider commerce, or even trade, so dishonourable as idleness and dependence. To facilitate the purchase of land, and the introduction of capital, is one of the first requisites for bringing the fertile island of Corfu to that state of prosperity that a few years of enlightened government would assuredly establish there; where nature has done so much, and man so very little. Then it might be hoped would finally disappear that deep animosity still subsisting (and hitherto only repressed, perhaps, by British bayonets and British influence) between a half-starved peasantry and an impoverished gentry, who cannot afford to be generous, and are too often tempted to be unjust and tyrannical.

Cephalonia has certainly made great progress, especially in civilization under British rule, in spite of the many errors committed under the latter. In Cephalonia as also in Zante, the superiority of the currants of the Morea may have affected the markets unfavourably. But the island has, nevertheless, prospered on the whole. It cannot be denied, however, that the Cephalonian navy has fallen into decay. But no one, worthy of credit, has ever attempted to show that the fault lay with the British Government. " In 1828," wrote Dr. Davy, " while Corfu had twelve, and Zante four, Cephalonia had 300 square-rigged vessels, with crews of from twenty to thirty men." This may be all true, but we are not told the tonnage of these 300 vessels; and, as a general rule, ships in 1828 were of much less tonnage than they are at the present day. But, allowing the fact of the decadence (to which the increase of the steam navigation of other nations has contributed), it is not a matter difficult of explanation. The chief commerce of the Cephalonians is carried on in the Black Sea; and there it is found more convenient to sail under the Russian than the Ionian flag. The Russian companies of merchants established at Odessa, Taganrog, and other ports, have also attracted the Ionian traders. The revenue of Cephalonia averages 45,000*l.* a year; about 35,000*l.* of which is raised from the customs. It exports from sixteen to eighteen millions of pounds of currants annually. In 1862, its total revenues were above the average, being upwards of 47,000*l.*

However much the shipping may have decayed since 1828, in Cephalonia, it has nevertheless greatly increased in the last ten years. In 1854, there were ninety ships of from one to twenty-five tons, forming a total of 1253 tons; and 146 ships of twenty-six tons and upwards, with a total of 1253 tons. But now, in 1864, there are 115 ships of from one to twenty-five tons with a total of 1461 tons; and 173 ships of twenty-six tons and upwards with a total of 29,466 tons.

Whether from poverty or increase of emigration, the population of Cephalonia has not of late years increased like that of Corfu, as has been already mentioned. The export of currants from Cephalonia has more than trebled in quantity since 1823. But owing to the great fall of prices the revenue has fallen off instead of increasing. To use round numbers, less than 56,000,000 lbs. of currants (from 1823 to 1830) produced more than 131,000*l.*; whilst more than 81,000,000 lbs. of currants from 1859 to 1863 produced less than 82,000*l.** The

* *Vide* Appendix O.

revenue of Cephalonia fluctuates less than that of Zante.*

Zante stands next to Corfu, and, indeed, rivals its commercial progress. But it does not appear to advance so rapidly in population. Yet in 1811 it had only 32,843 inhabitants, and in 1860 its population had risen to 39,455. Producing a considerable quantity of oil as well as of currants, its revenue is subject to fluctuations like that of Corfu.† This remark applies to the exports. Those of Zante, in 1853, were valued at 78,687*l.*, and in 1855, at only 66,600*l.* In 1856, they rose to 216,000*l.*; and in 1861, they were down to 125,588*l.* On the other hand the imports of Zante have steadily increased. In 1853, they were valued at 129,736*l.*, but in 1861, after a gradual rise, they were estimated at 192,868*l.*

Zante exports 13,000,000 lbs. of currants, and on an average 20,000 barrels of oil. In 1862, the revenues of Zante exceeded 53,000*l.* a year. The thirteen years' average gives only 38,000*l.*, of which the municipal part was 6,474*l.* But I believe that if the island should continue its present prosperous career, the next thirteen years' average, will be about 50,000*l.* a year.

* That is on the average. For if the worst year and the best of the thirteen years, often quoted, be made the criterion, the fluctuation is nearly the same. The revenue of Cephalonia was, in 1850, 45,435*l.*, and in 1852 only 26,134*l.*

† In 1852 the revenue of Zante was (municipal income not included) only 23,433*l.*, in 1856 it was 50,938*l.*—more than double.

Santa Maura exports oil and wine and flax, and has begun to cultivate and export currants. In 1862, her total revenues exceeded 17,000*l*. But their average has been about 10,000*l*. a year, of which 2,640*l*. formed the municipal part.

Ithaca exports currants principally, and a little oil and wine. Her revenue in 1862 exceeded 6,500*l*. The average has been about 4,000*l*., whereof 687*l*. formed the municipal part.

Paxo exports excellent oil. Her revenue in 1862 was more than 5,200*l*. The average was rather more than 4,000*l*., of which 493*l*. was municipal.

Cerigo had in 1862 a revenue of 2,162*l*. The average is 1,910*l*., of which 361*l*. is municipal. Poor, barren, and rocky *Cythera* exports little besides two representatives to the Assembly at Corfu, so illiterate that they sometimes could not answer the notes of invitation which they received at Corfu from the palace. She does, however (as I have before observed), export some wine made of the grapes imported from her neighbour Candia. What imaginations must those Greek poets have had in order to have given deathless renown to this desolate wind-bound, treeless, unfrequented island! It is only with certain winds that a landing can be effected there at all, and a more unsuitable place for Venus to have been born in or near to, it is difficult to conceive.

Most of the Cerigots abandon in youth their

own happy land to make money abroad, but it is said that when they have made it they usually return to their own homes.   Only three Jews live in the island, and they at Easter require the protection of the police.

We have seen that Cephalonia is considered to have decayed in shipping.   With regard, however, to the islands in general since 1840, the statistics are very satisfactory, and it is only from that date that they can be depended on for accuracy.   The Ionian marine has only slightly increased, it is true, but the numbers of ships of all nations that enter the Ionian ports have more than doubled. Austria figures as the largest on the list, for she has been granted very great privileges in the Seven Islands.*   These privileges (by the recent treaties regulating *the cession*) Austria is to retain for at least fifteen years ; amongst others that of carrying the mails.   Judging by her recent conduct to Denmark, she will be a great danger for Greece, now that England has ceased to rule in the Ionian Islands, and has left so many of the fortresses in ruins.

With regard to public establishments, there is a sad deficiency of hospitals, and charitable endowments, in most of the islands.   In this respect Cephalonia, I say it with regret, is unenviably distinguished.   Like Corfu and Zante, she boasts of

* *Vide* Appendix P, for the tonnage of the various nations in Ionian ports

a theatre, and it is perhaps the best in the Seven
Islands.   But she has neglected the more important matters, and figures but little in the statistics
of charity and benevolence.*   It is the fault of
her rulers, and not I think of her people.   She
has no poor-house, and yet has the greatest number of paupers of all the islands.

The following statistics on the exposed children
of the four principal islands, for five years may
interest the reader, as some test of their comparative immorality :

	1858.	1859.	1860.	1861.	1862.	Totals.
Corfu	45	48	49	63	59	264
Cephalonia	63	24	14	30	31	162
Zante	84	95	84	94	67	424
Santa Maura	55	48	51	54	52	260
Totals......	247	215	198	241	209	1110

I have used the words *some test;* because the
four islands are not in the same situation.   For in
Corfu and Zante, it is probable that the Foundling
Hospitals act as additional temptations to vice.
But comparing Corfu with Zante, and allowing,
moreover, for the great difference of their populations, and it must be confessed, that, "the flower
of the Levant" has a painful pre-eminence in vice,
but too much in keeping with its homicidal pro-
clivities.   Of all the islands it would appear that

* *Vide* Appendix Q.

Cephalonia is the smallest in morality, and I believe this to be really the case. Santa Maura, with its population of about 23,000, appears the next in immorality to Zante, its figures in the above list, being almost the same as Corfu, which has more than 73,000 inhabitants.

Soon after the Ionian Assembly had on the 5th October, 1863, voted unanimously for the Union with Greece, the debt of upwards of 90,000*l.* due to Great Britain by the Septinsular State, was wholly remitted. The remainder was, after due investigation, by order of the Assembly, declared to amount to 231,306*l.*, up to the end of August, 1863. The document speaks for itself, and is not creditable to the financial conduct of the Protectorate. The long delay in giving over the islands to the King of Greece will doubtless have increased the debt very considerably.*

But how can I write calmly of the disgraceful affair of the pensions? Although the Englishmen concerned have merited well of their own country, was it necessary that the burden of their recompense, should be thrown by *millionnaire* England upon *bankrupt* Greece? Most of them had no legal claims to pensions of any kind, either by Ionian or by English laws. And those who had were not entitled to a quarter of what has been

* *Vide* Appendix R, for the details of the Septinsular debt up to August, 1863.

decreed to them, by treaty. Moreover, these recipients are generally speaking young, and none of them are old men; and the obvious way to reward such services was to appoint them to similar situations in other parts of the world. For this, it was only necessary that ministers should have resolved to sacrifice a very trifling amount of their patronage for the honor of their country. Was it not, in fact, for England, that the brief services were performed, which are to saddle the Greek finances with life pensions to young Englishmen? Had the Ionians ever had any voice in their appointment to office in the Islands? But as it was made an indispensable condition of the Union it was submitted to, but with a very bad grace. A million sterling the Ionians had already paid to the Protectorate for fortifications and other military expenses; and now at parting (when all the so made additional fortifications are destroyed) the Islands are further saddled with life pensions to Englishmen not entitled to them. All the English in the Islands (even most of those who are to be benefited) felt ashamed of the whole transaction. Cannot Parliament at the eleventh hour suggest to the Chancellor of the Exchequer (formerly Lord High Commissioner) to have compassion on the Ionians, and not to let them suppose that he is seeking to revenge on them the failure of his famous mission. The total amount of the pensions though distressing to Greece, would be a mere drop of water in the ocean of the British budget. Moreover, if that drop cannot be allowed, there is (as already mentioned) a very obviously just manner of arranging the affair, free of all expense whatever. But enough of that disagreeable subject, which is calculated to make, and has made, many Englishmen blush for their country.

It is an unfortunate fact, that in modern Athens, which dates from only forty years back, education is more advanced than in the Ionian Islands, where Great Britain has ruled for fifty years with supreme power. But for these circumstances the political and religious prejudices of the Ionians are probably chiefly to blame. Before the cession there were 304 schoolmasters in the Islands, paid by the Government, 116 of whom were in Corfu. The total cost of the public education was 13,800*l.* But, owing to the very small salaries granted to the country schoolmasters, it was difficult to select suitable persons, and frequent vacancies in the office of teacher were the natural results.

The Ionian civil list was in 1857, 66,251*l.*, but is at present about 71,000*l* a year; and the total number of paid civilians was 1551, of whom only 26 were English, but with salaries very superior to those of the Ionians. Out of the civil list, also, was always paid the sum guaranteed to the Lord High Commissioner, and the subordinates of the Protectorate; which sum formerly amounted to 15,000*l.* a year, and was afterwards reduced to 13,000*l.* This grant defrayed the salaries of secretaries, treasurers, Residents, aide-de-camps, and many other officials.   In this manner the Ionians had disbursed little short of a second million sterling for the benefit of the British Protectorate.   Considering all these facts a little generosity at parting would have been scarcely more than justice; and Great Britain would have taken leave of the little country so long intrusted to her care in a more graceful and dignified manner, than has actually been the case.

Our country has undoubtedly performed a great and generous act in ceding the Islands to Greece; but it is to be regretted that her manner of conferring the boon has been but little calculated to arouse the gratitude of those for whose benefit the sacrifice was supposed to have been voluntarily made, in the face, and with the consent, of all the Great Powers.   And if in the case of the fortifications the blame lies chiefly with the latter, yet in the matter of the pensions, it must be confessed that Great Britain stands alone, in what cannot be called her glory.

CHAPTER XV.

CONCLUDING JOURNAL.[*]

Saturday, 23rd April.—Rode for the first time to-day to the *Val di Roppa*—the largest and most beautiful valley in the island of Corfu—and therefore well worthy of being visited by strangers; so that I have noted it here on that account. The richly-cultivated soil, and the verdure, especially at this season of the year, with the bold line of surrounding hills, make a charming picture, not easily forgotten even in this lovely island.

Sunday, 24th. — The Greek Palm Sunday. Grand procession of *Saint Spiro*, about noon, and lasting till two in the afternoon; the English, after

---

[*] From want both of space and time, this concluding chapter is taken chiefly from the author's diary of events, in which there was no room for more than a few lines daily.

Church, crowding to see the sight. The huge banners of all the churches of the town were there, with gilt lamps elevated on ornamented poles, and formed the principal part of the train, except where some great portrait of a saint was held aloft for veneration. As usual, the procession was on too straggling a plan for proper effect; and the parties with their banners too far apart from each other. In fact, the procession extended nearly half a mile. The Archbishop, surrounded by his clergy, and hedged in by the candle-bearers, walked in front of the saint, who, in his glass-case, was borne aloft under a canopy. All the gentry of Corfu, and a great rabble rout, escorted Saint Spiro through the crowds of spectators. When the procession arrived at Condi-terrace (the highest part of the town), a halt was made, and prayers were offered up by the Archbishop. After this, a man with a stiff arm (or some such misfortune), threw himself on the ground, and the saint was carried over him. The man arose, and his cure has, doubtless, swelled the long list of the bene-volent virtues of Saint Spiro, who appears to be never weary in well-doing. Some of the English spectators remarked that the arm of the patient appeared as stiff after · he got up as it had been when he laid down—a proof that he, at all events, was no impostor.

According to custom, the saint was carried under

the palace windows, where the Lord High Commissioner, with his secretaries and aide de camps
stood waiting to salute the Archbishop. The repeated bows of his Excellency, with the ac-
knowledgments of the Archbishop, formed part of
the ceremony. Finally, the mummy, or whatever
it may be, was carried back to the church which
bears its name. As soon as the saint returned
home, a salute of nineteen guns from the seven-
gun saluting battery in the citadel announced the
important fact. This was about two in the afternoon. Such was the first use made of the serviceable guns still left in the island after the removal
of the rest of the ordnance.

Thursday, 28th April.—We heard to-day of a
new change of ministers at Athens. As Bulgaris
had been succeeded by the veteran Canaris, so the
latter has been replaced by a gentleman of the
name of Balby, who is well spoken of generally.
It is reported that King George is anxious to take
over the Islands at once, in order to be able to get
rid of the National Convention, and to establish a
regular government. The new constitution cannot
be formed till the Ionian Islands have dispatched
their proportion of members to the convention at
Athens. Count Sponneck has become, it is said.
unpopular, from an idea that he too readily consented to the neutralization of Corfu and Paxo, to

the destruction of the fortifications, and to the job of the pensions.

Friday, 29th.—The Greek Good Friday. To-day arrived the order that the British officials, civil and military, should all simultaneously leave Corfu as soon as possible after the 1st of June, in four vessels that were about to be ordered out for the occasion. So, at length, there is a prospect of the cession becoming a fact, as well as a law. The usual torch-light procession (called that of our Saviour's body) takes place at midnight. Having often seen it, I shall stay away. It is, however, a sight worth witnessing.

Saturday, 30th.—The Greek Easter Eve. Walked out, at ten in the morning, to see the follies of the Greek Passover, as they call it. At half-past ten, bang went the gun; and immediately, from the tops and windows of the houses, down came the usual crash of crockery. At the same moment, fowling-pieces, pistols, and crackers, were fired in all directions—behind doors, out of windows, and from concealed nooks and corners. All of a sudden, a number of lambs were dragged along, and had their throats cruelly hacked at the thresholds of houses in the best streets of the town. Some of these creatures were ten minutes, or more, in parting with their lives, tortured in honor of the Greek Passover. It is curious, considering the hatred of the Greeks to the Jews, that they should thus keep *their* Passover. The firing continues for several days, as do the other fireworks—usually causing many accidents, and keeping nervous people in perpetual alarm. Many tradesmen shut their shops—or, at least, their shutters—for days. I am assured that at Easter, in Athens, these childish, and at the same time brutal, proceedings are no longer tolerated by the police; and it is disgraceful to the British Protectorate that they still occur in Corfu, and without any mitigation. The Jews are not visible anywhere lately out of their own quarters. In most parts of the town they would now con- sider themselves unsafe. What will happen when we are gone? Yet, perhaps, when the leading- strings by which the Ionians have been guided by the English are snapped, they may become men, and put away the childish things which now delight them. The nervous fear of tampering with religious scruples has caused the Protectorate to encourage follies, which it ought to have corrected. My able Cephalonian acquaintance of the Mills hit the right nail on the head, when he said to a Resident, "You English should either govern us or go away!" We would not properly govern them, and so we go away. By-the-by, since I left Cephalonia, that astute Greek has not only become a member of the Assembly of the thirteenth Par- liament, but was elected its Vice-president—an office which he still holds; for the Assembly is only prorogued, not dissolved, as yet.

Sunday, May 1st.—The Greek Easter Sunday. Early this morning, there was another procession in honor of Saint Spiro. Thus in eight days of the most solemn season we have had two processions in honor of Spiro, and one in honor of Christ, a not insignificant fact. On the south parade of the citadel I this day remarked, that the six long Venetian guns, and the four huge Venetian mortars (which our artillery-men had collected to leave behind) are no longer rusty, but beautifully cleaned and blackened, like guns on board of a man-of-war. I was glad to observe this becoming attention paid to the feelings of the Corfiots, which have of late been so little regarded.

Monday, 2nd May.—I learned from a Cephalonian friend, who visited me to-day, that Signor Zervo, the President of the Assembly in the twelfth Parliament had not been re-elected a member of the thirteenth Parliament. On the contrary he retired into private life, not desiring to advocate the Union in the present disturbed state of Greece.

I learned also, to-day, the behaviour of two of my Argostoli acquaintances, brothers of the name of Anino, which pleased me greatly. These gentlemen had long kept back from public affairs because they thought it useless folly to demand the Union from the British Protectorate, so long as the latter was determined not to grant it.   But when they found that the British Ministers themselves proposed and appeared to desire, the Union, they joyfully consented to represent their fellow citizens in the Assembly, where they joined in the unanimous vote of the 5th October, 1863.   It gave me great pleasure to hear of the wise and patriotic conduct of these amiable brothers, who (inseparable like Siamese twins) furnish an excellent example of that strong fraternal affection and concord which I have so often admired in Ionian families. What can be a more touching sight than to see many brothers living together in harmony, with a common purse, and never thinking of saying " give me my share and let me go?"   And yet this is not a rare case in the Islands.   Nay, a nobler example still is sometimes exhibited; the younger brother remaining single (though entitled to an equal share of property with his elder) to enable the latter to marry and keep up the family name with comfort and respectability.

I hear that a whole family, of five persons, have been just assassinated at Zante by an act of vengeance, in that land of frequent homicides.   A dark contrast to my previous narrative.

Tuesday, 3rd May.—This was a very fine day (between, as it turned out, two rainy ones), and most fortunately so; and I spent it most agreeably.   A party of four including a lady, drove

from Corfu to a country house above the village of
Benitzi to dine and pass the day with Sir Spiridion
and Lady Valaoriti. What with the drive there and
back in pleasant company, and the beautiful grounds
in which we strolled, and the picturesque terrace on
which we took our coffee; what with the beautiful
scenery and the charming hosts, it was decidedly
one of those occasions which are marked in the
memory with a white stone, if I may be allowed
to speak classically in such a land. Close in the
neighbourhood of the house (which belongs to
the Countess Flamburiari, sister of Sir Spiridion)
is situated the reservoir farthest from Corfu, to which
the first pipes, laid in a stone aqueduct above
ground, convey the springs of Benitzi : before they
are started on their way to the great reservoir. And
for nearly the whole of the year the mills and
gardens of the Countess benefit from a branch pipe
of the great aqueduct, which turns the mills and
irrigates the fields, and supplies the great want of
the Ionian Islands, namely, abundant water.

The man who has the charge of this upper reservoir receives 60*l.* a year for the care of it, which
in Corfu is considered no contemptible salary. At
our three o'clock dinner we were most hospitably
entertained, and the lamb, slaughtered expressly for
us, was of a delicacy and sweetness rarely found
out of, and not always found in, Great Britain itself. The guests, escorted down the first hill by

their hosts, and with magnificent bouquets of flowers culled by the ladies of the house, drove back to Corfu, on one of those bright lovely evenings, neither too hot nor too cold, for which this island is celebrated in the spring of the year.

Wednesday, 4th.—Rained all day; so that I the more rejoiced in our good fortune of yesterday. I received to-day some corrected details from Sir George Marcoran, by which it appears that more than a million sterling was paid to the Protectorate by the Ionians for military contributions, that is chiefly for the fortifications.*

I must leave to other pens the description of our approaching final departure; both from want of space, and also from want of time. I am consoled for this abrupt termination by the conviction that the final departure of the English will not have anything satisfactory or gratifying to our national pride. The ominous words " Neutralization," " Fortifications," " Pensions," all forbid us to expect many expressions of sympathy or respect on the occasion. But enough of this subject. The wisest course for us Britons is to retire quietly from the country, where we are not at present appreciated. And on certain occasions, the most prudent course is—to keep silence.†

* *Vide* Appendix E.
† " Mais enfin coupons aux discours,
　　Et que chacun doucement se retire :
　　Sur telles affaires toujours
　　Le meilleur est de ne rien dire."—Molière.

The plan of movement is, that the military and civilians shall both depart on the 1st of June ; the former for Malta, and the latter for Ancona ; and that day will assuredly be a memorable one in the history both of England and of Greece. I can only hope that the present causes of estrangement will soon disappear, and that the friendly feelings between the English and the Greek races, which displayed themselves so conspicuously a year ago, will once more resume their sway, and become permanently established, to the benefit of civilization and of genuine enlightened Christianity.

APPENDIX.

E.

In order to account for some difference from the text in this Appendix, it is necessary to state that after the author sent home the thirteenth Chapter of his second volume to be printed, Sir George Marcoran was enabled by some fresh information to prove that the total contributions of the Ionians to the Protectorate *have exceeded a million sterling.* Indeed, Sir George is disposed to put the amount at about 1,200,000*l.* But in this he includes sums supposed to have been spent by Sir Thomas Maitland; and for which his authority is the writings of a British statesman. But as I have no positive proof that Sir Thomas Maitland did raise any such contributions, I cannot contradict, without fuller evidence, the statements that I have inserted in my work. Omitting, therefore, the case of Sir T. Maitland, the contributions may be stated as follows:

AMOUNT OF CONTRIBUTIONS.

	£
In 1825, allotted by vote of the Assembly . .	164,000
In 1833, ditto ditto . .	15,000
In 1834, the contribution was fixed at 35,000*l.* a year, and kept till end of 1843 (nine years and two months)	320,833
In 1844 the Protectorate commuted the 35,000*l.* a year to one-fifth of the revenue, averaging 25,633*l.* a year, and this continued in force till end of 1849 (six years)	153,798
In 1850, contribution fixed at 25,000*l.* a year, up to 1863 (fourteen years)	350,000

Total . . £1,003,631

Thus, even supposing that Sir Thomas Maitland never called upon the Ionians for any military contributions, they have yet paid more than a million sterling to the protecting Government. But how much of the million was spent on the fortifications, and how much on lodging-money and other military expenses, is still unexplained. The following documents confirm the author's statements of the above details.

Translation of Act 24th of the second Parliament, passed on the 19th March, 1825.

PREAMBLE.

The fortifications of Corfu, being at present in a ruinous state, and those of the Island of Vido defective and imperfect, it is very important that their restoration by the necessary works, should secure them against a sudden attack. Considering the respected note of the Lord High Commissioner of the Protecting Sovereign, regarding the orders of his Majesty upon this important matter, it is decreed as follows:

Art. 1*st.* The fortifications of Corfu and those of Vido shall be restored and completed, with all the works necessary to render them perfect.

Art. 2*nd.* The list of expenses required for these works is adopted (as also for the posts and fortifications therein indicated), amounting to 164,000*l.*

Art. 3*rd.* The said sum shall be paid from the finances of these states, and disbursed at the rate of 20,000*l.* annually, until the payment of the whole of the said sum.

Art. 4*th.* The Treasurer-General will defray these distributed sums from the finances of these states.

Art. 5*th.* The present Act will be printed, published, and transmitted to the proper persons for its execution.

Extract from the English version of a Resolution passed in the Ionian Assembly at Corfu on the 18th of December, 1849:

Art. 28th . . . . substituted for Art. 12.

Sec. 2, chapter 7, of the Constitution . . . . is expunged, and the following article is substituted:

" Whereas, by the 6th Article of the Treaty of Paris, on the 5th day of November, 1815, between Great Britain, Austria, Russia, and Prussia, it is provided that everything which may relate to the maintenance of the fortresses already existing, as well as the subsistence and payment of the British garrisons, shall be regulated by means of a Convention with the Government of the United States of the Ionian Islands, it is now to be understood and enacted that, for the future, the United States shall pay annually into the military chest of her Majesty the Protecting Sovereign, the fixed sum of 25,000*l.*, in fulfilment of the obligations imposed upon the said States by the aforesaid Treaty of Paris, in respect to the subsistence and payment of the British garrisons, as well as the maintenance of the fortresses already existing.* The above annual payment of 25,000*l.* shall be made by the General Treasury, in virtue of the present Constitutional Clause, half-yearly, and in preference to all other charges on the Ionian revenue.

"*Art.* 29. The annual sum of 15,000*l.* placed at the disposal of the Lord High Commissioner . . . . for the salaries and contingent expenses of his establishment, comprising the Residents in the different Islands; the salaries of two of the members of the Supreme Council of Justice; the Secretary of the Senate for the General Department; and the Treasurer-General, whose nominations are reserved to the Protecting Power, in virtue of the Constitutional Charter, is now limited to 13,000*l.*, which may not be diminished without the previous assent and concurrence of her Majesty," &c.

* I do not believe that the pay and subsistence of the British garrisons were ever paid for by the Ionians. But besides the fortifications, it appears that at one time the lodging money of the troops for whom there was not room in barracks, was paid out of the military contribution in question.

F.

Return of the Number of Churches and Chapels in the United States of the Ionian Islands on the 31st December, 1857.

	Established Greek Church.								Latin Church.	English Chapels.
	Public.		Corporate Bodies.		Private.					
—	Number of Churches.	Annual Salaries of Priests.	Number of Churches.	Annual Salaries of Priests.	Number of Churches.	Annual Salaries of Priests.				
		£ s. d.		£ s. d.		£ s. d.				
Corfu............	23	286 15 6	240	669 2 10	518	... ...			4	2
Cephalonia	...	...	286	1,159 17 8	332	302 4 10			2	...
Zante	7	122 1 2	181	666 5 0	112	133 9 4			4	...
Santa Maura...	42	63 0 0	85	1,105 0 0	103	... ...			1	...
Ithaca...........	5	26 0 0	21	204 15 0	5	46 11 8			...	...
Cerigo	3	22 5 0	5	12 15 0	118	200 0 0			...	...
Paxo	...	... ...	54	8 0 0	7	5 0 0			...	...
Total......	80	520 1 8	872	3,825 15 6	1,190	687 5 10			11	2

RECAPITULATION.

—		Number of Churches and Chapels.	Number of Priests.	Amount of Annual Salaries of Priests.
				£ s. d.
Established Greek Church	Public	80	}	520 1 8
	Corporate Bodies	872	} 868	3,825 15 6
	Private	1,190	}	687 5 10
Latin Church		11	27	1,010 15 2
English Chapels	Corfu .... } Cephalonia ... }	2	3	215 0 0
Total......................		2,155	898	6,258 18 2

G.

Return of Ordnance in the Ionian Islands, 1864.

Nature.	Citadel.	Fort-Neuf.	Vido.	Ithaca.	Santa Maura.	Cephalonia.	Zante.	Total.
110 pounder Armstrong	3	...	2	...	...	...	...	5
68 ,, smooth bore	7	...	...	...	...	...	...	7
10 inch	7	...	...	...	...	...	...	7
8 ,,	21	11	11	...	...	...	2	48
32 pounder	24	...	...	...	...	...	3	27
24 ,,	59*	115	44	...	14	...	5	237
18 ,,	9	...	...	3	...	5	6	23
12 ,,	1	...	...	...	3	...	...	4
9 ,,	...	...	...	...	...	4	...	4
13 inch mortar	8	...	...	...	...	...	...	8
10 ,,	5	14	...	...	2	...	3	24
8 ,,	...	...	...	...	2	...	2	4
8 ,, howitzer	8	...	...	...	1	1	...	10
24 pounder carronade	...	...	2	...	8	5	9	24
12 ,,	...	...	...	...	2	...	...	2
Total	155	140	59	3	32	15	30	434

* Including seven saluting guns, and guns dismounted for alterations of works.

H.

List of the Ionian Islands lately ceded to Greece by Great Britain, commencing with the Northern and terminating with the Southern Islands.

Name.	Length in Miles	Breadth in Miles.	Square Miles.
CORFU (*Corcyra*)	41 }	19 at N. end 1¼ at S.	{ 227
Fano	4	3	
Merlera....................................	2½	2½	
Samotraki	2½		
Diaplo	1		
Vido	¾		
Kravia } Very small			
Lazaretto } Islands.			
Ulysses Rock.			
PAXO...	4	2	26
Anti Paxo...............................	2½		
Vascaglia Rock.			
SANTA MAURA (*Leucadia*)	22	8	156
Meganisi	8	2½	
Calamos*	7	2	
Castus*	5	½	
Sparti	1		
Skropio	1		
Arkudo	2	1	
CEPHALONIA (*Kephellenia*)	30	14	311
Guardiano. } Very small			
St. Helia. } Islands or			
St. Danista. } Rocks.			

The "Dependencies of Corfu," "Dependencies of Paxo," "Dependencies of Santa Maura," and "Dependencies of Cephalonia" are bracketed as sub-groups under their respective principal islands.

* The tenths, or taxes, of these two islands were granted to the Delladecima family of Cephalonia by the Venetian Government.   Vide page 29, vol. i.

Appendix II (continued).

Name.	Length in Miles	Breadth in Miles.	Square Miles.
ITHACA	14	3	44
Dependencies of Ithaca. Atoko	2	1	
Parapigadi. St. Nikolo. { Rocks or nearly so.			
ZANTE (*Zacynthus*).	24	13	161
Dependencies of Zante. { Trenta Nove. Peluso. Marathonissi. Yami. St. Nicolo. Strofades. } Small Islands or Rocks			
CERIGO (*Cythera*)...........................	21	13	116
Dependencies of Cerigo. { Sedro. Dragonera. Kouphenisia. Ovo. Elaphonesia. Milo Potamo. Plataues. } Small Islands or Rocks round Cerigo.			
Cerigotto	7	2½	
Porri. Poretti. Nautilus. { Rocks round Cerigotto.			

N.B. In that excellent publication, "The Almanack of Gotha," it was erroneously stated that *Petala* and *the Echinades* formed part of the United States of the Ionian Islands. They belonged, however, to the Kingdom of Greece ever since its formation.

I.

Population of the Ionian Islands under the Venetians, as far as known to Author.

	1558.	1578.	1588.	1601.	1602.	1611.	1613.	1616.	1620.	1622.	1760.
Corfu	...	19,221	19,635	...	22,170	23,800	25,460	27,051	...	...	48,484
Cephalonia	...	...	...	30,828	...	...	...	...	50,000	...	...
Zante	21,500	22,543	...	...	...	...	...	...	...	...	30,000
Santa Maura	...	...	...	...	...	...	...	...	...	...	...
Ithaca	...	...	...	...	...	...	...	...	...	2,500	...
Cerigo	...	3,263	...	...	...	...	...	...	...	...	...
Paxo	...	...	...	...	...	...	...	...	...	...	...

Population of the Ionian Islands in the present Century, as far as known to Author.

	1802.	1811.	1828.	1833.	1844.	1848.	1856.	1858.	1860.	1862.	1863.	1864.
Corfu...	45,000	...	...	40,000*	64,566	68,374	67,930	68,863	72,967	...	...	73,453
Cephalonia	...	...	...	60,000	65,614	69,403	69,926	71,747	71,482	72,787	...	...
Zante	...	32,843	...	30,000	...	...	...	37,257	39,455	39,693	40,141	...
Santa Maura	...	...	18,000	...	...	...	...	20,228	23,466	...	...	...
Ithaca	...	...	...	...	10,685	...	...	11,581	...	...	11,950	...
Cerigo	...	...	...	...	...	...	...	13,497	...	14,500†	...	...
Paxo	...	...	...	...	...	...	...	4,636	4,789	...	...	...

* An error in the calculations of Sir Charles Napier. 50,000 at least it should have been.

† As furnished by the Commandant of Cerigo; but it appears too great a number.

N.B. As a general rule the dependencies are included in the populations of the Seven Islands. But I suspect that this has not always been the case, as in the numbers given for Santa Maura in 1858. For in 1860 there is an improbably great increase in two years of more than 3000 souls.

K.

Return of the Population, and of the Marriages, Births, and Deaths in 1858.

Islands.	Males.	Females.	Aliens and Resident Strangers not included in the preceding Column.	Population to the Square Mile.	Persons employed in			Births.	Marriages.	Deaths.
					Agriculture.	Manufacture.	Commerce.			
Corfu	33,034	29,769	6,060	303	17,000	2,000	1,500	1,894	722	1,336
Cephalonia ...	39,918	31,829	1,927	231	16,957	3,252	1,046	1,754	457	1,192
Zante	19,651	17,308	298	230	7,738	1,368	539	1,287	351	850
Santa Maura .	10,658	9,470	100	129	3,140	200	385	243	213	150
Ithaca	6,080	5,487	14	262	3,000	300	1,900	268	76	211
Cerigo	7,281	6,174	42	116	2,550	660	810	326	74	210
Paxo	2,285	2,351	...	180	360	...	330	90	51	97
Total......	118,907	102,388	8,441	1,451	50,745	7,780	6,510	5,871	1,944	4,046

L.

Population in Detail of Corfu for three different years.

	1848.			1860.					1864.				
				Natives.		Foreigners.			Natives.		Foreigners.		
	Males.	Females.	Total.	Males.	Females.	Males.	Females.	Total.	Males.	Females.	Males.	Females.	Total.
Town	9,277	7,195	16,472	6,749	6,497	2,496	1,957	17,699	5,949	5,718	2,960	2,482	17,114
Suburbs ...	4,196	3,885	8,081	3,793	3,304	708	508	8,313	3,500	3,068	1,054	845	8,467
Country ...	22,653	19,558	42,211	23,659	20,584	531	440	45,214	24,053	20,990	623	489	46,155
Islets	844	766	1,610	874	858	7	2	1,741	840	851	13	13	1,717
Total ...	36,970	31,404	68,374	35,075	31,243	3,742	2,907	72,967	34,342	30,627	4,650	3,829	73,453

M.

Table of Births, Marriages, and Deaths in Corfu, from 1st January, 1854, to 31st December, 1863.—10 years.

Year.	Births.	Marriages.	Deaths.
1854	2,324	551	1,621
1855*	1,923	424	2,222
1856	1,918	718	1,553
1857	2,147	444	1,630
1858	2,106	717	1,541
1859	2,428	589	1,381
1860	2,274	447	1,561
1861	1,991	484	1,354
1862	2,589	513	1,639
1863†	2,303	503	2,464
Totals.	22,003	5,390	16,966

Total Births 22,003
Total Deaths 16,966

Surplus of Births over Deaths 5,037

* There was Cholera in Corfu this year.
† This year there was Small-pox.

List of Articles, both of Exports and Imports, the Duties on which form part of the Revenue of Corfu.

	1844.			1845.			1846.			1856.			1857.			1858.			1861.			1862.		
	£	s.	d.	£	s.	d.	£	s.	d.	£	s.	d.	£	s.	d.	£	s.	d.	£	s.	d.	£	s.	d.
Merchandise	12,735	5	3^{5}/.*	17,763	0	6^{5}/.	16,252	13	1^{9}/.	19,385	9	0^{8}/.	17,749	14	7^{2}/.	21,420	1	4^{2}/.	23,864	13	2^{4}/.	23,761	5	4^{2}/.
Oil (export)	6,383	5	7^{4}/.	21,308	1	10	4,746	4	6^{8}/.	30,766	9	8^{5}/.	4,925	5	0^{8}/.	56,777	0	10^{7}/.	21,552	12	7^{2}/.	15,343	19	7^{1}/.
Foreign Wines	233	2	1^{5}/.	262	15	8^{5}/.	253	14	7	449	18	6^{5}/.	212	19	11^{7}/.	358	7	2^{2}/.	250	10	8^{2}/.	420	18	6^{3}/.
Wines from the Islands (exported)	349	13	5^{6}/.	707	15	9^{4}/.	575	1	7^{2}/.	186	19	10^{1}/.	436	7	10^{1}/.	834	16	9^{4}/.	1,806	10	2^{6}/.	1,710	1	0^{4}/.
Foreign Spirits	654	17	9^{6}/.	734	4	0	799	15	10^{2}/.	4,141	12	0^{1}/.	2,887	11	8	2,340	13	4^{8}/.	2,050	19	8^{1}/.	1,734	0	6^{1}/.
Animals	1,335	10	8	1,564	0	2	1,318	1	10	1,631	7	10	1,157	13	0	1,319	1	4	2,000	16	2	1,532	5	4
Grains	8,493	8	6^{5}/.	7,978	12	8^{5}/.	7,727	15	0^{7}/.	7,302	10	2^{4}/.	7,195	18	1^{7}/.	8,524	2	6^{3}/.	8,796	8	1^{3}/.	9,276	15	1^{3}/.
Tobacco	1,045	14	8	1,171	12	10^{9}/.	765	14	8^{5}/.	1,611	7	2^{6}/.	1,065	10	9^{2}/.	1,469	2	1^{5}/.	1,711	10	5^{1}/.	1,578	19	2^{8}/.
Flour	83	19	7^{2}/.	86	18	9^{4}/.	93	17	10^{2}/.	346	9	8^{8}/.	294	16	9^{6}/.	268	5	0^{8}/.	331	12	4^{7}/.	443	19	8^{9}/.
Soap (export)	72	10	1^{8}/.	98	17	3^{6}/.	247	8	8	604	2	3^{6}/.	1,056	5	5^{1}/.	962	9	8^{4}/.	1,298	0	6^{3}/.	922	7	11^{1}/.
Acorns (chiefly exported)	...	...		23	6	5^{7}/.	2	18	1	0	1	7^{4}/.	13	14	11^{3}/.	29	14	5^{3}/.	10	14	0	13	5	6^{5}/.
Corfu Wines (export)	3	16	3^{6}/.	1	11	8^{5}/.	2	9	9	86	12	5^{4}/.	37	15	7^{4}/.	14	15	8^{6}/.	29	9	9^{7}/.	10	10	4^{7}/.
Transit	362	6	4^{4}/.	591	16	9	565	15	10^{2}/.	...	...		0	12	8^{3}/.	4	16	7^{7}/.	1	18	10^{2}/.	3	5	1^{3}/.
Custom House Fees	664	12	4^{8}/.	667	9	1^{2}/.	833	15	3^{9}/.	...	...		...	...		...	...		...	...		...	...	
Storeage	745	9	7^{7}/.	769	19	4	709	3	3^{7}/.	1,342	6	6^{3}/.	1,168	18	9	938	7	6	967	5	10^{2}/.	931	9	3^{5}/.
Contraband Goods, Fines, &c.	1	0	0	24	12	4	0	16	8^{9}/.	1	12	0^{4}/.	6	7	7^{5}/.	2	18	2^{8}/.	1	7	10^{5}/.	3	0	0^{7}/.
Coral Fishery	3	9	3^{6}/.	...	...		...	...		...	...		4	9	2^{8}/.	...	...		20	17	11^{6}/.	...	...	
Extra Store Fees, &c.	0	5	0	...	...		1	10	7^{9}/.	...	...		...	...		...	...		...	...		...	...	
Surplus Porterage	...	...		...	...		...	...		140	0	0	30	0	0	...	...		...	...		271	6	8^{9}/.
Home Productions and Manufactures, 1¼ per cent. (export duty)	644	4	6^{7}/.	1,899	16	2^{4}/.	556	0	3^{6}/.	2,867	6	1^{7}/.	826	3	5^{2}/.	5,087	1	10	2,254	19	6^{3}/.	1,664	12	11^{1}/.
Bullocks, 4s. 4d. each	1,298	1	0	1,477	0	4	1,213	11	0	1,537	9	4	1,093	19	0	1,259	14	0	1,018	10	4	1,480	9	6
Sheep, Lambs, Calves, 1s. 7½d. each	316	1	10^{5}/.	736	13	1^{5}/.	601	6	10^{5}/.	576	11	10^{5}/.	218	10	7^{5}/.	372	3	9	849	13	1^{5}/.	878	13	1^{5}/.
Sale by Government of — Salt	2,084	5	9^{4}/.	2,177	7	7^{6}/.	2,155	7	4^{5}/.	2,144	8	2	2,229	2	11	1,466	17	8^{4}/.	1,291	11	8	1,327	3	4^{7}/.
Powder	432	3	5^{3}/.	550	2	0^{3}/.	521	11	10^{7}/.	1,513	14	5	1,185	2	8^{2}/.	1,380	19	0^{7}/.	1,335	11	7^{4}/.	1,569	19	10^{8}/.
Stamped Paper	4,715	2	5^{9}/.	6,150	3	3^{2}/.	5,222	5	4^{7}/.	5,922	9	3^{8}/.	4,311	14	2	7,185	8	1^{5}/.	6,063	10	6^{1}/.	5,631	5	10^{1}/.
Debt of Signor Trombetta	188	7	5^{2}/.	...	...		...	...		...	...		...	...		...	...		1	15	6^{5}/.	49	4	11^{5}/.
Fees on Goods transferred in Custom House	...	...		...	...		...	...		2	17	6	4	5	0	3	2	6	1	2	6	5	2	6
	42,796	13	5^{8}/.	66,765	18	0^{4}/.	45,167	0	5^{1}/.	82,564	14	6^{8}/.	48,112	19	11^{3}/.	112,019	19	9^{8}/.	78,412	9	2	70,564	1	8^{9}/.

* The Fractions are in Ionian Currency of 10 Ceptas to a Penny.

O.

Export of Currants from Cephalonia and the Duty (altogether 19½ per cent.) paid thereon from the Year 1823 to 1863.

Year.	lbs.	£	s.	d.
1823	5,663,917	14,948	11	7
1824	5,199,491	12,947	6	0
1825	5,539,704	14,726	11	$6\frac{9}{15}$
1826	7,116,495	17,004	7	1
1827	6,781,725	17,147	8	$5\frac{5}{15}$
1828	8,299,630	19,914	6	$7\frac{4}{15}$
1829	7,795,951	15,671	10	10
1830	9,271,971	19,073	17	$3\frac{3}{15}$
Totals of 8 years...	55,668,884	131,433	19	$5\frac{3}{15}$

Year.	lbs.	£	s.	d.
1859	14,368,533	17,883	10	$11\frac{4}{15}$
1860	17,411,504	16,161	14	9
1861	14,083,687	14,133	2	7
1862	17,936,624	16,376	4	$7\frac{1}{15}$
1863	17,556,182	17,384	2	$10\frac{4}{15}$
Totals of 5 years...	81,356,530	81,938	15	$9\frac{4}{15}$

Amount of Tonnage of Vessels and Steamers Arrived and Sailed in the Ionian Islands during the following Years :

Flags.	1840.	1854.	1855.	1858.	1859.	1860.	1861.	1862.	1863.
Ionian	121,700	150,000	97,600	127,000	147,700	142,800	157,700	165,600	141,200
English	29,200	34,100	43,500	87,700	87,900	97,800	118,400	143,400	121,200
Austrian	42,600	163,000	139,400	191,800	155,800	196,000	215,400	222,700	225,600
French	770	3,310	3,500	2,400	300	1,300	1,700	1,900	3,500
Neapolitan	5,900	11,400	9,300	15,000	19,200	13,200 } Italian.	19,000	39,400	75,900
Papal	730	2,900	2,800	3,400	2,700	3,300 }			
Sardinian	4,100	5,700	2,500	2,200	1,800	4,500 }			
Ottoman	3,600	19,500	9,000	12,200	10,400	7,700	21,300	41,400	20,500
Greek	46,200	45,000	45,700	50,300	71,400	85,300	86,600	93,250	77,000
Russian	16,800	790	500	1,000	2,000	3,300	6,500	5,450	4,600
Other Nations	4,000	15,300	8,200	17,000	18,800	23,800	20,400	17,900	9,500
Totals	275,600	451,000	362,000	510,000	518,000	579,000	647,000	731,000	682,000

Q.

Miscellaneous Statistics.

Islands.	Population in 1858.		Freeholders.	Paupers.	Depositors in Savings Bank.	Hospitals.	Lunatic Asylums.	Almshouses.	Foundling Hospitals.	Number of Inmates.
	Males.	Females.								
Corfu	33,034	29,769	2,239	250	457	1	1	1	1	1053
Cephalonia	39,910	31,829	10,000	1000	10	1	...	...	...	193
Zante	19,651	17,308	1,117	937	90	2	...	1	1	470
Santa Maura	10,658	9,470	3,600	40	...	1	...	...	...	16
Ithaca	6,080	5,487	1,500	20	...	...	...	...	...	...
Cerigo	7,281	6,174	2,300	...	...	...	...	...	...	...
Paxo	2,285	2,351	580	...	...	...	...	...	...	...

R.

SUMMARY OF THE IONIAN ISLANDS' DEBT,

Made after the Debate in the Assembly on the Subject in October, 1863.

	Debt due 31st August, 1863.	Remarks.
	£ *s.* *d.*	
To the Civil List Pension Chest	97 13 11¹⁄.	
From the Pension Fund of the Constabulary	3,472 14 5°⁄.	

To the Mocenigo Legacy
    Capital £41,675   3   8
    Interest unpaid...   3,232   8   6
	44,007 12 2	

Government Orders	75,085 11 8	
Debts of Government to New Pension Fund	13,458 0 0	Capital to 31st August, 1863; since then the Treasury has contracted another Debt of £5,058.
Debts of Government to Private Funds...	2,693 18 7	
To Administration of the Revenue of the Salt Mines of Santa Maura	642 10 3°⁄.	
Money borrowed by the Government from the Ionian Bank.......................	70,800 0 0	
Borrowed from the Savings Banks of { Corfu ......£10,366 4 2²⁄. Cephalonia. 50 0 8 Zante ...... 30 18 9⁷⁄. Sta. Maura 9 7 10 Cerigo ...... 6 8 8 Paxo 0 5 0		
Public treasury... 2,214 4 9³⁄.		
Borrowed from Municipal Chests of { Corfu ...... 1,127 13 3¹⁄. Cephalonia. 1,651 16 6¹⁄. Zante ...... 1,233 9 7 Sta. Maura 645 12 6³⁄. Ithaca ...... 348 9 11¹⁄. Cerigo... ... 732 6 8¹⁄. Paxo ...... 387 1 4°⁄.	18,803 19 10⁷⁄.	
To the Convent of St. Gerassimo at Cephalonia	74 4 2³⁄.	For Land occupied as Fortifications by the French, the owners of which were indemnified by instalments for a certain number of years.
French Indemnity Fund	427 16 1°⁄.	
Carried forward............	229,959 1 4³⁄.	

Appendix R (*continued*).

				Debt due 31st August, 1863.			Remarks.
				£	s.	d.	
Brought forward......				229,950	1	4³/.	
To the chest of Indemnities and Succours	Cephalonia	£22	15	10⁹/.			
	Zante	48	12	0			
	Ithaca ...	58	19	2⁸/.			
	Paxo	8	2	4			
				138	9	5⁷/.	
Corfu Bank of Agriculture		0	15	4¹/.			
Cerigo.........		13	16	8³/.			
				14	12	0⁸/.	
Aqueduct of Corfu				1,863	3	0⁷/.	{ The administration of the Aqueduct is private.
Unsecularized Convents of Santa Maura				0	7	2³/.	
Penitentiary of Corfu.........................				100	8	2²/.	
Lyceum Fund (students' annual subscription of 4s. a head)				430	9	6¹/.	
Total debt of the Ionian Islands up to the 31st August, 1863				232,506	10	10¹/.	

THE END.

C. WHITING, BEAUFORT HOUSE, STRAND.

Four Years in the Ionian Islands:

Their Political and Social Condition; With
a History of the British Protectorate. In Two
Volumes. Edited by VISCOUNT KIRKWALL.

Chapman and Hall, 193, Piccadilly.

EXTRACTS FROM REVIEWS.

EXAMINER.

" This book is a very interesting one, full of information that
could hardly have been given by one not closely connected with the
English Protectorate, but also the result of independent thought and
impartial judgment."

SATURDAY REVIEW.

" Whoever he may be—military, civilian, diplomatic or unattached
traveller—he is a man gifted with a good deal of practical observation,
a strong generous sentiment, a certain power of sharp and sarcastic
writing........ He has taken not inconsiderable pains in gathering, and
rendering himself competent to gather, local information, as well as in
consulting the authorities in Ionian matters published before his own
times......... Our impartial Author can point out flaws in the policy
of almost every Lord High Commissioner, but he can also point to the
marks of excellent intentions well and wisely carried into execution.
.... The newest and most valuable portion of these volumes
is that which relates to Cephalonia........... Andrea Lascarato,
the great Ionian satirical writer, is, next to Napier, the most interesting
personage whom we come across in these pages."

SPECTATOR.

(Referring to the Introduction,) " Lord Kirkwall gives an able and
concise sketch of the more important features of the Venetian
Government." *(After reviewing the History of eight of the ten Lord
High Commissioners,)* " The remainder of his narrative is very clear

In post 8vo. 5s.

THE POCKET DATE BOOK;

Or, Classified Tables of Dates of the Principal Facts, Historical, Biographical, and Scientific, from the Beginning of the World to the Present Time.

By WILLIAM L. R. CATES.   [*Now ready.*

THE TIMES, *November 28, 1863.*

'Mr. Cates, in his *Pocket-book of Dates,* has really done good service. He is evidently a lover of historical accuracy, and wishes every one to be like himself. In addition to a catalogue of names the year of birth and death of each individual, his birth-place, and principal works, literary, military, artistic, or scientific, are also added, and the dry bones of chronology thereby made to assume a faint vitality. All this has been done carefully and well; great facts have not been over-laid by little ones, and much judgment has been shown in the omission of many subordinate events. We have only to add that the type and printing are clear and accurate, and that the "get up" of the book adds another merit to those already mentioned.'

DYCE'S SHAKESPEARE.

'The best text of Shakespeare which has yet appeared. . . . Mr. Dyce's edition is a great work, worthy of his reputation, and for the present it contains the standard text.'—*Times,* January 20, 1864.

A New Edition, to be completed in Eight Volumes, demy 8vo., 10s. each,

THE WORKS OF SHAKESPEARE.

Edited by the Rev. ALEXANDER DYCE.

This Edition is not a mere reprint of that which appeared in 1857; on the contrary, it will present a text very materially altered and amended from beginning to end, with a large body of critical Notes, almost entirely new, and with a Glossary, in which the language of the poet, his allusions to customs, &c., will be fully explained.

To be published every alternate Month. Vols. I. and II. now ready.

Sixth Edition, in Four Volumes, fcap. 8vo., with Portrait, 24s.

ELIZABETH BARRETT BROWNING'S POETICAL WORKS.

Including 'AURORA LEIGH.'   [*Now ready.*

A New Edition, in Three Volumes, fcap. 8vo.

ROBERT BROWNING'S POETICAL WORKS.

Vol. I.—LYRICS, ROMANCES, MEN AND WOMEN, 7s.   Vol. II.—TRAGEDIES, AND OTHER PLAYS, 8s
Vol. III.—PARACELSUS, CHRISTMAS-EVE AND EASTER-DAY, AND SORDELLO, 7s. 6d.

*** Sold separately.   [*Now ready.*

Collected Edition, in Three Volumes, fcap. 8vo., 16s.

HENRY TAYLOR'S PLAYS AND POEMS.

PHILIP VAN ARTEVELDE, &c.   [*Now ready.*

In One Volume, post 8vo. with Illustrations, 12s.

SPORT IN NORWAY, AND WHERE TO FIND IT.

Together with a Short Account of the Vegetable Productions of the Country. To which is added,
a List of the Alpine Flora of the Dovre Fjeld, and of the Norwegian Ferns.

By M. R. BARNARD, B.A.

Late Chaplain to the British Consulate, Christiania, Norway.

In One Volume, post 8vo., 8s. 6d.

CURIOSITIES OF INDO-EUROPEAN TRADITION AND FOLK LORE.

By WALTER K. KELLY.

In post 8vo., 4s. 6d.

THE GENTLEWOMAN.

By the Author of 'Dinners and Dinner Parties.'

New Edition, in One Volume post 8vo., with Illustrations by MARCUS STONE, 7s. 6d.

A CHILD'S HISTORY OF ENGLAND.

By CHARLES DICKENS.

NEW SERIALS.

NEW SERIAL BY ANTHONY TROLLOPE.

To be completed in Twenty Monthly Parts, uniform with 'ORLEY FARM.'

CAN YOU FORGIVE HER?

By ANTHONY TROLLOPE,

Author of 'Dr. Thorne,' 'Rachel Ray,' &c.

With Illustrations. Parts I. and II., price 1s. each.   [*Now ready.*

NEW SERIAL BY CHARLES LEVER.

LUTTRELL OF ARRAN.

By CHARLES LEVER.

Author of 'Harry Lorrequer,' 'Charles O'Malley,' &c.

With Illustrations by PHIZ. Parts I., II., and III., price 1s. each.   [*Now ready.*

NEW NOVELS.

GEORGE MEREDITH'S NEW NOVEL.
In 3 vols. post 8vo.

EMILIA IN ENGLAND.
By GEORGE MEREDITH.
Author of 'The Ordeal of Richard Feverel,' 'The Shaving of Shagpat,' &c.
[*In March.*

MR. THOMAS ADOLPHUS TROLLOPE'S NEW NOVEL.
In 2 vols. post 8vo.

BEPPO THE CONSCRIPT.
By THOMAS ADOLPHUS TROLLOPE.
Author of 'Marietta,' 'Giulio Malatesta,' &c.   [*23rd February.*

In 1 vol. post 8vo.

NOT QUITE THE THING.   [*In February.*

BY THE AUTHOR OF 'CHARLIE THORNHILL.'
In 2 vols. post 8vo., 21s.

A BOX FOR THE SEASON.
By CHARLES CLARKE.
Author of 'Charlie Thornhill.'   [*Now ready.*

In 2 vols. post 8vo., 21s.

THE TOWN OF THE CASCADES.
By MICHAEL BANIM,
Survivor of the O'Hara Family, and Author of several of the 'O'Hara Tales.'
[*Now ready.*

In post 8vo., 10s. 6d.

DAN TO BEERSHEBA.
Or, NORTHERN AND SOUTHERN FRIENDS.   [*Now ready.*

In 1 vol. post 8vo.

VLADIMIR AND CATHERINE;
Or, KEIV in the YEAR 1861. An Historical Romance.
By A THIRTY YEARS' RESIDENT IN RUSSIA.   [*Now ready.*

In 2 vols. post 8vo., 21*s*.

LLOYD PENNANT. A TALE OF THE WEST.

By RALPH NEVILLE.   *[Now ready.*

In 3 vols. post 8vo., 31*s*. 6*d*.

SIR GOODWIN'S FOLLY.

A STORY OF THE YEAR 1795.

By ARTHUR LOCKER.   *[Now ready.*

ANTHONY TROLLOPE'S NEW NOVEL.

In 2 vols. post 8vo.

RACHEL RAY.

By ANTHONY TROLLOPE.

[Sixth Edition now ready.

JUST PUBLISHED.

In royal 8vo., price 6*s*. No. III. (January, 1864).

THE FINE ARTS QUARTERLY REVIEW.

Editor—B. B. WOODWARD, F.S.A.,

Librarian in Ordinary to the Queen, and Keeper of Prints and Drawings, Windsor Castle.

CONTENTS.

I. THE CAMIRUS VASE (*with an Illustration in Chromo-Lithography*).
II. THE LOAN COLLECTION AT SOUTH KENSINGTON.—II.
III. RAPHAEL'S SCHOOL OF ATHENS.
IV. MODERN FRENCH ETCHINGS (*with Two Plates*).
V. EARLY HISTORY OF THE ROYAL ACADEMY.—II.
VI. HORACE VERNET.
VII. CATALOGUE OF PICTURES BELONGING TO THE SOCIETY OF ANTIQUARIES.
VIII. POUSSIN DRAWINGS IN THE ROYAL COLLECTION.—II.
IX. 'WHO WAS FRANCESCO DA BOLOGNA?'—II.
X. WORKS OF CORNELIUS VISSCHER.—III.
XI. RECENT ADDITIONS TO THE NATIONAL GALLERY.
XII. RECENT ADDITIONS TO THE NATIONAL PORTRAIT GALLERY.
XIII. RECORD OF THE FINE ARTS.
TITLE, PREFACE, AND INDEX TO VOL. I.

A CATALOGUE OF BOOKS

PUBLISHED BY

CHAPMAN AND HALL,

193, PICCADILLY.

ADAMS (EDWIN) — GEOGRAPHY CLASSIFIED:
a Systematic Manual of Mathematical, Physical, and Political Geography, with Geographical, Etymological, and Historical Notes. For the use of Teachers and Upper Forms in Schools. By EDWIN ADAMS, F.R.G.S., Author of 'The Geographical Word Expositor and Dictionary.' Crown 8vo. cloth. 7s. 6d.;

————— **(W. B.) — ROADS AND RAILS, AND THEIR**
PRACTICAL INFLUENCE ON HUMAN PROGRESS, PAST, PRESENT, AND TO COME. By W. BRIDGES ADAMS. 1 vol. post 8vo. 10s. 6d.

AINSWORTH — CARDINAL POLE; or, The Days of
Philip and Mary. An Historical Romance. By WILLIAM HARRISON AINSWORTH. 3 vols. post 8vo. cloth. 1l. 11s. 6d.

————————— **THE LORD MAYOR OF LONDON.**
By WILLIAM HARRISON AINSWORTH. 3 vols. post 8vo. 1l. 11s. 6d. New and Cheaper Edition, in 1 vol. crown 8vo. 5s.

————————— **THE CONSTABLE OF THE TOWER.**
Third Edition. 1 vol. crown 8vo. 5s.

ALL THE YEAR ROUND.
Conducted by CHARLES DICKENS. Vols. I. to VIII., handsomely bound. 5s. 6d. each.

ALISON — THE PHILOSOPHY AND HISTORY OF
CIVILIZATION. By ALEXANDER ALISON. Demy 8vo. cloth. 14s.

ATLASES AND MAPS,
FOR STUDENTS AND TRAVELLERS; with Railways and Telegraphs, accurately laid down.

SHARPE'S ATLAS. Constructed upon a System of Scale and Proportion, from the more recent Authorities. With a Copious Index. Fifty-four Maps. Large folio, half morocco, plain, 36s.; coloured, 42s.

SHARPE'S STUDENT'S ATLAS. With a Copious Index. Twenty-six Coloured Maps, selected from the above. Folio, half-bound. 21s.

LOWRY'S TABLE ATLAS. With a Copious Index. One Hundred Coloured Maps. Large 4to. half-bound. 12s.

SIDNEY HALL'S TRAVELLING ATLAS OF THE ENGLISH COUNTIES, containing Fifty Maps, bound in a portable 8vo. Volume, in roan tuck. 10s. 6d.

SIDNEY HALL'S ATLAS OF THE ENGLISH COUNTIES, Enlarged Series, with General Maps of Great Britain, Scotland, Ireland, and Wales. 4to. half-bound, 24s., and folio, half-bound, 24s.

ATLASES AND MAPS—*continued.*

SIDNEY HALL'S MAPS OF ENGLISH COUNTIES, Enlarged Series, with all the Railways and Country Seats. Coloured, in neat wrapper, price 6d. each.

SHARPE'S TRAVELLING MAP OF ENGLAND AND WALES, with Railways and Electric Telegraph laid down to the present time. Coloured and mounted, in cloth case, 2s. 6d.

SHARPE'S TRAVELLING MAP OF SCOTLAND, with Railways and Electric Telegraph laid down to the present time. Coloured and mounted, in cloth case, 1s. 6d.

SHARPE'S TRAVELLING MAP OF IRELAND, with Railways and Electric Telegraph laid down to the present time. Coloured and mounted, in cloth case 1s. 6d.

AUSTIN—TWO LETTERS ON GIRLS' SCHOOLS,
and on the Training of Working Women. By Mrs. AUSTIN. Post 8vo. sewed. 1s.

BAGEHOT—ESTIMATES OF SOME ENGLISHMEN
AND SCOTCHMEN: A Series of Essays contributed principally to the 'National Review.' By WALTER BAGEHOT. Demy 8vo. cloth. 14s.

BARHAM—PHILADELPHIA; OR, THE CLAIMS OF
HUMANITY: A PLEA FOR SOCIAL AND RELIGIOUS REFORM. By THOMAS FOSTER BARHAM, M.B. Cantab. Post 8vo. cloth. 6s. 6d.

BARNARD—SPORT IN NORWAY AND WHERE TO
FIND IT. Together with a Short Account of the Vegetable Productions of the Country. To which is added, a List of the Alpine Flora of the Dovre Fjeld, and of the Norwegian Ferns. By M. R. BARNARD, B.A., late Chaplain to the British Consulate, Christiania, Norway. With Illustrations. 1 vol. post 8vo., cloth. 12s.

BARRY CORNWALL—ENGLISH SONGS, AND
OTHER POEMS. By BARRY CORNWALL. New Edition, 24mo. sewed. 2s. 6d.

BEEVER (REV. W HOLT)—NOTES ON FIELDS
AND CATTLE, from the Diary of an Amateur Farmer. With Illustrations. 1 vol post 8vo. 8s. 6d.

BELLEW—LIFE IN CHRIST, AND CHRIST IN
LIFE. A NEW VOLUME OF SERMONS. By the Rev. J. M. BELLEW. 8vo. cloth. 12s.

BLAGDEN (ISABELLA)—THE COST OF A SECRET.
By the Author of 'Agnes Tremorne.' 3 vols. post 8vo. cloth. 31s. 6d.

BLANC (LOUIS) — HISTORICAL REVELATIONS.
Post 8vo., cloth. 10s. 6d.

BLANCHARD (SIDNEY LAMAN) — THE GANGES
AND THE SEINE: Scenes on the Banks of Both. By SIDNEY LAMAN BLANCHARD. 2 vols. post 8vo. cloth. 18s.

BLYTH (COLONEL)—WHIST-PLAYER.
Imp. 16mo. Second edition. 5s.

BORDER LANDS OF SPAIN AND FRANCE (THE);
WITH AN ACCOUNT OF A VISIT TO THE REPUBLIC OF ANDORRE. Post 8vo cloth. 10s. 6d.

BOURNE—A MEMOIR OF SIR PHILIP SIDNEY.
By H. H. R. FOX BOURNE. 1 vol. demy 8vo. 15s.

BRADLEY—ELEMENTS OF GEOMETRICAL DRAW-
ING, OR PRACTICAL GEOMETRY, PLANE AND SOLID. By THOMAS BRADLEY, of the Royal Military College, Woolwich. In Two Parts. Illustrated by Sixty Plates, engraved by J. W. Lowry. Oblong folio, cloth. Each 16s.

BROWNE—HUNTING BITS.
By H. K. BROWNE (Phiz). Twelve Coloured Illustrations. Oblong folio, half bound 1l. 1s.

————————————————————. Proofs. 1l. 11s. 6d.

BROWNING (E. B.) — POETICAL WORKS.
By ELIZABETH BARRETT BROWNING. Sixth Edition, with Portrait. Including AURORA LEIGH. Four vols. fcap. cloth. 24s.

———————————— AURORA LEIGH; A POEM.
IN NINE BOOKS. By ELIZABETH BARRETT BROWNING. Sixth Edition, with Portrait of Mrs. Browning. One vol. fcap. cloth. 7s.

———————————— LAST POEMS.
Second Edition. 1 vol. crown 8vo. 6s.

———————————— POEMS BEFORE CONGRESS.
By ELIZABETH BARRETT BROWNING. Crown 8vo. cloth. 4s.

———————————— THE GREEK CHRISTIAN
POETS, AND THE ENGLISH POETS. By ELIZABETH BARRETT BROWNING. Fcap. 8vo. cloth. 5s.

BROWNING (ROBERT) — THE POETICAL WORKS
OF ROBERT BROWNING. A New Edition, containing all the Poems formerly published in seven volumes. Complete in 3 vols. fcap. 8vo. Sold separately.

    Vol. 1. LYRICS, ROMANCES, MEN AND WOMEN 7/
    Vol. 2. TRAGEDIES, AND OTHER PLAYS 8/
    Vol. 3. PARACELSUS, CHRISTMAS-EVE AND EASTER-DAY, AND SORDELLO 7/6

———————————— MEN AND WOMEN.
BY ROBERT BROWNING. In two vols. fcap. 8vo. cloth. 12s.

———————————— CHRISTMAS - EVE AND
EASTER-DAY. A POEM. By ROBERT BROWNING. Fcap. 8vo. cloth. 6s.

———————————— A SELECTION FROM THE
POEMS OF ROBERT BROWNING. Fcap. 8vo. cloth. 6s.

BURCHETT — LINEAR PERSPECTIVE.
For the Use of Schools of Art. By R. BURCHETT, Head Master of the Training Schools for Art Masters of the Science and Art Department. Fifth Edition. Post 8vo. cloth, with Illustrations. 7s.

———————————— PRACTICAL GEOMETRY.
THE COURSE OF CONSTRUCTION OF PLANE GEOMETRICAL FIGURES. By R. BURCHETT. With 137 Diagrams. Fifth Edition. Post 8vo. cloth. 5s.

BURCHETT — DEFINITIONS OF GEOMETRY.
24mo. sewed. 5d.

BUTT — THE HISTORY OF ITALY FROM THE
ABDICATION OF NAPOLEON I.   With Introductory References to that of Earlier
Times. Two vols. 8vo. cloth. 36s.

CÆCILIA METELLA ;
Or, ROME ENSLAVED. Post 8vo. cloth. 10s. 6d.

CANNING — KILSORREL CASTLE.
By the Hon. ALBERT CANNING. 2 vols. post 8vo. cloth. 21s.

MR. THOMAS CARLYLE'S WORKS.
UNIFORM EDITION.
Handsomely printed in Crown Octavo, price Six Shillings per Volume.

THE FRENCH REVOLUTION: A HISTORY. In 2 Volumes. 12s.

OLIVER CROMWELL'S LETTERS AND SPEECHES. With Eluci-
dations and Connecting Narrative. In 3 Volumes. 18s.

LIFE OF JOHN STERLING.
LIFE OF SCHILLER.   } One Vol. 6s.

CRITICAL AND MISCELLANEOUS ESSAYS. In 4 Volumes. 24s.

SARTOR RESARTUS.
HERO WORSHIP.   } One Volume. 6s.

LATTER-DAY PAMPHLETS. One Volume. 6s.

CHARTISM.
PAST AND PRESENT.   } One Volume. 6s.

TRANSLATIONS OF GERMAN ROMANCE. One Volume. 6s.

WILHELM MEISTER. By GÖTHE. A Translation. In 2 Volumes. 12s.
Sets, in 16 vols., crown 8vo., cloth, 4l. 16s.

CARLYLE — HISTORY OF FRIEDRICH THE SECOND,
called FREDERICK THE GREAT. By THOMAS CARLYLE. With Portraits and Maps.
Third Edition. Vols. I. and II., Third Edition, demy 8vo. cloth. 40s. Vol. III., demy
8vo. cloth. 20s. Vol. IV., 20s., now ready.

CATES — THE POCKET DATE-BOOK ; or, Classified
Tables of Dates of the Principal Facts, Historical, Biographical, and Scientific, from the
Beginning of the World to the Present Time. By WILLIAM L. R. CATES. Small
Post 8vo. cloth. 6s.

CLARKE — BOX FOR THE SEASON.
By CHARLES CLARKE, Author of 'Charlie Thornhill.' 2 vols. post 8vo., cloth. 1l. 1s.

———— CHARLIE THORNHILL ; or, The Dunce of
the Family. A Sporting Novel. By CHARLES CLARKE. Crown 8vo. 5s.

Chapman & Hall's Select Library of Fiction.

PRICE TWO SHILLINGS EACH NOVEL.

MARY BARTON: a Tale of Manchester Life. By Mrs. GASKELL.

RUTH. A Novel. By the Author of 'Mary Barton.'

CRANFORD. By the Author of 'Mary Barton.'

LIZZIE LEIGH; and other Tales. By the Author of 'Mary Barton.'

THE HEAD OF THE FAMILY. A Novel. By Miss MULOCK.

AGATHA'S HUSBAND. By the Author of 'The Head of the Family.'

OLIVE. A Novel. By the Author of 'The Head of the Family.'

THE OGILVIES. A Novel. By the Author of 'The Head of the Family.'

THE BACHELOR OF THE ALBANY. By M. W. SAVAGE.

MY UNCLE THE CURATE. A Novel. By M. W. SAVAGE.

THE HALF SISTERS. A Tale. By Miss JEWSBURY.

THE BLITHEDALE ROMANCE. By NATHANIEL HAWTHORNE.

MAN OF THE WORLD. By S. FULLOM.

ROBERT BLAKE, Admiral and General at Sea. By HEPWORTH DIXON.

THE ORPHANS. By Mrs. OLIPHANT.

KATHERINE AND HER SISTERS. By Lady EMILY PONSONBY.

ELSIE VENNER. By O. W. HOLMES.

MARY SEAHAM. By Mrs. GREY, Author of 'The Gambler's Wife.'

THE LIFE AND ADVENTURES OF A CLEVER WOMAN. By Mrs. TROLLOPE.

THE BELLE OF THE VILLAGE. By the Author of 'The Old English Gentleman.'

CHARLES AUCHESTER. A Novel.

PRICE ONE SHILLING EACH NOVEL.

THE WHITEBOY. A Story of Ireland in 1822. By Mrs. S. C. HALL.

EUSTACE CONYERS. By JAMES HANNAY.

MARETIMO: a Story of Adventure. By BAYLE ST. JOHN.

MELINCOURT. By the Author of 'Headlong Hall.'

THE FALCON FAMILY; or, Young Ireland. A Satirical Novel. By M. W. SAVAGE.

TWO YEARS' RESIDENCE IN A LEVANTINE FAMILY. By BAYLE ST. JOHN.

Other Popular Novels will be issued in this Series.

A 4

Chapman and Hall's Standard Editions of Popular Authors.

Handsomely printed in Crown 8vo., Price 5s. each.

ANTHONY TROLLOPE'S WEST INDIES AND THE SPANISH MAIN. 5th Edition.

ANTHONY TROLLOPE'S CASTLE RICHMOND. 4th Edition.

ANTHONY TROLLOPE'S DOCTOR THORNE. 8th Edition.

ANTHONY TROLLOPE'S THE BERTRAMS. 6th Edition.

ANTHONY TROLLOPE'S THE KELLYS AND THE O'KELLYS. 5th Edition.

ANTHONY TROLLOPE'S THE MACDERMOTS OF BALLYCLORAN. 3rd Edition.

T. A. TROLLOPE'S LA BEATA (3rd Edition); and a TUSCAN ROMEO AND JULIET.

T. A. TROLLOPE'S MARIETTA. 3rd Edition.

W. M. THACKERAY'S IRISH SKETCH-BOOK. With Illustrations by the Author. 4th Edition.

ALBERT SMITH'S WILD OATS AND DEAD LEAVES. 2nd Edition.

W. H. WILLS'S OLD LEAVES GATHERED FROM HOUSEHOLD WORDS.'

W. H. AINSWORTH'S CONSTABLE OF THE TOWER. 3rd Edition.

W. H. AINSWORTH'S LORD MAYOR OF LONDON. 2nd Edition.

J. C. JEAFFRESON'S OLIVE BLAKE'S GOOD WORK. 3rd Edition.

ROBERT HOUDIN'S MEMOIRS. Written by Himself. 3rd Edition.

MRS. GASKELL'S NORTH AND SOUTH. 4th Edition.

G. A. SALA'S GASLIGHT AND DAYLIGHT. 2nd Edition.

MISS MULOCK'S THE HEAD OF THE FAMILY. 6th Edition.

MISS ANNA DRURY'S MISREPRESENTATION. 3rd Edition.

TILBURY NOGO. By the Author of 'Digby Grand.' 3rd Edition.

MARKET HARBOROUGH (5th Edition); and INSIDE THE BAR.

THE MASTER OF THE HOUNDS. By SCRUTATOR.

THE COUNTRY GENTLEMAN. By SCRUTATOR.

THE HOUSE OF ELMORE. By the Author of 'Grandmother's Money.'

CHARLIE THORNHILL. By CHARLES CLARKE.

COLLINS — A NEW SENTIMENTAL JOURNEY.

By CHARLES ALLSTON COLLINS. With Two Illustrations by the Author. Post 8vo. boards. 3s.

CONWAY (J.) — FORAYS AMONG SALMON AND

DEER. In post 8vo. cloth, price 6s.

COOPER (THOMAS)—PURGATORY OF SUICIDES.

New Edition. Fcap., cloth. 7s. 6d.

CORKRAN — BERTHA'S REPENTANCE. A Tale.

By J. FRAZER CORKRAN, Author of 'East and West; or, Once upon a Time,' &c. Post 8vo. cloth. 9s.

CRAIK—THE ENGLISH OF SHAKESPEARE;

Illustrated in a Philological Commentary on his Tragedy of 'Julius Cæsar.' By GEORGE LILLIE CRAIK, Professor of History and of English Literature in Queen's College, Belfast. Second Edition. Post 8vo., cloth. 5s.

——————— OUTLINES OF THE HISTORY OF THE

ENGLISH LANGUAGE. For the Use of the Junior Classes in Colleges, and the Higher Classes in Schools. By GEORGE L. CRAIK. Fourth Edition, revised and improved. Post 8vo. cloth. 2s. 6d.

DANTE'S DIVINE COMEDY, THE INFERNO.

A Literal Prose Translation, with the Text of the Original Collated with the best Editions, and Explanatory Notes. By JOHN A. CARLYLE, M.D. Post 8vo., with a Portrait, cloth. 14s.

DAVIDSON — DRAWING FOR ELEMENTARY

SCHOOLS. By ELLIS A. DAVIDSON, Head-Master of the Chester School of Art. Published under the sanction of the Science and Art Department of the Committee of Council on Education. Post 8vo. cloth. 3s.

DE PONTÈS—POETS AND POETRY OF GERMANY.

BIOGRAPHICAL AND CRITICAL NOTICES. By Madame L. DAVESIES DE PONTÈS. Two volumes, post 8vo. cloth. 18s.

DIAGRAMS, A SERIES OF,

ILLUSTRATIVE OF THE PRINCIPLES OF MECHANICAL PHILOSOPHY AND THEIR APPLICATION. Twenty-one large Plates, drawn on Stone. With descriptive Letterpress. Published under the Superintendence of the Society for the Diffusion of Useful Knowledge. One large folio Volume, cloth. 2l. 12s. 6d.

DINNERS AND DINNER PARTIES; or, The Ab-

surdities of Artificial Life. With Additions, including a short Catechism of Cookery, founded on the principles of Chemistry. 1 vol. Second edition, post 8vo. 3s. 6d.

DICKENS — CHILD'S HISTORY OF ENGLAND.

New and Cheaper Edition. With Illustrations by MARCUS STONE. Post 8vo. cloth. 7s. 6d.

——————— GREAT EXPECTATIONS.

New and Cheaper Edition, with Frontispiece and Vignette by MARCUS STONE. Post 8vo. 7s. 6d.

MR. CHARLES DICKENS'S WORKS.

ORIGINAL EDITIONS.

GREAT EXPECTATIONS. Fifth Edition. 3 vols. post 8vo., 31s. 6d.

THE PICKWICK PAPERS. With Forty-three Illustrations by SEYMOUR and 'PHIZ.' 8vo. 1l. 1s.

NICHOLAS NICKLEBY. With Forty Illustrations by 'PHIZ.' 8vo. 1l. 1s.

SKETCHES BY 'BOZ.' A New Edition, with Forty Illustrations by GEORGE CRUIKSHANK. 8vo. 1l. 1s.

MARTIN CHUZZLEWIT. With Forty Illustrations by 'PHIZ.' 8vo. 1l. 1s.

THE OLD CURIOSITY SHOP. With Seventy-five Illustrations by GEORGE CATTERMOLE and H. K. BROWNE. Imperial 8vo. 13s.

BARNABY RUDGE: A Tale of the Riots of 'Eighty. With Seventy-eight Illustrations by G. CATTERMOLE and H. K. BROWNE. Imperial 8vo. 13s.

AMERICAN NOTES, for General Circulation. Fourth Edition. 2 vols., post 8vo. 1l. 1s.

OLIVER TWIST; or, the Parish-Boy's Progress. Illustrated by GEORGE CRUIKSHANK. Third Edition. 3 vols., post 8vo. 1l. 5s.

OLIVER TWIST. 1 vol. 8vo., cloth. Illustrated. 11s.

DOMBEY AND SON. With Forty Illustrations by 'PHIZ.' 8vo., cloth. 1l. 1s.

DAVID COPPERFIELD. With Forty Illustrations by 'PHIZ.' 8vo., cloth. 1l. 1s.

LEAK HOUSE. With Forty Illustrations by 'PHIZ.' 8vo., cloth 1l. 1s.

LITTLE DORRIT. With Forty Illustrations by 'PHIZ.' 8vo., cloth. 1l. 1s.

HARD TIMES. Small 8vo., cloth. 5s.

THE UNCOMMERCIAL TRAVELLER. Third Edition. Post 8vo., cloth. 6s.

A TALE OF TWO CITIES. With Sixteen Illustrations by 'PHIZ.' 8vo. 9s.

CHILD'S HISTORY OF ENGLAND. 3 vols., square, cloth. 10s. 6d.

CHRISTMAS CAROL. With Illustrations. Fcap. 8vo., cloth. 5s.

CRICKET ON THE HEARTH. With Illustrations. Fcap. 8vo., cloth. 5s.

THE CHIMES. With Illustrations. Fcap. 8vo., cloth. 5s.

THE BATTLE OF LIFE. With Illustrations. Fcap. 8vo., cloth. 5s.

THE HAUNTED MAN AND THE GHOST'S BARGAIN. With Illustrations. Fcap. 8vo., cloth. 5s.

MR. CHARLES DICKENS'S WORKS.

THE ILLUSTRATED LIBRARY EDITION,

Beautifully printed in Post Octavo, and carefully revised by the Author.   With the Original Illustrations.   Price 7s. 6d. each.

Already Published.

PICKWICK PAPERS.	43 Illustrations	... ...	2 vols.	15s.
NICHOLAS NICKLEBY.	39 ditto	... ...	2 vols.	15s.
MARTIN CHUZZLEWIT.	40 ditto	... ...	2 vols.	15s.
OLD CURIOSITY SHOP.	36 ditto	... ...	2 vols.	15s.
BARNABY RUDGE.	36 ditto	... ...	2 vols.	15s.
SKETCHES BY BOZ.	39 ditto	... ...	1 vol.	7s. 6d.
OLIVER TWIST.	24 ditto	... ...	1 vol.	7s. 6d.
DOMBEY AND SON.	39 ditto	... ...	2 vols.	15s.
DAVID COPPERFIELD.	40 ditto	... ...	2 vols.	15s.
PICTURES FROM ITALY and AMERICAN NOTES.	8 ditto	... ...	1 vol.	7s. 6d.
BLEAK HOUSE.	40 ditto	... ...	2 vols.	15s.
LITTLE DORRIT.	40 ditto	... ...	2 vols.	15s.
CHRISTMAS BOOKS.	17 ditto	... ...	1 vol.	7s. 6d.
A TALE OF TWO CITIES.	16 ditto	... ...	1 vol.	7s. 6d.

CHEAP AND UNIFORM EDITION.

Handsomely printed in Crown Octavo, cloth, with Frontispieces.

	s.	d.
THE PICKWICK PAPERS	5	0
NICHOLAS NICKLEBY	5	0
MARTIN CHUZZLEWIT	5	0
DOMBEY AND SON	5	0
DAVID COPPERFIELD	5	0
BLEAK HOUSE	5	0
LITTLE DORRIT	5	0
BARNABY RUDGE	4	0
OLD CURIOSITY SHOP	4	0
OLIVER TWIST	3	6
SKETCHES BY BOZ	3	6
CHRISTMAS BOOKS	3	6
GREAT EXPECTATIONS	3	6
AMERICAN NOTES	2	6

MR. DICKENS' READINGS.   Fcap. 8vo.

	s.	d.
A CHRISTMAS CAROL IN PROSE	1	0
THE CRICKET ON THE HEARTH	1	0
THE CHIMES	1	0
THE STORY OF LITTLE DOMBEY	1	0
THE POOR TRAVELLER, BOOTS AT THE HOLLY-TREE INN, AND MRS. GAMP	1	0

DIREY—GRAMMAIRE FRANÇAISE.
Par L. DIREY. 12mo. cloth. 3s.

—————— LATIN GRAMMAR.
By L. DIREY. 12mo. cloth. 4s.

—————— AND FOGGO'S ENGLISH GRAMMAR.
12mo. cloth. 3s.

DIXON—ROBERT BLAKE, ADMIRAL AND GENE-
RAL AT SEA. Based on Family and State Papers. By HEPWORTH DIXON, Author of 'Life of William Penn.' Cheap edition, post 8vo. boards. 2s. Post 8vo. cloth, with portrait. 2s. 6d.

—————— WILLIAM PENN.
AN HISTORICAL BIOGRAPHY. By WILLIAM HEPWORTH DIXON, Author of 'Life of Howard.' With a portrait. Second edition, fcap. 8vo. cloth. 7s.

DODD — THREE WEEKS IN MAJORCA.
By the Rev. WILLIAM DODD. Post 8vo. cloth. 5s.

DOYLE RICHARD — PICTURES OF EXTRA AR-
TICLES AND VISITORS TO THE EXHIBITION. Eight Illustrations. 1s.

DRAYSON — PRACTICAL MILITARY SURVEYING
AND SKETCHING. By Captain DRAYSON, R.A. With illustrations. Post 8vo. cloth. 4s. 6d.

—————— THE COMMON SIGHTS IN THE HEA-
VENS, AND HOW TO SEE AND KNOW THEM. By Captain DRAYSON, R.A. 1 vol. fcap. 8vo. 8s.

DRURY (ANNA)—DEEP WATERS.
A Novel. By Miss ANNA DRURY, Author of 'Misrepresentation,' 'Friends and For tune.' 2 vols. post 8vo. cloth. 21s.

—————————————— MISREPRESENTATION.
By Miss ANNA DRURY. Third Edition. 1 vol. crown 8vo., cloth. 5s.

DYCE'S ELEMENTARY OUTLINES OF ORNAMENT
Fifty selected plates. Folio, sewed. 5s.

—————— SHAKESPEARE.
A New Edition in the press, to be completed in Eight Volumes, demy 8vo. THE WORKS OF SHAKESPEARE. Edited by the Rev. ALEXANDER DYCE. This edition is not a mere reprint of that which appeared in 1857. On the contrary, it will present a text very materially altered and amended from beginning to end, with a large body of critical Notes almost entirely new; and with a Glossary, in which the language of the poet, his allusions to customs, &c., will be fully explained. To be published every alternate month. Vols. I. and II. now ready, 10s. each.

EDINBURGH TALES.
In one thick volume, imperial 8vo. full gilt back. 8s. 6d.

EDWARDS (TENISON) — SHALL WE REGISTER
TITLE? Or, the Objections to Land and Title Registry Stated and Answered: combining a Popular Exposition of the Act 25 & 26 Vict. cap. 53. By TENISON EDWARDS, of the Inner Temple, Esq. Barrister-at-Law. Dedicated by permission to the Lord Chancellor. In crown 8vo., cloth. 4s. 6d.

ELEMENTARY DRAWING BOOK.

Directions for introducing the First Steps of Elementary Drawing in Schools, and among Workmen. With Lists of Materials, Objects, and Models. Prepared and published at the request of the Council of the Society of Arts. Small 4to. cloth. 4s. 6d.

ESQUIROS — THE ENGLISH AT HOME.

By ALPHONSE ESQUIROS. Translated by Sir LASCELLES WRAXALL, Bart. New Edition, in the Press.

———— THE ENGLISH AT HOME. Second Series.

By ALPHONSE ESQUIROS. 1 vol. post 8vo. cloth. 10s. 6d.

———— THE ENGLISH AT HOME. Third Series.

By ALPHONSE ESQUIROS. 1 vol. post 8vo. 10s. 6d.

————THE DUTCH AT HOME.

By ALPHONSE ESQUIROS. New Edition, in one vol. post 8vo. 9s.

FAIRHOLT—UP THE NILE AND HOME AGAIN.

A Handbook for Travellers, and a Travel-Book for the Library. By F. W. FAIRHOLT, F.S.A. With 100 Illustrations from Original Sketches by the Author. 1 vol. post 8vo. 16s.

FALSE POSITIONS.

2 vols. post 8vo. cloth. 21s.

FARM HOMESTEADS, THE.

To be completed in Twelve Monthly Parts, price 5s. each. A Collection of Plans of English Homesteads existing in different Districts of the Country, carefully selected from the most approved Specimens of Farm Architecture, to Illustrate the Accommodation required under various Modes of Husbandry; with a Digest of the Leading Principles recognised in the Construction and Arrangement of the Buildings. Edited by J. BAILEY DENTON, M. Inst. C.E., F.G.S., Engineer to the General Land Drainage and Improvement Company. Part IX., price 5s., just published.

FINE ARTS QUARTERLY REVIEW, THE.

Edited by B. B. WOODWARD, Esq., Her Majesty's Librarian. Imperial 8vo. Nos. 1, 2, and 3 published. 6s. each.

FINLAISON — NEW GOVERNMENT SUCCESSION-

DUTY TABLES. For the Use of Successors to Property, their Solicitors and Agents, and others concerned in the Payment of the Duties Levied on all Successions, under Authority of the present Statute, 16 & 17 Victoria, cap. 51. By ALEXANDER GLEN FINLAISON. Post 8vo., cloth. 5s. New Edition.

FOSTER—HISTORY OF ENGLAND FOR SCHOOLS

AND FAMILIES. By A. F. FOSTER. With numerous Illustrations. Post 8vo. cloth. 6s.

———— ELEMENTS OF GEOGRAPHY.

By A. F. FOSTER. Post, cloth. 5s.

FORSTER (JOHN) — OLIVER GOLDSMITH.

A Biography. By JOHN FORSTER. With Forty Illustrations. New Edition. Post 8vo. cloth. 7s. 6d.

FRANCATELLI—ROYAL CONFECTIONER.

By C. E. FRANCATELLI. With numerous Coloured Illustrations. Post 8vo. cloth. 12s.

FREYTAG — PICTURES FROM GERMAN LIFE, IN
THE FIFTEENTH, SIXTEENTH, AND SEVENTEENTH CENTURIES. By HERR FREYTAG, Author of ' Debit and Credit.' Translated by Mrs. MALCOLM. 14. 1s.
Also the SECOND PORTION, including the EIGHTEENTH and NINETEENTH CENTURIES. In 2 vols. post 8vo. 21s.

FROM HAY-TIME TO HOPPING.
By the Author of ' Our Farm of Four Acres.' Second edition, small 8vo. cloth. 5s.

GARDEN THAT PAID THE RENT (THE).
Fourth edition, post 8vo. boards. 2s.

GASKELL.—CRANFORD—MARY BARTON—RUTH—
LIZZIE LEIGH. By Mrs. GASKELL. Post 8vo. boards. Price 2s. each.

——————— NORTH AND SOUTH.
Fourth and cheaper edition. Crown 8vo. cloth. 5s.

——————— MOORLAND COTTAGE.
With Illustrations by BIRKET FOSTER. Fcap. 8vo. cloth. 2s. 6d.

GENTLEWOMAN, THE.
By the Author of ' Dinners and Dinner Parties.' With Illustrations. 1 vol. post 8vo., cloth. 4s. 6d.

GERMAN LOVE.
From the Papers of an Alien. Translated by SUSANNAH WINKWORTH. Fcap., cloth. 4s. 6d.

GRATTAN (THOMAS COLLEY.) — BEATEN PATHS,
AND THOSE WHO TROD THEM. Second Edition. 2 vols. post 8vo. 16s.

HARVEY (MRS.) — OUR CRUISE IN THE CLAY-
MORE ; WITH A VISIT TO DAMASCUS AND THE LEBANON. By MRS. HARVEY, of Ickwell-Bury. In post 8vo. cloth, with Illustrations. Price 10s. 6d.

HAWKINS — A COMPARATIVE VIEW OF THE
ANIMAL AND HUMAN FRAME. By B. WATERHOUSE HAWKINS, F.L.S., F.G.S., with Ten Illustrations from Nature by the Author. Folio, cloth. 12s.

HAXTHAUSEN—TRANSCAUCASIA.
Sketches of the Nations and Races between the Black Sea and the Caspian. By Baron VON HAXTHAUSEN. With Eight Coloured Illustrations by GRAEB. 8vo. cloth. 18s

——————————THE TRIBES OF THE CAUCASUS;
WITH AN ACCOUNT OF SCHAMYL AND THE MURIDS. By BARON VON HAXTHAUSEN. Post 8vo. cloth. 5s.

HEATON—THE THRESHOLD OF CHEMISTRY ;
An Experimental Introduction to the Science. By CHARLES HEATON. With numerous Illustrations. Post 8vo. cloth. 4s.

HEINRICH HEINE'S BOOK OF SONGS.
A Translation. By JOHN E. WALLIS. Crown 8vo. cloth. 9s.

HENSLOW—ILLUSTRATIONS TO BE EMPLOYED
IN THE PRACTICAL LESSONS ON BOTANY. Adapted to all classes. Prepared for the South Kensington Museum. By the Rev. PROFESSOR HENSLOW. With Illustrations. Post 8vo. 6d.

HOUDIN (ROBERT) — THE SHARPER DETECTED
AND EXPOSED. By ROBERT HOUDIN, Author of 'Memoirs of Robert Houdin.'
With Illustrations. Post 8vo. cloth. 6s.

————————————— MEMOIRS OF ROBERT HOUDIN,
AMBASSADOR, AUTHOR, AND CONJUROR. Written by himself. Third Edition
1 vol. crown 8vo. 5s.

HOUSEHOLD WORDS.
Conducted by CHARLES DICKENS. 19 vols. royal 8vo. cloth. 5s. 6d. each. (All the
back Numbers and Parts may now be had.)

HOUSEHOLD WORDS — CHRISTMAS STORIES
FROM. Royal 8vo. cloth. 2s. 6d.

INDUSTRIAL AND SOCIAL POSITION OF WOMEN,
IN THE MIDDLE AND LOWER RANKS. Post 8vo. cloth. 10s. 6d.

JEAFFRESON (JOHN CORDY) — OLIVE BLAKE'S
GOOD WORK. Third Edition. 1 vol. crown. 5s.

JERVIS—THE RIFLE-MUSKET.
A Practical Treatise on the Enfield-Prichett Rifle, recently adopted in the British Service.
By CAPTAIN JERVIS WHYTE JERVIS, M.P., Royal Artillery, Author of the 'Manual
of Field Operations.' Second and Cheaper Edition, with Additions. Post 8vo. cloth. 2s.

——————— OUR ENGINES OF WAR, AND HOW WE
GOT TO MAKE THEM. By CAPTAIN JERVIS WHYTE JERVIS, M.P., Royal
Artillery. With many Illustrations. Post 8vo. cloth. 6s.

——————— THE IONIAN ISLANDS DURING THE
PRESENT CENTURY. By Captain WHYTE-JERVIS, M.P. Post 8vo. cloth. 3s. 6d.

JEWSBURY—THE HALF-SISTERS.
A Novel. By GERALDINE E. JEWSBURY. Cheap Edition. Post 8vo., boards. 2s.

KEIGHTLEY—THE LIFE, OPINIONS, AND WRIT-
INGS OF JOHN MILTON. With an Introduction to 'Paradise Lost.' By THOMAS
KEIGHTLEY. Second Edition. Demy 8vo. cloth. 10s. 6d.

——————— THE POEMS OF JOHN MILTON.
WITH NOTES by THOMAS KEIGHTLEY. 2 vols. 8vo. cloth. 21s.

KELLY (W. K.)— CURIOSITIES OF INDO-EUROPEAN
TRADITION AND FOLK LORE. By WALTER K. KELLY. Post 8vo. cloth. 8s. 6d.

KELLY (T.)— LIFE IN VICTORIA IN 1853 AND IN
1858. By THOMAS KELLY. 2 vols. post 8vo., cloth. 21s.

KOHL (J. G.)—POPULAR HISTORY OF THE DIS-
COVERY OF AMERICA, FROM COLUMBUS TO FRANKLIN. Translated by
MAJOR R. R. NOEL. 2 vols. post 8vo. 16s.

——————— KITCHI-GAMI;
Wanderings round Lake Superior. 8vo., cloth. 13s.

MR. CHARLES LEVER'S WORKS.
LIBRARY EDITION.
IN DEMY OCTAVO, ILLUSTRATED BY PHIZ.

LUTTRELL OF ARRAN. A new serial. Parts I., II., and III. now ready. 1s. each.

BARRINGTON. Demy 8vo. cloth. With 26 Illustrations. 14s.

ONE OF THEM. Demy 8vo., cloth. With 30 Illustrations. 7s.

DAVENPORT DUNN; A Man of Our Day. 2 Vols., demy 8vo., cloth. With 44 Illustrations. 14s.

THE MARTINS OF CRO' MARTIN. 2 Vols. With 40 Illustrations. 14s.

HARRY LORREQUER. 1 Vol. With 22 Illustrations. 7s.

CHARLES O'MALLEY, THE IRISH DRAGOON. 2 Vols. With 44 Illustrations. 14s.

JACK HINTON, THE GUARDSMAN. 1 Vol. With 26 Illustrations. 7s.

TOM BURKE OF 'OURS.' 2 Vols. With 44 Illustrations. 14s.

THE O'DONOGHUE: A Tale of Ireland Fifty Years Ago. 1 Vol. With 26 Illustrations. 7s.

THE KNIGHT OF GWYNNE. 2 Vols. With 40 Illustrations. 14s.

ROLAND CASHEL. 2 Vols. With 40 Illustrations. 14s.

THE DALTONS; or, Three Roads in Life. 2 Vols. With 44 Illustrations. 14s.

THE DODD FAMILY ABROAD. 2 Vols. With 40 Illustrations. 14s.

CHEAP AND UNIFORM EDITION.

HARRY LORREQUER	with 8 Illustrations by Phiz,'		4s.
CHARLES O'MALLEY, 2 Vols.	16	„	„ 8s.
JACK HINTON	8	„	„ 4s.
TOM BURKE OF 'OURS,' 2 Vols.	16	„	„ 8s.
THE O'DONOGHUE	8	„	„ 4s.
THE KNIGHT OF GWYNNE, 2 Vols.	16	„	„ 8s.
ROLAND CASHEL, 2 Vols.	16	„	„ 8s.
THE DALTONS, 2 Vols.	16	„	„ 8s.
THE DODD FAMILY ABROAD, 2 Vols.	16	„	„ 8s.
MARTINS OF CRO' MARTIN, 2 Vols.	16	„	„ 8s.
FORTUNES OF GLENCOE, 1 Vol.	8	„	„ 4s.
ONE OF THEM, 1 Vol.	8	„	„ 4s.
DAVENPORT DUNN, 2 Vols.	16	„	„ 8s.

LEVER'S (CHARLES) WORKS. CHEAP EDITION.
TWO SHILLINGS EACH VOLUME.

JACK HINTON. 1 vol. 2s.	THE O'DONOGHUE. 1 vol. 2s.
CHARLES O'MALLEY. 2 vols. 4s.	ROLAND CASHEL. 2 vols. 4s.
THE DALTONS. 2 vols. 4s.	TOM BURKE. 2 vols. 4s.
HARRY LORREQUER. 1 vol. 2s.	DAVENPORT DUNN. 2 vols. 4s.
THE KNIGHT OF GWYNNE. 2 vols. 4s.	FORTUNES OF GLENCOE. 1 vol. 2s.
DODD FAMILY ABROAD. 2 v. 4s.	ONE OF THEM. 1 vol. 2s.

LEVER—A DAY'S RIDE: A Life's Romance.
By CHARLES LEVER. 2 vols. post 8vo. cloth. 21s.

LEAVES FROM THE DIARY OF AN OFFICER OF
THE GUARDS DURING THE PENINSULAR WAR. By LIEUT.-COL. STEPNEY COWELL STEPNEY, K.H., late Coldstream Guards. Fcap. cloth. 5s.

LENNARD—TALES FROM MOLIÈRE'S PLAYS.
By DACRE BARRETT LENNARD. Post 8vo. cloth. 10s. 6d.

LENOX-CONYNGHAM—EILER AND HELVIG.
A Danish Legend, by Mrs. GEORGE LENOX-CONYNGHAM. Demy 8vo., cloth. 2s. 6d.

LOWRY'S ATLAS.
With a Copious Index. 100 Coloured Maps. Large 4to., half-bound. 12s.

A New Series of Maps, in large 4to., price One Penny each Map plain, and Two Pence with the Boundaries coloured, completed in 100 Maps, any of which can be purchased separately, plain 1d., coloured 2d.

LIST OF THE MAPS.

Sheet.		Sheet.	
1, 2.	World in Hemispheres—2 Maps.	54, 55.	Turkey in Asia and Western Persia—2 Maps.
3, 4.	World on Mercator's Projection—2 Maps.	56.	Eastern Persia.
5.	Europe.	57, 58.	Syria and Arabia Petræa—2 Maps.
6.	British Isles.	59, 60.	China and Indian Seas—2 Maps.
7, 8.	England and Wales—2 Maps.	61.	Australia and New Zealand—General Map.
9.	Scotland—General.	62, 63.	Australia—2 Maps.
10.	Ireland—General.	64 to 66.	New South Wales—3 Maps.
11.	France, in Provinces.	67.	Victoria or Port Phillip District.
12 to 15.	France in Departments—4 Maps.	68.	New Zealand.
16.	Holland and Belgium.	69, 70.	Polynesia—2 Maps.
17.	Spain and Portugal—General.	71, 72.	Africa—2 Maps.
18 to 21.	Spain and Portugal—4 Maps.	73 to 75.	Egypt, Nubia, Abyssinia, and Red Sea—3 Maps.
22.	Italy—General.	76, 77.	North Africa—comprising Morocco, Algiers, and Tunis—2 Maps.
23 to 26.	Italy—4 Maps.	78 to 80.	West Africa—comprising Senegambia, Liberia, Soudan, and Guinea—3 Maps.
27.	Prussia and German States.	81, 82.	Southern Africa—2 Maps.
28 to 31.	Germany and Switzerland—4 Maps.	83.	British North America.
32.	Austrian Empire.	84.	Arctic Regions.
33, 34.	Hungary and Transylvania—2 Maps.	85, 86.	Canada, New Brunswick, and Nova Scotia—2 Maps.
35.	Turkey in Europe and Greece.	87.	North America—General.
36.	Bosphorus and Dardanelles.	88, 89.	United States—2 Maps—General.
37.	Greece and the Ionian Islands.	90 to 93.	United States—4 Maps.
38, 39.	Sweden and Norway—2 Maps.	94.	Mexico.
40.	Denmark.	95.	West Indies and Central America.
41.	Russia in Europe.	96.	South America—General.
42.	Asia, North.	97 to 100.	South America—4 Maps.
43, 44.	Asia, South, and Indian Seas—2 Maps.		
45.	India—General.		
46 to 52.	India—7 Maps.		
53.	Persia and Tartary.		

LIFE IN THE SOUTH FROM THE COMMENCE-

MENT OF THE WAR. By a Blockaded British Subject. Being a Social History of those who took part in the Battles, from a personal accquaintance with them in their own homes. 2 vols. post 8vo. cloth. 21s.

LLOYD PENNANT;

A Tale of the West. By RALPH NEVILLE. 2 vols. post 8vo., cloth. 1l. 1s.

LOCKER—SIR GOODWIN'S FOLLY.

A Story of the Year 1795. By ARTHUR LOCKER. 3 vols. post 8vo., cloth. 1l. 11s. 6d.

LYTTON—MONEY.

A Comedy, in Five Acts. By Sir EDWARD BULWER LYTTON. 8vo. sewed. 2s. 6d.

—————— NOT SO BAD AS WE SEEM;

OR, MANY SIDES TO A CHARACTER. A Comedy, in Five Acts. By Sir EDWARD BULWER LYTTON. 8vo. sewed. 2s. 6d.

—————— RICHELIEU ; OR, THE CONSPIRACY.

A Play, in Five Acts. By Sir EDWARD BULWER LYTTON. 8vo. sewed. 2s. 6d.

—————— THE LADY OF LYONS;

OR, LOVE AND PRIDE. A Play, in Five Acts. By Sir EDWARD BULWER LYTTON. 8vo. sewed. 2s. 6d.

M'CULLAGH — INDUSTRIAL HISTORY OF FREE

NATIONS. Considered in Relation to their Domestic Institutions and External Policy. By W. TORRENS M'CULLAGH. 2 vols. 8vo. cloth. 24s.

—————— USE AND STUDY OF HISTORY.

Being the Substance of a Course of Lectures delivered in Dublin. By W. TORRENS M'CULLAGH. Second edition, 8vo. cloth. 10s. 6d.

MACKNIGHT—HISTORY OF THE LIFE AND TIMES

OF EDMUND BURKE. By THOMAS MACKNIGHT, Author of 'The Right Hon. B. Disraeli, M.P., a Literary and Political Biography;' and 'Thirty Years of Foreign Policy, a History of the Secretaryships of the Earl of Aberdeen and Viscount Palmerston.' 3 vols. demy 8vo. cloth, price 56s.

—————— (THOMAS) — THE LIFE OF LORD

BOLINGBROKE, Secretary of State in the reign of Queen Anne. By THOMAS MACKNIGHT. Demy 8vo. cloth. 18s.

MACREADY—LEAVES FROM THE OLIVE MOUNT.

Poems. By CATHERINE FRANCES B. MACREADY. Fcap. 8vo. cloth. 5s.

MACPHERSON—VATICAN SCULPTURES.

Selected and arranged in the order in which they are found in the Galleries. Briefly explained by ROBERT MACPHERSON, Rome. With Illustrations. 1 vol. 18mo., cloth. 5s.

MALLET—COTTON :

The Chemical, Geological, and Meteorological Conditions involved in its Successful Cultivation. With an Account of the Actual Conditions and Practice of Culture in the Southern or Cotton States of North America. By Dr. JOHN WILLIAM MALLET, Ph. D. University of Gottingen, A.B. Trin. Coll. Dublin, Professor of Chemistry in the University of Alabama, Analytical Chemist of the State Geological Survey, and Chemical Professor to the State School of Medicine, Mobile. 1 vol. post 8vo. With Illustrations. 7s. 6d.

MALLET (ROBERT) — THE FIRST PRINCIPLES OF

OBSERVATIONAL SEISMOLOGY: as developed in the Report to the Royal Society of London, of the Expedition made by command of the Society into the interior of the kingdom of Naples, to investigate the circumstances of the great Neapolitan Earthquake of December, 1857. By ROBERT MALLETT, C.E., F.R.S., F.G.S., M.R.I.A., &c. &c. Published by the Authority and with the Aid of the Royal Society of London. In 2 vols. royal 8vo., with numerous Illustrations in Lithography and Wood, and Maps. £3. 3s.

MARIOTTI—ITALY IN 1848.

By L. MARIOTTI. 8vo. cloth. 12s.

MARKET HARBOROUGH; OR, HOW MR. SAWYER

WENT TO THE SHIRES. Fifth Edition. And INSIDE THE BAR, now first published. By the Author of 'Digby Grand.' 5s.

MARSHALL—POPULATION & TRADE IN FRANCE,

1861-62. By FREDERICK MARSHALL. 1 vol. post 8vo. 8s.

MAZZINI (JOSEPH) — THE DUTIES OF MAN.

By JOSEPH MAZZINI. Post 8vo. 7s.

MENZIES (HENRY)—EARLY ANCIENT HISTORY.

1 vol. post 8vo. 7s.

MELINCOURT;

OR, SIR ORAN HAUT-TON By the Author of 'Headlong Hall,' &c. Cheap Edition. Post 8vo. boards. 1s.

MEREDITH (L. A.)—OVER THE STRAITS.

By LOUISA ANNE MEREDITH. With Illustrations. Post 8vo. cloth. 9s.

MEREDITH (OWEN)—THE RING OF AMASIS. From

the Papers of a German Physician. Edited by OWEN MEREDITH. 2 vols. post 8vo. cloth. 21s.

———————— LUCILE. A POEM.

By OWEN MEREDITH. Crown 8vo. cloth. 12s.

———————— SERBSKI PESME;

OR, NATIONAL SONGS OF SERVIA. By OWEN MEREDITH. Fcap. cloth. 4s.

———————— THE WANDERER.

A Poem. By the Author of 'Clytemnestra,' &c. Second edition, foolscap 8vo. cloth. 9s. 6d.

MEREDITH (GEORGE)—THE SHAVING OF SHAG-

PAT. An Arabian Entertainment. By GEORGE MEREDITH. Post 8vo. cloth. 10s. 6d.

———————— THE ORDEAL OF RICHARD

FEVEREL. By GEORGE MEREDITH. 3 vols. post 8vo. cloth. 31s. 6d.

———————— MODERN LOVE:

And Poems of the English Roadside. 1 vol. fcap. 8vo. 6s.

MICHIELS—SECRET HISTORY OF THE AUSTRIAN

GOVERNMENT, AND OF ITS SYSTEMATIC PERSECUTIONS OF PROTESTANTS. Compiled from official documents. By ALFRED MICHIELS. Post 8vo. cloth. 12s. 6d.

MONEY — TWELVE MONTHS WITH THE BASHI-
BAZOUKS. By EDWARD MONEY. With Coloured Illustrations. Post 8vo. cloth. 7s

MOOR — VISIT TO RUSSIA IN THE AUTUMN OF
1862. By HENRY MOOR. With Illustrations. Post 8vo. cloth. 7s. 6d.

MORGAN—THE MIND OF SHAKSPERE, AS EX-
HIBITED IN HIS WORKS. By the Rev. A. A. MORGAN, M.A. Second edition
foolscap 8vo. cloth. 6s.

MORISON (J. COTTER) — LIFE AND TIMES OF
ST. BERNARD, ABBOT OF CLAIRVAUX. Demy 8vo. cloth. 14s.

MORLEY — ENGLISH WRITERS. The Writers before
Chaucer; with an Introductory Sketch of the Four Periods of English Literature. By
HENRY MORLEY. 1 vol. demy 8vo. 22s.

——— —— **MEMOIRS OF BARTHOLOMEW FAIR.**
By HENRY MORLEY. With Eighty Illustrations. Demy 8vo. cloth. 21s.

———————**THE LIFE OF HENRY CORNELIUS**
AGRIPPA VON NETTESHEIM, Doctor and Knight, commonly known as a Magician.
By HENRY MORLEY. In 2 vols. post 8vo. cloth. 18s.

———————**JEROME CARDAN.**
A BIOGRAPHY. By HENRY MORLEY. Two vols. post 8vo. cloth. 18s.

———————**THE LIFE OF BERNARD PALISSY, OF**
SAINTES. His Labours and Discoveries in Arts and Science. By HENRY MORLEY.
Post 8vo. cloth. Price 12s. Second and cheaper Edition.

——————— **HOW TO MAKE HOME UNHEALTHY.**
By HENRY MORLEY. Reprinted from the 'Examiner.' Second edition, small 8vo. stiff
wrapper. 1s.

——————— **A DEFENCE OF IGNORANCE.**
By HENRY MORLEY. Small 8vo. cloth. 3s.

MULOCK—THE HEAD OF THE FAMILY.
By Miss MULOCK. Sixth edition, crown 8vo. cloth, 5s. Cheap edition, post 8vo. boards. 2s.

———————**OLIVE; A NOVEL.**
By Miss MULOCK. Cheap edition, post 8vo. boards. 2s.

———————**THE OGILVIES; A NOVEL.**
By Miss MULOCK. Cheap edition, post 8vo. boards. 2s.

——— ———**AGATHA'S HUSBAND.**
By Miss MULOCK. Cheap edition, post 8vo. boards. 2s.

MUSHET—BOOK OF SYMBOLS.
A Series of Seventy-five Short Essays on Morals, Religion, and Philosophy. Each Essay
Illustrating an Ancient Symbol or Modern Precept. By ROBERT MUSHET. Second
edition, post 8vo. cloth. 6s.

NATIONAL REVIEW. Quarterly. 6s.

NORTH AND SOUTH.
By the White Republican of Fraser's Magazine. Post 8vo. cloth. 9s.

NORTON—CHILD OF THE ISLANDS; A POEM.
By the Hon. Mrs. NORTON. Second edition, square 8vo. cloth. 6s.

OUR FARM OF FOUR ACRES, AND THE MONEY
WE MADE BY IT. Nineteenth edition, small post 8vo. boards. 1s.

PACKET (A) OF SEEDS SAVED BY AN OLD GAR-
DENER. Second Edition, Enlarged. Crown 8vo. boards. 1s. 6d.

PEACOCK—GL' INGANNATI THE DECEIVED.
A Comedy. By T. L. PEACOCK. Fcap. cloth. 3s. 6d.

PETO (SIR S. MORTON, BART., M.P.)—TAXATION:
Its Levy and Expenditure Past and Future; being an Inquiry into our Financial Policy. By Sir S. MORTON PETO, Bart, M.P. for Finsbury. Demy 8vo. cloth. 10s. 6d.

RAMBLES AND RECOLLECTIONS OF A FLY-
FISHER. Illustrated. With an Appendix, containing ample Instructions to the Novice, inclusive of Fly-making, and a List of really useful Flies. By CLERICUS. With Eight Illustrations. Post 8vo. cloth. 7s.

RÉCAMIER, MADAME, with a Sketch of the History of
Society in France. By Madame M——. 1 vol. post 8vo. 9s.

REDGRAVE—A MANUAL AND CATECHISM ON
COLOUR. By RICHARD REDGRAVE, R.A. 24mo. cloth. 9d.

RICHMOND—A MEMOIR OF THE LATE DUKE OF
RICHMOND. With a Portrait. 1 vol. demy 8vo. 15s.

RIDGE—HEALTH AND DISEASE, THEIR LAWS;
WITH PLAIN PRACTICAL PRESCRIPTIONS FOR THE PEOPLE. By BENJAMIN RIDGE, M.D., F.R.C.S. Second Edition. Post 8vo., cloth. 12s.

—————— OURSELVES, OUR FOOD, AND OUR
PHYSIC. By Dr. BENJAMIN RIDGE. In fcap. 8vo. cloth. Third Edition. Price 1s. 6d.

ROBERT MORNAY.
By MAX FERRER. Post 8vo. cloth. 9s.

ROBINSON — THE ITALIAN SCULPTURE COLLEC-
TIONS OF THE SOUTH KENSINGTON MUSEUM. A Descriptive Catalogue, comprising an Account of the Acquisitions from the Gigli and Campana Collections. Illustrated with 20 Engravings. By J. C. ROBINSON, F.S.A., &c., Superintendent of the Art Collections of the South Kensington Museum. By Authority of the Committee of Council on Education. In a handsome royal 8vo. volume. 7s. 6d.

——————— (J. C.)—SOUTH KENSINGTON MUSEUM.
Italian Sculptures of the Middle Ages and Period of the Revival of Art. A Series of 50 Photographs of Works in the above Section of the Museum, Selected and Arranged by J. C. ROBINSON, F.S.A. The Photographs executed by C. THURSTON THOMPSON. In one large handsome folio volume. £6. 6s. Published by Authority of the Science and Art Department of the Committee of Council on Education. *₊* Separate Plates 3s. each.

RODENBERG—THE ISLAND OF THE SAINTS, A
PILGRIMAGE THROUGH IRELAND. By JULIUS RODENBERG. Translated by LASCELLES WRAXALL. Post 8vo., cloth. 9s.

ROMAN CANDLES.
Post 8vo. cloth. 8s.

ROSCOE—POEMS, TRAGEDIES, AND ESSAYS.
By WILLIAM CALDWELL ROSCOE. Edited, with a Prefatory Memoir, by his Brother-in-law, RICHARD HOLT HUTTON. Two vols. crown 8vo., cloth. 21s.

SALA—GASLIGHT AND DAYLIGHT, WITH SOME
LONDON SCENES THEY SHINE UPON. By GEORGE AUGUSTUS SALA. Crown 8vo., cloth. Second Edition. 5s.

ST. JOHN, BAYLE—THE SUBALPINE KINGDOM;
Or, EXPERIENCES AND STUDIES IN SAVOY, PIEDMONT, AND GENOA. By BAYLE ST. JOHN. 2 vols. Post 8vo., cloth. 21s.

———————————————— **TWO YEARS' RESIDENCE IN**
A LEVANTINE FAMILY. By BAYLE ST. JOHN. Cheap Edition. Post 8vo. boards. 1s.

———————————————— **MARETIMO;**
A STORY OF ADVENTURE. By BAYLE ST. JOHN. Reprinted from 'Chambers Journal.' Post 8vo., boards. 1s.

———————————————— **THE LOUVRE;**
Or, BIOGRAPHY OF A MUSEUM. By BAYLE ST. JOHN. Post 8vo., cloth. 10s. 6d.

ST. JOHN, J. A.—THE EDUCATION OF THE PEOPLE;
By JAMES AUGUSTUS ST. JOHN, Author of 'Isis,' 'Life of Louis Napoleon,' &c. Post 8vo., cloth. 8s. 6d. Dedicated to Sir John Pakington, M.P.

———————————————— **ISIS; AN EGYPTIAN PILGRIMAGE.**
By JAMES AUGUSTUS ST. JOHN. Second Edition. 2 vols., post 8vo., cloth. 12s.

———————————————— **THE NEMESIS OF POWER: Causes**
and Forms of Revolution. By JAMES AUGUSTUS ST. JOHN. Fcap. cloth. 5s.

———————————————— **PHILOSOPHY AT THE FOOT OF**
THE CROSS. By JAMES AUGUSTUS ST. JOHN. Fcap. cloth. 5s.

———————————————— **THE PREACHING OF CHRIST, ITS**
NATURE AND CONSEQUENCES. By JAMES AUGUSTUS ST. JOHN. Small 8vo., sewed. 1s. 6d.

SAVAGE—BACHELOR OF THE ALBANY. A Novel.
By M. W. SAVAGE. Cheap Edition. Post 8vo., boards. 2s.

———————————————— **THE FALCON FAMILY; or, YOUNG IRE-**
LAND. A Satirical Novel. By M. W. SAVAGE. Cheap Edition. Post 8vo., boards. 1s.

———————————————— **MY UNCLE THE CURATE.**
By M. W. SAVAGE. Cheap Edition. Post 8vo., boards. 2s.

———————————————— **CLOVER COTTAGE; or, I CAN'T GET IN.**
A Novelette. By the Author of 'The Falcon Family,' &c. With Illustrations. In fcap. 8vo., cloth. 5s.

SHARPE'S ATLAS:

Comprising Fifty-four Maps, constructed upon a System of Scale and Proportion from the most recent Authorities, and Engraved on Steel, by J. WILSON LOWRY. With a Copious Consulting Index. In a large folio volume. Half morocco, gilt back and edges, plain, 36s.; or with the maps coloured, 42s.

CONTENTS.

1. The World—Western Hemisphere.
2. The World—Eastern Hemisphere.
3. The World—Mercator's Projection.
4. Europe, with the Mediterranean.
5. Great Britain and Ireland.
6. England and Wales—Railway Map, North.
7. England and Wales—Railway Map, South.
8. Scotland.
9. Ireland.
10. France—Belgium—Switzerland.
11. Belgium and Holland.
12. Prussia, Holland, and German States.
13. Switzerland.
14. Austrian Empire.
15. Turkey and Greece.
16. Greece.
17. Italy.
18. Spain and Portugal.
19. Northern Sweden, and Frontier of Russia.
20. Denmark, Sweden, and Russia on the Baltic.
21. Western Russia, from the Baltic to the Euxine.
22. Russia on the Euxine.
23. Russia on the Caucasus.
24. Russia in Europe.
25. Northern Asia—Asiatic Russia.
26. South-West. Asia—Overland to India.
27. South-Eastern Asia — Birmah, China, and Japan.
28. Australia and New Zealand.
29. Egypt and Arabia Petræa.
30. Nubia and Abyssinia to Babel Mandeb Strait.
31. Asia Minor.
32. Syria and the Turkish Provinces on the Persian Gulf.
33. Western Persia.
34. Eastern Persia.
35. Affghanistan and the Punjab.
36. Beloochistan and Scinde.
37. Central India.
38. The Carnatic.
39. Bengal, &c.
40. India—General Map.
41. North Africa.
42. South Africa.
43. British North America.
44. Central America.
45. United States—General Map.
46. United States—North-East.
47. United States—South-East.
48. United States—South-West.
49. Jamaica, and Leeward and Windward Islands.
50. Mexico and Guatemala.
51. South America.
52. Columbian and Peruvian Republics, and Western Brazil.
53. La Plata, Chili, and Southern Brazil.
54. Eastern Brazil.

The above Maps are sold Separately. Each Map, Plain, 4d.; Coloured, 6d.

SHARPE—STUDENT'S ATLAS.

With a Copious Index. 26 Coloured Maps, selected from the preceding. Folio, half-bound. 21s.

SLACK — THE PHILOSOPHY OF PROGRESS IN HUMAN AFFAIRS. By HENRY JAMES SLACK, F.G.S., Barrister-at-Law. Post 8vo., cloth. 6s.

SMITH (ALBERT)—WILD OATS AND DEAD LEAVES.

By ALBERT SMITH. Second Edition. Crown 8vo., cloth. 5s.

———————————TO CHINA AND BACK:

BEING A DIARY KEPT OUT AND HOME. By ALBERT SMITH. 8vo. sewed. 1s.

——— (REV. JAMES)—THE DIVINE DRAMA OF HISTORY AND CIVILIZATION. By the Rev. JAMES SMITH. 8vo. cloth. 12s.

——— (MRS.) — PRACTICAL AND ECONOMICAL COOKERY, with a Series of Bills of Fare; also, Directions on Carving, Trussing, &c. By Mrs. SMITH, many years professed Cook to most of the leading families in the Metropolis. Post 8vo. cloth. 5s. 6d.

SPICER — STRANGE THINGS AMONG US.

By H. SPICER, Author of 'Old Styles.' New Edition. With Addenda. Post 8vo. cloth. 7s. 6d.

STEPNEY LIEUT.-COLONEL STEPNEY COWELL—
LEAVES FROM THE DIARY OF AN OFFICER DURING THE PENINSULAR WAR. Fcap., cloth. 5s.

STIGANT—A VISION OF BARBAROSSA, AND OTHER
POEMS. By WILLIAM STIGANT. Fcap. 8vo. cloth. 7s.

'STONEWALL' JACKSON, late General of the Confede-
rate States Army. A Biographical Sketch, and an Outline of his Virginian Campaigns. By the Author of 'Life in the South.' Post 8vo. 2s. 6d. boards, 3s. cloth.

STORY — ROBA DI ROMA.
By W. W. STORY. Third Edition, in 1 volume, crown 8vo. cloth. 7s. 6d.

———— POEMS.
By W. W. STORY. Post 8vo. cloth. 5s.

SYBEL (VON)—THE HISTORY AND LITERATURE
OF THE CRUSADES. By VON SYBEL. Translated by Lady DUFF GORDON. 1 vol. post 8vo. 10s. 6d.

TANNHÄUSER, OR, THE BATTLE OF THE BARDS.
A Poem. By NEVILLE TEMPLE and EDWARD TREVOR. Fcap. 8vo. cloth. Fourth Edition. 3s. 6d.

TAYLOR (HENRY)—PLAYS AND POEMS.
New and complete Edition. 3 vols. fcap. By HENRY TAYLOR, Author of 'Philip Van Artevelde,' 'St. Clement's Eve,' &c. 3 vols. fcap. cloth. 16s.

———————— EDWIN THE FAIR; ISAAC COMNENUS;
THE EVE OF THE CONQUEST, AND OTHER POEMS. By HENRY TAYLOR. Third edition. Fcap. 8vo. cloth. 3s. 6d.

———————— PHILIP VAN ARTEVELDE. By HENRY
TAYLOR. Sixth edition. Fcap. 8vo. cloth. 3s. 6d.

———————— ST. CLEMENT'S EVE: A DRAMA.
By HENRY TAYLOR, Author of 'Philip Van Artevelde,' &c. 1 vol. fcap. 5s.

THACKERAY—THE IRISH SKETCH-BOOK.
By M. A. TITMARSH. Fourth Edition, Uniform with Thackeray's 'Miscellaneous Essays.' In crown 8vo. cloth, with Illustrations. 5s.

———————————— NOTES OF A JOURNEY FROM CORN-
HILL TO GRAND CAIRO, BY WAY OF LISBON, ATHENS, CONSTANTINOPLE, AND JERUSALEM. By W. M. THACKERAY. With a Coloured Frontispiece. Second Edition. Small 8vo. cloth. New Edition, in the Press.

———————————— CHRISTMAS BOOKS:
Containing 'MRS. PERKINS' BALL,' 'DR. BIRCH,' 'OUR STREET.' Cheap Edition. In one square volume, cloth, with all the original Illustrations. 7s. 6d.

THURSTAN—THE PASSIONATE PILGRIM;
Or, EROS AND ANTEROS. By HENRY J. THURSTAN. Crown 8vo., cloth. 5s. 6d.

TILBURY NOGO;

Or, PASSAGES IN THE LIFE OF AN UNSUCCESSFUL MAN. By the Author of 'Digby Grand.' 2 vols. post 8vo. cloth. 21s. And New Edition, 1 vol. crown 8vo. 5s.

TOWNSHEND — DESCRIPTIVE TOUR IN SCOTLAND. By CHAUNCY HARE TOWNSHEND. With twelve Illustrations. 8vo. cloth. 9s.

———————— SERMONS IN SONNETS:

WITH A TEXT ON THE NEW YEAR: and other Poems. By CHAUNCY HARE TOWNSHEND. Small 8vo. cloth. 7s. 6d.

———————— THE THREE GATES.

IN VERSE. By CHAUNCY HARE TOWNSHEND. Second Edition, with additions and Portrait. Post 8vo. cloth. 10s. 6d.

TROLLOPE'S (ANTHONY) WORKS.

CAN YOU FORGIVE HER? A New Serial, with Illustrations, uniform with 'Orley Farm.' To be completed in 20 Parts. Parts. I. and II. now ready. 1s.

RACHEL RAY. 2 vols. post 8vo. cloth. 21s.

ORLEY FARM. With Forty Illustrations by J. E. Millais. Handsomely bound in cloth. 2 vols. demy 8vo. 1l. 2s.

TALES OF ALL COUNTRIES. 1 vol. post 8vo. 10s. 6d.

————————————————————. Second Series. 10s. 6d.

DR. THORNE. Eighth Edition. 5s.

THE BERTRAMS. Sixth Edition. 5s.

WEST INDIES AND THE SPANISH MAIN. Fifth Edition. 5s.

THE KELLYS AND THE O'KELLYS. Fifth Edition. 5s.

THE MACDERMOTS OF BALLYCLORAN. Third Edition. 5s.

CASTLE RICHMOND. Fourth Edition. 5s.

WORKS (uniform edition), containing the last named six works, crown 8vo., handsomely bound in red cloth. 5s. each.

NORTH AMERICA. Third Edition. 2 vols. demy 8vo. 1l. 14s.

TROLLOPE (THOMAS ADOLPHUS) — GIULIO MALATESTA. By THOMAS ADOLPHUS TROLLOPE, Author of 'La Beata,' 'Marietta,' &c. 3 vols. post 8vo. cloth, 1l. 11s. 6d.

———————— LA BEATA (Third Edition); and a

TUSCAN ROMEO AND JULIET. 1 vol. crown 8vo. 5s.

———————— PAUL THE POPE AND PAUL

THE FRIAR: A STORY OF AN INTERDICT. By THOMAS ADOLPHUS TROLLOPE. With a Portrait. Po 8vo. cloth. 12s.

———————— FILIPPO STROZZI. A Biography.

By THOMAS ADOLPHUS TROLLOPE. Post 8vo. cloth. 12s.

———————— MARIETTA.

Second Edition. Crown 8vo. 7s. 6d. And Third Edition, crown 8vo., 5s.

———————— THE GIRLHOOD OF CATHE-

RINE DE' MEDICI. By T. ADOLPHUS TROLLOPE. In 1 vol. post 8vo. cloth. 10s. 6d.

TROLLOPE (T. A.) A DECADE OF ITALIAN

WOMEN. By THOMAS ADOLPHUS TROLLOPE. With Portraits. 2 vols. post 8vo. cloth. 22s.

——————————— TUSCANY in 1849 and in 1859.

By THOMAS ADOLPHUS TROLLOPE. Post 8vo. cloth. 10s. 6d.

——————————— A LENTEN JOURNEY IN UM-

BRIA AND THE MARCHES OF ANCONA. By THOS. ADOLPHUS TROLLOPE. Post 8vo. cloth. 10s.

TROLLOPE (THEODOSIA) — SOCIAL ASPECTS OF

REVOLUTION, IN A SERIES OF LETTERS FROM FLORENCE. Reprinted from the 'Athenæum.' With a Sketch of Subsequent Events up to the Present Time. By THEODOSIA TROLLOPE. Post 8vo. cloth. 8s. 6d.

TWILIGHT THOUGHTS. By M. S. C.,

Author of ' Little Poems for Little People.' Second Edition, with a Frontispiece. Fcap. cloth. 1s. 6d.

TWINING — THE ELEMENTS OF PICTURESQUE

SCENERY; or, STUDIES OF NATURE MADE IN TRAVEL, with a View to Improvement in Landscape Painting. By HENRY TWINING. Vol. II. Imp. 8vo. cloth. 8s.

VANCE (ALEXANDER) — ROMANTIC EPISODES

OF CHIVALRIC AMD MEDIÆVAL FRANCE; to which are appended some few Passages from Montaigne. Now done into English by ALEXANDER VANCE. Post 8vo. cloth. 10s. 6d.

——————————————— THE HISTORY AND

PLEASANT CHRONICLE OF LITTLE JEHAN DE SAINTRÉ, AND OF THE LADY OF THE FAIR COUSINS. Together with the Book of the Knight of the Tower Landry, which he made for the Instruction of his Daughters. Now done into English by ALEXANDER VANCE. Post 8vo., cloth, 10s. 6d.

WAYFARING SKETCHES AMONG THE GREEKS

AND TURKS, AND ON THE SHORES OF THE DANUBE. By a Seven Years' Resident in Greece. Second Edition. Post 8vo. cloth. 9s.

WHIST-PLAYER (THE).

THE LAWS AND PRACTICE OF SHORT WHIST. EXPLAINED AND ILLUSTRATED BY COLONEL BLYTH. With numerous Diagrams printed in Colours. Imp. 16mo. Second Edition. 5s.

WHITE — A LONDONER'S WALK TO THE LAND'S

END, AND A TRIP TO THE SCILLY ISLES. Second Edition. Post 8vo. cloth. With four Maps. 4s.

——————— A MONTH IN YORKSHIRE.

By WALTER WHITE. Fourth Edition. With a Map. Post 8vo. cloth. 4s.

——————— ALL ROUND THE WREKIN.

By WALTER WHITE. Second Edition, post 8vo. cloth. 9s.

——————— NORTHUMBERLAND AND THE BORDER.

By WALTER WHITE. Second Edition. With a Map. Post 8vo. cloth. 10s. 6d.

WHITE—A JULY HOLIDAY IN SAXONY, BOHE-
MIA AND SILESIA. By WALTER WHITE. Post 8vo. cloth. 9s.

————ON FOOT THROUGH TYROL ;
IN THE SUMMER OF 1855. By WALTER WHITE. Post 8vo. cloth. 9s.

————A SAILOR-BOY'S LOG-BOOK.
From Portsmouth to Peiho. With a Portrait. Edited by WALTER WHITE. 1 vol.
crown 8vo. 5s.

WILKINSON (J. J. G.)—THE HUMAN BODY AND ITS
CONNEXION WITH MAN. Illustrated by the principal Organs. By JAMES JOHN
GARTH WILKINSON. Post 8vo. cloth. 5s.

WILKINSON (W. M.)—THE REVIVAL IN ITS PHY-
SICAL, PSYCHICAL, AND RELIGIOUS ASPECTS. By W. M. WILKINSON. Second
Edition. Small 8vo. cloth. 3s. 6d.

WILLIAMS—HINTS ON THE CULTIVATION OF
BRITISH AND EXOTIC FERNS AND LYCOPODIUMS; with Descriptions of One Hundred and Fifty Species and Varieties. By BENJAMIN SAMUEL WILLIAMS. 8vo.
cloth. 3s. 6d.

———————— THE ORCHID-GROWER'S MANUAL ;
Containing a Brief Description of upwards of Two Hundred and Sixty Orchidaceous Plants,
together with Notices of their times of Flowering, and most approved Modes of Treatment.
By BENJAMIN SAMUEL WILLIAMS. With a Coloured Frontispiece. Second Edition.
Post 8vo. cloth. 5s.

WILLS—OLD LEAVES GATHERED FROM 'HOUSE-
HOLD WORDS.' By W. HENRY WILLS. Post 8vo. cloth. 5s.

WORNUM—THE CHARACTERISTICS OF STYLES ;
An Introduction to the Study of the History of Ornamental Art. By RALPH N. WOR-
NUM. In royal 8vo. cloth, with very many Illustrations. Second Edition. 8s.

WRIGHT—A HISTORY OF DOMESTIC MANNERS
AND SENTIMENTS IN ENGLAND DURING THE MIDDLE AGES. By THOMAS
WRIGHT, M.A., F.S.A., Hon. M.R.S.L., &c.; Corresponding Member of the Imperial
Institute of France (Académie des Inscriptions et Belles Lettres). Illustrated by upwards
of 300 Engravings on Wood; with Illustrations from the Illuminations in Contemporary
Manuscripts, and other sources, drawn and engraved by F. W. FAIRHOLT, F.S.A. In
1 vol. fcap. quarto, price 21s., bound in an appropriate ornamental cover.

YONGE—THE LIFE OF FIELD-MARSHAL ARTHUR,
DUKE OF WELLINGTON. By CHARLES DUKE YONGE. With Portrait, Plans, and
Maps. 2 vols. 8vo. cloth. 40s.

———————— PARALLEL LIVES OF ANCIENT AND
MODERN HEROES, of EPAMINONDAS, PHILIP OF MACEDON, GUSTAVUS ADOLPHUS, AND
FREDERICK THE GREAT. By CHARLES DUKE YONGE, Author of 'A History of
England,' &c. Small 8vo. cloth. 4s. 6d.

BOOKS FOR THE  USE OF SCHOOLS,

ISSUED UNDER THE   AUTHORITY OF THE

SCIENCE AND ART   DEPARTMENT,

SOUTH   KENSINGTON.

THE CHARACTERISTICS OF STYLES. An Introduction to the Study of the History of Ornamental Art. By RALPH N. WORNUM. Second Edition. In royal 8vo., with very many Illustrations. 8s.

BURCHETT'S LINEAR PERSPECTIVE. By R. BURCHETT, Fifth Edition. Post 8vo. With Illustrations. 7s.

BURCHETT'S DEFINITIONS OF GEOMETRY. 24mo. sewed. Third Edition. Price 5d.

BURCHETT'S PRACTICAL GEOMETRY. Fourth Edition. 8vo. cloth. Price 5s.

DYCE'S ELEMENTARY OUTLINES OF ORNAMENT. 50 Selected Plates, small folio, sewed. Price 5s.

TEXT TO DYCE'S DRAWING ROOM. Fcap. 8vo. Price 6d.

REDGRAVE'S MANUAL AND CATECHISM ON COLOUR. Second Edition. 24mo. sewed. Price 9d.

REDGRAVE ON THE NECESSITY OF PRINCIPLES IN TEACHING DESIGN. Fcap. sewed. Price 6d.

A DIAGRAM TO ILLUSTRATE THE HARMONIOUS RELATIONS OF COLOUR. Small folio. Price 9d.

PRINCIPLES OF DECORATIVE ART. Folio. sewed. Price 1s.

LINDLEY'S SYMMETRY OF VEGETATION. 8vo. sewed. Price 1s.

ROBINSON'S LECTURES ON THE MUSEUM. Fcap. sewed. Price 6d.

AN ALPHABET OF COLOUR. Reduced from the works of Field, Hay, Chevreull. 4to. sewed. Price 3s.

DIRECTIONS FOR INTRODUCING ELEMENTARY DRAWING IN SCHOOLS AND AMONG WORKMEN. Published at the request of the Society of Arts. Small 4to. cloth. Price 4s. 6d.

ILLUSTRATIONS TO BE EMPLOYED IN THE PRACTICAL LESSONS ON BOTANY. Adapted to all classes. Prepared for the South Kensington Museum. By the REV. PROF. HENSLOW. With Illustrations. Post 8vo. Price 6d.

DRAWING FOR ELEMENTARY SCHOOLS: Being a Manual of the Method of Teaching Drawing, specially adapted for the Use of Masters of National and Parochial Schools. By ELLIS A. DAVIDSON, Head Master of the Chester School of Art. Published under the sanction of the Science and Art Department of the Committee of Council of Education. Post 8vo. cloth. 3s.

ELEMENTS OF GEOMETRICAL DRAWING; or Practical Geometry, Plane and Solid, including both Orthographic and Perspective Projection. Illustrated by Sixty Plates, engraved by J. W. Lowry, from original drawings. By THOMAS BRADLEY, of the Royal Military Academy, Woolwich, and Professor of Geometrical Drawing at King's College, London. Published for the Committee of Council on Education. In Two Parts, oblong folio, cloth, 16s. each.